Beyond the Blue

About the Author

TJ O'Shea is a New Jerseyian by location and a New Yorker by vocation. When not working in the video game industry or writing angsty queer romances, she enjoys playing video games (this time for fun), shouting answers at *Jeopardy!* reruns, amateurishly baking, spending time with her wife, and singing to their cat.

Beyond the Blue

TJ O'Shea

BELLA BOOKS

2022

Bella Books, Inc.
P.O. Box 10543
Tallahassee, FL 32302

Printed in the United States of America on acid-free paper.

First Edition - 2022

Editor: Heather Flournoy
Cover Designer: Heather Honeywell

ISBN: 978-1-64247-343-8

PUBLISHER'S NOTE

Acknowledgments

This book came to life on the NJ Transit train back and forth to Manhattan. Over the course of months, for the forty minutes of solitude between work and home, the characters of Mei and Morgan told me their story. I'm honored and grateful to have this novel published, and cannot thank enough the many folks who put in the time to get this story out there. Thank you to Bella Books for not only publishing the novel, but also their support and the community of writers whose world I can't believe I'm a part of. My editor Heather, to whom I owe a great amount of thanks for shaping this novel into something worth reading, and for her humor, encouragement, and kindness. To anyone and everyone who's read something I've written and offered their feedback, I appreciate you. And of course, my wife, who is the best beta reader around despite her egregious bias.

Dedication

To my wife, without whom this book would not have happened, and more importantly, would not have been worth it.

CHAPTER ONE

Chunky, stupid snowflakes dropped from chunky, stupid clouds and piled upon the other chunky, stupid snowflakes blanketing Mei's car. Though her windshield wipers bravely fought the hellish white onslaught it was a Sisyphean task, as the snow impeded her vision regardless of their efforts. Trembling hands turned down the heat as she waited on the side of the desolate highway. No other soul would brave this sudden blizzard, especially on Valentine's Day. Having agreed only to an early dinner with her daughter's family, Mei expected to be home before the worst of the snow set in. She would be curled in front of her fireplace already had her tire not taken this most auspicious occasion to pop, flatten, and force her to stop, thus placing her directly in the path of the snowstorm and its chunky, stupid snow.

Because, of course, the universe would punish her for brushing off what used to be Allan's favorite holiday. Marrying a hopeless romantic was an eye-opening experience for someone whose parents barely knew each other prior to their wedding day. Allan never needed a special occasion or corporate holiday to be romantic, but he could not contain his excitement for the kitsch and camp of Valentine's Day. Over thirty years it became a tradition for Mei to spoil Allan on Valentine's Day, and though she wasn't inclined toward romantic overtures, she did her best.

On this second Valentine's Day without him, her eldest daughter insisted Mei drive out to her suburban home for dinner assuming she would otherwise sit at home, melancholic and pathetic. Normally Mei would decline the invitation, but the more she declined the more insistent her daughters became about her attendance on these superfluous holidays. The more insistent they became, the more they visited unannounced or scheduled lunches to make sure Mei hadn't dissolved into a puddle of human remains.

Now she regretted giving in to Grace's demands as she sat on the side of the highway, in the middle of a blizzard, her tire flat against the asphalt. Roadside assistance insisted they were on their way, but no doubt predictably busy and reluctant to send a mechanic in the midst of this torrential snow. Keeping the heat as low as she could stand, Mei tried to reserve her car's gas and battery, wrapping her head in a thick wool gaiter. A glimmer of hope in the form of a pair of headlights passed in the other direction, but they did not belong to a truck. Simply another fool out in this damnable weather, though Mei envied them their mobility.

Not long after that car passed, two yellow lights shone behind her, refracted in the snowflakes. As the car crunched through the freshly fallen snow, it surprised her to see it did not belong to a tow truck, but rather a two-door sedan. Grabbing the emergency safety hammer from her center console, Mei waited as the figure approached her. She was not about to be murdered on top of all the other inconveniences this night wrought.

The stranger knocked on the window. Mei clenched her hammer and rolled the window down about an inch. "I'm fine."

She rolled it back up and the person knocked again.

This time, she rolled it down two inches. "I have called for help, thank you," she stated in a tone she thought stern, and rolled the window up.

They knocked again.

Mei tightened her grip on the hammer and rolled the window all the way down.

It was a woman. Too dark to tell what she looked like, but Mei did see a smiling face tucked between a wool beanie and scarf. "Is everything okay?"

She nodded as the flakes began falling into her vehicle, onto the conditioned leather. "Yes. My car has a flat. I called my roadside assistance."

Glancing left and right down the quiet highway, she inquired, "How long ago did you call?"

Already too many questions for Mei's liking. "Thirty minutes. It's fine, I imagine they're busy."

"Yeah, I bet," she replied. "Do you have a spare tire in the trunk?"

Allan's fastidious nature in regard to car ownership meant the spare tire remained inflated and in good condition. Mei hadn't bothered with it in the last two years. "I believe so."

"All right. I have a jack in my car. I can get that changed out for you in no time."

Mei blinked in astonishment. Noticing the snow falling into her vehicle, the woman used a gloved hand to wipe the snow from the car door out into the highway. "Why?"

Pulling her scarf up by her chin, the woman narrowed her eyes. "Why? Why would you ask me why?"

"Because we're in snowstorm and you are a stranger. How do I know you won't use your altruism as an excuse to lure me out of my vehicle for malignant purposes?"

"You know what? That's fair. It is a total serial killer move. Like a reverse Ted Bundy." This made Mei chuckle unexpectedly as the woman graciously stepped away from her car. "Roadside is gonna take a while. I'm not comfortable leaving you here alone, but if you don't want me to change your tire, I understand. I can wait in my car until roadside arrives."

A generous offer considering the conditions. Mei released the hammer and placed it on the passenger seat. "I would hate for you to be on the ground in this weather."

"Better than you freezing out here for the next hour, I'd think," she responded, jamming her hands in her pockets. "I can change the tire in a few minutes."

Mei should drive her car right to an asylum for taking up this stranger on her offer, but at least it wasn't a man. "Okay. Thank you. It's the rear left tire."

"Sure thing." Turning on her heel, she trotted back to her car. Mei turned off her engine and reluctantly stepped out into the harsh weather to open her trunk as well. Upon her return, the woman whistled and dropped her duffel bag next to them. "Wow, that is the cleanest trunk I've ever seen. Are you sure you're not the serial killer?"

It was bare—a bag of emergency supplies tucked neatly into one corner, a first aid kit in the other, the rest a flat expanse of freshly vacuumed thin carpet. "If I were a serial killer I wouldn't be foolish enough to transport a body in my own trunk."

The woman paused, giving Mei a strange, amused smile. "I feel like I should've been the one with the emergency hammer," she remarked. Lifting the carpet and the false bottom, the woman tugged the tire out of its place. She rolled it to the left and knelt down next to the offending wheel. Using a palm-sized flashlight, she lit the tire and searched it. "Oh, there it is. Looks like you caught a nail. Not surprising on this highway. If it's not construction materials, it's a pothole."

Mei retrieved her emergency blanket from the bag and laid it on the ground. "Here. I don't want you catching your death out here because of the state's inability to use my taxpayer money correctly."

"Boy, you said it." Kneeling on the blanket, the woman started her work loosening the lug nuts on the tire. "So, what are you doing out so late on Valentine's Day? Hot date? Or, cold date?"

Mei snickered, taking up a position next to the tire leaning on her car. "No, no. I had dinner with my daughter and my grandchildren."

"Oh, nice. Sounds like a good time. Although, you did leave in the middle of a blizzard, so maybe not."

"In my defense, I left before the blizzard started. And it would've been fine if not for that pesky nail." The woman wiped snow from beneath the vehicle, then placed a piece of wood down. She put the jack on top and began cranking the car up. Mei had observed Allan do this at least once or twice and it took such considerable strength. It duly impressed Mei how effortless this woman made it look. Three cheers for feminism. "What about you? Spending the night perched atop a gargoyle, waiting to rescue those in need?"

This made the woman laugh heartily, and Mei smiled. "Totally. I forgot my mask and cape in the car." Pulling the tire off the car, she set it aside and brushed her hands off. "Uh, I actually am on a date. A blind date. Well, it was a blind date, but we've seen each other by now. So, a regular date."

"Oh no. I'm so sorry, I never would've asked you to do this if I'd known." Glancing to her left, Mei barely made out the shape of a person in the passenger seat of this woman's car.

"You didn't ask. I offered," the woman replied. "And it's fine. What kind of person gets mad at someone for doing a favor?" Mounting the spare tire, she took to tightening the lug nuts.

"I suppose that's fair. This is far and beyond a favor, though. Changing a tire in a snowstorm for a stranger is rather extreme."

"Nah, it's not. Any decent person would do it." Not a consistent truth in Mei's experience, but she remained mute. "Besides, between you and me, this date is a disaster. In fact, sitting on this blanket talking to you is the most fun I've had all night."

Mei put her hand over her mouth to stifle her laughter. "Blind dates are the worst, aren't they?"

"They truly and deeply are. Would you mind?" Taking off her jacket, the woman handed it to Mei and lowered the jack. Underneath, the woman wore a mauve blazer, the sleeves of which she shoved up before tightening the lug nuts again, with much more effort. The coat in Mei's hands smelled wonderful, like wood and citrus. "It's not my style. I'd rather go on a date with someone I have a connection with, you know? And I know instantly if there is one. I don't feel it with her." Placing the tools into her bag, the woman stood and brought the blanket up with her. "Plus, it's Valentine's Day, so there's all sorts of weird expectations to be romantic with someone you just met. I don't know a whole lot about love, but I do know it's not something you're given. It is something you earn."

Shaking out the snow, she folded the blanket and stuck it back in the trunk. Mei handed over her jacket. "I have to say I agree. Though I suppose a gallant roadside rescue in this incredible snow is rather romantic. Perhaps your date will think so."

Scrunching her face, she slid her jacket back on. "Is it terrible if I say I hope not?"

Mei snickered. "My lips are sealed."

The woman hefted the bag over her shoulder, brushing snow from her pants. "She was rude to the valet *and* our waiter. That's a hard no for me. I'm trying to keep an open mind, but I can't stand when people are discourteous for no reason."

"No, I'm sure the sort of magnanimous person who interrupts a date to help a total stranger in a blizzard is not turned on by boorishness," Mei said, though the term *stranger* bothered something in the back of her mind.

Apparently reading her mind, the woman took off her glove and extended her hand. "Well, who says we have to be strangers? I'm Morgan."

"Mei," she replied, taking her hand and shaking it. They stood, hands clasped, as film-ready snow fell from the sky. A dying wind allowed a gentle stream of flakes to cascade around them. Mei withdrew her hand, shivering. "I'll let you get back to your date. Thank you again."

Morgan stared at her, unmoving. Suddenly, she shook her head and blinked a few times. "Right, anytime. Well, anytime, but hopefully not again when it's below zero. Anyway, get home safe. Don't drive too fast on the spare, okay? And you can't go very far on it."

"I won't transport any dead bodies across state lines, scout's honor," she promised, grinning behind her scarf. "Have a good night."

"Yeah. You too."

Less impeded by snow, Mei eyed the irate woman in the passenger seat with her arms crossed, glaring daggers at her through the windshield. Morgan waved as she got into the car, and Mei waved back.

She slid into her driver's seat, grateful for the meager warmth. As she watched Morgan's brake lights fade into the distance, a feeling crossed between déjà vu and premonition came over her. Mei did not consider herself sensitive to the inner workings of the universe, preferring to plant herself directly in her beloved sciences, but her otherwise methodical brain entreated she remember this unspectacular moment. Like a late-night *As Seen On TV* advertisement, the universe insisted: wait, there's more.

The wind picked up, bending snow-covered trees toward the road. Whatever the universe was trying to say, it had to wait. Mei could not rely on two good Samaritans in one night. Shaking herself from a trance, she locked her seat belt and maneuvered her car carefully back onto the white highway.

CHAPTER TWO

Downstairs, the mechanical whir and drip of the coffeemaker rattled loud enough to rouse Mei from slumber, bleary eyes blinked at the clock on the other nightstand. A soft, green *5:00 a.m.* greeted her. Today, an unusual blip interrupted her usual morning routine of skincare and business-casual dress: an invitation to spin class. Turning away from a closet of gray and blue blazers and slacks, she rummaged through her dresser drawer filled with neatly folded piles of athletic wear. Not a lot to choose from—her athletic regimen was limited to the home gym in her basement and somewhat weekly jogging—so she nabbed a black-on-black ensemble of athletic shorts and a tank top, complete with what she thought to be a fanciful stripe of mint green down the hem. Compiling a simple outfit for work, she hung it in a garment bag and swiped her phone from the nightstand. Eyes on her phone, she descended the stairs, following the aroma of dark blend. Only a few emails, Mei noted with relief, all of which could wait for a response until she got into the office.

Her house felt still. Early mornings used to be frenetic with the great boom of a bass and the two high-pitched trumpets of her daughters. A cacophony of clarinet lessons and debate team prep and is-that-my-jacket-give-it-back. Sometimes Mei waxed nostalgic for those days when socked feet scurried across her hardwood floors, when the melody of petty squabbles floated above the percussive clack of a typewriter in another room. Other times, the silence was a blessing.

In her current life, silence was the norm. The house didn't feel empty, Mei thought as she dumped the fresh mug of coffee down the drain, but it was still. Peaceful, one could say if one felt generous. Like a secluded garden, or a cemetery.

Outside, the sky glowed a pale greenish blue as the sun climbed over the matching roofs of neatly identical suburban homes. Snagging the morning paper from her porch, she plunked it into the recycling bin on her way to her car. Eventually, she would remember to cancel the subscription.

"Good morning, Dr. Sharpe."

Startled, Mei regarded her next-door neighbor, who, for some godforsaken reason, was awake this early. "Good morning, Evelyn."

"You know," Evelyn began, and Mei did not know, but she did know she did not want to know. "Henry and I are having a little shindig this weekend. We were wondering if you'd want to come. Nothing crazy—a few neighbors having an end-of-winter potluck."

"That sounds—" Truly and deeply awful. "Lovely."

"We would love it if you could join us," Evelyn called over the tops of her trimmed hedges.

"Oh, no thank you," Mei replied. "I mean, thank you for the invitation. I have a lot of work to get through this weekend, unfortunately."

"Okay," Evelyn said, cheerfully pruning her bushes. "Next time!"

Not a chance in hell. "Sure. Have a good day, Evelyn. Give Henry my best."

Mei tried to find a good speed with which to get into the

car—not so fast where Evelyn would know she was rushing, but fast enough to avoid further conversation.

The spin class took place in a strip mall about five minutes away, run by a portly former baseball player named Rod. Rod's Fitness, between the laundromat and the generic Italian pizza restaurant, named for a man who never quite made the major leagues but somehow maintained a local celebrity status despite his athletic mediocrity. Rod's fitness and Rod's Fitness both left something to be desired.

Outside the entrance stood Shanvi Klein, waving at Mei as she drove past to find a parking spot. Shanvi was the type of friend for whom Mei did not have to feign excitement for this early class, but did dutifully agree to attend. Good friendships require balance.

A rare pre-marriage friend, Shanvi remained in her life even as the rest of her social circle dwindled down after Allan passed. Shanvi did not pity her or talk to her in vague platitudes, and Mei appreciated the refreshing honesty and normalcy she brought to her life. If one more well-meaning acquaintance trotted out a phrase about God closing doors or opening windows, Mei was liable to burst. God needed to keep her hands off Mei's doors and windows, which Mei locked and secured with the app on her phone, thank you very much.

"I'm shocked you picked spin for us to try, considering your infamous diatribes against bicyclists."

Triggered, Shanvi grimaced as they entered the gym and she signed Mei in as her guest. "I hate bicyclists on the street. I am fine with these bicycles, here inside a building, where they cannot flagrantly disobey the rules of both the sidewalk and the road."

With a chuckle she followed her friend past the overachievers pumping iron and pounding away on treadmills. The mixture of smells—body odor, rubber, and sweat—bombarded Mei as they wove in and out of equipment. A departure from the pine-scented cleaner and vanilla smell of home, or the antiseptic smell of work. But maintaining perhaps her only significant friendship was worth the olfactory onslaught.

Dropping their bags off in the locker room, Shanvi laughed

as they mounted their bikes, side by side. "I see you somehow managed to find the most demure gym clothes you own."

In accordance with her personality, Shanvi wore the daring choice of a blaring red paisley tank top and fire-engine-red shorts. The rest of their class showcased a sea of neon pinks, lime greens, and other colors one might find inside of a gumball machine. Mei lifted her arm. "Green."

"Color me shocked."

"Hilarious. Besides, for whom should I have dressed up like a peacock? These co-eds?"

Shanvi shrugged. "You never know when you're going to run into a hottie with a body. And they should know you are also a hottie with a body."

"Please, never use that phrase again."

Forty-five minutes of cycling through digital forests later, Mei and Shanvi finally received the instruction to dismount their bikes. Shanvi panted, wrapping her towel around her neck and pressing her face into it with a groan. "I think I died in that forest somewhere. Don't worry about an autopsy, the cause of death was exhaustion and hubris."

Mei laughed, dabbing her face with a towel and shouldering her gym bag. Squirting water into her mouth, she shrugged. "This was—"

"My idea, yes I know. But you, the reasonable one, are supposed to talk me out of this nonsense," she replied. "And not let me spin myself into a coma. Let's get out of here."

Just outside the doors, Mei and Shanvi politely exchanged smiles with the other class members filing out and tried not to look as exhausted as they felt in front of the much younger patrons. "Well, this was fun."

"Was it?" Shanvi replied, desperately sucking down water.

"It was fun for me to watch you struggle."

"First, you're mean. Second, tomorrow, back to the café. This was a disaster."

Mei thought about the coffeemaker. Another routine she never disrupted. Pulled along by an unseen current, she still bought the beans and filled the grinder, setting the program each night to brew in the morning. Then, bright and early, she'd dump the fresh brew into the sink and meet Shanvi at the café for tea. She always preferred tea. "I'll see you tomorrow."

Sparing a glance down at her phone, Mei opened a new email from her youngest daughter on her walk back to her car. She read a short, impersonal request to meet for lunch with both her daughters, tomorrow. That would be rare treat. Lara's late-night bartending gig meant she slept until nearly noon and spent her other free time wandering in an academic fog on a path to a Master's. Her eldest, Grace, usually proved even harder to pin down. She worked nonstop as a corporate pilot flying across the globe at the whim of a wealthy CEO. Grace loved it, allegedly, and relished the unpredictable and hectic schedule. According to this email, she'd been granted a week off and wanted to "reconnect."

Reconnect. What a stupid word, Mei thought as she drove the short distance across the county to her job. It sounded very corporate, very Grace, but also devoid of meaning. When had they disconnected? Though now adults living in their own personal spheres, they kept in touch. But, she relented over the hum of talk radio, since their father's death, reaching her had become more difficult. Allan coordinated family holidays, scheduled lunches with their globetrotting daughter, provided moral support to their aimless youngest. He stayed home with them through their adolescence, coaching teams and ferrying to practices and recitals, being soft where Mei was hard. When they needed practical advice, they came to her. When they cried over crushes, they went to Allan. Now, with him gone, she could not fill the gap he left. She could not be both soft and hard.

Perhaps, Mei thought as she pressed her badge against the electronic buzzer and unlocked the stairwell, perhaps they did need to make a reconnection.

A quick shower and redress later, Mei gave herself a once-over in the mirror. While nobody worth impressing ever ventured down to her office, she made an effort to look presentable should someone show up who was not a corpse. Rarely did any of her colleagues deign to come down to the "dungeon," as they referred to it when they thought Mei wasn't listening. She the dungeon-master, she supposed.

As per her routine she responded to emails, fielding questions from her colleagues about the degradation of bodies in warm climates or the prevalence of poison in hair samples, and ignored the invitation to next month's surprise birthday party for the sheriff. No response means plausible deniability if asked why she did not attend. Emails get lost all the time. It's not like anyone would come looking for her.

Robed in her lab coat, she pulled out the first cadaver of the day. Male, forty-nine, six foot three, Caucasian. Frederick Solomon. Two gunshot wounds to the chest. Well, it did not take several advanced degrees to know what killed him. However, upstairs marked it as high priority, so she did her due diligence and began laying out her tools. Dungeon-master, indeed.

Hours later Mei stood at the slab, deeply involved in a gunshot wound in the man's chest. Flecks of fabric embedded in the wound she removed for analysis. Two different colors and two different fabrics, to be specific. One, a navy blue knit—possibly a polo shirt—and the other a puffy white. This wound entered straight on, directly in the heart. The other wound, where Mei only discovered one fabric, entered on a diagonal. Odd for a victim this size, six foot three, to have a wound diagonally downward in the upper pectoral.

"Hello?"

She jerked, nearly dropping her pair of tweezers on poor Frederick. The elevator must have dinged upon arrival, but so engrossed in her victim Mei hadn't heard it. Unless the elevator dinger was broken—she never used it, so anything was possible. Lots of superfluous machinery didn't work in her dungeon, but to ask for a fix would be to not only file a grievous amount of paperwork, but also invite someone into her workspace. She did not suffer interlopers in her sanctuary.

"Hello?" Mei called back.

"Dr. Sharpe?"

She clicked off the recorder, removing her gloves and mask. "Yes, over here."

Two officers rounded the corner toward where she stood next to Frederick. One of them, Sergeant Ruiz, grimaced as the scent of formaldehyde hit her nostrils. Sergeant Ruiz was young, maybe late twenties or early thirties, heavily tattooed and stocky like a shot-put player, with an Army pedigree expressed in a rigid demeanor and dress, her lips and suit both pressed into stern lines. Office gossip filtered down to Mei, uninvited, indicated the sergeant's matter-of-factness and intolerance for bullshit put off most officers, but economical personalities went appreciated in the dungeon.

Twenty-five years working in the county medical examiner's office, Mei knew—at least, peripherally—almost everyone who worked homicides and other crimes that might result in death. Her companion, however, Mei never had seen before. Tall for a woman, casually dressed in a button-down plaid shirt tucked into black jeans with a black belt, and a dimpling smile at the ready.

"Hey, Dr. Sharpe," Sergeant Ruiz greeted in her gruff monotone. "Cap asked for an update on the vic." The woman next to her aggressively cleared her throat and without turning, she introduced the officer. "Dr. Sharpe, this is Lieutenant Kelly."

Lieutenant Kelly must be older than she looks. Mei didn't know a single lieutenant under thirty, which was how old her stylish teenage-heartthrob undercut, blond hair hanging to her prominent cheekbone and combed entirely to one side, made her look. "Nice to meet you, Lieutenant Kelly."

"Morgan, please. Lieutenant Kelly is my father." Morgan chuckled, but upon seeing neither of the other women laughing, stopped short. "I'm kidding, my dad's not a cop. He hates cops, actually. He's not really my dad," Morgan quickly corrected. "Just—anyway, about that vic?"

Unperturbed, Mei raised an eyebrow. "Exactly what information did Captain Williams hope to find that you did not already know?"

"Basically anything you can tell us. The scene is still being picked over but it was fairly clean and the vic had no rap sheet," the sergeant explained.

"Ah, well. I've only done a preliminary examination. I

haven't gotten to the stomach contents or to poke around any of the organs."

"Not any of the fun stuff," Morgan interjected with a grin. Scoffing, Ruiz gestured for Mei to continue.

"However, I did pull fabric from the first wound. I'll have to run tests but on first glance, it looks like several different sources. Was he wearing a jacket? Or an undershirt?"

Producing a folder from behind her back, the gruff sergeant leafed through it. "Pics say no. He was wearing a plain blue polo shirt, khakis, a belt, athletic socks, old white man sneakers, and glasses. Nothing about a tank top or a jacket. Not even a sweater. Are you sure?"

Ignoring the affront to her skills, Mei nodded. "Like I said, I haven't analyzed them yet, but my educated guess is they originated from two different sources."

"Well, how does that happen? We only got two people at the scene: our buddy here, and the shooter. We know the shooter was let into the victim's home between twenty-hundred and zero-three-hundred hours, shot him in the living room—bang bang—fled the scene. No prints, nobody heard the shots. Neighbors on either side of the home were not present at the time and none of the neighbors saw anything suspicious. Now you're telling me there is someone else involved?"

"No, I am telling you I found unidentified fabric in the wound," Mei replied evenly. Morgan stepped around her partner, narrowing her eyes and leaning in closer to the cadaver than Mei could witness comfortably. "Can I help you, Lieutenant?"

The operating table lamp illuminated two sparkling blue eyes flicking up to her. "Nope. Please, continue."

"How the hell does a bullet catch fabric on its way from the damn gun to the victim?" Sergeant Ruiz crossed her arms over her chest.

"Shot him with the gun in his jacket pocket," Morgan mumbled absentmindedly as she hovered over the victim's torso. "Maybe?"

Now almost nose-to-skin near the victim's chest, Morgan cocked her head like a German Shepard. "Lieutenant, are you looking for something?" Mei asked, barely preventing her tone from clipping.

"Yeah, I think I dropped my earring," she replied. "Kidding. Did you—would you be able to tell me what this thing is in the wound here?" Morgan gingerly pointed at a speck of material in the margin of abrasion.

Grabbing her tweezers, Mei plucked the material. It wasn't a stray fiber, but a minuscule clump of fibers together. Malleable under the pressure of the tweezers.

"A feather?" Morgan asked, standing up straight. "Lint?"

Mei pulled her magnifying glass down and placed the fabric beneath it. "White, puffy, closely knit. Like something you'd pump into a stuffed animal."

"A pillow silencer." A voice said aloud the thought forming in Mei's head. Morgan nudged Sergeant Ruiz. "The victim's shirt was stained so weird."

"You think the killer used a pillow to silence the gun?"

"Do you know which shot killed him?" Morgan asked suddenly.

Unusually riveted by the real-time unraveling of this crime, Mei swallowed her eagerness and proceeded calmly. "The first one, right in the heart. He was killed instantly."

"It was an execution," Morgan announced to the room, but clearly to herself. "But how did he..." She nabbed the folder from Sergeant Ruiz's hands and pointed at it with her fingers in the shape of a gun, the tip of her index finger pressed against the folder. "If you do it like this, how do you know you're aimed in the right place?"

"A hitman would know where to shoot," the sergeant retorted.

Morgan held the folder to her chest. "Or our vic was holding it. He stands there, like this, holding the pillow to him. The killer shoots—" Morgan flapped her hand for Mei to come around. "Here, Dr. Sharpe. Shoot me."

Mei raised her eyebrow. "Absolutely not."

"Not like for real," Morgan said, chuckling. "I'd ask Ruiz, but I know for a fact she's a spoilsport."

With a sigh, Mei rubbed the bridge of her nose. "Lieutenant Kelly, I'm very busy, and I—"

"Just for a second." The lieutenant pouted. "Please? It'll help with the case."

Defenses breached, Mei rounded the table and reluctantly pointed her finger gun at the officer. "Bang."

"No, no. Get yourself a weapon." Mei quickly searched for a weapon and decided on her lead mallet. She held the mallet by the head. "Okay, now press the barrel against the folder." Mei walked forward and held the mallet out, pressing the handle's end into the officer's chest. Standing much closer to the younger woman, she inhaled the scent of citrus and cedar, staring into bright, expectant eyes. Her memory slapped her so hard she nearly blacked out. She recognized that smell, and those eyes. The Morgan who rescued her off the side of the road a month ago now stood in front of her. How many other well-built, female Morgans could there possibly be?

"Go on."

Her gentle encouragement snapped Mei out of it. Morgan didn't recognize her. No reason to interrupt their job to bring up the time she was foolish enough to drive in a blizzard. "Bang."

Morgan dropped to her knees. "It hits me in the heart, right? I'm dead, can't keep myself from falling." She lurched forward.

"Bang." A bit of exhilaration ran through her, but also a bit of absurdity.

Morgan dramatically snapped backward, hitting the ground in a pratfall. In all her years as medical examiner, Mei had never witnessed—or allowed—such buffoonery in her office. "They shot him again to be sure, blowing him onto his back. It would explain why we found his body in such a weird position and the fabric in the wound. We don't have the whole story. Nobody executes a civilian."

Ruiz stared down at her partner on the floor, seemingly unperturbed by this bizarre behavior from the high-ranking officer. "He was an upstanding citizen. Not even a moving violation. There's nothing on this guy. The house was as WASP-y as it gets."

"We know he let his killer in. We thought he was duped, but maybe they knew each other. Execution is personal."

While Ruiz offered resistance, Mei observed the calculation in her dark brown eyes as she considered Morgan's theory. "You don't have evidence of a pillow, or evidence the victim held it when he got shot."

"Yet." Morgan leapt to her feet. "I don't have the evidence *yet*. But what I do have is my tingling detective Spidey sense and an excellent investigative partner," she said, throwing her arm over Ruiz's shoulder. The sergeant shrugged her off, but Mei noted the fond half smile she failed to hide.

"We gotta go back to the house, don't we?"

"Yup!"

Despite Morgan's cheer, Ruiz groaned. "I hate the suburbs. Gives me the *escalofríos*."

"Heebie-jeebies or not, we have to comb the house and see if we can find a pillow. I doubt our killer waltzed in or out of this home with a Bed, Bath and Beyond bag in their hand. Let's re-interview the relatives. Look at his job again. Something about Mr. Solomon here isn't adding up." Morgan rummaged in her back pocket and withdrew a leather wallet. Sliding a card out, she handed it to Mei, who took it with a raised brow. "When you finish the autopsy, can you send me an email? Even his stomach contents could give us something to go on."

"Absolutely, Lieutenant. I'll be sure to pin down the materials I found and let you know as soon as I have something accurate and verifiable. And anything else I find in the 'fun stuff,'" she said with a small smile.

In an instant, the professional engrossment in Morgan's expression changed into genuine amusement, an infectious smile breaking on her face. "Thanks, Doc. You're gonna be the one who breaks this case open. I can feel it."

"Oh, I doubt that." Heat blooming on her cheeks, Mei waved in dismissal. "I'll leave that to you and your spider sense."

"My spider sense," Morgan repeated softly, gazing at Mei with such an unexpected fondness it made her heart leap into her throat. Morgan's unrelenting, penetrative stare caught her.

"Right, um. Well, I should get back to my autopsy," Mei said, but she didn't move.

"Yeah," Ruiz drawled, glancing between the two women in vague suspicion. She nabbed Morgan by the elbow to lead her away. "We'll leave you alone now, Dr. Sharpe. Thanks for your help. Let's go, Lieutenant." Escorting her partner as she would a perpetrator, Ruiz corralled Morgan toward the elevator.

Newly invigorated, Mei donned a fresh pair of gloves and dove back into her work. If a smile grew behind her mask, well, it wasn't as if Frederick would tell anyone.

CHAPTER THREE

Morgan became a good detective almost entirely by accident. When she solved her first homicide, her mentor at the time slapped her on the back and asked the popular question: how did you do it? The answer, Morgan realized, was easy. She didn't know how not to do it. Solving crimes came naturally, like chefs to cooking or dancers to rhythm. She thrived in the dizzying labyrinth between the crime and the solve. Connecting dots, interviewing witnesses, collecting evidence, and constructing the brick-and-mortar foundation of an eventual arrest. Collars were fine and accolades dandy—her medals collected dust in a box somewhere—but the puzzle brought her the most joy.

Dozens of her childhood memories revolved around puzzles. Exhausted by Morgan's boundless energy, her mother would sit her down in front of any available task—jigsaw puzzles, board games, or fixing a broken appliance—and she wasn't allowed to get up until she finished. One time, she threw Morgan a ring of fifty keys and a safety deposit box, and told her she could only move after she unlocked the box. Years of this laissez-faire parenting incidentally gave Morgan the ability to funnel her overwhelming energy into patience, cunning, and focus. She realized every crime, every witness, every criminal, even just regular people—they were all safety deposit boxes, and Morgan just needed the patience to find the right key.

And so, by applying the coping mechanism she'd utilized as a kid to block out the noise of her childhood, Morgan developed into one of the best detectives in the state. Which worked well for her today, as Ruiz had asked her to comb the house for evidence in the Solomon murder. A tedious job for most—the other two officers grumbled in another room—but Ruiz knew she wouldn't mind, so her partner stood next to her as Morgan sifted through the kitchen.

"This would go a lot faster if you were looking, too," Morgan said, handing Ruiz two cans of tomato sauce from Solomon's pantry.

"Nope. You're reaping what you sowed by trying to show off in front of Dr. Sharpe," Ruiz replied, stacking the cans on the counter.

Shoving cans of peas in her direction, Morgan glared. "I was not showing off."

"Uh-huh. 'Oh, Dr. Sharpe, you're gonna solve the case,'" she mimicked in a breathless, high-pitched voice that didn't sound a thing like Morgan. "Thought I was going to have to mop the floor after us."

"Rude," Morgan thought but did not articulate because Ruiz didn't need any more ammunition, as she was already incredibly accurate. The moment she laid eyes on Dr. Sharpe she turned into a Looney Tunes character, jaw on the floor and pupils shaped into hearts. She recalled with perfect clarity the moment when the small smile broke out on Dr. Sharpe's face and evacuated all the oxygen in the room. The opening bass to Roy Orbison's "Pretty Woman" struck up in her head and her brains swiftly made for the exit.

Pulling out a value pack of cereal, Morgan casually muttered, "Whatever, Dr. Sharpe is cool."

Leaning against the wall, Ruiz crossed her arms and stared down at her. Despite having at least five inches of height on her, Ruiz felt larger than Morgan. This intimidating stance worked well for interrogations, but right now it gave Morgan the disapproving-older-sister vibe she wanted to avoid. "Is that right?"

"Yeah, you hyped her up like she was gonna unhinge her jaw and consume us, but she was nice."

Handing Ruiz three bags of chips, Morgan continued her search and Ruiz piled them into the section of Things That Are Not Pillows. "What are you getting at, Kelly?"

"Nothing," Morgan replied immediately, diving back into the pantry to evade detection. One wrong look at Ruiz and she would be found out. Ruiz's knack for seeing through any farce made her a great detective but a rather impossible best friend. Not that Morgan lied to her—she despised lying in general—but she couldn't even keep her cards close around Ruiz. "Just making conversation, Sergeant Ruiz, gee whiz."

Getting to her feet, Morgan perused the shelves, using a gloved hand to shove away boring bric-a-brac. Next to her, Ruiz shrugged and swung one leg over the other. "The officers don't like her because she doesn't suffer fools. They go down there and swing their dicks and she shuts them down. That's why I like her, but I know not to fuck around and waste her time making her re-enact a murder."

Jerking back out of the pantry, Morgan peeked at her friend. "Okay, but she was game, though? So, that's something."

"That's nothing, Kelly." As Morgan ducked back in to continue her search, Ruiz grabbed her by the shoulder and yanked her out. "Wait a second. You want it to be something, don't you?"

"No," Morgan denied immediately, her cheeks growing warm. "I'm just saying she wasn't as bad as you made her seem, that's all."

Holding Morgan still with a surprising amount of strength, Ruiz inspected her with her unrelenting dark brown gaze. Within moments, Morgan knew she was doomed. The look of recognition rippled across Ruiz's face and Morgan's hopes for casually inquiring about Dr. Sharpe crashed to the ground like a cartoon piano. "Don't even start with this one, Kelly. I see that look in your eyes."

"There's no look." Pouting, Morgan dropped her gaze to the expensive tile beneath them and sighed deeply. "Okay, fine. I can't help it. Gosh, she is gorgeous."

"I knew it."

"Well, what am I supposed to do?" Morgan whined. "Not be attracted to her?"

"Yes!" Ruiz threw up her hands. "Kelly, for once think with your big brain and not with your *pinga*, please. Don't go batting your big blue puppy dog eyes at her."

"I am not batting anything, I—" Huffing, she turned fully to face Ruiz and implored her, "I felt the connection. Like, immediately."

"You talked to her for five minutes," Ruiz replied flatly. "And you said the same thing about that lady whose tire you swapped."

"I felt it both times!"

At this point, many years into their friendship, Ruiz had to know her skepticism wasn't a deterrent. "Look, I know it's been a while since you had a girlfriend. You and Georgia broke up before Christmas, right? You're dumb and horny right now—"

"I am not," Morgan protested. "It's not like that."

"Okay. Whatever it is 'like,' Sharpe is straight."

Morgan's face fell. Knowing a woman's sexuality presented a unique problem for her. On the one hand, compulsory heterosexuality meant some women turned out less straight than they thought and Morgan enjoyed guiding them on that journey. On the other hand, she rejected the notion of "turning" a woman gay. So, she optimistically pursued women who showed interest in her and hoped for the best. Her "date first, ask questions later" approach didn't have a high success rate, but it beat being alone. "Oh. How do you know?"

"Besides the fact that she couldn't ping a gaydar with a mallet and a gong?" Ruiz inquired, raising an eyebrow. "A while back I needed a stupid form from the examiner and instead of Sharpe it was some idiot who didn't understand what I wanted, so I asked the sheriff why the hell I had to deal with this moron and he told me she was on bereavement because her husband died."

Her heart ached and she felt the delicate string of fate slowly tying itself around the two of them. Despite their obvious differences, loss bound them in a way only those left emotionally bereft by death could understand. The tendrils of her grief slithered out to grab another, to pull them close and say: I get it; sometimes I'm in the darkness, too.

Darkness aside, Morgan knew her silly crush would go tragically unrequited. A woman like Dr. Sharpe—intelligent, poised, probably ate her dinners off a non-disposable plate— didn't fall for oversized dorks like herself. "Right."

"So," Ruiz began slowly, "we're not going to skirt-chase a straight, much older woman who showed no interest in you, right?"

"I don't skirt-chase," Morgan replied, grimacing. With her focus all but lost due to the mere idea of Dr. Sharpe, Morgan finally noticed the rumbling of her stomach. Food would be a good distraction from the discussion of her workplace crush, as well as restore the energy needed to search the rest of the house. "All right, I'll check the fridge and then we can break for lunch. What do you think he's got in here?"

"Hummus? Plain yogurt? A Tupperware container of unseasoned chicken breast? If you find a pillow in there, I'm quitting the force," Ruiz stated, chuckling at the look of disdain Morgan shot her on the way to the fridge. Yanking the door open, Morgan stepped back in surprise as pooling water trickled out. This was a fancy fridge—one with a touchscreen on it and sleek stainless steel exterior—and it should not have been malfunctioning. Inside, the produce wilted and lay sadly soggy in the drawers. "Yikes. Did it get unplugged or something?"

"Or the condenser coils are clogged?" Morgan posited. Ruiz raised an eyebrow. "What? I know stuff sometimes. Help me move this."

With a few grunts of effort the two women pulled the fridge away from the wall as far as they could, sliding it out of its fitted place between the counters. Lo and behold, their smoking gun in the form of a bloodied, now moist pillow stuffed between the wall and the back of the refrigerator. "How the fuck did this get back there?"

Morgan grinned. "Maybe the refrigerator was tired from running."

"The only thing I hate more than one of your weird little mind palace hunches turning out right is your puns, and you know this." With a heavy sigh and a shake of her head, Ruiz called over her shoulder. "Jensen, Fiore, get in here."

Two uniformed officers rushed into the room, and stood at attention. Morgan technically outranked Ruiz, but this wasn't her case and throwing weight around couldn't be further from her nature. Besides, she relished the opportunity to see Ruiz boss around someone other than her.

Snapping off her gloves, Morgan stretched and got out of the way of the officers. "Okay, lunchtime, and you're buying because you made me sad trying to dash my dreams of being Mrs. Doctor Sharpe."

"I'll buy you lunch every day if I don't have to hear you pine after yet another of your femme crushes," Ruiz replied, leading them out of the Solomon house. Waiting at the car, Morgan turned to regard the house as a whole. A little ostentatious for the block, she mused. Stucco exterior and pillars on the entrance, as opposed to the more cookie-cutter siding-and-screen porch of the others. After delegating to the officers, Ruiz approached her from the side. "What's up?"

"Do you think the house is a bit much? Solomon was what, an accountant for a mid-level firm? How does a man like that make a salary to afford this?" she said, gesturing to the extravagant exterior.

"By being an overpaid, underachieving white man. Why?"

"We should look at this house. Where is this money coming from?" Turning to Ruiz, Morgan smirked. "Fifty bucks says the mortgage was paid off in cash."

Ruiz looked from her to the house. "You think he was embezzling?"

"Not sure yet, but something doesn't add up here. Anyway, fifty bucks?"

Ruiz shook her hand. "Fifty bucks."

Pulling away from their scene, Morgan watched the suburbs roll by out the passenger window. She knew Ruiz would disapprove of her pursuing Dr. Sharpe. Negativity was the dialect of Ruiz's love language, and Morgan spoke it well. After doggedly seeking her friendship at the academy, Morgan peeled away the layers of Anna-Maria Ruiz and found beneath her hard shell beat the steadfast heart of the greatest friend Morgan ever had. Their friendship forged itself in the fires of the academy and their subsequent police work, but it cured in the moments of life in between. No matter what nonsense Morgan pulled, through successes and failures, Ruiz lifted her up. Ruiz never wavered.

"Kelly, why are you smiling at me like that?" Ruiz asked, and only then did Morgan realize she'd looked over at some point and stared at her.

"Sorry, was just thinking about how long we've been friends."

"Yeah, I still can't believe I let you trick me into a friendship," Ruiz replied, but she glanced at Morgan and smirked, her eyes soft. "Why were you thinking about that?"

"Because I'm mad at how good your advice is, and why you're always right." Ruiz pursed her lips, as if finding this incredibly reasonable. They parked outside a deli somewhere between the city and the suburbs in an upscale strip mall with a fancy white brick façade. Anchored on one end by a new Italian restaurant, Morgan glanced at the pretty alfresco dining area. "Aw, man, I wish we had time to eat outside. It's such a nice day."

"*Lo siento.* I'll let you sit on the hood and eat, though," Ruiz said, standing in the queue with Morgan beside her.

"That's 'cause you don't let me eat in the car," Morgan lamented. "Not after the Incident of 2013."

"It took me two weeks to get the gravy out of the car mats."

Morgan frowned. "I know." As they waited for their turn to order, Morgan wrung her fingers together. Normally she heeded Ruiz's warnings against certain women, as her own romantic instincts often led her astray. In this instance, Morgan felt herself rebelling. "Anna-Maria, can you answer me honestly?"

Surprised by the intimate address, Ruiz grew somber. "I never lie to you, Morgan."

"Do you really think I shouldn't try with Dr. Sharpe? Because I don't know if I can…not," she admitted softly.

"Okay. I'm going to say this one time and that's it, all right? This is not a tacit endorsement, this is an observation." Morgan nodded. "I caught a vibe between you and Sharpe, too."

Ruiz groaned aloud when she saw Morgan's elated reaction. Admittedly, the elation she allowed to cross her face didn't even measure up to the overflowing fountain of pure joy bubbling inside her. "Okay. Thank you."

"You're welcome." Eyeing the way Morgan bounced on her heels, Ruiz reached out and grabbed her arm. "Just tread carefully, okay? I don't know if Sharpe is hetero-flexible or what, but...she lost her husband, you know? She might be a tougher nut to crack than you think even if she is somehow open to your Sapphic energy."

"I'm a great nutcracker," Morgan replied immediately, brightening. "Not one of those chintzy Christmas ones, either. Like an all-year-round, solid stainless steel nutcracker."

"*Cristo*, I hope she's into dorks."

"Me too."

CHAPTER FOUR

Tucked away safely in the corner of a cheerful café, Mei read quietly amidst the morning bustle. With Shanvi due any moment Mei enjoyed the solitude, or as much solitude as one could expect in a busy corner bakery. Sipping on her tea, she leafed to a new page of her book and looked up only when Shanvi shouted to get her attention. After exchanging a wave, she continued to peruse her novel while Shanvi waited in line and received her order from a disinterested, blue-haired barista.

"Early, as always," Shanvi declared, smiling as she sat down across from Mei. "Though it does get us the best seat." She nodded at the floor-to-ceiling windows facing the street next to them. The corner table also provided Mei with a view of the entire café, as well as the patrons. As averse as she was to socializing, she did enjoy people-watching. "You know, some people think compulsive punctuality is an intimidation tactic."

Mei raised an eyebrow. "Some people? And what scientific study did 'some people' say this in?"

Shanvi shrugged, sipping her coffee. "Google it. Anyway, how's work?"

"Oh, you know. Same as always," came Mei's automatic response. Not satisfactory enough, judging by the look on Shanvi's face, so Mei prepared to elaborate. "Well, not exactly. I did have a rather odd conversation with two detectives."

"A conversation? And honest-to-god conversation?" Shanvi opened her eyes wide, smiling devilishly. "Do tell."

"I'm performing the autopsy on a murder victim. Apparently, Captain Williams has little to go on and sent them down to push me along. Normally, the cops don't like to hang around the morgue."

"Unsurprising."

"Exactly. But Sergeant Ruiz—I think I've told you about her, haven't I?"

Shanvi paused in thought. "Yeah, I think so. Former military, right? No bullshit?"

"Precisely. She brought with her a woman I'd never seen before. Or at least, I thought I hadn't seen her before."

"Oh, intriguing. But you had seen her before?"

"Yes," Mei replied. "Remember when I got that flat on Valentine's Day?"

"Yes, and your romantic roadside rescue," Shanvi recalled with a wistful sigh.

"That is not how I described it, but yes. So, um, as it turns out, the stranger who helped me is a new officer at the county."

If Mei had any other friend to tell, she would have. Shanvi's obsession with mysticism and fate ran directly counter to Mei's strict adherence to an orderly world. Two chance meetings with the same person struck her as slightly odd. Meanwhile, Shanvi's eyes practically burst from her head. "Oh, my goodness! Mei-be!"

"You know perfectly well that is not my name."

"Mei, that is kismet if I ever heard it. What did she say?"

Mei ventured a look outside at the sun pouring its golden light into the street. "Nothing, she didn't recognize me. Instead, thinking I'm a perfect stranger she just met, she made me re-enact the murder with her."

Shanvi snorted into her drink. "Wow. How did she manage to get the woman who won't even participate in charades to do such a thing?"

Reclining her chair, Mei considered that question for long moments. She hadn't given any thought to why she'd gone along with Lieutenant Kelly's request. "I—I don't know. She asked. She did change my tire in a blizzard."

"And I was the maid of honor at your wedding and you won't even play Pictionary with Paul and me."

Glaring at her friend, Mei continued. "Anyway, I finished the autopsy earlier than usual and sent a prelim report to the captain and the lieutenant. I've received no response from either." Mei nursed a bit of disappointment having not heard back from the lieutenant, considering she was the one who'd extended contact to Mei. She cupped her mug in both hands. "What about you?"

Shanvi launched into a humorous story of a woman who did not "believe in floss," and Mei listened with her full attention. Until, over Shanvi's shoulder, the lieutenant strolled through the door, side-swept and tousled blond hair glinting in the early morning sunlight. In place of a plaid shirt she wore an untucked crisp white button-down with a slim navy blue tie, her badge dangling around her neck from a beaded metal necklace. Eyes glued to her phone, Mei went unnoticed by Morgan as she kept her gaze on the officer and her ears tuned in to Shanvi.

"I tell her floss is not a scam invented by dentists. If she would just do it, she could see me less. Trust me, I want to see her less."

Once at her turn, Morgan flashed a brilliant smile and ordered something Mei couldn't hear. Sharing a genial laugh with the cashier, she paid her bill and moved along to the pickup counter. Leaning on the counter with one elbow, she continued to swipe through whatever kept her engrossed in her phone.

"Hey, Morgan," the barista greeted. She slid a wax bag toward the officer, who snatched it and excitedly peeked inside. "How are you?"

"Oh, you know me, Amira," Morgan replied, taking a bite of her pastry with a halfhearted shrug. "Self-soothing with sugar. How are you? Any new developments in the field of microbiology I need to be aware of?"

Amira giggled, bashfully chewing on the inside of her cheek. Mei could not stop the eyebrow on her face from rising straight off her forehead. Was this young woman flirting with the lieutenant? At her place of employment? Mei must've made a noise out loud because Shanvi stopped talking and followed the direction of Mei's intent stare. "Do you know her?"

Mei shook her head. "No. I mean, yes. That's the woman who came down with Sergeant Ruiz yesterday." Morgan, oblivious to the two women now staring at her, allowed the barista to fondle the badge around her neck.

"That's your blizzard heroine?" Shanvi raised her eyebrows. "You neglected to mention her being built like an Ancient Greek Olympian."

"That's because I would never describe someone in those terms," Mei replied flatly. "Plus, it was winter and we were in our coats. What is she doing here?"

"Probably for coffee, like we are." Mei shot her a look. "Looks like she's definitely been here before. We've been coming for months and we don't know that barista's name." She paused. "Are we assholes?"

"No, that woman is egregiously friendly," Mei complained, tuning in to Morgan's conversation with her rapt barista.

"Oh, well, it depends on the day."

"So," the barista purred, batting her eyelashes, "if you made dinner plans, say, tonight? Would your schedule allow for that?" Mouth full of pastry, Morgan bobbed her head in agreement. Again, the barista let out a giggle that niggled its way beneath Mei's skin. How unprofessional, to proposition a customer. Amira released the officer's badge and slid the coffee toward her. "My number's on the cup. Don't throw it out."

"Okay." Morgan raised the cup and bag. "Thanks!" As the officer spun toward the door, Mei returned her attention to Shanvi. Apparently a moment too late, because Morgan stopped in her tracks. "Dr. Sharpe?"

"Hello, Lieutenant," Mei greeted, smiling softly.

"Hey, fancy meeting you here," Morgan said, smiling back with her megawatt grin. Mei thought she might need sunglasses just to look at her. "Not that I'm a regular. Do you—do you come here often?"

"When I can convince her to leave her house, yes," Shanvi interjected with a devious grin. "Hi, I'm Shanvi."

Tucking her pastry under her arm, she extended her hand to Shanvi. "Nice to meet you. I'm Morgan. Wow, Shanvi is a beautiful name. Is that Hindi?"

With mischief painted all over Shanvi's face, Mei knew she could not prevent her friend from engaging her coworker. "It is. So, *Morgan*, we come here almost every day. How come we only saw you today for the first time?"

Morgan anxiously hovered her items over the table. "May I? Only for a minute, I don't want to intrude."

"No intrusion," Shanvi answered. Mei knew, deep in her heart, Shanvi's insistence was punishment. Morgan silently asked Mei for additional approval and she reluctantly consented.

"Great!" Morgan grabbed a chair from behind them and slid it across, straddling it backward. "I only started coming here two weeks ago, and usually not this early. Ruiz insists we start our day before everyone else. So, while I appreciate her work ethic, I do need a coffee and a pastry to handle it."

Gleefully engaging in conversation in the wake of Mei's obvious discomfort, Shanvi inquired further. "And what division do you work in?"

Morgan took a big bite of her pastry, holding up a finger as she chewed. Swallowing, she offered an apologetic smile. "Sorry, Ruiz doesn't let me eat in the squad car so I have to inhale this or I won't see sustenance again until lunch. I'm in investigations. I was transferred to lead the cold case unit."

"Cold case unit?" Mei asked, finally catching up to the conversation after shooting death glares at her friend. "I wasn't aware we had one."

"It's new," Morgan replied, a shadow crossing her otherwise permanently smiling face. "It got worked into my promotion."

"I see." Mei sipped her tea, eyeing the phone number and winking face scrawled on Morgan's cup. "Why are you working the Solomon case with Ruiz? Isn't that a bit below your title, Lieutenant?"

"I do as I'm told. Cap asked that I step in before diving into the cold case files."

"Why you?" Shanvi pressed. A homicidal urge thrummed through Mei, encouraging her to strangle her only friend. Lieutenant Kelly engendered disquiet in her, like removing a bone fragment whilst needing to sneeze. Mei did not like that feeling. "Surely there are other officers with less to do?"

"Probably, but I am a very good detective, Shanvi," Morgan drawled. Suddenly, she shot back in her seat. "Oh! Speaking of." Whipping out her phone from her pocket, she tapped a few buttons and handed the phone to Mei. "Look what I found at the Solomon residence."

Mei took the phone and stared down at the blurry image of a forensic photo of a bloodied pillow. "A pillow."

Morgan stared at Shanvi, narrowing her gaze. "Gosh, your eyes are lovely. They should have you, like, model glasses or contacts or something." She turned to Mei, just in time for Shanvi to bashfully glance away. "Yes, we found it. Stuffed behind the refrigerator in the kitchen. Forensics is matching the blood to the vic, but the fibers are already a match for the ones you found. That's why I never got back to you about the email, things got pretty crazy after that. But your finds totally blew the case open, Dr. Sharpe." Like ping-pong, she looked to Shanvi. "Your friend is a stellar medical examiner."

"She works hard at it," Shanvi concurred.

"She sure does. I've read several of her reports," Morgan said, tearing off another piece of her pastry.

Mei pushed the phone back across the table. "You have?"

Morgan nodded, as if reading old autopsy reports was commonplace and not an extremely odd extracurricular activity. "Yeah. I dug into the cold cases while I help Ruiz, some of which you were the medical examiner on. Your reports are obsessively thorough. They're some of the most well-written and incredibly intelligent autopsy results I've ever read." She canted her head. "You know that, right? That you're, like, brilliant?"

Mei blushed, silently cursing herself for the inability to school her features. She must look like a fool, like the blue-haired barista staring longingly from behind the counter at the back of Morgan's head, but nobody had ever fawned over her boring autopsy reports before. "Well, I am always happy to be of use."

Swallowing the last bite of whatever blood-sugar-spiking confection she purchased, Morgan took a swig of her beverage and returned her chair to the proper table. "Thanks for letting me crash your party. I'm glad to have run into you, Dr. Sharpe. I hope we see each other again soon. You're always welcome to visit my dungeon."

Again, Morgan's eye contact pulled her into a trance. "Your dungeon?"

"Yeah, the cold case unit is in the basement. Well, I say 'unit' but it's a couple storage rooms full of boxes and binders. Anyway, I should get going. Ruiz will have my head if I'm late to the briefing again." She extended her hand to Shanvi. "It was nice to meet you, Shanvi."

"Likewise, Morgan," Shanvi replied, shaking her hand. "You can crash our party anytime."

Morgan laughed gently and shook her head. "Ah, be careful. I am not known for being able to turn down a wonderful time with not one, but two fascinating women. Enjoy the rest of your day."

Shanvi's eyes followed Morgan out, only to see her nearly bump into a woman walking her dog. Morgan knelt down, matching the dog's excitement with effusive, two-handed petting. The dog licked her face and she laughed, chatting with the woman above her. Morgan took out her phone and snapped a picture of the dog, then shook the dog's paw politely. They parted with short waves, and the woman turned around with a grin to check Morgan out as she walked away.

"Wow. How is anyone that pleasant? Especially a cop." Shanvi sighed. "You were right, though. She is a lot."

Mei grumbled into her tea. "I know. I appreciate you bringing her show to our table and inviting her back for an encore."

"Please, you like her."

Coughing in surprise, Mei dabbed her mouth with a napkin. "Excuse me?"

"You like her, I can tell."

"A: I barely know her," Mei countered. "B: She's a cop. You've been around enough of them by now to know they're all muscle, no meat."

"She looked like plenty of meat to me," Shanvi said with a waggle of her eyebrows. "And muscle."

"Please do not objectify my colleagues."

Shanvi grinned. "Oh, she's a *colleague*." Off Mei's exasperated look, Shanvi raised her hands in surrender. "I'm just saying you were not your usual icy self. More of a gentle frost."

"I sometimes genuinely wonder how we remain friends."

"Because I am one of the few people in the world who knows you this well and still likes you." Mei glared at her, but Shanvi did nothing but smile in return. "Besides, I think it would be good for you to make a friend. I will continue to be your best and closest friend, but still."

Mei relaxed, releasing the breath she held in her chest. Pressing her finger against the window, she dragged it down the dewy condensation on the pane and scoffed. "Gentle frost."

After an uneventful rest of her morning, Mei arrived (predictably, but not intentionally) early to lunch with her daughters. Sitting outside in a comfortable wooden chair, she closed her eyes and allowed the spring sun to warm her up. Mild for early March; weather Allan used to love. He would set up the patio furniture in the backyard, insisting on taking all his meals in the fresh air, disregarding their perfectly acceptable dining room. When the girls were little he dug them a firepit and took them "camping" in the yard, complete with a tent and s'mores. Mei rarely joined them—the thought of sleeping amongst the bugs was particularly off-putting—but they always had a good time.

"Earth to Mom." Mei opened her eyes to see her youngest staring down at her, concerned, with her black hair tossed haphazardly in a bun atop her head and makeup dark. She wore a T-shirt with a band Mei had never heard of scrawled across the chest, and a pair of low-slung, ripped black jeans. Punk rock couture. "Aren't you a little young for the midday naps?"

"Hello, Lara."

"Hello, Mother." Lara sat down, waving over the attention of an anxious waitress. After ordering a tame cocktail, she folded her jacket over her chair and clasped her hands. "Well, this is a nice place."

"Fairly adequate American Italian. They recently opened the alfresco dining. I thought the three of us could do with a little sunshine."

Lara snorted. "You sound like Daddy."

"Thirty years of marriage will do that, no matter how hard I resisted his influence," Mei replied with a fond smile. "Do you know why your sister arranged this date?"

"No," Lara said, the lie written plainly across her face. Her youngest was brilliant, but also an awful liar. Domineering since birth, Grace always took the lead in their sisterly scheming. This submissiveness was painted all over Lara—her string of failed relationships, her aimless job-hunting, and the constant existential crises. Lara rubbed the blood-red ink tattoo on her forearm. One of her many tells. "I found out when you did."

"Is that right?" Mei didn't push it. Grace would be here soon enough and they could lay their cards out on the table. "How is school going?"

Lara shrugged, tugging at one of her short shirtsleeves. "Same as always. Misogynist professors. Patriarchal textbooks. I'm this close to switching to Women's Studies so I don't have to hear another old white guy mansplain Jane Austen to me."

Between British Literature and Women's Studies, Mei could see no practical application for her daughter's future, but she knew better than to try going down that road. These children would be the ones picking her senior home, and she'd like a nice room facing the sunset. "Fair enough. Ah, there she is."

Grace, in her business-suited glory, came powering through the restaurant. Where Lara got Allan's softness, his sensitivity, and the artist in him, Grace seemed to have sucked up all Mei's straightforwardness. Designer sunglasses on, she put her purse on the ground and sat in the chair next to her sister. "Am I late?"

"No, Mom insists on being early enough to make us feel late."

"Why does everyone think I do that on purpose?" Mei asked, baffled.

"Because you do." Grace ordered a drink from the waitress and let out a long sigh. "How are you, Mom?"

Mei eyed her suspiciously. "As I told you over the phone, I am fine. Keeping busy, as always. I tried a spin class."

"Did Shanvi drag you?" Lara asked, teasing. "She loves yanking you out of your comfort zone."

"Yes, when she can. It does bring her a strange glee." Unable to bear an awkward silence, Mei placed her folded hands on the table. "You may tell me why we are here now. Not that I don't love a chance to see my wonderful daughters, but you are less than subtle."

A brief reprieve arrived with their waitress. After completing the task of ordering food, Grace shot her sister an anxious look. "To be frank, Mom, we're worried about you. We worry that you're closing yourself up. You know, since Dad died."

"Closing myself up? When I was so open before?" Mei cocked an eyebrow, a tad insulted. A mutiny from her own spawn. How dare they insinuate she used to be extroverted?

Lara touched Mei's elbow. "No, but Daddy was always the one who got you to socialize. I mean, how long has it been since you hung out with anyone besides us or Shanvi?"

"That hardly seems relevant." In fact, no one. It was easy to avoid people after Allan's death—nobody wanted to make awkward small talk with a bereaved widow, and this bereaved widow didn't want to make small talk.

Grace cocked an eyebrow over her Manhattan. "Lots of widowed spouses have trouble reconnecting after their partners die. And you, you're the queen of Shouldering-A-Burden, so we know you're not going to ask for help. Or, god forbid, seek therapy."

"Therapy?" Mei scrunched her face. She possessed no bias against therapy, but she could not see herself on an expensive bonded leather couch, pouring her soul out to someone paid to scribble notes. "Is there something I've done to warrant this intervention?"

"Mom." Lara implored her with her big expressive brown eyes and cherubic face. "We're concerned. You haven't talked to anyone about Daddy's death. Grace and I are both in therapy for it. And we're, you know, mostly functional adults. Grace flies giant death machines and she still struggles with grief. It's not an admission of weakness."

"I am aware of that," Mei returned, pausing to smile politely at the waitress delivering their meals. Staring down at her ravioli, she sighed. "Honestly, I am grateful you girls are worried about me. But I assure you, I am fine."

It wasn't a total lie. She ably completed her days without a breakdown. Her work had not suffered, other than the few weeks of catching up she had to do upon returning from her bereavement. The house sparkled with cleanliness, the lawn trimmed and green, and her hygiene immaculate. She had one friend. All things considered, she did pretty well.

From her purse, Grace withdrew a folded sheet of letter-sized paper and handed it to her mother. "There's a casual group in your town for people who are grieving. Widows, widowers, basically anyone who has lost a family member or whoever. A nice woman who's like…maybe some sort of nun? She runs it. A former nun, maybe? I'm not sure what the deal is. But it's secular and chill."

A thankfully low-key flyer; Mei had thrown out enough brochures splattered with pictures of sun-drenched beaches and breathtaking mountaintops to last a lifetime. This paper consisted of a short introduction to a "Sister Laura" and a location and time. Held in the local high school gymnasium, once a week on Tuesday nights. Attendance was at will, coffee and pastries provided. No mantras, no promises of a better future, just a place to sit and talk. "I don't know."

Lara grasped her mother by the wrist. "We miss you, is all. You've gone to a place where I feel like I can't reach you. Other than birthdays or major holidays, you disappear for weeks or months. I know you think going to work and getting up and dressed is living, but Mom, it's not. It's a fraction of who you are. I think…I think you'd benefit from getting out there. Talking to people. I don't know, go on a date or something."

"A date?" Grace glared at Lara with an inherited icy stare. Lara cowered as Mei glanced between them. "Is that what this is leading up to?"

"No," Grace assuaged. "We only want you to try this out. You don't have to talk and share, but listening to other people share their experiences can be cathartic. We thought joining a group with other people going through a similar experience might help you right the ship."

This was not the first intervention her daughters had staged in the past year. Eight months after Allan's death, they told her she needed to go on vacation with them. She did, enjoying a lovely week at Grace's lake house, and then returned to her solitary life. And perhaps it wasn't all that healthy. As far as dates, well, Lara and Shanvi each sent Mei on a blind date, and they both ended with Mei convinced the effort required to rummage up interest in those mediocre occasions was not even worth the dinner. Mei had no use for these dates. She'd had her great love—why waste time with futile attempts at another?

Going to a group chat—one time, to assuage the worry of her daughters—sounded infinitely better than her loved ones playing Cupid.

"Okay."

Lara's face lit up. "Really? You'll go?"

"Yes. I will go at least once and see what it's like. No promises on my continued attendance, but I will go." Mei folded the paper and slid it into her bag. "Now, can we have a nice lunch without further delving into my alleged depression? Lara, do you have anything exciting going on? You must be getting up to something fun once in a while."

Grace primly slid a bite of her salad off her fork and cast a glance at her sister. "Lara is sleeping with the much older TA of her Black Poetry and Poets course."

"Oh my god, Grace, you suck." Blushing furiously, Lara hid her face in her hands. "She is not that much older and you are a jerk."

Mei held her fork midway to her mouth. "And how—how is that going?"

Lara groaned. "It is not going. It was a one time thing."

"You know how Lara's fancies change with the wind," Grace retorted with a teasing smile. "I remember one year there was the bartender."

"Tall Drink Lady," Lara replied with a dreamy stare.

"The officer whose stakeout you interrupted."

"Detective Dimples."

"The realtor trying to show an apartment across from yours."

"Agent Blazer."

"All of that within a year."

Lara rolled her eyes. "It's not like I slept with all of them. Forgive me for keeping my options open. Not everyone can find their soul mate at a high school pep rally."

As usual, Grace did not give an inch. "I am not to blame for my romantic efficiency. I found a mate, married him, and propagated. Loving him is a nice bonus."

Mei swallowed her bite and shook her head. "How is Mateo?"

"He's good. Decided to build a deck this spring, despite having zero experience with construction. But he's certainly capable of watching YouTube tutorials, so I'm not worried."

"Yes, you are," Lara said.

Scowling, Grace relented. "Fine, I am, but it makes him happy so I've decided to find it charming."

"And my grandchildren?"

"They're great. Nathan got a red belt in karate. Julia is tutoring."

Lara snorted. "Tutoring what, dolls? She's nine."

"A very advanced nine, scholastically speaking," Grace corrected. "Her mathematics are well above average, so the teacher asked if she wouldn't mind helping other students in the class."

"You would manifest a little teacher's pet, wouldn't you? Couldn't pry you from the asscheeks of any teacher you had. Every time I got into a new grade, 'Oh, you're *Grace's* sister! She was one of my favorites! You have big shoes to fill, young lady,'" Lara bemoaned.

Grace laughed, downing the rest of her cocktail and signaling the waitress for another. "Is that why you're so pale? From living in my shadow all these years?"

"I'm pale because we're Asian and we don't tan," Lara replied, pointing her fork at her sister.

"I tan," Grace replied. Across both her daughters, Mei could see the complex way their genetics expressed. Grace inherited Allan's Anglo-Saxon bone structure and darker skin, but Mei's black hair and her eyes. In Lara, Mei could see her female ancestors right up the family tree, a Lin through and through. "Don't be racist, Lara."

"You're both beautiful," Mei cut in. "And more importantly, you're both smart. If it's any consolation, Lara, your sister's teachers pulled me aside every year to ask if I would tell Grace to allow the other students to participate. Every one of them. She was, and I quote, 'a handful.'"

"A domineering top even in childhood," Lara sassed with a shake of her head. Mei furrowed her brow in confusion, but Grace understood and scoffed.

"Not all of us are sappy bottoms content to spend her life on her back getting driven into a mattress."

Mei's eyes widened. She wasn't one hundred percent sure what Grace referred to, but she knew it sounded overtly sexual and this was uncharted territory for them. "Ladies."

"She started it," Grace accused, gesturing toward her sister.

Lara gaped widely. "I did not! Grace is the one who brought up me having sex with the TA. What was I supposed to do? Just take it?"

"Isn't that what bottoms do?"

"I don't know, why don't we ask Mateo?"

Pausing to be momentarily appalled, Grace burst into laughter. "Turnabout is fair play."

Mei sighed. "This conversation took a regretful turn."

"We could talk about you going on dates again," Lara offered with a smile.

Mei took a moment to consider it. "Fine, continue. What is a 'sappy bottom'?"

CHAPTER FIVE

A single, bright white light slid up the dark line in between the elevator doors, crawling vertically from floor to ceiling. Morgan impatiently tapped her shoe against the thin carpet as the elevator shook and creaked to a stop. The doors chugged open and she walked out, stopping short. To her left, the morgue, and inside, Dr. Sharpe and her stunning intellect, her charming half smile, and the soft cadence of her voice. To her right, her new office.

She strolled down the hallway, lunch bag swinging in hand, beneath the flickering fluorescent lights beckoning her toward the office. While Dr. Sharpe's morgue boasted state-of-the-art equipment, the rest of the basement was like the bus in *Speed*—stuck in the seventies. The stale, gray hallway with thin, government carpeting and unflattering lights led her to a nondescript white door. Eventually, this would have COLD CASE UNIT written on it but nobody cared enough to send maintenance down here to affix the plaque. Which was just as well, as Morgan didn't want to have anyone in her office who wasn't there to help. Additionally, between her desk and the dozen towers of case file boxes, there was no room for anyone else to help. She'd gotten to a few of the box stacks but others stood unmolested, with impressively thick spiderwebs strung from the cardboard to the ceiling. Two additional storage rooms buttressed this one, each filled with metal shelving units stuffed with more binders and case boxes, where eventually Morgan would store all the cases. But first she had to solve one.

With her first cold case thumbtacked to her corkboard, Morgan sat on top of her desk and faced it cross-legged, her takeout in her lap. Using her phone to play music from the Bluetooth speaker perched perilously atop one of her many stacks of boxes, she dug into her lo mein as she worked over the case in her head. The assault and murder of a young girl, no DNA matches, no witnesses, interviews that went nowhere, a case cold for nearly two decades. However, in flipping through the case notes she discovered major holes in the investigative team's reports. Certain more swiss-cheese cases remained, Morgan knew she could make the solves required to get a team.

With vintage soul music on blast, Morgan lay back on her desk and ate upside down, snaking noodles into her mouth from her chopsticks held aloft. Staring into the perforated ceiling tiles emptied her mind, clearing space for the evidentiary puzzle of her case.

That is, until a faint "Ah, Lieutenant?" called from near the door. Startled, Morgan dropped a knot of noodles and vegetables directly into the back of her throat. She sat up with a start, choking on the un-chewed food fighting its way down her esophagus. Dr. Sharpe took a step forward in a gesture to assist but Morgan waved her off, using her phone to turn down the music to a conversation-level volume.

"I didn't mean to startle you, I'm sorry," Dr. Sharpe said, chuckling.

"It's—" *Cough.* "Fine. It's not you—" *Cough.* "Stupid baby corn. You're not even real corn." She collected herself as best she could, straightening her tie. Of course she'd make a complete fool of herself the moment Dr. Sharpe appeared—she really had to put all her eggs in the hope-she-likes-dorks basket. "Good to see you again, Dr. Sharpe."

Giving her "office" an inspection, Dr. Sharpe took in the towers of boxes covered in layers of dust. It reminded Morgan of grade school, her strict second grade teacher walking primly up and down the aisles making sure each student's desk sparkled. The authority exuding from her made Morgan hot beneath the collar of her suit. Though not required to suit up every day, Dr. Sharpe's unexpected visit made her glad she did. Her gray blazer and fitted trousers complemented perfectly with her navy button-down and polished navy shoes. The kind of put-together look she hoped someone as fastidious as Dr. Sharpe might appreciate.

"You know, my mother would say it serves you right for eating scandalously Americanized Chinese food."

Morgan tapped on the takeout box. "Well, unless your mother wants to come to my apartment and cook for me, this is the best I can do."

"No, don't say that. Somehow, she'll hear you and then not only is she cooking you food, but also doing your laundry, your zodiac—Western and Eastern—and by the end of it she'll have rearranged your house and maybe tried to marry you off." Exhaling a fond sigh, Dr. Sharpe tacked on, "She means well, but she says whatever she wants and nobody can stop her."

Morgan chuckled, digging back into her pint of takeout. "And what do you say?"

"I say live your life, but since it's only noodles and an absurd amount of oil, you probably could've made it yourself and forgone the offending baby corn." Dr. Sharpe ran her finger along the lid of a cardboard box, rubbing the dust between her fingers.

"You overestimate me, I'm afraid," Morgan replied, carefully extracting noodles from the container. "I make boiling water look difficult."

"Is that so?" Standing next to a tower of boxes, Dr. Sharpe crossed her arms and leveled a look of disbelief at her. "So you're a 'very good' detective, but not a 'very good' cook?"

"You've figured me out exactly, Doctor."

"Oh, I don't think that's true at all." An indiscernible look crossed Dr. Sharpe's face and an ache ran through Morgan. A desire to get to know the doctor so well she could read her facial expressions like a map. "Settling in okay? It's not quite a top-floor suite with a view."

"Ah, it's not so bad. A couple throw pillows will really tie the place together," she replied, smirking. "But to be honest, I've lived in places worse than this. Plus, there's always the spiders to keep me company."

"That's depressing."

"Which part?"

Dr. Sharpe paused. "Both."

Laughing and coughing, Morgan sat on the edge of her desk. "So, what brings you to my neck of the dungeon?"

"I received word from Sergeant Ruiz you solved the Solomon murder. I came by to congratulate you." Morgan nodded. With their perp in custody, the captain immediately sent Morgan down to cold cases, not giving her any time to thank Dr. Sharpe for her work. "So, congratulations."

"Thanks, Doctor. Honestly, it's you who should be congratulated. I only connected the dots. You put them there."

"I did?"

"The pillow and the execution solved the case. A few counties over, the 'hold the pillow while I shoot you' song and dance is popular with a specific drug cartel. Once we went through the vic's finances again, we made headway. Turns out, Mr. Solomon was laundering money. Decided to shave a little off the top."

"Evidently that did not go over well."

"They are surprisingly fastidious with the bookkeeping." Morgan put her container on the desk. "An informant who wanted to keep the cops away from the main outfit turned in the hitman. Cap is still going to try to link up with the other counties and get a task force going on the operation. But for now, at least Solomon gets justice."

"Unlike all these poor, unfortunate souls." Dr. Sharpe jerked her thumb at the boxes. "How are there so many?"

"Ah, you know. Older cases didn't have DNA analysis available, some poorly investigated, and others overlooked entirely. Lack of resources, lack of suspects, lack of evidence, and lack of effort. Take your pick."

"And they expect you to solve them alone?" The room barely held enough space for two people to hold a conversation, never mind a whole unit, so she understood Dr. Sharpe's confusion. "In this factory for respiratory ailments? Very good detective or not, this is a Herculean undertaking."

Gazing around at the mini-skyline of boxes, Morgan agreed. "Once I get a solve, Cap will green-light a full team. 'Til then, it's just me."

"Well, if you come across anything you think I can help with, don't hesitate to reach out. I am only down the hall, after all," Dr. Sharpe offered.

An open door, an invitation, a means to keep the doctor firmly within her orbit, and Morgan would not let it go to waste. Getting to see her more, plus getting an expert opinion on old cases? A no-brainer. Which was good, because the longer Dr. Sharpe stayed in her presence, the less brains Morgan had.

"Really? Gosh, it would be such a help to get another pair of eyes every so often. Especially yours." Earnestly excited, Morgan brightened at the idea of collaborating with such a brilliant woman. However, she instinctively tempered her excitement. The internalized voice shouting, *Shut up, kid* reminded her how she put people off with her unchecked exuberance. "Are you sure? I wouldn't want to be a bother."

"It's not a bother at all," Dr. Sharpe replied. Glancing to the floor a moment, she asked, "Why? Do I seem difficult to you? I know the other officers think I am."

Morgan knit her brows together. Insecurity had to be a rare look on the urbane doctor. "Difficult? Why?"

"I don't know," Dr. Sharpe deflected, shrugging. "Many of them find me intimidating."

"And? Them being scared of an accomplished woman is their problem. My mom used to say intimidating is a word men use for intelligent women who don't take shit. In my experience, she's been one hundred percent right about that."

Much to Morgan's delight, Dr. Sharpe laughed again. "Funny and, quite sadly, true. Well, um, my offer stands. Swing by, or send me an email if you don't want to possibly come in the middle of an autopsy. I don't know how much help I can be elbows-deep in someone's chest cavity."

"Duly noted."

"I should get back, let you finish your lunch without another baby corn attack."

"There is no end to their treachery," Morgan replied, grinning ear to ear. "See you around, Dr. Sharpe."

Once home and redressed, Morgan stopped to check herself out in her hall mirror before heading out. For grief meetings she dressed down, avoiding any stylistic clues she might be a cop. No suits or badges, just ripped jeans, raglan leather jacket, and wool beanie. All of the regular attendees knew her profession, but she didn't like to signal it if she could help it.

Locking up behind her, Morgan shivered at the cold breeze rustling the garden. Cutting through the front yard, the motion sensor light illuminated the driveway, casting a garish yellow spotlight on her car. Before she could get in, a voice called from above, "You all right, Morgan?"

Squinting up into the light, Morgan just made out the plump figure of her upstairs neighbor, Mrs. Vern, leaning out her second-story window. "Yes, Mrs. Vern. Going to my meeting."

"Okay, dear, have fun. Don't be out too late, it's getting cold. I heard there was some snow on the way."

"Thank you, Mrs. Vern," Morgan replied, chuckling. "Have a good night."

Backing out of her driveway, Morgan slowly cruised down her block. The neighborhood was more upscale than she could afford, sitting just outside the city limits in a gentrified neighborhood with an organic grocery and French-press coffee shop. However, when she apartment-hunted years ago, a spot opened up at a rent so low Morgan would've moved in even if it had been haunted. Mrs. Vern lived upstairs and owned the entire duplex, and in her retirement sought a low-key renter whom she could trust. After revealing herself as both a police officer and an orphan, Morgan received an adopted grandmother and a beautiful, affordable one-bedroom apartment on a scenic block.

She didn't venture to the suburbs much, not for anything other than work or her grief meeting. Well-manicured lawns, shiny vehicles, pristine mailboxes, all the hallmarks of an upper-middle-class neighborhood—and Morgan felt like an outsider. The warm lights of their garden lanterns acted as torches keeping away the Frankenstein monster Morgan imagined she was, treading upon their precious land.

Already late, Morgan parked her car in a hurry. The night grew colder and Morgan jogged across the high school parking lot to the entrance of the gym, practically bursting through the doors. Her loud entrance cut off Sister Laura mid-sentence, and Morgan grimaced as all eyes turned to her. Scurrying to her seat, she stopped midway between the open folding chair and the folding table full of treats. Not homemade, Morgan noted sadly, but a brownie was a still brownie. Nabbing the treat, she sat down next to Sister Laura and shucked off her coat. "I'm so sorry I'm late, Sister Laura."

"That's quite all right, Morgan. I'm glad you're here." Sister Laura was sixty-five with long hair, blond and graying, and the weathered look of someone who lived on a houseboat full time. She didn't wear a habit, instead dressing in flouncy sweaters and bell-bottom jeans, but her nun vibe put Morgan at ease. Morgan had attended a lot of grief meetings since fifteen years old, but Sister Laura's was the only one that ever took.

"I just finished my introduction as we have two new folks here today."

"Oh?" Morgan looked up, scanning the semicircle for new faces. Most of them were old faces, literally and figuratively. For weeks now, Morgan was the only person in the grief meeting under retirement age. Tonight, interrupting the sea of white sat a brown-haired, bushy-bearded, middle-aged man in a brown suit, and—

Morgan nearly dropped her brownie. Across from her, dressed casually in trousers and a violet sweater under a wool coat, sat Dr. Sharpe. Like a deer in headlights, the doctor stared at her in open shock.

"All right," Sister Laura said, opening her arms out into the semicircle. "Would either of our new members like to introduce themselves?"

Pulling off her beanie, Morgan watched her colleague seize with social anxiety. Thankfully, the man piped up. "Um, I can start. My name is Jonathan."

"Welcome, Jonathan," Sister Laura replied. "Is there anything you'd like to share?"

"Oh." Jonathan twisted his gloves in his hands. "I'm forty-three. I'm a liberal arts professor, have been for quite some time. I lost my husband five months ago. So, that's…that's why I'm here."

"Thank you for sharing, Jonathan." Turning her attention to the other side of the circle, Sister Laura inquired, "Would our other newest member like to introduce herself?"

Startling in her seat, Dr. Sharpe visibly recoiled and shook her head. "Oh, me? No, I—no."

"That's all right, dear," Sister Laura soothed. "In your own time."

"I'm Mei," she blurted out. "Mei Sharpe."

Heart thudding in her ears, Morgan didn't hear anything else Sister Laura said. In her mind she got sucked back into the past, *Ratatouille* style, to the snowy night on the highway. Meeting a woman named May whose voice and humor instantly charmed her, and whose energy hummed with Morgan's own. Shaking her hand, having her moment of connection. Flashing to the morgue, the name *Dr. Mei Sharpe* emblazoned on the door as she walked in.

"Would anyone like to get us started?"

Thrust back into the present, Morgan shook herself out of a trance and raised her hand. "Maybe I can get us going," she said, drumming on the tops of her thighs. "It's been a tough week, to be honest. Next week will be the twentieth anniversary of my mom's death."

"That must be very hard," Sister Laura replied.

"I miss her, every day. It gets easier, but it's so goddamn slow." Morgan winced. "Sorry, Sister."

"That's all right," she said, reaching over to pat Morgan's leg. "Keep going."

"I've lived on this earth without her longer than I did with her, and I'm still not able to get beyond it," Morgan admitted. "It's so scary. There's a lot of fear in grief, you know? I don't think we talk about that enough."

"What do you mean?" Sister Laura inquired gently.

"Living without someone. Living with loss. Living with this interminable void, it's—it's…"

"Terrifying," Dr. Sharpe supplied from across the room. Morgan looked up from the floor, gazing at her. "Nobody tells you how scary it's going to be."

"Exactly," Morgan agreed, relieved. "It's scary, right? We're meant to move on and live our lives, and everyone tells you it's okay to be sad, but nobody tells you it's okay to be scared."

"Especially in the second year," she said, giving a glance over to fellow newbie Jonathan. "I lost my husband in February, two years ago. And that first year was fine because, well, it was expected. First Father's Day without him. First Thanksgiving, first Christmas. You know to expect this hole. But that second year? When what was first an anomaly becomes the standard? That's absolutely terrifying. The normalcy is frightening."

"The normalcy is frightening," Morgan repeated, staring directly at her from across the semicircle. "That's absolutely it. Thank you."

The doctor offered a weak smile and took off her coat. Others in the group echoed Morgan's sentiment of fright. Their losses varied from spouses to siblings, parents or children, but they all circled back to fear in their own way. When Sister Laura called it a night the elderly folks swarmed Morgan before she could take a step.

"Lieutenant, how's crime?"

"Did you get that email I sent you?"

"When are you going to call my granddaughter?"

Unable to break the testudo formation of seniors enveloping her, Morgan attentively fielded their inquiries, peering between them to watch Dr. Sharpe hurry out the door. Excusing herself as politely as possible, Morgan jogged out of the blue double doors and into the parking lot. Spotting the doctor bent over near a luxury sedan, Morgan waved and ran toward her.

"Hey, Dr. Sharpe, wait!"

As Morgan approached, the wary smile on her coworker's face turned into a frown. "Lieutenant, you're not wearing a jacket."

Looking down, Morgan's eyes widened in surprise. "Oh. Right. Well, I wanted to say goodbye, but I got jumped."

Dr. Sharpe shivered, leaning toward her car as if it would protect her from the wind. "That's okay. I didn't want to elbow my way through your throng of admirers in there."

"Oh, man." Morgan groaned, shaking her head. "Some of it is that Boomer cop-worship, but they're sweet. Early on I made the mistake of letting them know I don't have any living grandparents, and, well. Now I have a surfeit of grandparents." Morgan pointed to the beanie on her head. "Eleanor knit me this hat."

Chuckling, the petite doctor suppressed another shiver as the wind whipped around them. "You must be freezing."

Morgan shrugged. "Strong constitution, I'll be fine. Anyway, so, you are the woman whose tire I changed on Valentine's Day." Dr. Sharpe bobbed her head in confirmation. "Did you know when Ruiz introduced us?"

"Not immediately," she admitted. "Eventually I remembered your name and then connected it with your face. You look very different indoors. And not, you know, covered in snow."

Morgan scratched the back of her neck. "Yeah. I mean, I didn't know at all. All I had to go on were two brown eyes and the make and model of your car. Not that I was like, looking for you or anything. I never expected to see you again."

"You know, I did wonder, how did that date go?"

"Poorly," Morgan said with a snicker. "She was livid I changed your tire and accused me of intentionally sabotaging our date."

Balking, Dr. Sharpe put her hand on her chest. "Sabotage how? Like you put those nails in the road?"

"No, because I..." Morgan trailed off, embarrassed. That date went so remarkably bad it should have a place in a museum. "It's not important. Long story short, I felt more of a connection with you, a total stranger, than I did my supposed date. Needless to say, I haven't heard from her since."

"I would apologize, but it sounds like I did you a favor."

Cheeks dimpling, Morgan smiled and took off her hat, rustling her fingers through her hair. "I, um, I don't mean to sound too forward, but I'm happy to see you again. It's sort of crazy we ended up working together, right? And then here— honestly the last place I expected to see one of my colleagues. It's mostly just me and the golden gang."

"I'll admit when my daughters suggested this to me I was reluctant to join a care-share circle. Being forthright with strangers is not my forte, but seeing you here made it easier." Ducking her head, the blushing doctor scoffed. "I'm sure that sounds ridiculous, we barely know each other."

"It's not ridiculous," Morgan replied quickly. "I feel the same way."

A light dusting of snow began to fall, coating Morgan's hat and the tips of her eyelashes. She watched the perfect crystals land amongst Dr. Sharpe's lovely black hair, shimmering like ancient constellations. "I can't believe it's snowing again."

Morgan peered up at the weighty blanket of gray clouds looming overhead. "It's kind of our thing now, huh?" She took a step away from the car, motioning toward it. "Gosh, get inside, you're shivering like crazy. Have a good night, Doc."

"Mei," she said. "You can—please, call me Mei."

"Okay, Mei." Morgan's lips spread into a giant grin and Mei smiled back. "Get home safely. I don't want to have to get my mask and cape out of the car again."

"Very funny, Lieutenant." A smile still plastered on her face, Morgan stepped away from the car as she got in. Engine coming on with a quiet purr, Mei rolled down her window. "Please go get your jacket."

Morgan saluted her. "Yes, ma'am."

Rolling her eyes, Mei closed the window and backed up, slowly navigating out of the parking lot. Morgan stood amidst the snow, waving to the car driving away from her. As Mei's backlights faded into the night, Morgan closed her eyes and imprinted the moment in her mind. Morgan never forgot a new beginning, and she had the strong feeling this one would be one to cherish.

CHAPTER SIX

"Mei, what do you think about this?"

Without looking up from her autopsy, Mei knew Morgan was powering into the room. Over the course of a few weeks Morgan developed an expertise in maneuvering around the equipment tables and finding Mei. Bone saw in hand, Mei waited patiently for Morgan finally to realize she'd interrupted a rather delicate procedure. Between them a cadaver lay with its rib cage wide open, matter sprayed on Mei's protective mask.

"Whoops." Seemingly unperturbed by the body, Morgan boosted herself up onto the empty metal slab on the other side. "Sorry, please keep going."

"I cannot use a bone saw with you in here without protective gear, Morgan. Not after last time."

"Oh yeah, I forgot. You know, some of it was still in the cuff of my shirt when I went home?"

Placing the saw on the table, Mei flipped the shield of her mask open. "What can I do for you?"

Morgan paused, clearly contemplating whether to continue with her interruption. Ultimately, she couldn't contain herself.

"Okay. Remember the Harris homicide I asked you about last Monday?"

"Yes. The home invasion."

"Right. So, the examiner's report is pretty good. Not like, Dr.-Sharpe-level good, but decent. The stomach content section is crazy thorough. 'Roasted potato, undetermined type of red meat, fibrous green vegetable, possibly string bean or asparagus.'" Morgan glanced up. "Doesn't that sound extra specific? Aren't they usually more vague?"

"It depends," Mei replied, crossing her arms over her protective anorak. "There's analysis that can be done to determine what the food is, if the officers deem it necessary to establish timeline. For example, if the examiner finds undigested curly fries in the stomach—"

"Gnarly."

"—then you know the victim was killed within a few hours of eating the curly fries, maybe from an Arby's. It takes about six hours for the stomach to empty. If I can identify or estimate the foods, I do."

Morgan closed the folder, staring down at it. Accustomed to this idiosyncrasy, Mei waited in silence as the detective worked the case in her head. Morgan suddenly refocused. "The timeline is all screwy, but that at least narrows down the time of the murder. You don't eat steak and potatoes for breakfast, even if it is 1974."

"I can tell you for certain I did not eat steak and potatoes for breakfast in 1974." Morgan snickered and peered up at the clock. Following her gaze, Mei frowned. "Oh, when did it get so late?"

"It can't be too late." Lifting her wrist, Morgan proved the opposite with a grimace. "Never mind, it's almost seven."

"That's not late for you," Mei replied casually. "When I leave your car is usually still here."

Her grimace now a sly grin, Morgan playfully raised an eyebrow. "Are you tailing me, Dr. Sharpe?"

Far too late to walk back on that comment, Mei attempted indifference. "Your car is not an easy thing to miss. It's a statement vehicle and you know it, Lieutenant Kelly."

"She is a beaut." Mei rolled her eyes and pulled the shield back down, ready to continue her sawing. "Listen, do you—do you want to grab dinner? Off the clock, I won't make you explain anything about any dead person's half-digested food. And we definitely won't get Arby's. I may never eat it again. Which is a shame, 'cause, you know, the milkshakes."

What else did Mei have going on? Nothing waiting at home but a dinner for one and a random documentary. Totally normal, right? Two colleagues going out to dinner on a Thursday night? Plenty of employees fraternized outside of work; this wasn't an aberration. Technically they didn't even work together, other than the past two weeks of her unofficial assistance on the unsolveds.

She must've taken too long to answer because Morgan raised the folder and waved her off. "It's okay, I didn't mean to put you on the spot. I'll—I'll go."

Warring with herself, Mei watched her take a few steps before speaking up. "No, I'd love to. I just need to put all this away and clean up. Shouldn't be more than ten minutes."

Morgan brightened considerably. "Great! Where to? Any dietary preferences?"

"Nope, I'm pretty open. Lean vegetarian but I'm not strict about it."

"Cool. I know a good spot not too far. I'll meet you outside."

Normally she preferred to finish her autopsies, but the crestfallen look on Morgan's face at a perceived rejection made her heart hurt. Perhaps she was more empathetic than she thought.

Twenty minutes later, Mei emerged into the parking lot and found Morgan waiting against the exterior of the building, round headphones over her ears. An overhead floodlight cast a pale yellow glow around her, picking out the darker golden streaks in her hair. Unseen, she watched Morgan bob her head to an unheard song, tapping on her phone with her thumbs. Mei, only five foot four on a good day, estimated Morgan's height to be closer to five nine. Generally slender but athletic, the outline of her biceps visible through her shirt and the flexor muscles in her exposed forearms. Built like a basketball player, or maybe a soccer player, if she had to guess. Years of observing nude corpses made Mei more of an expert in what people looked like beneath their clothes than she'd ever admit out loud.

Walking into her view, Mei tugged her coat closed. "Sorry, cleanup took a little longer than normal. I didn't want to have any surprises in the cuffs of my shirt." It definitely wasn't because she touched up her minimal makeup or re-combed her hair several times, because that sort of behavior would be bizarre for a platonic dinner between acquaintances.

Laughing as she tucked her headphones into a bag slung around her shoulders, Morgan shrugged. "It's all good. Since you know what my car looks like, I figure you can stalk me—I'm sorry, *follow me* there."

"Uh-huh. Lead the way."

Nestled in a trendy part of downtown, the restaurant stood out on a block full of brick-façade bars and matte black awnings. Twinkling multicolored lights hung from strings across the top of the windows, curtained by heavy navy blue drapes. A pungent and pleasant aroma of cooking could be smelled from the sidewalk. Stepping inside, Mei took stock of the cozy interior. Cross-regional Mediterranean, she estimated, with Turkish-inspired decor.

Morgan shrugged off her coat and took Mei's, hanging them up in a corner. "Ever been here?"

"No." The scent of spice hung heavily in the air, clinging to the fabric pillows on the wicker chairs and penetrating into the wood-paneled walls. "I don't do a lot of eating out."

Morgan snorted, though Mei wasn't sure what was so funny. "Right. Well, Yumel is a hidden gem in this part of the city. Everything is made on-site and from scratch. Trust me, you're gonna love it. Now, I am famished. Where is—"

"Morgana!" A large older woman burst from the kitchen door, startling the other three patrons sitting at a corner table. Draped in a mauve tunic sweeping the floor, the woman's sandaled feet slid against the tiles toward them. She embraced

Morgan tightly, kissing her on both her cheeks. "Morgana, you're here!"

"*Merhaba*," Morgan greeted. "It's nice to see you, Meltem. Where's Yusuf?"

Meltem squished Morgan's face between her hands. "Oh, you know he is back there, hands sticky in the dough. I will tell him you are here." Wide eyes with lids painted blue took in Mei. "Is this your guest?"

"Yes. Mei, this is Mrs. Yalaz. She and her husband Yusuf own Yumel. Mrs. Yalaz, this is Mei Sharpe. She works with me."

"Call me Meltem. Any friend of Morgana is a friend of ours. Please, please, sit. You get your favorite seat." Meltem ushered them toward a table by the window. "Yusuf! Morgana is here!"

As Mei started in her seat at the woman's booming voice, a man's face popped into the serving counter window between the dining area and the kitchen, his bushy beard stuffed into a hair net. "I heard you! The whole neighborhood heard you!"

"Then come say hello!" Meltem uttered what Mei assumed were exasperated remarks in Turkish, then clapped her hands together, startling Mei again. "Okay, I will get you all you need."

In short order strong drinks and numerous unordered appetizers appeared at their table. By the time their entrées arrived, the warm, tingly buzz of good alcohol spread through her bloodstream. Despite Mei's reservations about befriending a police officer, Morgan was lively and full of intelligent conversation, entertaining Mei with funny anecdotes and asking her lots of questions about her life. Whether due to the company or the liquor, Mei spoke at length about herself with unexpected ease. By the time Mei realized Morgan cracked her open, she'd already discussed her daughters, her career, and even the origin of her friendship with Shanvi. Eager to talk about something other than herself, Mei pivoted the conversation.

"So, what's the story with the muscle car?" she asked, jerking her thumb out the window where Morgan's car asserted itself against the curb, shining brilliantly against the lights. She drove a vintage model Mei couldn't name with a dictionary, painted sleek crimson red with a white streak across the side. Of course her car would be a lot. Everything about Morgan was a hair shy of too much.

Morgan raised an eyebrow as she happily dunked her pita into hummus. "What makes you think there's a story?"

"It's a beautiful car you clearly take good care of. Nobody spends that much time on something they don't want to talk about."

Chuckling with a piece of pita hanging from her mouth, the officer finished her food and swallowed. "Fine, *Detective*. There is no great tale," she began, deflecting a bit. "My mom loved muscle cars, but we could never afford one. I found Dorothy online ten years ago, and—"

"Wait, I'm sorry, Dorothy? You named the car?"

"Of course I named the car." Morgan scoffed. "She is a member of my family, she has to have a name. It's a 1971 Mercury Cyclone. It took about five years of my life to painstakingly and lovingly restore her."

"I see." Mei narrowed her eyes. "Dorothy, like from *The Wizard of Oz*?"

"Yep. 'We must be up inside the cyclone!'" She exclaimed, pitching her voice high. "Get it?"

Mei put her hand over her mouth. "Is that—was that your impression of Dorothy Gale?"

"Yes," Morgan said defensively. "It's pretty good, right?"

"It is not good at all," Mei replied, laughing. Morgan's face twisted into a cartoonish frown. "You made her sound like Betty Boop."

"She does sound like Betty Boop!" Morgan crossed her arms. "How dare you, what if I was really proud of that impression?"

Mei raised an eyebrow, sipping her beer. "Are you?"

"Maybe."

"Then I'd hope you'd appreciate my helping rid you of that delusion."

Morgan stuck out her tongue and lobbed a piece of bread toward Mei's plate. "Ouch. Fair, but also, ouch."

Mei was busy laughing as Yusuf arrived to clear their table. "Okay, I am ready to hear how wonderful my food was."

The warm adoration in Morgan's eyes was sweet, Mei reluctantly admitted. Her friendliness wasn't egregious, as she'd initially said to Shanvi. She genuinely liked other people, and these other people liked her back. Her ability to connect with others was organic, real. So while Mei, cozy inside her shell, could not relate, she did appreciate it.

"Yusuf, it was the best I've had in days. Weeks. It was *lezzetli.*"

"You flatter me," Yusuf said, turning on his heel with the plates in hand. "Did you hear that? Morgana say my food is the most delicious she had in her life."

"That is not what she said, Yusuf," Meltem called from the kitchen.

"Close enough," he cheered, backing into the kitchen with a big smile.

Gluttonously full, Mei leaned back in her wicker chair and placed her hand over her stomach. Allowing the alcohol to work its way through her bloodstream, Mei nursed a water as she regarded the woman across from her. "They seem fond of you."

"Oh, I've been coming here for years. Since I joined the force, at least," Morgan said. "Part of my beat included this block and I'd pop in. Helped them out a time or two."

"Ah. Perks of the job."

A light dusting of pink colored Morgan's otherwise pale cheeks. "I promise I don't come here to be fawned upon or get free food."

"I didn't think you would," Mei responded gently.

"The meals are delicious, and Mr. and Mrs. Yalaz are good people. Nearly every night they pass out food to the homeless on their way home. Plus, their daughter lives in Vancouver so they don't see her much. I'm the ersatz version they stuff with food."

"I think it's sweet," Mei replied. "It does feel a bit parental, the way they dote on you."

"It's a mutually beneficial agreement. They get to spoil a daughter and I go home with doggy bags full of food to keep me alive," Morgan explained. "Speaking of, excuse me a moment. They won't let me out of here without lunch and dinner for the next three days."

Morgan rose from her seat and strode into the kitchen as if she worked there. Mei took the moment alone to reach into her bag and retrieve her phone. Engrossed in her conversation with Morgan, she hadn't looked at it all night. Her eyes bulged wide at the time. Nearly midnight! Between trading work-related horror stories and their discovery of a mutual love of *Frasier*, Mei forgot all about how it was Thursday and she was due to be up for work in six hours.

As Mei gathered her purse, Morgan returned with six knee-high brown paper shopping bags. She put one on the table in front of Mei. "For you. They insisted."

Standing to peek inside, Mei uncovered a troubling number of to-go containers. "This can't possibly be left from what we ate."

"It's not. It's the end of the night so we get the closing-up goodies."

"The rest is for you?" Mei did not hide her alarm.

"Oh, geez, no," Morgan replied, putting the bags on the ground and retrieving their coats from the hooks in the corner. "I'm gonna swing by Eighth Street and drop these off on my way home. Well, most of them. One is for me. A girl's got to eat."

Living in the suburbs for so long, Mei had little to no grasp on the neighborhoods in the city. "What's on Eighth Street?"

Pulling her coat over her shoulders, Morgan fished her hat out of her pocket and plunked it on her head. "A women's shelter. The food bank provides meals most nights but it's not anything like this. It's a bit late for dinner, but all of this will hold for a few days."

Tying the belt of her coat closed, Mei reached for her purse. "So it's not just saving fair maidens on the side of the road, is it? You do this sort of heroism daily."

"I wouldn't call it heroism," Morgan demurred, brushing her off. "I'm only doing a little good. It is sort of my duty to give back."

"Is that why you became a cop?" Mei followed Morgan out the door after waving goodbye to the owners. Morgan turned to her. "To give back?"

"Oh, I think why I became a cop is another dinner altogether. But the short story is I may have watched a little too much *Law and Order* growing up." Morgan shifted the bags in her hands, stretching out her arm to look down at her watch. "Shoot, I should get going. Sorry I kept you out so late."

"Nonsense, I had a great time." Mei tucked her hair behind her ear. "Oh wait, the bill. I totally forgot. I waltzed out of there with all their food."

"You dined and dashed? You know that means I have to arrest you."

"You don't even have your handcuffs with you."

Morgan arched an eyebrow. "Says who?"

"Let me get my wallet. I didn't mean to leave without paying, I—"

"Relax, I took care of it." Mei opened her mouth to protest but Morgan raised her free hand. "Trust me, they give me a hard enough time as it is when I try to pay. If you offer, it adds another variable in what is already a complicated transaction. You can get next time. If you...if you want there to be a next time. No pressure."

"Yeah, I'd like that," Mei answered honestly, feeling bold. Finding friends was a well-worn topic between she and her daughters, as well as Shanvi. Well, here she was, with a friend. Perhaps not quite who Mei expected, but how can one predict these things? Making friends as an adult is like bobbing for apples, except instead of apples they're live goldfish. It's like bobbing for goldfish. "I'll see you tomorrow."

"I sure hope so."

After changing into casual attire from her lab clothes, Mei lingered in the morgue longer than usual, double-checking her tools for proper sanitation and organization, going over the log, doing temperature reads on the cold chambers, and other tasks she would not normally do on a Friday night. But as the clock neared six thirty and she still hadn't seen the lieutenant, it occurred to Mei perhaps Morgan wasn't in and she was a stalker.

Concluding her behavior was borderline ridiculous, Mei turned off the lights and locked the doors, heading up the stairs toward the parking lot. She scanned the lot upon entering, but Morgan's loud vehicle was nowhere in sight. Perhaps she'd left early. That would be rare, but it was a Friday. Mei swallowed her disappointment. She tried to shake the feeling as she walked to her car, head down toward the gravel.

"Dr. Sharpe?"

The somewhat familiar voice of Sergeant Ruiz drew her attention to a truck a couple spaces over from her own. Out of uniform, in an oversized sweater and leather pants, Ruiz's outfit reflected softness contradictory to her professional nature. "Hi, Sergeant Ruiz. Going home?"

"I wish." She groaned, leaning against her car. Unlike Morgan's low, sleek muscle car, Ruiz drove a hefty SUV, black and daunting, dwarfing the already diminutive officer. "Kelly is making me go on a date with her. I'm waiting for her to text me directions to this club."

Mei cocked her head to the side. "Kelly? Is that another officer?"

"You know Kelly," Ruiz said, gesturing. Mei stared back blankly and the sergeant snapped her fingers. "Oh, right. *Lieutenant* Kelly."

"Oh, Morgan." The tiniest barb nestled in Mei's heart as she pieced together what she was told. "You two are going on a date?"

"*Mierda*, not together," she said with a dramatic scoff and an expression of pure disgust. "Jesus, it would be like giving it to my sister."

"Would it? I didn't know you two were close." In their talks last night Morgan only brought up Sergeant Ruiz in a professional story, not a personal one. Their friendship mirrored hers and Shanvi's: Morgan's easygoing personality, her desperation to be liked, quick to smile just like Shanvi, all in direct opposition to Mei; and Sergeant Ruiz, closed off, aggressive, and suspicious of others. Maybe that's why Morgan took to her—she had years of experience handling a prickly woman.

"Yeah, we attended the academy together. Lived together for a while too. That's why I agreed to tag along on this date.

Otherwise, I wouldn't be caught dead in a trendy nightclub on a Friday night."

"Oh."

"But you hang around Kelly long enough, she makes you soft," she muttered, smiling a little. Affection colored her words, the same shade Mei spoke in when talking about her own family. "I don't know why she's going out with this woman she's barely into."

"Oh." Mei knew she should probably be making better conversation than this. At least another letter of the alphabet besides *O*. She didn't have reason to speak to Sergeant Ruiz much, though she did like her. However, something about this topic of conversation caused a sickness to churn in her stomach. That salmon for the sushi she'd made did seem a little suspicious. "Morgan wanted to go to a nightclub?"

"Nah, she hates them. I used to have to drag her out, back when we were both single. But her date said it's the 'hottest spot in town' and Kelly's real bad at saying no."

Mei held her purse closer to her stomach, fidgeting. "She is rather easygoing."

"Easygoing, a people-pleaser, a total pushover," Ruiz revealed with exasperation. "She's the best detective I've ever worked with, but she can't figure out women for her life."

Without any frame of reference for this information, Mei took her word for it. "Well, I won't keep you. Enjoy your date, Sergeant Ruiz."

"Just Ruiz is fine. We're off the clock."

"Right, okay. Um, please tell Morgan I said hello. I didn't see her today."

A sly expression crossed the officer's face. "Yeah, she had some off-site research to run down. You two have been seeing a lot of each other lately, huh? Kelly won't shut up about it."

"She won't?"

"God, no. She's obnoxious. Every day it's, 'Then Dr. Sharpe said this.' 'Mei thinks that.' I don't know how you deal with her. It took me six weeks to even want to talk to her at the academy. Another six weeks to be friends." Ruiz pushed off her truck. "I hope you know what you're getting into. Once you get close to Kelly, it's hard to get away."

Mei had difficulty discerning whether to take her words as an invitation or a warning. "I'll keep that in mind."

"All right. *Adiós*, Doctor."

As Mei drove away, she chose to ignore the gnawing sensation in the pit of stomach. Bad fish, that's all.

CHAPTER SEVEN

Out of breath, Morgan slowed down her ten-mile run near a park bench and leaned on it. One of those fake "summer" days in spring, the heat seared the back of her neck and sweat dripped down her spine beneath her tank top. This was her favorite park to run in because it had the best dog-to-person ratio, which meant she got to pet a significant amount of good boys and girls. It didn't, however, have enough shaded coverage and so she spent most of her run baking in the irregular heat.

Pulling her cell phone from the arm holster, Morgan scrolled through her contacts to find Mei. On her last trip to the natural history museum she noticed a sign advertising the traveling exhibition on forensics and the history of human medicine. To Morgan, it presented the perfect opportunity to slowly integrate Mei into seeing her on a less professional basis. Their casual interactions over the past few weeks—mostly lunches in Mei's lab and midday walks talking shop—revolved around work, at least in an official capacity. Here, though, it would be about work in a recreational sense, but also equally about getting to know one another. Like a gateway date.

Bringing up her text messages with Mei, Morgan smiled at their last exchange. A harmless argument over the best character on *CSI* (Morgan a *CSI* Willows stan, Mei, predictably, liked Al Robbins). She also had an unread message from Amira, the barista she'd gone out with last night, and she frowned. Even though she'd dragged Ruiz with her, it was a disaster. Ruiz told her it would be good to keep her options open should Mei prove to be a dead end, and Morgan did her best to be chivalrous and open-minded. They ended up in Morgan's bed and Amira held unfortunate, porn-addled ideas of what having sex with a cop should be like, and Morgan spent the night extremely uncomfortable. Evidently, Amira either didn't mind or didn't notice, and sent her a "thanks 4 last night, hope 2 hear from u soon."

Blowing it off for now, she instead sent a text to Mei, asking if she was free tomorrow to see the exhibit at the museum.

Every moment that passed by without an answer was agony. Pacing back and forth, Morgan's sneakers scuffed the asphalt of the jogging path impatiently. Dots appeared and disappeared. What if she blew it? What if this was a step too far, and Mei had no interest in even being her friend? What if she was just being polite because they worked together and she didn't want to see Morgan if she didn't have to? What if—

Her phone buzzed.

Yes.

"Ha! Ha! She said yes!" Morgan pumped her fist as passing joggers stared in her direction. She shook her phone at them. "She said yes!"

A woman gave her a strange look as she jogged by. "Good for you?"

"Thank you!" Morgan bounced up and down at the short but positive response. Quickly, she fired back a series of texts.

Great! See you at 2.

I'll meet you by the quesadilla.

:)

Glancing over the words, Morgan groaned loudly at her typo. It was one thing to flub her words when Mei was around, but it was another to be a complete idiot via text.

... *Quetzalcoatlus. That was autocorrect but now I'm hungry.*
Whooping in celebration, Morgan turned up the volume on her headphones and worked back into her run. Navigating the waters of Dr. Mei Sharpe proved to be tricky, but Morgan stayed the course. Beauty existed on the edge of the horizon; Morgan just needed the patience to get there.

Grand, automatic doors brushed against the carpet as they opened, welcoming in the visitors. Children rushed passed Morgan on all sides, chased by their accompanying guardians, and took off in different directions upon entering. Cavernous ceilings ricocheted the sound of kids and din of chatter. Twenty minutes early, Morgan instinctively navigated to the food court and bought the largest slushie they offered. Pleased with her purchase, she walked back to the lobby and stood beneath the fossil of the Quetzalcoatlus, forever immortalized mid-flight. The museum functioned as a place of worship for Morgan in childhood, a Sunday school where she learned about dinosaurs, geology, and how to entertain herself for hours on end without attracting the attention of security guards. The taste of blue-raspberry in her mouth and the familiar scent of floor cleaner and popcorn transported her back to calmer, fonder memories of her childhood. Wandering exhibits, slushie in hand, staring up in open wonder at the ancient relics.

The sharp click of heels caught her attention and she saw Mei walk in through the automatic doors. Stunning in any environment, Mei in a casual setting was one of her favorite looks. Her incredible, angular bone structure made her look austere a lot of the time, but she wore supple fabrics—silk, cashmere, designer cotton with a higher thread count than Morgan's sheets—and it softened her. Not to say Morgan didn't enjoy Mei in her starched lab coats and goggles, but she appreciated the tenderness of off-the-clock Mei.

Most appreciated, though, was the way Mei's face brightened at the sight of Morgan, making her heart flutter uncontrollably in her chest.

"That's quite a beverage."

Lips still wrapped around the wide pink straw, Morgan grinned. "It's the greatest flavor of all: blue." She tipped the straw toward Mei, who declined with a wave of her hand. "Good idea. I'm almost done anyway. The dregs are never as good as that first sip."

"I'll take your word for it." Slurping up the last of her drink, Morgan tossed it in a nearby trash can and put her hands in the pockets of her olive-green combat jacket. Mei glanced up at her expectantly. "Did you want to see any other exhibits, or right to the medicine?"

"Traditionally I swing by the dinos," Morgan replied, leading them toward an exhibit entrance.

"Traditionally?"

"Hey, Ted!" Morgan high-fived the museum guard, an older man with a bristly white mustache. "How are the dinos looking today?"

"Not a day over two hundred million years old, Ms. Kelly," Ted said, belly heaving with laughter.

"You, or them?" Morgan ribbed, patting him on the shoulder. "Good to see you, Ted. Tell Debbie I said hi."

"I sure will, Ms. Kelly. Enjoy your visit."

Mei followed on her heels through winding carpeted halls of glass-enclosed replicas of dinosaurs or incidental fossils. Once inside the dinosaur exhibit proper, Mei caught up to her side. "Am I to assume you're a regular patron of the museum?"

Morgan bobbed her head, staring up at another flying dinosaur. "Oh, yeah. I practically grew up here. My mom worked long hours, so on weekdays I'd hang out at the library after school until she got home. But on Sundays the library closed, so she'd bring me here. Ted's worked here for forty-five years, if you can believe it. He's known me almost my whole life. He always kept an eye on me as a kid."

"Why? Were you trouble?"

"No, no. I think Ted felt bad I was by myself." Morgan peered down at the carpet. "In any case, I kept visiting long after she died. I try to come about once a month, if I can. Ted should be retired by now, as I'm sure you could tell. His wife,

Debbie, recently retired as a schoolteacher but Ted can't seem to quit even though his sciatica acts up because he's on his feet all day. But I can't blame him. When you find a job you love, it's hard to leave it."

As they stopped in front of the next dinosaur, Morgan's eyes followed the escalating vertebrae of an Apatosaurus. Its exposed grin bore down at them, perhaps menacing in intent but Morgan found him really goofy. As she turned to Mei to mention it, the other woman chuckled and gestured to her face. "Your lips and tongue are blue."

Morgan licked her lips. "Is it becoming on me?"

"Terribly." Mei laughed as Morgan escorted her toward a rafter of Velociraptors. "Did your mother work here?"

"No, the bus to her job stopped out front. She'd buy me a slushie and then take the bus to work. I'd entertain myself for a few hours and, as a treat, we sometimes ate in the food court when she came back." Morgan stopped in front of an odd-looking duck-billed dinosaur. "This is one of my favorites. His name is Larry."

Cocking her head at the strange creature, Mei side-eyed Morgan. "I assume you named him."

"That's correct. He's a Lambeosaurus. Named after Lawrence Lambe, a famous Canadian paleontologist. He also has a mountain named for him." A few kids gathered around them as she rattled off more facts about Larry, but Morgan only had eyes for Mei, who continued to humor her by listening intently. Embarrassed by her babbling, Morgan wrapped it up. "The showstopper is that crest. Apparently, they think it was used to make noise to recognize other lambies. It's basically hollow. You could probably blow through it like a horn."

Leaving Larry behind, they started down another corridor. "What about your father, couldn't he have watched you?"

"Nope," Morgan replied, popping the p. "I didn't know my biological father until after Mom died. My mom's ex-boyfriend was out of the picture, and—Oh, look! It's Brad!"

The Brachiosaurus stood alone in his own exhibit, surrounded by fake vegetation crawling from his feet up to the ceiling. A truly breathtaking size, they both bent backward to take in all of Brad's wonder. "Brad."

"Brad the Brachiosaurus," Morgan said fondly. "He's my favorite."

"Oh, really? Why's that?"

"Look at this dork. Why is his neck so long? Why are his front legs so much bigger than his back legs?" Morgan put her hands on her hips. "He's so awkward. Not a skilled hunter or a fierce predator. Not one of the horned ones who fight, or the tiny asshole dinosaurs that'll leap out at you for no reason and tear you to shreds with those freaky Freddy Krueger claws. Brad's sole desire is to eat leaves. He's a gentle giant. I dig his energy, you know?"

"It does seem peaceful," Mei agreed, staring up at the creature. "They could've at least put one of those plastic leaves in his mouth for him."

Morgan looked over to his head with a mournful gaze. "That is somewhat cruel, now that you mention it. Poor Brad. I'll talk to Ted about it. He's got no real authority other than reprimanding rambunctious teens, but he'll like that I think he has the authority."

Casually strolling through other exhibits, it took another hour to find the humans in medicine. The exhibit began chronologically, and they walked through the history of medicine via precious relics and replicas. Morgan let Mei lead, being the expert between them, and stopped when Mei paused beside a replica bust of Julius Caesar.

"Why is Caesar here?"

"Allegedly, his corpse was one of the first recorded autopsies," Mei said. "The physician recorded that the second stab wound to the breast was the killing blow."

Both in casework and casual conversation, Mei's smooth elucidations never condescended or sought to do anything other than inform, and Morgan eagerly absorbed whatever Mei wanted to tell her. It was easier for Morgan to listen than contribute, as her own efforts to be charming often took flight with the grace of a rotund penguin. Still, she tried. *"The evil that men do lives after them, the good is oft interred with their bones."*

"Apropos."

Nearly tipping over the velvet rope keeping them away from the exhibit, Morgan squinted to read the plaque affixed below the bust. "No kidding, his doc invented forensics?"

"Not so much invented. The whole thing is shoddy at best, historically. It's not until Medieval England where you start to see people caring more about cause of death. Well, the cause of death for the important dead."

"Peasants got the 'bring out yer dead' treatment, presumably."

"More or less."

More visitors crowded the rest of the exhibit, with familiar instruments of early medicine shown off by mannequins dressed as medieval coroners or early nineteenth-century quack doctors. Mei kept close to Morgan, who took the lead weaving them in and out of the collections, keeping a gentle hand on the small of Mei's back.

Perusing a collection of antique knights' helmets Mei trailed behind her, running her palm along the velvet rope barrier. "So, um, how was your date?"

Pivoting, Morgan flipped up the visor on the toy knight's helmet she wore, eyes wide. A nearby museum employee gave them to children, but Morgan gleefully convinced him to let her have one as well.

"My what?"

"Your date? I ran into Sergeant Ruiz on my way out the other day. She said something about a club or a rave?"

"A rave?" Morgan canted her head. "Mei, nobody living above the Mason-Dixon Line has been to a rave since 1999."

Mei rolled her eyes. "You know what I mean."

"Uh. It was fine." Morgan shut the visor and shimmied to the right, away from Mei.

Despite her prayers to the contrary, Morgan knew there was no higher power because instead of dropping it, Mei inquired further. "Just fine?"

"Pretty much. I—I don't even know why I went." Morgan took off her helmet, hoisting it onto her hip. "I mean, I do. I went because she seemed nice. I don't know. We had no connection. She isn't my type, maybe."

"Let me guess." Mei strode beside her, plucking the helmet from her hip and plunking it on Morgan's head. "Sir Morgan Kelly prefers herself a maiden fair."

Morgan pushed up the visor, irked. "She needn't be a maiden and she needn't be fair. She need be...I don't know. Interesting, at least. Able to hold a conversation. Interested in more than sleeping with me would be nice."

Hoping this admission would deter her, Morgan moved to the next piece in the exhibit. The last thing she wanted to do was project an image of herself as someone who flagrantly philandered with anyone willing. "Oh. Is that a—a frequent problem for you?"

"I wouldn't say frequent," Morgan replied, placing her helmet into a basket of used ones at the end of the exhibit. Tousling her hair with her fingers, she then shoved them back into her coat pockets. "But it happens. I thought she liked me, but I think she wanted to notch a cop on her bedpost."

Mei's features twisted in confusion. "I didn't know people had that...predilection."

"Yeah, sometimes," Morgan replied tiredly, skimming her fingers along a touch-friendly piece of petrified wood. "Honestly, it's not a big deal. It's disappointing. I can understand how it's hard for civilians to look past the job...the mythos around it is a lot and the optics are not always great. But to assume my job is my whole personality is insulting, you know? I have other interests."

"Dinosaurs, for one." Fingers outstretched, Mei followed the trail of Morgan's touch along the wood. Placing her fingertips on top of Morgan's own, she smiled when Morgan turned to her. "For what it's worth, they're missing out."

"Thanks," Morgan said, ducking her head bashfully. "I appreciate that."

Three hours later they exited the exhibits and returned to the main hall. A lovely sense of quiet swirled in the domed lobby, less trafficked near dinnertime. Morgan rested against a directory in the middle of the floor beside the gift shop, peering inside its neon wonder. "Such cool stuff. I wanted everything in there as a kid. The plush dinosaurs, the magnets with your name printed on them, those stupid erasers that erased nothing but had pictures of animals on them."

"I'm stunned you didn't have a bedroom full of merchandise, considering how often you were here," Mei said.

"I barely had a bedroom. Plus, all of that was too expensive." Like a hologram, Morgan's younger self appeared in front of them, being dragged away from the gift shop. Her mother threatening under her breath, warning Morgan against making a scene. The iron grip of her hand clenching Morgan's. Fear coursing through her, knowing any escaped tear invited punishment. Shaking the memory away like an Etch A Sketch, Morgan smiled and turned to Mei. "I appreciate you coming with me. And humoring me with the dinosaur exhibit."

"No, this was great. Thank you for inviting me. It's not the sort of thing most people are interested in. Plus the breadth of your dinosaur knowledge was truly something to behold."

"Okay, now I don't believe you," Morgan joked, nudging Mei with her elbow. "Well, unless you want an overpriced, constellation-themed pencil case, I think we can go."

Together they walked to Mei's car, parked not too far from the entrance. Pressing the key fob to open her doors, Mei peered around for Morgan's obvious vehicle. "I walked," Morgan said with a grin. "I know you miss Dorothy, but the lady deserves a rest."

"Would you like a ride home? It got quite late."

The sun, now a deep, lovely shade of cerise, dipped below the city skyscrapers. As much as Morgan desperately wanted to spend more time with Mei, she needed the walk home to clear her head. "No, thank you. That spectacular sunset demands to be witnessed in the open air."

Mei's eyes moved to the sun behind Morgan's head, its orange glory lighting up the amber flecks in her irises. Instantly, Morgan decided every sunset should be seen reflected in those deep brown eyes. "All right. Good night, Morgan."

"Good night, Mei."

Outlining cases usually made Morgan too excited to eat, but she shoveled Mei's delicious homemade fried rice into her mouth as she gesticulated at her whiteboard. Behind her, Mei sat on a desk and plucked rice from her bowl, observing with rapt attention as Morgan passionately made connections between pieces of evidence.

Swallowing first, Morgan took a step back to admire her work. "So, I'm thinking the uncle needs to be re-examined. He had opportunity, means, and if the DNA on file isn't too degraded to test, we can match his DNA if he offers it. I don't have nearly enough for a warrant yet."

"What about motive?" Mei asked, digging in her lunch. "What motive does the uncle have for killing the niece? That seems like it would be uncommon."

"You know, there's no word for that: killing one's own niece. They've got words for killing infants, uncles, fathers, mothers, brothers, sisters, nephews, what have you," Morgan listed, shaking her head. "Anyway, yes, it is definitely uncommon. I've reread the interviews with the family, the neighbors, the boyfriends, friends, but something sticks out to me about the uncle. I'm not sure about motive yet, but—" Morgan picked up a nearby stack of folders and shook them. "I did some digging, and that county had a string of unsolved attempted kidnappings and abductions leading up to the murder. There are also around a dozen sexual assaults with a similar MO to what happened to the victim, though all those girls survived. It could be the same man. All of it could've been escalation."

Mei leafed through the case file, skimming through until she got to what had to be the mug shot of the uncle. "Yikes."

"The mustache, right?" Morgan grimaced. "That's not why I suspect it's him, but it doesn't help."

"Yeah, it really doesn't."

Morgan sat on top of her desk, cross-legged with her meal in her lap. "I'm going to re-interview the relatives in a couple days."

Normally Morgan relished the opportunity to interview witnesses because the human element of her investigations meant the most to her. But, after spending the last several weeks since the museum frequently in Mei's company, she loathed to leave. She risked losing the spellbinding magic of early courtship, or perhaps losing Mei's interest altogether. The latter would devastate her, but taking a look around at the hundreds of other unsolved cases, Morgan knew somewhere in those files was someone just like her, waiting for their chance at a resolution.

"Do people want to talk about it? Typically? I can't imagine the emotional trauma of dredging up a murder like that again."

The buoyancy of her mood dipping considerably, Morgan stared down into her rice. "I can relate. But, um, people don't have a hard time talking to me. I'm open and always myself, instead of like a Super Cop Here To Solve The Crimes. I try to make them understand that I want to bring them closure. Justice, if I can, but closure at the least."

Mei paused. "Why didn't you tell me you were a cop when you offered to change my tire? I've thought about it since and, I imagine, if I were a police officer, I would introduce myself as such, if I were trying to help. Gain trust, so the person doesn't think I'm a murderer."

Morgan let out something between a snort and a scoff. "Telling people I'm a cop doesn't always make them feel safe. I only announce myself as police if I'm doing something I can only do as an officer. Otherwise, a good deed's a good deed. Don't want to complicate it unnecessarily."

As a wealthy person, Mei probably interacted with cops less than the average citizen, so Morgan didn't begrudge her this relatively naïve position on law enforcement. It took Morgan a long time to realize her own naïveté as well.

"Will you be taking backup?"

"Not for the interviews. Most of the family members involved are well into their sixties and seventies, and I don't think they pose much of a threat. The uncle has a couple of priors but the family is clean."

"Isn't that dangerous?" Mei asked, an adorable amount of concern in her tone.

"I don't know. Probably not."

"That's not comforting, Morgan."

Light, rhythmic knocking interrupted them. "Come in."

Officer Lopez approached, taking in the relative disorder with a grimace. Despite the strides Morgan had made in the past few weeks to organize the chaos, towers of case boxes took up every available surface of carpet. "Hi, Lieutenant. Uh, Sergeant Ruiz sent me down here to get you. She said to tell you there was cake."

"Ooh, cake." Morgan cheered, hopping off the edge of the desk. She looked at Mei. "You want to come up for cake?"

A store-bought sheet cake served buffet-style probably sounded as appealing to Mei as a bat to the face, as Morgan knew her distaste for highly processed foods, especially sugar-laden confections. However, contrary to Morgan's assumption, she nodded. "Sure."

Morgan fist-pumped in victory, at which Mei fondly rolled her eyes. "Lead the way, Officer Lopez."

After chugging upstairs in the silent elevator, they emerged into a bullpen buzzing with energy. Concrete walls and floors made it seem more like a jail than an office, but the sheriff's birthday party was in full swing and quite lively. Streamers, signs, balloons, even a scant amount of officers in party hats. Before Morgan could make a beeline for the cake, a very smug Sergeant Ruiz intercepted her and Mei. "Dr. Sharpe, your very first office birthday party." Leaning in conspiratorially but not lowering her voice, she asked, "Kelly made you come, didn't she?"

"Morgan did not make me attend." Ruiz shot the doctor her patented you're-full-of-shit look and Morgan stifled her laughter. Mei relented. "She asked, and it took little convincing. Happy?"

"Soft," Ruiz teased. "I told you she has that effect."

Slinging her arm over Ruiz's shoulder, Morgan jostled her. "And Ruiz is glad for it, as my overwhelmingly positive influence helped her woo her smoking hot fiancée, so…"

Blushing, Ruiz shoved Morgan away. "Shoo, Kelly, go get your cake."

"I can and I will," Morgan announced, turning on her heel toward the serving table. After chatting briefly with Officer Lopez, she found Ruiz and Mei near the punch bowl. Holding a plate with a softball-sized square slice of cake piled high with frosting, Morgan grinned around her fork with unapologetic glee. Mei and Ruiz shared a look and the detective shook her head. "That's all you, Doctor."

Using the napkin, Mei reached up and removed frosting from Morgan's nose with a gentle wipe. A fierce blush spread across Morgan's cheeks, but Mei smiled at her. "I take it the cake is good?"

"No, it's terrible, I'm just not picky. Especially not picky about cake. Do you want me to get you a piece?"

"After that rave review? Somehow, I think I'll pass." Next to them, an officer blew into a noisemaker and startled Ruiz.

"Knock it off, Chen, I swear to god. I'll shove that noisemaker up—" Ruiz glanced at Mei and clamped up. "You know where I'll shove it. *Vamos.*"

Blowing out a much softer, incredibly pathetic whir from the noisemaker, Officer Chen bowed his head and scurried away. Morgan briefly glanced to check in with Ruiz, who gave her a short nod in return.

Scraping the frosting from the paper plate, Morgan looked up to see the flummoxed look on Mei's face. "What? Do I have more frosting on my nose?"

"No, you—you finished your cake."

"Dr. Sharpe doesn't know whether to be disgusted or impressed," Ruiz remarked. "Fortunately, she's never seen you eat a slice of pizza."

"Oh, but I have. The odd way she takes a bite of the end, then eats the crust, and then eats the rest of the pizza? Truly fascinating."

"Are you sure it's fascinating and not disturbing?"

"I choose fascinating."

Ruiz rolled her eyes, tipping back her drink and tossing the cup in a nearby bin. "Right. I guess when you spend your time with dead people this freak seems perfectly normal."

"My bar for normal is rather low."

Morgan's eyes shifted between them at their teasing. "This is tantamount to bullying! And here I am, inviting you up here for cake."

"I know, I know, I'm sorry," Mei cooed. "You're not odd or freakish. Perhaps, quirky?"

Aghast, Morgan placed her hand over her heart. "How could you? Quirky is worse than odd and freakish."

"I don't see how that's even remotely true."

"Well it is. I don't have to stand here and take this," Morgan said, straightening her back. "I am getting more cake. The cake doesn't call me names. The cake is my friend."

As Morgan walked away, Ruiz followed close behind. "Do you always eat your friends, Kelly? Seen you make that mistake once or twice."

"I hate you."

"No, you don't."

Exhausted from a week of interviews on her cold case, Morgan flopped back on her hotel bed and reached for her beer. Unwinding was necessary after cases like this—dredging the waters of other people's trauma, hers often got caught in the net as well. Morgan's empathy made her good at extracting information that might otherwise be withheld, but it also left her feeling fraught and open, like an exposed nerve.

Her phone buzzed from the nightstand, vibrating the bottle of beer next to it. Grabbing both, Morgan tapped her phone. "Hey, Ruiz."

"Kelly," Ruiz greeted. "How're the interviews going? Getting anywhere?"

"Yeah, I think so." Morgan tipped back her beer. "The focus is tunneling on the uncle, but I got other POIs to dig into when I get back."

Morgan could hear Ruiz humming in acknowledgment on the other side. "*Bueno.* And how you holding up?"

Smiling fondly, Morgan leaned back and sighed. "I'm okay, thanks for asking. It gets a little hairy sometimes, but I want to help them. I have to help them."

"Yeah, well, as much as I hate to say it, if anyone can help them, you can. Don't forget to take care of yourself, too, *comprende*? And not just with the sauce."

Morgan looked at the beer in her hand. "It's not like that."

"It's not, but it could be." As if she could sense the walls coming down inside Morgan, Ruiz asked, "And how's it going with Sharpe?"

"Ah, you know. Slow." *Slow* was generous. While their dates increased in frequency, Morgan took great care not to attempt anything too intimate. Their messages, once short and professional, now included inside jokes and teases, late-night confessions, and the occasional photo of a cute dog. Nothing Morgan couldn't walk back on if Mei didn't want a relationship. "Casual. I don't...I don't want to spook her."

Ruiz chuckled. "I can't picture Dr. Sharpe being afraid of anything, least of all you, Kelly."

"Maybe." Though Morgan wouldn't admit it to Ruiz, she did sometimes catch a bit of fear in Mei's eyes when the tension between them veered into the non-platonic. Hard as she tried to keep it light and casual, their relationship remained delicate. In spite of the agonizing speed, Morgan persevered. Beautiful things required time to build. "I'm letting her set the boundaries. I'm here waiting on the other side whenever she decides to cross them."

"What if she doesn't?"

"I'll let you handle the negativity. You're better at it." Morgan snickered. "The real question is: what if she does?"

"All right, Romeo. Get back to it." Ruiz shuffled on the other end, speaking Spanish in low tones. "Reyna says hi and she loves you. And she wants me to remind you that even though I'm being a 'party pooper,' we're rooting for you."

"Tell my *cuñada* I love her very much. I'll see you guys when I get back. *Adiós*."

Ending the call, Morgan tossed her empty beer bottle into the little blue bin and exchanged it for a piece of chocolate cake she'd ordered from room service. Swiping through her scene photos, Morgan came across a smiling, muscly blue pitbull she encountered on a walk, and giddily sent the photo over to Mei. Her last message was another of Mei's "check-ins" making sure a clan of geriatrics hadn't murdered Morgan.

Look how cute he is!

Despite the late hour, the response was immediate.

That is indeed a cute dog.

His name is BUMBLEBEE!!!

If I could get a dog, I'd name him Eddie. What would you name your dog?

Eddie is a fine name. How are your interviews going? Will you be back soon?

I'm making good progress here, she wrote. *Should be back in the office by Monday. Might have enough for a warrant.*

Maybe it was the beer. Maybe it was the emotional heft of the past few days. Maybe it was thinking about Mei on the other end of the line staring at her phone, smiling at the messages from Morgan. Dressed in silk pajamas—rich ladies always wore silk pajamas—curled up on her couch with a glass of wine. Or maybe, Morgan thought, in her bed, communicating with Morgan from her place of comfort. Whatever the reason, she hurriedly sent the text and braced for the worst.

Why, miss me?

Two minutes later, the response came through and Morgan excitedly, and carelessly, dropped her cake on her blanket.

Very much so.

CHAPTER EIGHT

Slowly, the way water erodes rock, Morgan wore away any objections or hesitations Mei possessed about their friendship. Before she knew it their routine became normal: constant contact through text, Mei's homemade lunches either shared in the office or at the nearby park, occasional evening meals at restaurants or bars, and seeing a movie or a play after work. Mei's weekends evolved from solitary gardening to day trips to local attractions, talks at the museum, or indie movies at the cineplex in the city. The new ritual of getting out had her calling up Shanvi and visiting Lara more often, sharing more meals with Grace, Mateo, and her grandchildren. Her days vibrated with life.

As they walked out of a talk on the real-life physics of *Star Trek*, Mei watched as Morgan took a deep breath of the warm outside air. "Smells like summer is coming. Oh, that reminds me. I'll have to take you to the river I kayaked in last year. It was super calming, I think you'd like it."

"Sounds good," Mei agreed, though she'd never once in her life sat inside a kayak. Before she got in the car, she leveled a look at Morgan over the top. "How did you do this?"

Morgan leaned her elbows on the roof. "How did I do what?"

"Get me to do all this. The talks, the movies, the nights at the bar. I was never like this."

Squinting into the sunset, Morgan tilted her head. "Would you like me to stop?"

"No, I don't think I do." Mei slid into her driver's side seat and waited for Morgan to get in as well. She did, looking at Mei as she buckled her seat belt. "I'm sorry, that probably sounded odd."

"It did, but I get it." Over the rumble of the road and a lite radio station playing in the background, Morgan added, "I'm a good climber."

Glancing sidelong, Mei raised an eyebrow. "Okay?"

"You asked how I did it. Well, like I told you, people build high fences. But once you find the right ladder, you can climb any fence if you put in the effort." Morgan shrugged. "I'm a good climber, and you're worth the effort."

Touched, Mei turned away and kept her attention on the road as they neared Morgan's home in a charming residential neighborhood just outside the city limits, composed of brownstone-styled apartments, with short front lawns and close neighbors. The city-block-party aesthetic fit Morgan and her extroverted nature, as evidenced by how many of her neighbors waved and spoke to her as she came and went from her building with Mei.

Lost in her thoughts, Mei almost didn't hear Morgan softly ask, "Do you want to come over for dinner?"

While she'd picked Morgan up many times, or left her car to take Morgan's on their way to an adventure, she'd only ventured inside once or twice, and never for longer than a few minutes. "At—at your place?"

"Yeah. Not tonight, I wouldn't—such short notice. But tomorrow? If you're free?" Tugging on the hem of her shirt,

Morgan avoided Mei's glances by staring directly out the windshield. "I know tomorrow's Saturday and I'm sure you already have plans. You can say no, don't feel pressured."

"No, no, I'd love to," Mei replied. "I'm free."

"Cool." Morgan smiled her trademark grin. "I've got a new puzzle that's absolutely killing me. I also saw a new documentary on HBO I thought you'd like. So, you know, eating and hanging out."

Pulling up to the curb outside Morgan's home, she parked the car and turned to her with an impish grin. "Are you going to cook?"

Morgan frowned and crossed her arms. "I feel like you're patronizing me, Dr. Sharpe."

She touched Morgan's shoulder in a conciliatory gesture. "I'm sure it'll be fine. What time?"

"Around five?"

"Perfect." Morgan hesitated, stuck in suspended animation debating whether to say or do something—Mei wasn't sure which. But a feeling she felt often in Morgan's presence, especially over the past few weeks, resurfaced. The feeling of standing on a precipice. Without saying anything, Morgan smiled and unlocked her door. Relief and possibly disappointment slowed Mei's heartbeat. "See you tomorrow."

Peeking back in, Morgan gave her a thumbs-up. "Yep! Don't worry about bringing anything. Just, um, yourself."

Once Morgan retreated into her home, Mei U-turned and drove toward her own. Something prickled the back of her neck. Anxiousness? Anticipation? She couldn't decipher it, so she employed her preferred method of burying it deep inside.

Upon arriving at Morgan's apartment the following afternoon, Mei's nerves shook with fraught energy. Not since college, or perhaps even high school, had she experienced this level of naked anticipation and surge of nerves. Turning the bottle of wine over in her hands, she debated knocking again when, through the door, she heard a flurry of PG-13 curses, followed by the shrill beep of a fire alarm.

Feet scuffled behind the door until it finally swung open and revealed a slightly disheveled Morgan in the foreground, and a haze of gray behind her. Morgan pushed back her hair and smiled. "Everything's fine."

"Okay." Morgan allowed her in, running on socked feet back to the kitchen. Climbing a nearby kitchen chair, she tore the batteries out of the alarm. Mei wasn't but a few steps in before she could hear a voice calling from outside.

"Morgan, is that you?"

Head hung in defeat, Morgan craned over the sink, shouting out the window above it. "Yes, Mrs. Vern."

"Are you cooking again?"

Mei snickered into her palm and Morgan looked back at her helplessly, then turned to the window. "Yes," she called up solemnly. "It was a little oil smoke."

"All right, dear. Let me know if you need anything," the woman yelled down. "You know I always have a lasagna in the freezer for you."

"Thank you, Mrs. Vern. Have a good night." Morgan turned around, back against the sink. Frazzled was an exceptionally adorable look on her. "There has been a bit of an incident."

"I see." Mei held on to the wine, attempting to school her features neutrally. "What happened?"

"I was supposed to be 'sweating the onions' but instead I burned the onions and nearly set the place on fire." Taking a pan from the stove, Morgan glared down at it in disdain. "'It's so easy,' Ruiz said. 'There's no way you could fuck up a burrito,' Ruiz said."

Ingredients strewn haphazardly on the available counter surfaces, many half-opened, made it clear Morgan had not gotten very far in her cooking adventure. Setting the wine down on the table, Mei drew closer to Morgan, close enough to spot the white bandage wrapped around Morgan's left index finger. She took Morgan's hand from the counter and held it in her own. "Another incident?"

"Cutting the onions."

"Okay." Mei inspected the carnage. "Why don't you let me help you? This all looks salvageable."

Dropping her eyes to the ground, Morgan shifted from foot to foot. "Because you're my guest."

Mei tugged on the string of Morgan's apron. "Please, I'd love to help. Do you have another of these?"

"Aprons? No, I bought this one today." Morgan untied it and pulled it over her head. Underneath, she wore a beige button-down tank top tucked into a pair of black linen pants. Decidedly less casual than what she normally wore outside of work. She held out the apron to Mei in defeat. "All yours."

Mei put the apron on and tied it around her waist. She, too, had worn a nicer outfit than usual and didn't want to risk ruining it. A silk, lavender blouse that cut off mid-biceps, as well as one of her black trousers she didn't wear to work. She didn't like to wear the same thing in the morgue and out of it. Seemed a bit morbid, even for her.

"All right. Let's get started."

Easing into the cooking over their natural banter, Mei relaxed as she walked Morgan through the steps of cooking. It brought back memories of cooking side by side with her mother in their tiny kitchen during Mei's childhood, dutifully learning the ancient technique to perfect the twist on dim sum. Ages since Mei talked about her childhood and adolescence, she almost forgot how much she enjoyed the nostalgia. Cooking with her mother was some of the only bonding they'd ever done, and neither Grace nor Lara shared her affinity for working in the kitchen. It helped that Morgan was excellent at following directions, and within only thirty minutes they'd salvaged her meal into two presentable burritos. They sat in front of two place settings waiting atop a tiny kitchen table next to a window overlooking the neighbor's neat garden packed with flowers.

"So, did you do much of the cooking with Allan?" Morgan asked, biting into her burrito. Mei didn't talk about Allan much with Morgan, only sometimes at group and if the subject matter was relevant. Not on purpose; it felt like a door that needed to stay closed.

"No, actually." Collecting her thoughts, Mei sipped her wine. "Allan was an excellent cook. I like to think we split the cooking equally, but he was home a lot more than me."

"Oh, that's right. You said he worked from home most of the time. It must've been great for your girls to get to know their father so well," Morgan stated, tearing into her burrito again. After she swallowed and washed her food down with wine, Morgan leaned on her hand. "Grace is a pilot, right?" Mei nodded. "What does Lara do?"

Mei sighed, taking a forkful of the burrito she'd deconstructed and giving herself a moment to enjoy it. "Lara is a bartender. She's in graduate school currently, working on her Master's."

"Good for her. What's the Master's in?"

"Arts in Literature, specializing in British literature." Mei held back a wince. Lara didn't lack a work ethic and Mei was proud of her, just—

"You don't sound pleased."

Cringing at Morgan catching her casual condescension, Mei exhaled softly. "I am not displeased. Lara works hard and she's incredibly smart. I worry about her future." Mei knew she sounded like an overbearing mother, but she was an overbearing mother. The daughter of another overbearing mother. "I don't want her to waste her time being in school forever."

While Morgan chewed in contemplation, Mei did not feel judged in the silence. Mei admired her thoughtfulness. "Maybe she will be in school forever. That wouldn't be so bad, would it? To be a lifelong academic?"

Shrugging, Mei managed a casual, "I suppose not," but it came out as disingenuous as she thought. However, as she gazed across the table, it was clear Morgan did not hold it against her. Her eyes were wide, pensive, and sympathetic.

"She could become a scholar, write papers and theses. Maybe she'll write the next great critique on Elizabeth Gaskell. I'd read that."

"Perhaps."

Morgan pressed on. "From how you've described her, Lara seems capable and intelligent. Openhearted and kind. I'm sure whatever she puts her mind to she will succeed in. Plus, she's got a great mom on her side. I can't imagine her future being anything but wide open."

Mei pointed her fork at Morgan. "Your indefatigable optimism is both exhausting and charming."

"'Exhausting and charming' is my Tinder profile bio." Off the displeased look on Mei's face, Morgan chuckled and waved her off. "I'm kidding, I don't have a Tinder. I find the chemistry algorithm creepy."

"One could argue all of attraction is a creepy chemistry algorithm," Mei posed, carefully cutting into her burrito. "One is organic, one is binary, but they produce similar results."

"The binary version doesn't allow for random chance." A wistful but serious look crossed Morgan's face. "I find the most meaningful connections are ones I never intended to make at all."

After Morgan insisted upon cleaning up alone, Mei perused her living room. She traced the spines of Blu-ray discs, though most titles she did not recognize. Off to the side was a record player—because of course a woman who owned a vehicle from the early 1970s would also own a vinyl record player—along with a neat stack of albums. Tasteful but minimal décor led her into the living room proper. The small space held a single midcentury modern sofa and matching chair, a rug, and the bare minimum of shelves to keep electronics off the ground. It had the look of a newly moved-in tenant, with a couple of broken-down cardboard boxes leaned against a wall in the corner. Next to a far wall, Mei found a short side table shoved into a corner with one case file box sitting on top of it. Above it was a lone shelf, only a few feet across, holding three pictures frames.

"I thought you weren't allowed to take case files home," Mei called, bending down to inspect the name written in short black marker on the side. Gray with a wide blue stripe, the box did not have the same color scheme as the ones stuffed floor to ceiling in Morgan's office.

"Not my case," Morgan called back. Mei squinted, and finally saw the name printed on the side: KELLY, CHARLOTTE.

Morgan's mother's case box. Mei snapped backward as if she'd uncovered a secret, though Morgan kept it out in plain view. "I didn't mean to intrude," Mei murmured as Morgan neared her from behind.

"You didn't," Morgan replied. "I'll give you the abridged version. After my mom died, I was put into foster care because I was still a minor—"

"But what about your biological father?" Mei tilted her head, unsure whether to continue. Based on the fragility in Morgan's voice, it was a sensitive subject. "Or your mother's boyfriend? Nobody could take you in?"

Morgan's face turned hard. All her cheerfulness evaporated in an instant. "My biological father was in jail at the time on drug charges. My mother's ex-boyfriend fled the state. It was—it was ruled a suicide."

Both inside and outside their group grief meetings, Morgan spoke at length about her mother and their relationship. She sang a melody Mei knew well—exalting her but purposely avoiding the notes she couldn't quite hit. While Mei didn't know the full breadth of what Morgan's childhood was like, she knew there were pieces missing, just as she pushed aside segments of her own marriage in favor of the easier memories.

"Were you there when…?"

"No. I discovered the body."

"Holy shit." If Mei's language surprised her, she didn't say anything. She merely stood staring at the box, bunching the dishtowel in her hands.

"Yeah. I showed up at the station every day telling them to open her case, that there was no way she killed herself," Morgan said, her tone fragile. "Eventually, one detective listened to me and took down my statement. It never went anywhere—the chief thought it was a waste of resources—but the detective kept in touch with me, Detective Carol Kowalski. The foster home I got placed in was bad, but as an older minor I didn't have a lot of options. Luckily I was smart, so Carol helped me graduate early and got me legally emancipated. She helped me enroll in college, get scholarships, way above and beyond the call of duty. I think she—she saw I was lost and didn't want me to fall through the cracks of the system."

"So, naturally, you became a cop," Mei supplied with a warm smile.

"Naturally. Carol showed me all the good that can come from being a public servant. When she retired and moved to Florida, the lazy bum, she pulled some strings and got me the file. I keep it to remind me of why I do what I do. It isn't always rewarding, but if I can help one person the way Carol helped me, then it's worth it."

Her eyes tracked upward to the shelf above the box, to the only photos Mei saw anywhere in the home. A four-by-nine of Morgan and Ruiz in their dress uniforms graduating the academy. The second a candid shot of a college-aged Morgan stuffed into a pub booth with about five other co-eds, faces painted in the colors of an English soccer team. The final photo, weathered and bent on the corners, featured a grade-school-aged Morgan in a baseball cap, an oversized hockey jersey and wrinkled jeans, gazing up adoringly at the woman holding her hand. The woman stood model-height, gorgeous, with waist-length brown hair and the dimpled, infectious grin Morgan clearly inherited aimed directly at the camera.

"Is that her?"

"Yeah, that's my mom. That was a good year. We didn't have a lot of those, but she was the best." All at once the need to comfort Morgan consumed Mei, but she lacked the language to express such a desire. Instead, she took Morgan's hand in her own and squeezed it. Catching Morgan's gaze as she looked down at their connected hands, the glossiness in Morgan's eyes startled her. She squeezed Mei's hand back. "Ah, well. That was a depressing interlude. Can I get you a drink?"

"Sure, whatever you're having is fine."

As Morgan departed for the kitchen, Mei entered the living room proper and noted the half-finished puzzle on the coffee table. Going off the pieces already together, she gathered the whole image was an old-fashioned popcorn machine. Much of the machine was constructed, but the main part of the image—the repeating images of popcorn—remained in the box. Morgan handed her a bottle of beer and took a long swig from her own. "You puzzle?"

"I have been known to put a puzzle or two together on occasion. You?"

"I love them." Morgan sat down cross-legged on the floor with her back to her couch. "It was one of the only things I had to do as a kid, so I got good at it. Well, do puzzles and watch a lot of *Law and Order*."

Mei slid down, bringing her knees to her chest as Morgan started putting the pieces together. "Shanvi has told me on more than one occasion that putting puzzles together is 'for recluses.'"

"Good thing she's not here," Morgan replied with a cheerful grin. "If you want, I'll put on music and we can finish this puzzle. These popcorn pieces are killing me, but with you? It's gonna be a breeze."

"Sounds like fun." Standing on her knees, Mei peered into the box of leftover pieces.

Morgan paused in her step. "Does it? We can do something else? Watch TV, or go out. Or, you can go home if you want. I don't want you to think you're a prisoner here with me and my puzzle addiction and my murder boxes."

Mei smiled. "Morgan, put the music on."

Two hours and several beers later they'd finished the puzzle. Gentle indie folk music poured from speakers set up on either side of Morgan's generously sized television, stationed against a lovely exposed brick wall. The whole apartment radiated coziness and warmth, the night's summer air blowing in from three bay windows off to the side. The good alcohol and good company gave Mei a pleasant buzz.

"All right, all right, that's enough stories about Morgan Kelly, Pre-Pubescent PI. What about you?"

Not at all to avoid talking about herself, Mei took a long pull from her beer, nearly finishing it. "What about me? What do you want to know?"

"Everything," Morgan scoffed. "I feel like all I do is talk about me."

"That's not true, I tell you a lot." Mei looked away. "I tell you more than I tell most people."

"Okay, then. Tell me something about you nobody else knows."

Mei paused thoughtfully. She had Morgan's full attention, with the younger woman resting her elbow on the couch cushion, her head in her hand. Lit by the glow of a nearby lamp, Morgan enchanted her with her button-down shirt now a few buttons open, exposing a well-defined collarbone and cleavage Mei definitely wasn't thinking about. Like how she wasn't thinking about Morgan's visible biceps, the curve and shape of the muscle gleaming in the light. Nor did she think about the warm curiosity in Morgan's eyes causing her heart to flutter. Suddenly at a loss for words, Mei shook her head.

"I—I don't know. You go first."

"Fair enough." She peered off in thought, finishing her beer and placing it on top of the finished puzzle. Mei had the brief thought she would leave a stained ring on their masterpiece, but she swallowed it. Either the heat or Morgan's relentless baby blue eyes, but something made the moment feel heavier than before. Bloated with emotion. "I was married."

Her dark eyes widened so much it almost hurt, looking back and forth between Morgan's face and her hand, upon which no ring sat. Not even a tan line. "What? When? To whom? What?"

Using her blunt nails to scrape the label on her beer, Morgan shifted in her seat and averted her gaze. "When I was in the UK for school, I met a DCI named Gemma Thomas, fell madly in love with her, and we were married less than a month later."

"A month?" Hiding her shock proved impossible. She took more than a month to pick out furniture, never mind a spouse. Allan spent weeks courting her for a single date. Another emotion edged in after the shock, easily recognizable as jealousy. "That sounds intense."

"It was a whirlwind. Passionate and consuming. I was totally and completely enamored with her. I think she was in love with me too." Morgan's voice trailed off, and the shock to Mei's system abated a bit. A deep pain crossed Morgan's face, not unlike the faraway sadness she got in her eyes talking about her mother. It made Mei want to reach out and comfort her again. "It was a messy, messy relationship, but we were crazy about each other. Then she...left."

"Oh, Morgan." Mei put down her beer and covered Morgan's hand with her own, shuffling to her on the floor. How could anyone look into those guileless blue eyes and cause her pain? Who could break the heart she wore so readily on her sleeve? "What happened?"

"About a month before I finished my degree she got hired for some high-profile secret espionage stuff and had to cut off contact. I let her annul the marriage or dissolve the union, whatever. It was complicated and legally ambiguous then. I never saw or heard from her again. She didn't even say goodbye."

"How painful," Mei murmured, running her thumb over the knuckles of Morgan's fist. "I'm so sorry, darling."

"Thanks. And you know, I never would've stopped her from taking a dream job like that. So, it's not so much the leaving that fucked me up, it's knowing no matter how much I loved her, she never would have stayed." Clearing her throat, Morgan managed a smile. "So, what's yours?"

"Oh, right." So incensed at this woman for breaking Morgan's large, generous heart, Mei forgot about the reciprocal nature of the question. She did not possess a dark past romance—she and Allan were college sweethearts, and he was Mei's first and only serious romance. No skeletons in her closet, so to speak. "Well, I...I was accepted into the Royal Ballet School when I was eleven, but my mother would not let me attend. She let me get all the way through the audition, get accepted, and then denied it."

Morgan's features drew together in deep sorrow. "Jesus. Why do you think she did that?"

This memory exposed the ugly parts of Mei's relationship with her mother, the complicated sense of pride and possession that tainted their bond. The resentment she bottled inside and swore never to release on her own children, but enough unintentionally leaked out that Mei knew Grace and Lara probably resented her, too. Luckily, they had Allan to counterbalance Mei's tiger parenting tendencies. Mei was not as fortunate. "I think she wanted to know I had enough talent to get in. Or, I don't know, that she achieved enough to get me in. We moved to America when I was little; I barely remember anything about living in Taiwan at all. But I know my mother had a lot of pride in creating the opportunity to live here. *Bàba* died not long after we immigrated, so we lived alone together for quite a while."

"That's an incredible feat for anyone, not to mention a single mother," Morgan replied, eyes wide in amazement. "You must have faced enormous pressure."

"Yes. Without any siblings it was on me to bear the fruits of her labor," Mei said, harshness in her tone. "I have a lot of successful cousins, so when my grandparents chose to move here to be closer to us, the expectations they brought with them buried my mother. And, in turn, she buried me in them."

"The expectation for what?"

"To be successful. To have tangible proof of success. To be the American Dream. An advanced degree, an impressive job, a good husband. Achievements they could hold on to and tell people back home. Being a dancer, it was…That's a dream, not a reality. Not to them, at least."

"But that's extraordinary. The Royal Ballet School! You must've been so good." Genuine heartbreak squeezed Morgan's voice, and Mei loved her a little bit for it.

"I was great. But ballet dancers have short careers, and what do they do after?" Mei closed her eyes, faded memories of opera houses and cramped audition rooms bloomed in full Technicolor after years of lying dormant in her mind. "We never spoke about it again, but I—I don't think I ever forgave her for taking that chance away from me."

And she hadn't told anyone else. Not Shanvi, not even Allan. It was a deep pain, and a deep scar, one she never intended to show to anyone. But Morgan, with her imploring eyes and open heart, somehow got inside her and rooted it out. Mei wanted to feel violated, but instead relief flooded through her.

Lost in her thoughts, she didn't notice Morgan move closer, or the heavy look in her eyes. That is, until she spoke.

"Can I—may I kiss you?"

"What?" she asked, more breathless than she intended.

"I want to kiss you but I won't without your enthusiastic consent. It's okay if you're not ready—"

Cutting her off, Mei closed the distance and pushed her lips against Morgan's moving ones. Their kiss moved slow and sensual, and different. Soft. Morgan ran her fingers through Mei's hair, cradling the back of her head. Her thumb traced little circles behind Mei's ear and she pressed against her with barely restrained yearning. Desire rose and fell like a high striker at a traveling fair, pinging the bell in her brain and then settling deep down in her stomach. Sliding her free hand up Morgan's side to her arm, she gripped the strong muscles with a squeeze. Morgan gently probed her lips and skimmed across her tongue with her own.

As they broke apart, Mei's mind began catching up with the rest of her. She'd kissed Morgan. Another woman. Her coworker. Her younger, lesbian coworker. The contented, dazed look on Morgan's face almost prevented Mei from saying the words forming in her mouth.

"I'm sorry."

Blinking away her distraction, Morgan furrowed her brow. "Why?"

"I'm sorry. I'm not—I should not have done that."

"Why not?"

Mei shifted backward and then abruptly stood up, nearly knocking over their painstakingly put together puzzle. Morgan rose as well, confusion etched across her face. "I—it's—it's inappropriate."

"Says who? I—I thought our date was going well. Was it—was it not going well? Am I moving too fast? I know it's been three months, I didn't want to push you."

"Our...date?" Attempting to shake the arousal clouding her brain, Mei struggled to catch up. "Three months?" With another look around the apartment, Mei felt more stupid than someone with two PhDs ought to. Dim lighting, the attempted home-cooked meal, the intimate bonding activity, how unusually dressed up Morgan was. "This was a date."

Morgan's eyes went wide. "I mean, yeah? We've been dating for three months."

"We have?"

An awful, terrible pause fell between them. "We *haven't*?"

"N-no?"

Morgan took a few steps back, the horrified look on her face matching the astonishment Mei felt. "Oh my god. You... you didn't think we were dating. These were not dates. Oh my god. No. No, no, no."

"No, I—" Every interaction was suddenly different as Mei's mind played them back. The dinners, the plays, the late-night texting, the casual trips to bars, the lunchtime talks: many of those were dates. They looked like dates. They sounded like dates. Had they happened to anyone else, Mei would've thought they were dates. "I'm so sorry, Morgan. I feel like I misled you. I'm not—I'm not gay."

The pure disbelief on Morgan's face rapidly turned into hysterical horror. "Oh my god, you're not gay. You're not gay! I kissed you and you are not gay."

"Technically, I kissed you."

"I am such an idiot. Ruiz said it right to me, she said: 'Dr. Sharpe isn't queer, Kelly. Get your brains out of your *chonies*.' And I ignored her. Oh, god, I want to bail out the window like the Cowardly Lion in *The Wizard of Oz*. Full-on, headfirst, no looking back."

Morgan plopped down on the couch, her head in her palms. Torn between alleviating the situation or just leaving it, Mei firmed her resolve and stayed put. Ultimately, she could only take so much cowardice from herself in one day. "It's not your fault."

"I have become the lesbian trope I feared most." Morgan aggressively rubbed her face in her hands. "I'm so embarrassed."

Mei sat down next to her, folding her hands in her lap. She wanted to give a touch of reassurance, but she didn't think physical contact was a good idea. "You have no reason to be embarrassed. I'm the one who should be embarrassed. I feel like I missed some rather obvious signs."

"You think?" Morgan asked, peeking through her fingers to level an incredulous look in Mei's direction. "You can leave me here to die now, thank you."

"No, Morgan, please." Panic rose in her chest. "I don't want to lose your friendship. It's become rather important to me. You're important to me."

When Morgan finally lifted her head, it stung Mei's chest to see the pained look on her face. "Of course we'll still be friends, Mei. I just need time. I have to…reset myself."

"Reset yourself?"

"Yeah, I thought we were dating. I mean, casually, but still."

This perplexed Mei. "You never made a move—"

"I was taking it slow!"

"That's extremely slow. That's practically glacial."

Morgan scoffed, rising from her seat to pace the floor. "I was being respectful. Sure, it was slow, but it was going well. I'd have—I was willing to go as slowly as you needed."

Like an idiot, Morgan's chivalry and heartfelt vulnerability charmed Mei instantly. She resisted the urge to close the gap between them and forget about whether she was gay, or the age difference, or Allan. "Wait, at the museum when you'd just slept with someone else, you were under the impression we were on a date?"

"Kind of?"

Planting her hands on her hips, Mei found the audacity to be miffed. "I'll have you know that if I knew we were dating, it would not be acceptable for you to be sleeping with other women."

"Okay, great, Mei. Thanks." Morgan's face contorted into a sneer. "Trust me, I didn't want to. I was doing anything and everything I could to not get so deeply into this, but it was impossible. I…well, no use in trying to deny it now, is there? I have feelings for you. Feelings that are decidedly unfriendly, and if we're going to salvage our friendship—all is lost for my dignity, but that's fine—I need space. We can't be friends if every time I look at you I get the belly swoops."

Mei paused. "I'm sorry, you get the what?"

"You know, the belly swoops."

"Morgan, I have never heard that expression before in my life."

Evidently exasperated with Mei's ignorance, Morgan gestured around. "It's like when you're on a roller coaster and it crests the peak? Suddenly it plunges and your belly swoops. It feels like that."

"I make you feel that way?" Mei's heart screamed in her chest, begging her to reconsider.

Shoulders sagging, Morgan nodded dejectedly. "All the time."

"Oh."

"Right, and obviously that doesn't go away overnight. I need time to get over you. It's not going to be easy, but I will work through this. I don't want to lose your friendship, either." Morgan rubbed her forehead with two fingers. "And I'm deeply sorry if I ever made you uncomfortable. I'll rectify my behavior going forward, I promise."

"Please, stop apologizing. You never made me uncomfortable, not once." Thinking about Morgan casually slinging her arm over the back of her chair, or touching her back to guide her through a crowd, or generally in close proximity—it never made Mei feel encroached upon. Her touch was always welcome and reassuring. Mei grieved losing this touch, but she was not willing to unpack that feeling. Instead, she focused on the relief of knowing Morgan would not forsake their friendship. Though tonight took a turn, Mei knew one thing for certain: she needed Morgan in her life more than the younger woman would ever know. "Okay. So, I should probably go?"

"Yeah, I think you should."

Following a few steps behind to the door, Morgan watched Mei slip her feet into her shoes. In the foyer, avoiding each other's gazes, they remained suspended in an unbearably awkward silence. When Mei met Morgan's eyes, they glistened with unshed tears. Fighting every impulse in her, Mei kept her hands at her sides. *It shouldn't be this difficult to resist someone you didn't even know you wanted.* "I'm sorry."

"You have nothing to apologize for," Morgan replied curtly. "It isn't your fault you aren't gay and don't have feelings for me."

Mei could not, and would not, consider the veracity of that sentence. "I suppose."

"Yeah, so. Text me so I know you got home safe. And I'll— I'll call you, okay?"

"Okay." Pivoting on her heel, Mei walked away from Morgan's slouched figure in the doorway. Every step felt like walking against wind, or storming up a hill. She didn't look back as she got into her car. If she looked back she might reconsider, and this was the right call. Getting involved with her young coworker could only end in disaster.

For all the questions the night raised, Mei revealed the answer to at least one. Who could break such a heart?

Turns out, she could.

CHAPTER NINE

Plaintive singing burst from Morgan's apartment, echoing out the open windows and into the street. Her front door opened and closed, and the heavy gait would be recognizable as Ruiz's even if Morgan hadn't called her over. Sprawled on her couch with liquor in hand, Morgan didn't move but continued to stare at the rerun of *Frasier* playing on mute.

"Brandi Carlile," Morgan announced to Ruiz, who had not asked. She took a swig of her drink and sighed. "The patron saint of lesbian heartbreak. She is the only one who understands what I'm going through. You can hear it in her voice. That is a woman whose heart has been broken by another woman. She has felt The Pain."

Ruiz sat on the edge of the armchair next to the couch, resting her elbows on her knees and observing the scene. Breakups sporadically spotted the timeline of their friendship, more on Morgan's end than Ruiz's, and this was their tradition: seeing each other through it.

"Isn't Melissa Etheridge the patron saint of lesbian heartbreak?"

"No, that's more lesbian angst."

"Tegan and Sara?"

"Longing. Pining, maybe."

"Joan Armatrading?"

A pause hung in the air, much longer than necessitated by the question. "Okay, yeah, that's fair. You're welcome to put her on. I've got *Walk Under Ladders* somewhere over there," she said, waving with her liquor in the direction of the vinyl player.

"I'm good." Ruiz waited patiently, but all Morgan did was stare at the ceiling and drink from a mason jar for a solid ten minutes. "Are you going to tell me what happened, or do you want me to guess?"

"Oh, sure, allow me to give you the play-by-play, Sergeant Ruiz." Swinging her legs over to sit upright, Morgan halted to wait for the world to stop spinning without her. "I invited Dr. Sharpe over for dinner, as you know. Ruined dinner, by the way, no thanks to you and your 'foolproof' directions."

"*Mala cocinera.*"

"We made dinner together, had a nice time. Sat right here, right where I am, and we did that puzzle you see now all over the floor. But it was together because we'd finished it. I asked her if I could kiss her, she didn't say yes, but she kissed me. And then she went into a full-blown gay panic and told me she had no idea we were dating and she isn't gay."

While the situation could've called for an I-told-you-so, she knew Ruiz wouldn't say it. In the same way it's easier to ask for forgiveness than permission, it's easier to provide support than objection.

"Ouch, I'm sorry," Ruiz replied with a sympathetic wince. "How did she go all this time without realizing you were dating? Didn't you like, take her on dates?"

"Yes, I did, Ruiz, so ecstatic you're here to point that out. We did, in fact, go on several dates. Nice dinners, movies, plays, talks over drinks. But I guess I forgot to say the word 'date' at any point over the last three months, so Mei figured all of this exceptional amount of effort was appropriate for a friendship."

"Wow, I can't believe it."

"Me either."

"No, I can't believe you finally found someone more oblivious than you are."

"I am too fragile for your insults right now, Anna-Maria." Dramatically flopping back and heaving a world-weary sigh, Morgan lamented further. "She wants to be friends. Friends! I have lusted after her for months and then I caught feelings for her like a tried-and-true dumbass, and then she tells me—after we share a kiss I feel in the marrow of my bones—she would like to be friends. Being friends is very important to her."

Picking up Morgan's discarded bottles, Ruiz stopped short. "So, are you telling me you thought you were dating this woman you're crazy about and you waited three months to kiss her?"

"That sounds like an accusation and not a question and I do not appreciate it." Arms crossed, Morgan huffed in her direction. "Need I remind you we went to Reyna's family's restaurant every week for two months before you worked up the courage to ask her out? Because I remember having to work out twice as much because of all the enchiladas you made me eat."

"Nobody told you to eat so much."

"You know I have a hard time saying no. To women, to food, and especially to women *with* food."

"*Mira*, you tried. Now, we pick it up and we move on." Piling bottles into the recycling bin, she returned to her friend. "Next week is the department's charity basketball game. You can flex your muscles and some cute little pillow princess will be all over you in a second. You'll forget all about Sharpe."

"I don't want to forget about her," Morgan murmured. "I like her."

The hard look on Ruiz's features softened. "I know you do. Plus she checks all your usual boxes."

Morgan narrowed her eyes. "My usual boxes?"

"You like them dark-haired, you like them older than you, and you like them a little bit mean." With Morgan gaping like she'd sucker-punched her mother, Ruiz held her hands up. "Don't look at me like that. You're the one with the type. All of your exes are dark-haired ice queens and Dr. Sharpe is no different."

Rather than taking offense to the astute observation, Morgan was offended by how aptly it described her ex-wife, and she wondered how long she'd chased the same type of woman who broke her heart. That couldn't be healthy. It also didn't help that it somewhat described her own mother. That was definitely unhealthy. That was like, mythologically unhealthy.

"Mei is different, though," Morgan countered softly. "Even months ago when we met on the highway, remember?"

"I remember. I also remember how you talked about her so much to your actual date she never wanted to see you again."

"Yeah, that was my bad, but I maintain that I dodged a bullet. Did I tell you she hated apples? She was like, against apples as a fruit. It was such a weird stand to take."

"At least Sharpe is leagues better than your other exes. She's smart, polite, holds down a real job, a little icy but not a total *bruja*. She's mean, but in a hot way."

"Like in a hot-smart way. Like Lilith on *Frasier*," Morgan said with a dreamy sigh. "Oh my god, are all my exes Lilith from *Frasier*? Okay, be honest: do you think I have a shot with Bebe Neuwirth?"

Predictably, Ruiz ignored her tangent and mini existential crisis. "Regardless, she's different with you. I don't blame you for going for it. She put out all the signs, whether she knew it or not." Sniffing one of the bottles, Ruiz grimaced and shot Morgan a disdainful look for her poor taste. "Figuring out if you're queer is a tough road at any age. Figuring out you're queer and you're attracted to a woman twenty years younger who is law enforcement's answer to Elle Woods? That's enough to make anyone panic."

"I know the Elle Woods comparison is meant to be unflattering, but you know how much I love *Legally Blonde*." Ignoring Ruiz's exasperation, Morgan groaned and buried herself in the couch. "She said she wants to be friends and I respect that, so I asked for space. But I don't want to be just friends with her, Ruiz. I don't know if I can. I can't un-feel the way my heart flutters when she enters a room. I can't un-think all the ways I thought about loving her. I was—I am—falling for her."

The two friends sat in silence as the album ended and filled the room with the muted noise of an electrified, empty speaker. All this heartache because of one simple fact: Morgan was incapable of small love. How desperately she wanted love to come to her like it came to others: slowly, like falling asleep, they said. For Morgan, it wasn't falling asleep. It was passing out behind the wheel and careening off a cliff. It happened first on the playground, tucked in the tunnel between the slide and the rope ladder, getting her first kiss from another girl and feeling the world drop out beneath her. Again, in college, when knee-deep in her Master's DCI Gemma Thomas took her on a date. Exhausted from a string of late-night studying, Morgan fell asleep standing up in their private pod on the London Eye. Gemma didn't move, and Morgan awoke at the top of the Eye looking out into the sunset with Gemma smiling at her, crazily fond.

Most recently, it happened strolling the perimeter of a lake with Mei, watching her try cotton candy for the first time. Her face lit up in pure glee and embarrassment, mouth bursting with blush pink sugar. Beneath a circus of brilliant stars and the glow of a harvest moon spilling over the water, Morgan's heart walked right out of her chest and into Mei's hands.

Ruiz, genetically unable to stand mess, slid off the couch to put the puzzle pieces back into the box. "Maybe she'll come around, who knows? I warned you about her when you started this 'friendship' not because I don't like Dr. Sharpe, but because I worry about you. You give your heart away and most of the time they don't deserve it."

"*Suavecita*," Morgan interjected with a smile.

Glaring, Ruiz continued. "If she comes around, great. In the meantime, we move on. Your homicide is getting hot, right? Then Cap will get you rolling with a squad. You'll be okay."

Under normal circumstances it would be Morgan supplying the optimism for Ruiz, a worrier of legendary proportions. But when she needed it, Ruiz capably provided sensible advice for which Morgan was eternally grateful. "She's not the first straight woman I've ever gone after like an idiot."

"She sure as shit isn't," Ruiz replied. "Hannah, Lena, Jillian A and Jillian K, Yolanda…"

"Okay, I get it."

"Mandip, Julie Waters, Julie Waterson, Mackenzie—"

"All right, you've made your point." Descending to the floor, Morgan grumbled as she retrieved the strewn pieces. "Your memory is scary, but your tough love is appreciated."

"I only do it because I love you." Ruiz plopped a handful of puzzle pieces into the box. "Also because I resent how much you pull for someone who chases a disproportionate amount of straight tail and has zero game."

"Ugh, you know I hate the word 'pull.'" Morgan tossed a puzzle piece at her face, which Ruiz deflected with ease. "I have game."

"Sure." Ruiz stood up, kicking a few pieces to Morgan from the edges of the living room. "Remember when you met that woman at the dog park and she gave you her number and instead of asking her on a date, you walked her dog for two months?"

"That was one time!"

With a fresh warrant issued for the uncle in her cold case and the burden of choosing a new squad on her shoulders, Morgan had little time to focus on her total misfire with Mei. However, without being able to talk to Mei about the new developments in her job, Morgan found it hard to rustle up any excitement about them.

Respectful of her wishes, Mei didn't come by for lunch. Morgan ate alone, forcing down a sad sub sandwich filled with floppy cold cuts and shredded lettuce bearing an unfortunate resemblance to plastic Easter basket grass. So, while she dearly missed Mei's home cooking, she missed their conversations even more. She missed the way the corner of Mei's mouth curled up before she laughed. Or how adamant she became about the virtues of eating rice once a day. Her riveting stories about her daughters and the trials and tribulations of raising two remarkably different young women. The way she made a lab coat and sensible pumps look effortlessly attractive. When she wore glasses and pushed them up the bridge of her nose after making a point.

Morgan skipped the café because she didn't want to intrude on Shanvi and Mei's morning ritual. It would only serve to complicate matters if she saw Mei before she was ready. Of course, who could tell when that would be? If only undoing her affections could be as efficient as plucking out a splinter or a thorn. It was certainly as painful.

After a long week of paperwork, chasing down evidence, instructing officers, and avoiding Mei, the County Basketball Tournament waited for her like an oasis. Hauling out her matte black Jordans from a box in her closet and dressed in her polyester jersey and matching shorts, Morgan felt a little bit more herself. A little bit more like the collegiate athlete she used to be, bursting with confidence and swagger.

She rode that high to the tournament, held in the city center's basketball courts. Surrounded by parks, it was one of the few expanses of green within the city limits. Fragrant trees blocked out much of the city's pollution in an arboreal phalanx of protection and Morgan gratefully inhaled the fresh, sweet summer air and basked in the mellow heat from the sun.

In the distance she spotted the row of four back-to-back courts, each side buttressed with steel bleachers already crammed with crowds. Refreshment stands and local artisans surrounded the perimeter selling their wares to families, shouting about fresh zeppole and how to get a new tub fitted in their bathroom. Attendees jam-packed the remaining grass, hoping to cheer or jeer the civil servants participating in the tournament.

Her team, three officers from courts and one from the K9 unit, waited near the sideline bench when she arrived. Volunteer participants had been sorted into teams, and they'd only met once before to choose a team name (Rockets) and pick up their police jerseys. Plunking her bag down on the bench, Morgan eyed their opponents across the court. Firefighters, three of them, plus two city cops. She grabbed a ball from the rack and headed into the empty court to run drills. Dribbling, shooting, a few crisscrosses—enough to get her loose and ready to play.

"Kelly!" Morgan spotted Ruiz and Reyna approaching the court, so she passed the ball to another teammate before jogging to the fence. "Lookin' good, Hoops."

"Thanks." Morgan smiled at Ruiz's partner. "Hey, Reyna. How've you been? I feel like it's been ages."

"Since the engagement party," Reyna said.

"Oh yeah. Boy, that party knocked me out."

"We did tell you not to drink so much tequila," Reyna replied with a teasing grin. "Though, Liliana did not complain."

Running her tongue along her teeth, Morgan fought back a blush. She knew it was poor form to engage in a hookup with the future sister-in-law of her best friend, but Liliana was pushy and demanding and exceptionally hot. And, according to Ruiz, that was her type. Morgan possessed very little in the way of resisting powerful women. "Oh, well, good. How is she doing, by the way?"

Reyna smirked. "She's fine. She asks about you from time to time."

"Oh?"

"Don't even think about it, Kelly," Ruiz warned. "You couldn't handle Liliana with a chair and a whip. That woman eats people. You're not tough enough for her."

Morgan pouted. "I'm tough."

"Aw, sure you are," Ruiz teased, reaching up to pat the top of Morgan's head. "Good luck. We'll come back when the game starts, *domadora*."

Pouting after their retreating figures, Morgan turned her attention to the court. She stayed on one half, running more drills to clear her mind. Like riding a bike, the muscle memory returned to her without fail. Attempting to dribble through her legs, she hit herself on the shin and the ball rolled over toward the fence. She gave chase, snatching it from the ground and looking up dead into the eyes of an attractive woman. "Hello."

"Hey." The woman shooed away her friends, waiting for Morgan to stand to her full height. Morgan could smell the alcohol on her, probably from the foot-tall plastic margarita glass in her hand, but she wasn't drunk. After giving Morgan an aggressive up-and-down, the woman tucked her lip into her teeth, and then popped it out. "What's your name?"

"Lieutenant Kelly." Should she use her title? She was technically there as an officer, but also technically off-duty. "Morgan. Uh, Lieutenant Morgan Kelly."

"Lieutenant Morgan Kelly. Two first names, huh?"

"Yep, like a serial killer," Morgan replied, immediately wincing. Ruiz told her, more than once, to stop dropping serial killer stuff into casual conversations. "Well, at least I said the least cool thing I'll say all day to a beautiful woman."

The woman dropped her gaze to her expensive, dazzlingly diamonded watch. "It's only noon, there's always time for another. You may surprise yourself."

"Unfortunately, it wouldn't be a surprise," Morgan replied, hoisting the ball onto her hip.

The woman reached through the fence and tugged on Morgan's tank top. "You're cute when you're flustered, Lieutenant Morgan Kelly."

"Thank you?"

"Good luck out there. I'll be watching." With a wink and a wiggle of her hips, the woman sashayed over to where her friends staked a claim on the bleachers.

Morgan watched after her and sullenly came to the conclusion Ruiz was right: she had no game, at least not with women. Basketball, thankfully, was a different story. Heading back to her team, they hyped each other up in a huddle before breaking for the tip-off. For Morgan, it was like stealing candy from a baby. Within the first five seconds of play she scored a basket. The opposing team barely made it past half-court before Morgan dispossessed them again and scored with an easy layup. Exchanging high fives with her teammates, Morgan jeered their opponents as she jogged backward into their half.

"Ooh, looks like you're late to put out the fire."

By halftime Morgan's team was twenty points ahead, due in no small part to Morgan's efforts. Dripping with sweat, she hiked up her jersey and wiped down her face and neck.

"Oh, yeah, take it off, Lieutenant Six-Pack," someone called from the bleachers. That someone, Morgan realized as she peered out into the bleachers and a woman pretended to fan herself, was the flirtatious woman she'd spoken with earlier. Fortunately her windedness hid her blush, but she took her time pulling her jersey back down.

Only seconds into the third quarter, the firefighters began fouling Morgan as often as possible. Whether due to her friendly taunting or the twenty-point deficit she'd put them in she didn't know, but Morgan matched their aggression with outright skill. Snatching the ball from their useless point guard, Morgan took off in a breakaway. Four steps into their half Morgan felt a foot near her ankle. Sprawling into the air, the basketball bounced away as she tripped and skidded across the asphalt.

Gazing up from the ground, she stared into the snarling face of the man who'd tripped her. "Rat."

Before Morgan could respond, her teammate quickly appeared by her side to help her up, shoving the opposing player away. "Hey, you're bleeding. You want a time-out?"

"No." Gesturing for a towel, Morgan caught it from the ball boy and held it against her calf. Only a skid, no real harm done except to Morgan's ego. "Let's win this thing already."

By the end of the game Morgan single-handedly scored forty-seven of their total seventy-one points, versus the firefighters' total of a measly forty-two. The crowd cheered for them as they celebrated their victory, and Morgan got unexpectedly doused in blue Gatorade by one of the K9 cops. These teammates, members of her office who barely spoke to her under normal circumstances, clapped her on the back and congratulated her. Their joviality buoyed Morgan. It was nice to feel accepted, for once.

With thirty minutes between games, Morgan nabbed her water bottle and walked through the crowd toward the first aid tent. She sprayed the water bottle over her head, trying to rinse the Gatorade from her hair. No other players were present inside the spacious tent, which gave Morgan the unfortunate distinction of receiving the first injury of the day. Parked in a neat row were three beds, two supply carts, and at the very end, one doctor with their back turned.

"What's up, Doc?"

And, because the gods are cruel and life is a terrible mistress, the doctor was, of course, Mei. Clad in jeans instead of her usual trousers and a pair of sensible white sneakers, she possessed the same elegance and radiance as she did in professional attire. When she turned time moved in slow motion, like the first shot of a hot female love interest in any eighties movie.

Morgan froze. "Oh."

"Morgan," Mei exclaimed, breathless in surprise. Her cheeks blushed a light pink as she pointed to Morgan's head. "Why are you wet?"

Running her fingers through her hair, Morgan slicked back the unfortunate combination of Gatorade and water now acting as hairspray. "We won."

"I see." Morgan hoped she wasn't imagining the heat in Mei's dark eyes as she took stock of her, soaked and flushed from exercise. Shaking off her shock, Mei inspected her more closely and spotted the blood on her calf. "Oh, you're hurt."

"Yeah." She bowed her head, embarrassed. "I got cut."

"Well, you're my first patient. Lucky me. Have a seat." Obediently Morgan hoisted herself up onto the table, wincing at the pain in her ribs. One of the larger men had elbowed her pretty hard in an attempt to steal possession. "How'd this happen?"

Shrugging, Morgan stilled her swinging legs as Mei approached her with disinfectant and wiped the scrape. "Some hose jockey tripped me."

"By 'hose jockey,'" Mei repeated, chuckling, "do you mean a firefighter?"

"Unfortunately, yes. They took exception to my exceptional playing and got physical with me. Caught a few fouls for it, but a lot went unnoticed by our volunteer ref." Feeling Mei's soft, strong hands on her calf definitely wasn't doing anything to Morgan's insides. They were still firmly organs and certainly not a pile of goo. "How did you get roped into this?"

"I volunteered," Mei replied, tossing the disinfecting wipe into a nearby trash bin. Inwardly, this surprised her. As she understood it, Mei intentionally kept herself away from most of the goings-on within the sheriff's department. "Not a bad way to spend a Saturday. I haven't done first aid in a long time, but it's like riding a bike."

"Your usual patients are less rowdy, I'm sure." Mei snickered and opened up a bandage to apply to Morgan's leg. "It's, um, it's good to see you."

Clearing her throat, Morgan watched Mei wrap her hands around her calf to gently apply the adhesive to her skin. Her hair was tied up in its usual bun, but not as tightly. An immediate flashback of threading her fingers through it as they kissed clouded Morgan's brain. Gazing at her with a soft look, Mei nodded. "It's good to see you too."

Morgan was certain she didn't imagine Mei's eyes darting to her lips, and then she licked her own. Hopping off the table, she flinched again. "Ow."

Blinking the dazed look in her eyes away, Mei zeroed in on Morgan as a whole. "What's wrong? Is it your leg?"

"No, my ribs." Perhaps it was a ploy to test the waters of Mei's supposed heterosexuality, but Morgan couldn't help herself. It worked once today, it might work twice. Rucking up her tank top over the top of her breasts, she peered down to get a look at her ribs. "One of the big dudes jabbed me. It's a little tender. How does it look?"

Much to Morgan's delight, Mei's reaction was not entirely professional. Morgan paid close attention to the way Mei's throat bobbed and her mouth opened, the slight dilation of her pupils, the less-than-straight admiration of Morgan's muscle tone and maybe even her cleavage. Gingerly placing her hand below Morgan's injured rib, Mei furrowed her brow. "Looks like you'll have some bruising in a bit. It's discolored currently. I'll grab you an ice pack."

Hurrying away from Morgan, who stared after her with a pleased expression, Mei rummaged in the nearby cooler. Morgan opened her mouth to say something, but someone else sauntered into the tent before she could speak. The woman from earlier, oversized margarita in hand, breezed in with a grin. "There you are."

Morgan tilted her head. "Here I am."

As another injured player hobbled in, Mei reluctantly went to their side to guide them to an open table, her eyes carefully watching the exchange. Smiling wide and predatorily, the woman stalked toward Morgan. Her sharp detective instincts mentally sized her up before she got close enough to touch. Expensive clothes, a haughty air born from either money or education (possibly both), and knowledge of her own attractiveness. She was beautiful, with russet skin and dark hair professionally styled with intentionally messy curls. Maybe forty or forty-five years old, she checked at least two of Morgan's alleged boxes. So, maybe she did have a type.

With an appreciative look at Morgan's chest, she raised her eyebrow. "And here I thought that little show on the court was for me."

Morgan smirked. She had exactly the confidence she assumed this woman would have. "Now, how could that have been for you? I don't even know your name."

"Andrea."

She held out her hand. "Nice to meet you, Andrea."

"Congrats on the impressive win, Lieutenant Morgan Kelly," she said, shaking the offered hand. Her palm and fingers felt smooth, almost baby soft, in contrast to Morgan's calloused hands. Definitely money, she thought.

"Thank you."

"I wish I could stay and watch you play more, but we have to go." Sounding genuinely regretful, Andrea motioned to her friends who waited outside the tent. "Perhaps you and I can get dinner one night. Assuming you clean up as well as I think you do."

"Why? Is the 'drenched in blue Gatorade' look not doing it for you?"

"Honey, it does it for me just fine," Andrea replied with a chuckle, lowering her voice. "But if I'm going to see you wet, I'd like to be the cause of it."

A resounding clatter interrupted Morgan's response, drawing both her and Andrea's attention to Mei, who stared down in betrayal at a dropped tray of tools. Waving off their concern,

Morgan turned to Andrea and found her with a business card pinched between two fingers. She looked at the card, then down at her outfit with a frown. "I don't—these shorts don't have pockets."

Emitting a sultry chuckle, Andrea advanced on Morgan and slid her fingers beneath the waistband of her shorts, tucking the card there. Looking up at her from beneath hooded lids, she winked. "Keep it safe."

Without waiting for a goodbye she spun around and joined her friends, getting lost in the sea of people moving away from the tent. Morgan shifted, pulling the card out of her shorts. "That's gonna poke my belly."

Mei returned holding out the ice pack, face wiped clean of expression. "Keep this on until your next game. You can bring it back when you're done."

Holding the ice pack against her bruise, Morgan inhaled a sharp breath at the invasion of cold against her overly heated skin. "Thanks for your help."

"Sure. Enjoy the rest of your day, Lieutenant."

Flinching at the clipped tone and professional address, Morgan moved away from Mei. "Right. You too."

Once outside the tent, Morgan peered down at the business card in her hand and chuckled. *Andrea Pierce, MD. Proctologist. Put your colon problems in the rear view.* Maybe it would require the intervention of a romantic interloper to slash the vines of Mei that wrapped themselves around her head and heart. She plugged the number into her phone and set a reminder to send a text later on that night.

Back at work, Morgan's cold case team finally took shape and they dug into the other case files Morgan borrowed from the suspect's county. Establishing a timeline decades later was difficult, but Morgan had no doubt they'd make the connections necessary to bring justice to not only the young woman from her cold case, but perhaps other victims in the area as well.

"I don't understand this," one of the officers announced, tossing a folder down onto his desk. Having moved and organized the unsolved case boxes and two of the binder shelves into an adjacent room, the squad pushed their desks into a loose L shape with Morgan at the helm. On the wall behind her desk hung a whiteboard upon which she outlined her thoughts, next to the pinboard holding photos and copies of evidence. From his desk at the end of the L, Officer Daniels huffed. "We're going in circles."

"Well, Daniels, that's how planes land, so perhaps we will find similar success." Daniels didn't move. Morgan tore herself from her work and walked to his desk, glancing down at the report. "What don't you understand?"

"We got him on the murder. There's no evidence he was involved in any of these other crimes."

Peeved, she tilted her head only an inch. "That is precisely what you are here to find. Establish a timeline of events, collect evidence, and then put the suspect within those parameters. I want him held accountable for all he may have done, and eliminate him from what he did not do. Some might say that's our job."

Daniels let out another scoff and crossed his arms, slouching in his chair. "Yeah, whatever."

Angling forward, Morgan tented her fingers on the officer's desk, hardening her stare. Daniels often tested Morgan's patience with bouts of insubordination. Upstairs, Morgan's reputation was well known, and nobody wanted to get stuck in cold cases with another precinct's pariah. However, this was their job, and it was her job to make sure they did it to the best of their abilities. "Daniels, I am only going to say this to you once. If you have an issue following orders, you are welcome to ask the captain to assign you to another team. If you do not think you are capable of establishing a criminal timeline, I suggest you also take that up with the captain. Perhaps there is a spot for you in transpo for the courts. It's an integral department and doesn't require any difficult deductions." She got closer. "If your problem is with me, don't be a coward. Say what you'd like to say."

For a moment, Daniels stuck his chin out in defiance. It

thrilled Morgan to think he'd found the courage to be open and honest about his thinly disguised contempt for her. Disappointingly, he shook his head, mumbled a "no, ma'am" under his breath, snatched the file, and proceeded to look engrossed. Morgan backed away, turning in time to see Mei standing in the threshold of the office.

"Dr. Sharpe." In an instant, Morgan's expression brightened. "To what do we owe the pleasure?"

Looking befuddled or perhaps lost, Mei stared directly at Morgan, eyes blank. Her hand shot up between them, a manila folder white-knuckle-gripped in her fist. "The Haley case. I did the analysis, as you asked."

"Oh. Oh!" With a cheerful smile, Morgan took the folder. "Great, thanks, Dr. Sharpe."

Normally, Mei would hang around and ask how the case was going, which Morgan knew was her polite way of opening the door for Morgan to ask her advice. Now, though, Morgan had three other people whose job was exactly that, and she'd asked Mei for space. Space she desperately needed, as being in Mei's presence for any length of time rendered her a mess.

"Okay. Well. I'll leave you to it."

"Right. Cool." Morgan slapped the folder against her palm a few times for no good reason and Mei rushed through the exit. All three officers stared at her. "What?"

Corporal Gilland, a newly promoted young detective, smirked. "That was so awkward. Why was that so awkward?"

Cheeks heating up, Morgan scoffed. "No, it wasn't. Why would that be awkward? It definitely was not awkward."

Officer Polzar, the final member of their team, nodded her head. "Yeah, it was, Lieutenant."

"I don't know. We're both awkward, I guess. I think working in the basement has siphoned us of our ability to socialize like normal people."

"Oh, good," Gilland chirped, turning back to her case file. "Something to look forward to."

CHAPTER TEN

Hurt and embarrassed after her disaster with Morgan, Mei wished to convalesce in private, like a wounded wild animal. Crawl into a dark cave and hope the blood trail didn't attract any attention. Normally she could do this unbothered, as she had in the months following Allan's death. However, Morgan effectually opening her up and making her accessible meant this time her sudden withdrawal went noticed by Shanvi and her daughters. Even her mother inquired about her reversion in demeanor, and Mei was at a loss. No longer could she recede into her cave; Morgan's residual light shone too bright for her to hide in the shadows.

Divulging her social catastrophe to her progeny was out of the question, so Mei opted for the easiest route: a Friday afternoon lunch date with Shanvi. Shanvi knew Morgan well enough by now to perhaps provide Mei the clarity she desperately needed.

But first she had to tell her what happened.

After many minutes of intense, silent staring, Mei relented. "Okay, so, I kissed Morgan."

Shanvi visibly relaxed, as if she'd been anticipating bad news. "That's it?"

"What do you mean, 'that's it'? I kissed another woman," Mei replied. "That's a big deal."

"Is it? To be honest, I figured you two had been doing that for a while. I've been mad at you this whole time because I thought you were keeping me out of the loop and I was so jealous you prohibited me from living vicariously." Uncrossing her arms to brace them on the table, Shanvi scooted her chair in. "Get it all out. Let's go. Gimme the whole story, top to bottom."

Glancing away, Mei wished she had more courage to have this conversation. She was severely deficient in bravery recently. "Morgan invited me over for dinner, we had a lovely night, and she asked if she could kiss me."

"Oh my goodness, she asked?" Shanvi slapped her hands on either side of her face. "That's so precious. Continue."

"I cut her off and kissed her myself."

"And how was it?"

"It was…" The most confusing, amazing kiss she'd ever had in her life. "Soft. Lovely."

"I bet she had those baby blues twinkling, muscles rippling, dimples…dimpling." She paused. "Huh. Turns out I may have a crush on your girlfriend."

"Almost certainly, but she's not my girlfriend. We are friends. Except Morgan thought we'd been 'casually dating' for the past three months."

Without warning, Shanvi reached across the table and slapped the top of Mei's hand. "What? How did you not know?"

"I thought we were hanging out as friends! You're my only friend, I have no idea what other people do." Clearly not finding that remotely convincing, Shanvi gave her a droll look. "What? It's not like she ever made a move on me. I would have noticed, I'm sure."

"Would you? If being obtuse was a sport, you'd have more medals than Babe Zaharias."

With a hapless shrug, Mei elaborated. "She said she was being respectful of me. I imagine she mistook my total obliviousness for apprehension."

The amusement on Shanvi's face morphed into sympathy, and she rested her head on one hand. "That's understandable. So, then what happened?"

Putting her forehead in her palms, Mei shielded her face from Shanvi. "I told her I'm not gay and asked if we could remain friends. She told me she has romantic feelings for me and needed space to 'get over me.'"

Suitably appalled, Shanvi gasped. "You kissed her and then friend-zoned her?"

"You know the friend zone is an imaginary masculine construct wherein men feel entitled to a woman's romances and—"

"Oh, spare me. I'm a feminist too. You probably gave the poor thing whiplash."

"I know. And now I—I don't know." Two chatty café patrons sat down at a table near theirs, and Mei lowered her voice. "At first I thought it was a fluke, because I am not gay. I have always been heterosexual, always attracted to men. Well, not men, only Allan. I find most other people annoying and generally unattractive."

"Present company excluded," Shanvi interjected.

"Yes. But I don't find her annoying despite all the reasons why I normally would. Which, sure, fine. In a bubble, that's a perfectly reasonable basis for a platonic friendship. Then I kiss her and it feels…it feels amazing. But we're both a little drunk and emotional. Then I saw her at the charity basketball game."

"The charity basketball game you volunteered for, the first time I've ever seen you volunteer for anything at work, knowing perfectly well your little paramour was a collegiate basketball player and would almost certainly attend," Shanvi said with a smug grin.

Mei went flush. "Yes, well, she sauntered into the first aid tent absolutely soaking wet and I was so physically attracted to her I had to pick my jaw up off the floor. I felt like a teenager."

"Ooh, Horny Mei. Now that's a Mei I don't think I've ever seen." Shanvi's brown eyes twinkled with delight.

"I suppose I've always been attracted to her, but I didn't know what it was. So I thought, well it's not a big deal to be attracted to another woman. It happens. Doesn't mean I want to be in a relationship with this person. Then some woman flirted with her right in front of me and it made me so mad."

"Somebody moved in on your girl and you were jealous."

"Not only jealous, but forlorn. It made me sick to think someone else was going to kiss her, or laugh at her dumb jokes, or wipe the cake frosting from her nose."

"That's specific."

"Ultimately, all of these events pointed to the rather obvious conclusion I am not only attracted to Morgan, but I have also developed feelings for her. So, I began to think about it hypothetically. If I pursue this, how would it work? We're so different, and that's not to mention the age difference."

"Has she?"

Mei furrowed her brow. "Has she what?"

"Mentioned the age difference."

She paused. In fact, Morgan had not. Any time she talked about her daughters or her marriage, or any single experience in the past fifty years, Morgan never once commented on how she was not even in existence for the first twenty years of Mei's life. "No. It's never come up. It doesn't—it never feels like that. It always feels like we're on the same page. To use a term I detest, she feels like a kindred spirit."

"It's not as if she's some doe-eyed co-ed. I mean she is doe-eyed, but she's also in her midthirties. She's a grown woman and knows what she wants; I don't see how it doesn't work. You two get along, and you have a lot of similar interests despite the fact that she is fun and you are not."

"Fun is certainly a word for it. She's so goofy. How can I be with someone who devours store-bought sheet cake? Jumps in puddles without proper footwear? Takes photos of other people's pets because they're cute? Engages total strangers in long, intimate conversations?" Though Mei rattled off supposedly negative behaviors, she smiled. "Then I saw her at work yesterday."

Absolutely riveted in her seat, Shanvi coaxed, "Yes, and?"

"I walked in on her giving a subordinate a tough, serious dressing down and it turned me on so much I forgot why I was in the room." Mei put her head down on her hands. "Shan, what do I do? I'm too old for this kind of crisis."

This conversation marked the first time in years Mei actively sought Shanvi's advice. Even when Allan pursued her in college, she went out with him three times before mentioning it to her closest and only real friend. She valued Shanvi's advice, but knew she would tell her things Mei didn't want to hear.

"First of all, you are not too old for love, or sex, or romance. So, shut that down. Second, you already know what to do. You've attempted some impressive mental gymnastics, but romance isn't one of your neat little equations. Third, I can't imagine it came as a big surprise to you that you developed feelings for this woman with whom you spend all your free time. And, despite what you said, she is your type. Or, you know, the lady version of your type."

Mei sat back. "My type? I married one guy and I have a type?"

"Mei-be, Morgan is very much like Allan." Shanvi's deep brown eyes grew so wide the irises nearly melted into her pupils. Mei's jaw slipped open. "Obviously not physically, but her buoyant personality? Friends with everyone, disarming personality, possesses the rare ability to pull you out of your shell? I'm not saying you found or sought another Allan, but it is reasonable to be attracted to someone with similar qualities to the first love of your life."

All of that information hit Mei with the force of an eighteen-wheeler. It had not occurred to her how strongly Morgan's and Allan's personalities overlapped. They came from different worlds, too disparate to ever be compared. Lining them up side by side caused her a bout of intense cognitive dissonance. "I feel guilty."

"Guilty?"

"After I kissed Morgan, I felt guilty. Not like I was cheating on Allan, but...I did something he can never do. He'll never get the chance to feel romance again. He'll always be married to me, but I—I can choose to not be married to him anymore."

Features softening, Shanvi leaned forward. "That doesn't mean you are not allowed to commit the act of happiness again.

You didn't choose not to be married, you were made single by tragedy. The only choice is whether you want to stay that way."

A profound silence fell between them. Scientifically, Mei knew sexuality existed as a spectrum and she wasn't overly fond of her heterosexuality anyway. But the fear of opening herself up, the guilt of moving on from the love of her life, kept her from a woman who made her feel wanted, desirable, and supported.

The choice before her required a backbone Mei didn't know if she possessed.

"It's a lot to put on a young woman," Mei acknowledged. "It's complicated. Dealing with a widow is complicated. A widow with two adult children is even more complicated. A widow who, until quite recently, thought she was heterosexual is so complicated it might as well be advanced quantum physics."

"What is she, without problems or faults? Without a past you'll have to parse through?" Shanvi arched her eyebrow. "We all bring baggage into a relationship. That's part of the work, unpacking it with someone you care about, who cares about you. She would be a fool not to want to put in the work to be with you. And I say that as a totally unbiased third party."

Mei snickered in disbelief. "Of course. You know, you're probably right."

"Of course I am. And for the sake of transparency, I recorded you telling me I'm right and I plan on playing it as a lullaby for myself."

She playfully swatted Shanvi. "Shut up."

"Like white noise, or rainfall." Turning her smirk into a genuine smile, Shanvi lightly continued. "I'm not a lesbian love guru, but I am your friend. You want this new love, and you deserve it. It's a love that makes you want to wake up in the morning. How long has it been since anything, never mind anyone, made you feel that way?"

Musing on that question, Mei came to the uncomfortable conclusion she'd never felt this way before. Morgan awoke something deep inside her heart. A lockbox she'd hidden and buried, filled with the wants and desires she'd circumvented in favor of her career, her children, and her husband. Now, she peeked into the box to see what life could be like if she chased her own desires. It was scary, but exciting.

"Forget all the complications for a second. How did you *feel* when you kissed her? Not as a wife or a widow or a mother. As a woman. How did it make you feel?"

Mei pressed her eyes closed. It took no effort to recall that moment; she replayed in her mind so often it was closer to an instinct than a memory. Desire rushed through her, yearning, excitement, and a sense of relief.

"Wanted and wanton."

When she opened her eyes, Shanvi gave her an obvious, willful look. "Then I have to ask you, with all due respect: what the hell are you doing here?"

Mei couldn't concentrate.

Rarely in all her fifty-five years did she have trouble concentrating. Her ability to focus was legendary—she once crammed for a test at a boisterous outdoor pep rally in the middle of winter. It was an extreme version of tunnel vision Mei employed when she worked. Sensitive work such as an autopsy required that level of concern.

But she couldn't concentrate.

In fact, she hadn't the ability to focus on a single thing since having dinner at Morgan's apartment. Since having dinner at Morgan's apartment where she'd kissed Morgan, broke her heart, and left her alone within a ruthlessly efficient twenty minutes. All due to an attack of cowardice that struck without warning. Now, she stood at a crossroads where she may have to watch Morgan walk away, bringing her light and her joy to someone who could appreciate it without feeling terrified.

After her third glass of wine and second empty crossword puzzle, Mei drew in a deep breath and picked up her phone. Squeezing her eyes shut, she tapped the name in her contacts and held the phone to her ear.

It rang four times. Then, finally, "Mom?"

"Hello, Lara. Are you busy?" Mei stared into the unlit fireplace in the center of her living room. Curled up on her couch, she tucked her feet beneath her legs and took another gulp of wine.

"No, I was about to make dinner. What's up? Is everything okay?"

The worry in Lara's tone was palpable. One of the few memorable times Mei called her daughters was to tell them to come to the hospital because Allan was close to passing. This may have scarred Lara for life. "Everything is fine. I have a rather sensitive question I'd like to ask you."

Reasonably, a long pause occurred before Lara responded. "Okay."

"I am going to request you not ask me any questions in return," Mei said, keeping her voice firm but kind. "Rather, I ask that you answer me as honestly as possible."

Lara's apprehension emanated through the phone. "This is very weird, but I'm intrigued."

Taking another deep breath and an additional sip of wine, Mei bit the bullet. "How did you know for certain you were a lesbian? Was there ever a time when you were attracted to men? If so, how did you come to the conclusion you were not in fact bisexual, but a lesbian?"

"Wow." Lara sighed on the other side of the phone, and Mei heard more shuffling, presumably as Lara got comfortable to answer a series of uncomfortable questions. "I am *dying* to ask you why you need to know this information many years into my being out, but I won't."

"Thank you, I appreciate that."

"Okay, so, I will say I always knew I was interested in girls. Even as a child, I had crushes on girls the way other girls had crushes on boys. I wanted to be near them, I wanted them to like me. As I got older, that feeling became romantic and I understood it more clearly as attraction. You and Daddy always spoke openly about queerness and the differences of other people, so I didn't struggle with compulsory heterosexuality as a pubescent teen."

Chewing on her lip, Mei drew a bit of courage from the wine. "Is it common for people to develop same-sex attraction much later?"

Another pregnant pause. While Lara was indeed a daddy's girl, Mei knew she'd called the right child. Lara's open sexuality was one of her greatest characteristics, an unabashed commitment to who she was and encouraging others to follow this truth. Grace was far too judgmental, but Lara understood. She had Allan's unwavering gift for empathy, and Mei adored them both for it.

"Human sexuality is so complex, I find it easier to believe that one's individual fluidity changes rather than stays the same," Lara said. "From experience I can tell you a lot of women come out later in life. I could deep-dive into the patriarchal reasons that happens, but it's not really pertinent. The most important thing is to not exclude any relationship that brings us joy. Living in a box may be comfortable, but it's never made anyone happy."

"I see."

Mei was silent for a long time. Lara sat on the other end of the line, breathing quietly into the receiver. Finally, gently, she prodded. "Mom, are you okay? You know you can talk to me. I won't tell Grace."

Chuckling softly, Mei sighed and finished her wine. "No, it's all right. I have some thinking to do. Thank you for your honesty."

"You're welcome. Good luck, Mom."

"Thank you. Good night, love."

Staring ahead, Mei knew if she sat on her couch any longer she'd think herself into knots and do nothing. She'd grown tired of doing nothing. Sliding her band off her finger, she left it next to the framed photo of her and Allan at the Grand Canyon sitting on her side table.

Mei lost the courage to knock four times before rapping the door with her knuckles. Steeling herself, she waited for Morgan with a limited reserve of patience. Thankfully she didn't take long, and the door swung open to reveal a confused and freshly showered lieutenant. Her cropped hair hung in half-dried curls, eclipsing one of her eyes, and clad only in a pair of terry-cotton lounge shorts and a thin tank top.

"Mei?" Morgan spoke around the toothbrush in her mouth. "What—are you okay?"

"Yes, I'm fine. I'm sorry to drop by unannounced. May I come in?"

Blinking, Morgan seemed to process Mei's presence slowly. Finally, she stepped back. "Um, yeah."

Mei paused in the doorway. Should she take off her shoes? What if Morgan kicked her out? She wouldn't want to be scrambling for her shoes in that devastating situation. Going with her instincts she kicked off her shoes, following Morgan into the living room. Hip-hop music bounced off every wall until Morgan grabbed a nearby remote to shut it off. Excusing herself, she darted into her bathroom and reemerged without the toothbrush in her mouth. Purse in hand, Mei clenched it tightly as she met eyes with Morgan. "I...I don't know how to begin saying what I need to say."

"All right." Morgan ran her fingers through her damp hair, pushing it off to the side, worry etched across her face. "Here, have a seat. Can I get you something to drink?"

Sitting down near the spot on the floor where she'd kissed Morgan, Mei shook her head and put her purse on the coffee table. "No, thank you. Please, sit down."

Morgan sat down next to her, and the scent of coconut and fresh spring soap filled Mei's nostrils. Different from the mixture of outdoors and sweat from the basketball game, or Morgan's usual scent of cedar and citrus. Combined with her tousled, soaked hair and gorgeous blue eyes, Mei hadn't the clear head she usually did. Maybe having a clear head was overrated.

Morgan's open expression turned worried. "Mei?"

"I know you asked for space, and I want to apologize for violating that agreement."

"I forgive you," Morgan replied with a shrug.

"Thank you." Clearing her throat, Mei dove right in. "I'm here because I need to ask a favor of you. I absolutely do not deserve it after what I put you through, but I am asking nonetheless because I am desperate."

"Of course, anything." It was clear she meant it, too, and Mei knew she would never deserve her steadfast loyalty.

Reaching up, she carded her fingers through Morgan's hair, following the silky tendrils the short distance from her scalp to the ends. "Please, don't get over me."

Drawing back only an inch, Morgan canted her head. "What?"

"Don't get over me. Don't get over me, because if you do, then I have to get over you. And I'm not sure I can."

Hopeful blue eyes gazed at her. "Over *me*?"

"Morgan, I can't tell you if I'm queer or bisexual or whatever, but you make me feel something I've never felt before, and quite honestly it scares the shit out of me. I don't...I don't know what it means yet, but I do know this: I want you. I want you, and I want you to kiss me so badly I can barely think of anything else."

Evidently, she didn't need to be told twice. Immediately Morgan took her in a searing kiss defying all sense of decency. Unlike their first kiss with all of its gentle probing, this one was full of intense purpose, open-mouthed and about as desperate as Mei felt. Lips moving against lips, Morgan's hand came to rest on her hip, fingers digging in. Mei cradled Morgan's neck in her hands and pulled her in harder, increasing the intensity of their embrace as Morgan slipped her tongue into her mouth and stoked a fire inside her.

Under her spell, Mei boldly vaulted one leg over Morgan's lap and straddled her, pressing their bodies flush. Morgan gasped, but the reprieve from their kiss lasted only a moment as she splayed her hands on either of Mei's hips and enveloped her in a tight embrace. Desire thrummed through her, pounding from her heart out to each of her extremities in a way no other kiss had ever done. She cursed the need to breathe as she popped away from Morgan's lips to suck in oxygen. Panting against the soft plush of Morgan's lips, she was unprepared when Morgan blurted out, "I have a date tonight."

It would be so easy to kiss Morgan again, to selfishly rob her of the chance to back out of this. Patiently, she ran her fingers through Morgan's hair and cupped her jaw with the other hand. "Okay. Would you like me to leave?"

"No." Morgan's voice sounded rough, like rubbing velvet in the wrong direction. Mei shuddered. "Don't move. Please."

Wordlessly, Morgan reached an arm to the side and picked up her phone. Mei didn't look. She knew who it was—the attractive, confident young woman who'd visited Morgan in the first aid tent. The insane jealousy that possessed her watching someone give Morgan the attention she deserved without reservation. Witnessing this "Andrea" try to stand where she stood. Blinking out of the memory, she stared at Morgan's face and admired the slopes of her cheekbones, the opaque freckles along her cheeks, the faint pink marks of old blemishes. How had she not succumbed to this terrible attraction before? It was so obvious now, her deep denial about what was right in front of her.

The clatter of the phone hitting the table snapped her attention to Morgan's eyes. She stared up at Mei in pure wonder, unflinchingly affectionate. "I never stood a chance."

Mei held her breath. "A chance of what?"

"Of getting over you."

Without preamble, Morgan surged forward to kiss her harder than before. It surprised Mei, and then pleased her, to have aroused Morgan's passions. Using the height differential of their positions, Morgan pecked hot, open-mouthed kisses against Mei's jaw, then down the side of her neck. Her hands, warm, slightly calloused, and unyielding, roamed the expanse of Mei's back, creeping beneath the fabric with an insistent touch. The drag of Morgan's blunt nails down her spine culled a helpless whimper, and Morgan slowed down.

"Too much?" Morgan asked, breathless.

"No. Don't you dare stop."

And she didn't. Mei couldn't tell how long they stayed like that, entangled like horny teenagers, aggressively making out on a couch. Time was irrelevant. All that mattered was Morgan's lips and hands and the way she would groan and whimper beneath Mei's touch. Morgan kissed with a skillful confidence, but also softness and care. Mei fought to keep up, gaining and losing control of their kiss in a pleasurable back-and-forth. Pulling away for another round of precious air, Morgan reached up to push Mei's hair behind her ears.

"Do you—" Morgan swallowed, biting her swollen bottom lip. Her eyes focused to the right, to the short hallway presumably leading to her bedroom. "We can stop if you want. Or we can just kiss, that's okay, too."

Stopping was quite literally the last thing on Mei's mind, muddled as it was from dizzying arousal. Mei took Morgan's chin between her fingers. "What do you want?"

Chest heaving, Morgan gazed up through hooded lids, her answer firm and undeniable. "I want you in every possible way I can have you."

Well. Her brains now between her legs, Mei climbed off Morgan's lap. Holding her hand out, she flicked her head toward the bedroom. "Then take me to bed."

Taking her hand, Morgan led her down the hallway into her bedroom. While Morgan drew the curtains over her open windows, Mei gave the room a sweeping inspection. It was sparse like the rest of her apartment. A deep navy blue paint on the walls gave way to a charming bright white wainscoting. Her queen-sized antique poster bed sat against a wall, flanked by one bedside table with only a single lamp on it, a lone oak wood dresser flush against another wall, and a vintage chest at the foot of her bed with clothes thrown over it. Original hardwood floors stretched from wall to wall, shiny and well kept. It could use a rug, but Mei filed that away.

Somehow, Morgan radiated more nervous energy than Mei. Anxiously standing next to her bed, she gazed around her own bedroom as if seeing it for the first time. Mei picked up the clothes and held them out, raising an eyebrow at a one-piece black denim jumpsuit Mei had never seen Morgan wear. "It was, for my, ah, my date."

Mei folded the jumpsuit and placed it neatly on the top of the chest. She stepped into her space and settled a hand upon Morgan's chest, dropping her voice. "What a shame she'll never see you in it."

Sitting down on the edge of the bed, Mei scooted backward and Morgan followed, crawling over her. Successful in assuaging Morgan of a portion of her anxiety, Mei watched the cocky grin fix itself on her face. "Oh, it's a shame, is it?"

"Truly a pity." Mei gathered a fistful of Morgan's tank top and yanked her in for another kiss. Morgan obliged, holding her torso above Mei and pressing their hips and legs together. Heat rose between them, exchanged through their clothes, pushing their pulses to a gallop. Mei's hands probed beneath the fabric of Morgan's tank top, over the curves of her back, and down the unfairly firm plane of her stomach. Morgan sat back, her butt on Mei's legs, and whipped her tank top over her head, discarding it without looking. Her tempting, chiseled map of muscle on display, Mei traced the ins and outs of her abs under Morgan's watchful eye. The appearance of muscles didn't arouse her, but rather the implied dedication to fitness that accompanied it. Discipline turned her on. No time to dwell on what psychological recess that impulse came from. For long moments Morgan allowed Mei to discover her upper body through touch, the muscles of her biceps and triceps, the softness of her breasts, the sharp lines of her sternum. Each part of her elicited different reactions from Morgan, from breathless whimpers to short grunts of pleasure, and Mei was obsessed with all of them.

Reaching down, Morgan tugged at the hem of Mei's blouse. "May I?"

Oh, right, this would require undressing on her part as well. Mei couldn't remember the last time she disrobed in front of another person. Years, well before Allan died. Would Morgan find her attractive? Was she still attractive? Mei consented, but her apprehension did not go unnoticed.

"If you would prefer to stay dressed, that's okay." Despite the aching desire plain in Morgan's face, she knew Morgan would do as she asked. However, needing to feel Morgan's skin against her own dashed her initial hesitation.

"No, go ahead." Whereas Morgan's tank top and shorts went flying in different directions, Morgan carefully and methodically undressed Mei, respectfully placing all her garments in the same pile near the bed. Both fully nude, Morgan lowered herself until their skin touched, cautious not to press the entirety of her weight on Mei, and kissed her slowly, with languid but ardent intent. Bare skin sliding against bare skin, Mei reveled in the softness and athletic rigidity of Morgan's body atop her own. Clutching Morgan's shoulders, she writhed against her as Morgan laced kisses down her cheek, neck, and the top of her breasts. As Morgan explored her body with an almost holy reverence, Mei became acutely aware of the imperfections on her person in a way she'd long forgotten how. Every hair, every mole, every stretch mark, every inch of cellulite came rushing back to her all at once.

Her grip on Morgan's shoulders loosened, and Morgan looked up from her task. "You okay?"

"I feel…exposed," Mei replied in a whisper.

Morgan smiled and gave a sly, appreciative glance at her breasts. "By some blessed miracle, you are." Chuckling at the cheekiness, she swatted Morgan's arm. "You mean like self-conscious?" Off Mei's confirmation, Morgan shrugged. "Yeah, me too."

Mei's eyebrow nearly flew off her face. "You? But you're—look at you. You look like what I imagine superheroes look like beneath their costumes."

With a gentle laugh, Morgan nosed the line of Mei's collarbone. "That is patently untrue," she murmured against her skin. "Besides, you are ridiculously beautiful. Not to objectify you too much, but you're, like, crazy hot." Mei rolled her eyes and glanced away. Morgan's light touch on her cheek brought her attention back. "I'm not kidding. I am so painfully attracted to you I'm pretty sure it's the reason being gay is a punishable crime in so many countries."

"You are absolutely absurd, but thank you." Mei tipped Morgan's chin up so she could kiss her. "Sorry, I'm just—I'm nervous."

"So am I," Morgan admitted. "I feel like I have a lot to prove. They might take away my lesbian license if I'm not any good."

Lacing her fingers through and underneath Morgan's hair, she laughed under her breath and brought her down for a long, soft kiss. Mei attempted to convey her desire, her overwhelming need for Morgan, in every movement of their lips, every stroke of her tongue. "There's nothing to prove. I want this. I want you."

Nodding, Morgan moved her weight to one arm so she could cup Mei's face in her hand. "I see your fear and I promise to earn your trust, okay? I'll tell you everything I do before I do it. I won't do anything you're uncomfortable with. If you need me to stop, just say so. Anytime, no questions."

"Okay." Morgan's intensely serious expression made Mei want to alleviate her sudden change in demeanor. "I have had sex before. I do have two daughters."

"Sure, but not like, with another woman, right? I mean, you said you weren't—" Morgan cut herself off after watching Mei's face light up with nefarious glee. "You're teasing me."

"Nice solve, Detective."

"Wow. You're in for it now, you know that?"

Mei raised her eyebrow and peered between them at their nakedness. "God, I certainly hope so."

The growl of Mei's stomach rumbled long and loud, like a starving lion in the savannah. They'd taken a few "hydration breaks," as Morgan called them, but after having her heart rate elevated for several hours, she was ravenous. With neither the energy nor desire to make food, Morgan ordered takeout while they took turns cleaning up, and then relaxed against her plush pillows, tucked underneath a thin summer comforter as they waited for dinner to arrive.

In addition to hunger, many previously unused parts of her body pulsed in soreness. To be expected after the marathon of athletic sex she'd been party to, and she had the good sense not to complain about it, but her muscles ached with fatigue. Morgan knew techniques Mei never heard of and put her through more positions than an advanced yoga class. Things Morgan did with her hands and her mouth and a strap-on she'd introduced about halfway through...the walk to Morgan's bathroom was more of a waddle than she'd like to admit. Most surprising was the unexpected ease of having sex with another woman. A bit of a learning curve, but pleasurable and exciting. In fact, Mei grappled with the fact that it might've been the best sex of her fifty-five years. As a scientist, it was her duty to investigate this hypothesis further. It had nothing at all to do with the identity crisis birthing itself in the back of her mind.

"May I ask you a question?" Morgan propped herself up on her elbow, nodding. "I need you to be honest with me."

"Always."

"On a scale of one to ten, how would you rate your typical sexual performance? One is horrible, ten is mind-blowing."

Morgan blinked in open stupefaction. "Oh. Um, geez. I don't know how to answer that."

"Honestly. Compared to other lovers you've had, how would you rate yourself?"

Eyes narrowed, Morgan licked her lips. "I feel like this is a trick question."

"It's not," Mei replied. "I am curious about something, but I need more information."

As usual, Morgan took her seriously, pausing in sincere contemplation. "I would say I'm usually somewhere between a seven and an eight."

"Then it would be accurate to state you're above average, but been with lovers you'd consider better than you?"

"At least one, yeah."

For the sake of science, Mei ignored the immediate twinge of jealousy piercing her insides. "Your performance today, would you say that was about average for you, or better?"

Morgan chuckled. "This is some bedside manner, Doctor. Do you usually ask your partners to rate their 'performance' directly after sex?"

"Considering you are one of only two, no, I have not."

Mei herself neared laughter as she watched Morgan's face grow sober. "I'm sorry, I'm feeling a lot of emotions about that piece of information at the moment."

"I see that."

"But, um, please know I feel extremely privileged to have earned enough of your trust that you'd allow me to—"

"Ruin me for sex with anyone else?" Positioning a calming hand on Morgan's chest, she shook her head. "I'm only asking because that was incredible and I was wondering if it was you, or if I am perhaps much gayer than I anticipated."

"Oh. Well. I'm going to try valiantly to not let that get to my ego. Just so you know, it is not working and I plan to be insufferable." Deep blue eyes twinkled, crinkling at the corners as she traced her fingers over the top of Mei's hand. "It's probably a bit of both. I've slept with women who previously only slept with men and nine times out of ten, that's the reaction."

"Nine times out of ten?" Mei parroted.

"An approximation," Morgan said, grinning. "It differs from person to person. To put it simply, sometimes it's *women*, and sometimes it's *a woman*. The only way for you to know conclusively would be for you to sleep with another woman." The grin fell from Morgan's face. "Can I ask you something?"

"Fair's fair."

Peering down, Morgan tugged on her bottom lip. "I probably should've said something before all this happened, but I don't exactly do my most fruitful thinking with a beautiful woman on my lap."

"Flatterer. Go on."

"I—I'm not interested in casual sex. I do it on occasion because I'm pretty terrible at saying no. But I, um, I don't like it." Her chest expanded with a deep breath. "I really, really like you. And while obviously you're not under any obligation to return my feelings, you deserve to know I won't be able to have anything casual with you. If you want to sleep with other women to better understand yourself, I would understand. But if that's all you want from me, this will have to be our first and only time. Is that all you want from me?"

"Oh, Morgan." Mei dipped beneath the blanket to grab Morgan's hand, bringing it up and brushing her lips against Morgan's knuckles. "I admit I'm a little confused as to what this means for me, but I am not confused about you. I have feelings for you too. You'll have to be patient with me as I haven't dated in a long time and there's a good chance I will be awful at it. But I don't want something casual with you, either. I...I don't want to be with anyone else."

Sighing with relief, Morgan clutched Mei's fingers in her own. "Okay, good. That's all I needed to hear."

She snuggled in close, her cheek flush against Morgan's sternum. The young lieutenant's heart beat strongly, rhythmically, and as they got comfortable against the pillows curled in one another, it became a soft, predictable thump. Mei kissed the bare skin above Morgan's heart and whispered, "You give me the belly swoops too."

CHAPTER ELEVEN

Morgan didn't know what time it was when she pulled in the lot at work. She parked her car and sailed through the doors of the bullpen, right into the meeting room.

Morgan didn't participate in their morning briefing, choosing instead to let Gilland field the cold case questions.

Morgan didn't pet the dog on her way to the coffee shop to pick up her order, nor did she pay any attention to the amount of money she dropped in the tip jar, though her wallet would be a surprising twenty dollars lighter later on.

Morgan didn't see Ruiz intentionally get into the elevator with her until she gave her a little shove. "So, what the hell is that look on your face? I realize you got laid, but you're usually not so smug about a fling."

A smile permanently fixed on her face, Morgan waited in silence for the elevator to bring them downstairs. It creaked open and Morgan walked out into the hallway. Before she could take another step, Ruiz grabbed her by the arm and forced her attention. "Morgan. Is everything okay?"

She stood still as Ruiz took stock of her, narrowed eyes scrutinizing her and the cups in her hand. One a sugar-laden coffee and the other a tea, its little tag hanging out of the side of the cup. Finally, she met Ruiz's eyes and they shared a soft, knowing smile. "Ah."

Morgan pivoted left toward the morgue, shouldering open the door with a now incredibly intrigued friend tailing her.

"Good morning," Mei greeted, taking the hot cup Morgan offered. She touched her cheek and pecked a gentle kiss on her lips, eyeing the gawking Sergeant Ruiz. "I see you brought company."

"Hmm?" Morgan shrugged. "She followed me."

Mei smirked, wiping powdered sugar from the corner of Morgan's mouth. "How are you, Sergeant Ruiz?"

"Honestly, Doctor, I don't even know." Ruiz chuckled, shaking her head in disbelief. "This is why Kelly didn't answer her phone all weekend and why she's had that dumbass head-in-the-clouds look on her face this morning. *Felicidades.*"

As Mei blushed at the insinuation, Morgan didn't flinch. Friday night with Mei rapidly turned into all day Saturday, which sort of melted into Sunday morning. Their weekend was a total blur of decent television, excellent sex, indulgent food, and lazy naps. Hedonistic and wholesome in equal measure, it was the single greatest weekend of Morgan's life.

"All right, you are way too saccharine." Ruiz backed away from where Morgan sat on the edge of Mei's desk and shot heart-eyes at her. "Unlike Kelly, I can't consume this much sugar this early in the morning. I am leaving."

Morgan waved in her direction. "Bye."

"You should be leaving too," she suggested with a purposeful firmness. "You have three little saplings in your office who need your guidance."

"Uh-huh. They're fine, I left the TV on and they have snacks. Goodbye, Anna-Maria."

Despite Ruiz's niggling, Morgan made no attempt to move. She sat with her coffee between her hands, smiling down at Mei as the noise of the door closing behind Ruiz reached them. "I missed you."

Mei blushed. "You did not. You saw me"—she glanced at the time on her wrist—"less than twelve hours ago."

Morgan put her coffee down and shrugged. "Still missed you."

While Morgan had no issue—okay, some issue—going slowly with Mei, it wasn't in her nature to be obtuse about her feelings. She didn't lie, and she didn't see the need to hide how she felt. Morgan strongly believed time was precious and any moment spent obscuring the truth was time wasted.

Standing from her chair, Mei left her tea and wedged herself between Morgan's legs. She held her face in her hands, stroking Morgan's cheekbone with her thumb. "I will admit it was alarmingly easy to fall asleep with you, and even more alarmingly difficult without."

Turning her head, Morgan kissed Mei's palm, sliding her hands around the bottom of Mei's waist. The top of her butt, to be specific, as Morgan made known her proclivity for Mei's butt several times over the last three days. "I don't mean to jump too fast."

"In fairness to you, you did think this weekend was the continuation of three months of dating." Mei rested her hands on the base of Morgan's neck. "It was I who perhaps jumped too fast."

Gaze dropping to the floor, Morgan let out a dejected, "Oh."

Tilting her head down, Mei pressed her lips against Morgan's and brought her attention back up. "I didn't mean it like that. I don't regret it."

The dread flooding her washed away in an instant. "No?"

"No, darling, not even a little bit." Morgan beamed at her and Mei chuckled, kissing her with more purpose. Morgan responded eagerly, with the reckless abandon of an infatuated teenager. A hunger gnawed at her, one she knew no amount of kissing would ever sate. Breaking apart slowly, Mei stayed within easy kissing distance and ran her fingers through Morgan's hair. "I only meant that I was the one who slammed on the brakes and then threw us into drive. It's understandable you may have emotional whiplash."

"It's not that," Morgan murmured, hooking her leg around the back of Mei's calf. "I've had feelings for you for months. So, where this feels natural to me, I don't want to make you uncomfortable. Just because we had sex doesn't mean we can't go slowly." Bashful, Mei bit her lip and looked down. Morgan laughed. "Oh, now you're embarrassed? Don't act coy. You certainly weren't shy this weekend."

"I am not acting coy. This is a workplace, Lieutenant," Mei teased, nudging Morgan in the shoulder. "And what do you mean by that?"

"Nothing. For someone who never had lesbian sex, you're a quick study. I never imagined you'd be so enthusiastic and bossy in bed."

"I'm bossy?" As Morgan's mouth opened Mei pressed a finger against her lips, narrowing her eyes in suspicion. "Before you answer that, when did you imagine what I was like in bed?"

"For the first time?" Pausing, Morgan canted her head to think about it. Imagining sex with Mei became a shameful hobby of hers rather early on. Safe to say it was better than she could have ever imagined. "Ah, here, talking to you about a case. You were in the middle of an autopsy and got hung up. You made this…frustrated noise of effort and I thought maybe that's what you might sound like in bed. Then I, uh, thought about it a couple of times since then."

"Right. We'll come back to that another time. You said I'm bossy?"

Morgan grinned. No way to know what Mei's sex life was like with her husband, and she would never ask, but it struck her as hilarious that Mei might not know she was incredibly bossy. "Well, yeah. You know what you like and you're not afraid to ask for it. I thought I'd be the expert, but you took control. Most people are not like that the first time."

Though Morgan diligently acquired consent and prepped her for each position or method of intercourse, Mei caught on quickly. It wasn't long into their night before she started receiving directions and Morgan would've died sooner than deny Mei a single thing. "Is that…does that work for you?"

"Does that work for me? You're so cute." Based upon the instant, tiny frown on Mei's face, *cute* was not the adjective she wanted to hear, but Morgan couldn't help but be a little smug. It wasn't often she had the upper hand between them. "There is very little you could do to me, or ask me to do to you, that would not work for me."

"I see." Sinfully close, Mei ran her fingers through Morgan's hair and then abruptly gave the ends a sharp tug. Morgan gasped, tilting her head back, instinctively submissive. Mei brushed her lips along the column of Morgan's exposed throat before lingering over her ear. "So, if I were to tell you that I wanted to take you here, on my desk, and that you have to be so, so quiet…would *that* work for you?"

Nodding her head furiously, Morgan choked on air. "Y-yes."

"Excellent." Mei bit the lobe of Morgan's ear tenderly, then moved to kiss her on the cheek. "Another time, perhaps. I have a lot of work to do."

How was it possible this was the same woman who didn't even know they were dating only a few weeks ago? "I am in over my head, aren't I?"

"Oh, I don't know, darling," Mei replied with a cheeky grin. "You're the expert."

Fortunately for Morgan, work allowed no time to dwell on Mei's sudden sexual confidence and her complete helplessness to withstand it. Not that she didn't think about it after departing Mei's office, but with her suspect in custody the captain had approved her and her squad to branch out to other projects, and brain time had to be devoted to work. Work, and not the drop-dead gorgeous scientist she'd spent the better part of the weekend turning out with some of the hottest sex she'd ever had in her life.

For Morgan, sex was a currency she exchanged for affection. It was easy, fun, a way to get girls to like her, and it allowed her to feel something during times when feeling anything required an exorbitant amount of effort. Not until she met Gemma did she finally have a partner who made love to her and loved her. She earnestly sought this bond in every partner since, but it never materialized. However, Mei was different. Morgan felt wanted and desired for the first time in a long time.

Caught in a daydream, she returned to reality to find Corporal Gilland staring at her with a smirk on her face. She frowned. "What?"

"Nothing. You looked like you were in a much more pleasant place than a room full of musty boxes," Gilland replied. "Have a good weekend, Lieutenant?"

And, right, yeah, they were prioritizing the case files. The young officer proved excellent at figuring out which cases would be the quickest solves. She had good instincts and reminded Morgan of herself, adept at solving puzzles and an astute judge of character. Morgan secretly had a favorite of her three new coworkers, and it was Gilland. Unassuming to look at—mousy with wiry brown hair and pale gray eyes, maybe reaching five foot four in her boots and a buck twenty-five soaking wet—Gilland possessed a quick wit, using other people's tendency to underestimate her to her advantage. Morgan admired little more than someone who took the cards dealt to them and played to win.

"The best." Of course, as her boss she declined to elaborate. Especially since she and Mei had not discussed going public. "The best I've had in a long time."

"Good for you." Gilland took a couple steps toward Morgan, shooting a glance at the door leading back into the shared open office. "I want you to know I respect what you did. Honestly, it's one of the reasons why I jumped at this assignment."

"You did?"

"I did. Actually, Daniels and I both did."

"Daniels?" Her eyes bulged. Officer Daniels made no effort to show more than the minimum amount of interest or respect. "Really?"

"Daniels is in the process of shedding the toxic masculinity slimed on him at the academy," Gilland explained. "Him being an asshole toward you is solely based on what he heard from other dumbass officers with more guns than brains. Underneath that he's a good cop and wants to make a difference. Plus, we can develop careers down here and not have to ass-kiss some old white man." Gilland eyed a box and walked it over to another stack. "Anyway, I came here for my career, but I also did it for you. You're probably the best detective in the state, and you have integrity. How could I not?"

"Thanks, Gilland." Morgan rested her elbow on one of the boxes. "That means a lot to me."

"I know it does, because I'm your favorite," she said, stacking a box above her height. "And look, your ambitions and talent are going to take you far beyond this basement, but while you're here, I'll learn what I can from the woman who cracked the Bodega Burglar case."

The first case Morgan ever got commended for. A string of midnight burglaries committed at bodegas across the city: a masked man demanded cash and left no trace of himself. No cameras caught him, no witnesses other than scared cashiers, no prints, no DNA. As a rookie, Morgan broke the case open by identifying the motive as race related. "What a case."

"Well, if you're in the mood to nerd-out about case solving, I'm all ears."

"Gilland, it is not an exaggeration to say I am always in the mood to nerd-out about case solving."

As they stacked and organized case files, Morgan explained part of the methodology that helped catch the Bodega Burglar. It made her career and sent her right to the front of the bullpen. Everything about it exemplified why she got into police work— solving puzzles and helping people, especially those in the margins of society.

In the middle of waxing nostalgic about a riveting stakeout, a light knock on the door interrupted them. Morgan popped up from behind boxes. "Mei!" Eyes wide, she cleared her throat. "Ah, Dr. Sharpe. How—how are you?"

Of all her supposed gifts, subtlety was not one of them. Her stilted attempt to be professional garnered an incredulous look from Mei. "I'm well, Lieutenant, thank you. I wondered if you might want to have lunch with me."

Corporal Gilland blew dust off the top of a box. "Lieutenant Kelly talks a lot about how delicious your cooking is."

"That's very kind of her. Unfortunately, I was too busy this weekend to prepare any lunches."

Morgan bit her lip so hard it nearly drew blood. Gilland most certainly connected the dots in her head, a sly grin growing on her face. "Oh. Right. You know, I'm going to check with Polzar about...um, crime? Crime. Crime and crime-related activities." Sliding by Mei in the doorway, she gave Morgan a thumbs-up over the back of Mei's head.

Mei crossed her arms. "What was that?"

"I mentioned to Corporal Gilland I had a nice weekend, and I think she has made an inference."

"Impressive deduction," she said, stalking toward Morgan. "So? Are you free?"

"Sure, where did you want to go?"

Like always Morgan wore a pristine, pressed, button-down shirt and tie, but today over a pair of skintight jeans instead of slacks. By the hungry look in Mei's eyes, she'd chosen well. "What's on the way back from your place?"

Morgan scrunched her nose in thought. "Hmm, well, there's Carlo's Pizza, or the halal joint with the amazing falafel, or—" Upon seeing the sultry, amused look on Mei's face, Morgan realized she was an idiot. "Oh! How long do you have for lunch?"

"My colleagues can wait indefinitely."

"Is that right? What happened to 'I have a lot of work to do'?" Mei snickered and stroked the fabric of her tie. "Well, I'm sure they can do without me for an hour." Mei shook her head. "Or two?"

"Better."

After bringing Mei to three climaxes, Morgan finally began building to her own orgasm in earnest, thrusting quickly and roughly as she chased an angle to bring her release. Digging her nails into Morgan's back, Mei spoke the right combination of encouraging words to drive her over the edge. She clenched her teeth into the meat of Mei's shoulder, letting out a high-pitched grunt as her hips stuttered and slowed, until she ran out of energy entirely.

Sweaty and smiling, Morgan lifted her head and kissed Mei deeply with a postcoital surge of affection, which was enthusiastically returned. Mei spread her hands out on Morgan's back, rubbing her muscles in soothing circles. Reaching down between them, Morgan maneuvered out of the harness and tossed it over the side of the bed. She scooped Mei in her arms and pulled them together, rolling onto her side. Morgan didn't expect or need much reciprocation from her partners, but she did require aftercare. Mei instinctively provided this, cuddling her and keeping her in a gentle embrace with skin-on-skin closeness.

A wayward breeze blew in through an open window, sticking to the aerosol droplets of sweat along their bodies. For long moments it was quiet, as the oxytocin and dopamine rushed through them and produced a shared calm.

"That was fantastic," Morgan said, tilting her head back. "Good god."

"You're telling me." Mei pulled the back of Morgan's knee to wrap her leg around her hips. "By far my best work lunch."

"Yeah, that's at least top five for me." Mei bit down where she kissed Morgan's neck. "Okay, okay. Top three."

"Brat."

"What? I have eaten some excellent food," Morgan said with a prim sniff, prompting Mei to roll on top of her and pin her wrists on either side of her head. Her lover's gaze roamed hungrily up and down before settling on her eyes with a heady stare. "Careful, Doctor. We have to return to our 'workplace' soon. Let's not start something we don't intend to finish."

"Is that a challenge?" Mei sat back, releasing her hands to brace her weight on Morgan's stomach.

Morgan pushed locks of hair from Mei's face. "I wouldn't dream of it."

Leaning in, Mei kissed down the center of Morgan's throat, across her sternum and between her breasts, giving them a squeeze on her way down. "No? Why not?"

"You're still new at this. I wouldn't want you to be disappointed if you couldn't do it."

Every square inch of her words were a direct challenge and Morgan keenly understood Mei's incapability to back down. With a sardonic chuckle, Mei pecked a chaste kiss against Morgan's lips.

"Oh, okay." Slowly, predatorily, she skimmed her mouth across Morgan's cheekbone to the outer shell of her ear. "Spread your legs."

This was stuck on loop in Morgan's mind as she sat next to Mei in their group grief meeting. Sister Laura pontificated in her usual, profound way, but Morgan's mind replayed the previous afternoon's encounter in high definition. Mind in the gutter, she turned to gaze at Mei, who listened intently to Sister Laura's quasi-sermon. She had cute ears, tiny and round. Pierced with a single diamond earring she figured was a gift— Mei's practicality prevented her from purchasing extravagant jewelry. Pin-straight strands of black hair, nearly the color of black cocoa, fell down around her face and neck, spread out over her blouse. Unfairly perfect skin, soft and flawless. Faint wrinkles lay around her eyes, the corners of her mouth, and along her forehead, vestiges of smiles and laughs, of years and experience. And her eyes. Morgan sighed. Gorgeous and deep, constantly calculating and twinkling. Equally beautiful in body and mind, Mei was unlike anyone she'd ever met, orbiting alone outside the stratosphere of ordinary.

Instantly upon meeting her in the morgue Morgan felt it, a pull toward Mei as easy to identify as a pulse. Getting to know her better only served to worsen the crush. Knowing your crush is beautiful is one thing; beauty is common enough. Knowing your beautiful crush is also smart, kind, funny, and a little bossy? Morgan was a goner before they'd begun.

Ruiz told her she was a dweeb. While perhaps true, now she was a dweeb with a girlfriend. Maybe. So, there.

"Morgan?"

Uh-oh. Snapping back to attention, many pairs of eyes landed on her as she struggled to orient herself within the conversation around her. All of Sister Laura's words melted into a drone she'd tuned out in favor of ogling Mei, and the room of surrogate grandparents saw her do it.

"Uh, yes?"

Sister Laura smiled in her infinite, holy patience. "I asked if you had anything you'd like to contribute. You're uncharacteristically quiet tonight."

A smirk curled up on the side of Mei's face but she didn't look over. Morgan cleared her throat. "No, Sister, I'm fine. What a great meeting. Everyone's...everyone's doing so well. Such a—so productive. Proud...proud of you...all."

Bless the grace of Sister Laura, who saw through Morgan entirely but stood to end their meeting. "That's all for tonight, folks. Feel free to take home any goodies from the table. See you all next week."

Within seconds Morgan leapt to her feet, ready to fight blue-hairs for the scrumptious cookies Rosie brought, but got swarmed before she could make the dash. Barry, a retired US Army captain, got to her first. "Lieutenant Kelly, how the hell are you?"

"I'm fine, Captain Greene, thank you," Morgan replied. "How's your physical therapy going? Leg still giving you trouble?"

Barry shook his left leg, clad in his baggy neon blue nylon pants, to show his dexterity. "No ma'am. Feelin' much better. The boys are takin' me fishin' this weekend. Gonna catch me a big ol' bass, I tell you that, Lieutenant."

"I believe you, Captain. None of those fish stand a chance."

Frannie barged in between Morgan and Barry, shuffling in her orthopedic shoes and flouncy white shirt to interrupt them. "Now, Morgan, I talked to my niece this weekend. You remember Danielle, the one I told you about? Well, I told her all about you. I said, 'Danni, I know this lovely police officer. She's got great manners and she's good lookin' and you'd be a fool not to go on a date with her.' That's what I said. And my niece, she's a looker."

"That's sweet of you, Frannie. If she's even half as beautiful as you, she's already out of my league."

"Oh, now you stop that," Frannie chided, blushing beneath her rouge. "And she's not just pretty, either. She's smart, got a degree. Here, let me get a photo for you." Frannie looked over her glasses at her phone, holding it far away from her face. "How do I get to the photos? Hit camera?"

As Frannie took a photo of either herself or the floor, Morgan grew anxious. Setups were common amongst these folks; they loved to play matchmaker. At first she encountered reticence about her sexuality, but once they came around Morgan drowned in their adult granddaughters, nieces, even a few stray young cousins as they tried to marry her off.

"It's all right, thank you. I am...I am seeing someone, actually."

With a dramatic gasp, Frannie nearly dropped her phone on the ground. "You've got a girlfriend? Why didn't you say so? Who is it? What does she do?"

Her loud inquisition caught the attention of lingering group members who closed in around Morgan as she helplessly watched Mei make a quiet exit out of the gym. "It's new. It's...it's really new, but I'm crazy about her. I'm sorry I can't take your niece out on a date. I'm certain she's lovely, but it wouldn't be fair to her since my heart is elsewhere."

Declining to elaborate further, Morgan extricated herself from the well-wishing group of seniors and regretfully left Rosie's cookies behind. She raced out into the parking lot, heaving a sigh of relief when she spotted Mei outside her car. She jogged over as quickly as she could without looking desperate, and Mei peered up from the ground with a gentle smile. "Hey."

"Hey. You bailed and left me to the sharks."

Mei snorted, raising her eyebrow. "Who in that harmless gaggle of seniors is a shark?"

"All of them, are you kidding? You should see them play bingo. It is ruthless." Examining her sneakers, she stubbed the gravel with her toe. "Listen, I didn't say anything to them about us. I mean, honestly, I wouldn't know what to tell them."

Looking a little relieved, Mei reclined against her car. "Neither do I. I don't think their pacemakers could handle the reality of what is going on between us."

"Right," Morgan replied, snickering. "I just wanted you to know. I wouldn't broadcast any information you didn't want me to. Not that I want to hide, but I respect your privacy."

"I know you do." Mei hooked her arms around Morgan's elbow and squeezed. "You're incredibly kind and more considerate than I deserve."

"That's not true."

"It is, but I appreciate it. All of this is new to me." Mei fiddled with the hem of Morgan's sleeve. "I didn't date before I met Allan. My academics didn't leave time for it, and frankly, it didn't interest me at all. It took him three weeks of convincing just to get me to dinner. I wouldn't want you to be frustrated with me."

Peering up, Morgan stared into the depths of coagulating storm clouds. The night sky swirled in gray and white, like milky tea. Waiting wasn't a problem for them. The problem would be convincing Mei she was worth waiting for. "I'm not in a rush, Mei. I waited three months to kiss you. I think you'll find I'm fairly patient."

"Until you discover I'm not worth that amount of effort."

Using her free hand, Morgan tilted Mei's chin toward her. "You never have to worry about that. Even if this doesn't work out, you would still be worth the effort."

To Morgan's surprise, Mei wrapped her hand around the back of her neck and pulled her down for a kiss, not at all chaste. Morgan's insides stirred as she moved her hand down to Mei's waist. It didn't seem to faze her that a few of the seniors trickled out of the gym and, if any had decent eyesight, they'd be seen. When she opened her eyes, Mei's gaze reflected back unexpectedly vulnerable, shiny brown orbs capturing the moonlight. "Can I come home with you?"

Weakness for women or not, nothing short of a five-alarm house fire would've prevented Morgan from saying yes. But, she stayed cool and smiled. "Of course. I'll see you in a few."

Once she turned to walk toward her car, she allowed the giant, giddy smile to stretch across her face.

CHAPTER TWELVE

Time moved differently when Allan was sick. Slow, grueling, but not enough time at all. Waiting in the lobby for him to finish chemo, those hours dragged. Not enough magazines, audiobooks, or distractions in the world existed to make that time go faster. But when they crashed through his bucket list—getting drenched at Niagara Falls, screaming into the Grand Canyon, for some reason going bobsledding—it moved all too fast. After he passed the rhythm changed, like the set list at a ballroom dance. For two years, Mei struggled to find the tempo.

Now, Mei woke up, met Shanvi or Morgan (or on particularly trying days, both) at the café for breakfast, worked until the end of her shift, and either went to Morgan's apartment or out to dinner with her. Some nights she'd spend at Morgan's, others they were either too tired or busy and she'd sleep alone at home. But Mei found the rhythm again. Her life resembled normalcy.

By late summer, dating Morgan became part of that new normal. She seamlessly integrated herself into Mei's life; they'd even celebrated Mei's birthday together at an intimate lakeside restaurant. Summer breezed by as they did many of the same things they did during those first three months when Mei was an idiot. Except now, other than Shanvi, Sergeant Ruiz, and probably Morgan's cold case squad, nobody knew about them. Her daughters didn't know. She hadn't brought Morgan to her house where the neighbors could spot her, or gone to any restaurants she and Allan used to frequent. To her credit, Morgan was as she said she would be: perfectly content to take things slowly. But Mei knew it was coming. Eventually, she'd have to stop half dating Morgan and either commit to this or risk losing her entirely.

The moment arrived with the autumn breeze as it ushered out the summer heat.

Morgan perched on the edge of her bed in the robe Mei purchased for her after discovering, much to her shock, that Morgan did not own a bathrobe. She simply toweled off and dressed, which felt like a crime. Leaving it carelessly (or intentionally) open to reveal a sliver of damp, pinkish skin between her breasts and down to her navel, Morgan nervously tugged on the end of the plush sleeve as she revealed the upcoming nuptials of Sergeant Ruiz and her fiancée, Reyna.

"Despite being allergic to friendliness, Ruiz has a lot of friends. A big portion of the office is coming. The deputy sheriff, a few district attorneys, a prosecutor or two. And, so, I hope you...want to go with me. As my date. As my wedding date. To the wedding."

"I see."

Shuffling forward, Morgan continued to make her case. "This means people at work will know about us. If that makes you uncomfortable, I understand. We can attend together, but not together-together."

Ultimately, the department's awareness of her dating Morgan would not change the function of her occupation. As a separate entity she did what she pleased, including their new lieutenant. "Would you like us to attend as...I'm not sure of the terminology. Girlfriends feels a bit juvenile. As lovers? Oh, that sounds terrible."

"We're not septuagenarians in a hot tub," Morgan replied with a grimace. "Would I like us to attend as a couple? Yes. I would be honored and humbled to be your date."

How exactly was she meant to say no to this woman? Batting her baby blue eyes, smiling like Mei hung the moon and stars? It wasn't possible. "Of course I'll go with you. If it means outing ourselves, so to speak, to your colleagues, that's okay."

Morgan lit up like a Christmas tree. "Really?" She practically leapt the two feet between them and hugged Mei tightly. Her scent, fresh from the shower, enveloped Mei, and she inhaled a deep breath through her nose.

Pulling back, she cupped Morgan's cheek in her hand. "I never want you to think I'm ashamed of you. I can't tell you how much it means to me that you're so considerate of my feelings. It's shocking."

Morgan narrowed her eyes. "Shocking? Why?"

"Well, I've told you a bit about my mother. How I felt about things didn't matter much to her. And, you know, Allan was such a huge personality, I think over the years I got used to my voice getting drowned out. Not that he didn't care what I thought, but he was so charismatic—and frustratingly right all the time—I often went along with what he thought without considering myself."

Listening attentively, Morgan took Mei's hand from her face and clasped it between her own. Her left hand, on which her wedding ring remained wrapped around her finger. "I'm happy you're comfortable telling me how you feel. I know it doesn't come easily to you, and I'm grateful that you try."

Mei sighed, pushing an errant lock of Morgan's hair away from her face. "How are you real?" Drawing close, she placed a warm, soft kiss against Morgan's lips. "Don't say anything else charming or you'll end up right back in that shower."

Humming into their kiss, Morgan pushed forward and gently coaxed Mei onto her back. She shrugged off her robe and let it slip onto the floor. "You could join me."

Heart pounding, she let Morgan untie her robe and shove the material away, exposing her and raising goose bumps along her skin. "It would save water."

Morgan lay between her legs, grinning wickedly. "If you think about it, this is very responsible of us."

As the best woman, Morgan was wrapped up in a flurry of wedding preparations for the rest of the week, so Mei found herself in the familiar embrace of solitude once again. It was strange to not see her for days, but Morgan frequently updated her via text. This included such pertinent information as sightings of cute deer and squirrels, last-minute clothing emergencies, and Ruiz's uncharacteristic bridezilla behavior, which tickled Morgan to death.

Years since her last formal occasion that wasn't a funeral, it delighted Mei to change into something beautiful and flattering, as opposed to her tried-and-true blazers and pants or skirts. She wore a dress made of violet satin with a wide belt tied below her ribs. The deep V-neck worked well with her modest cleavage and the sharp bones of her clavicle, something she knew Morgan admired, so she also wore an eye-grabbing sterling silver chain upon it. Hair up and secured with a diamond barrette, she slipped into her matching heels and appraised herself in the mirror.

She debated her ring. Leaving it on felt most natural, but she worried about the office rumor mill churning away at their expense when they saw an older widow on the arm of her younger, lesbian coworker. Mei went with her gut and left it on.

Leaving the city and the suburbs behind, she drove the forty-five minutes to the wooded estate printed on the invitation. A winding, tree-lined driveway led her to a gargantuan mansion built from logs, a hunting lodge of epic proportion with floor-to-ceiling windows reflecting the late afternoon sun like embers. Adjacent, the reception hall Morgan sent photos of—a rustic, elegantly decorated barn—stood proudly in the thicket of trees. The actual ceremony took place upon the shores of a placid lake not far from the rest of the property. Dozens of guests milled about by the time Mei gave her car to the valet. No expense had been spared, as Mei heard the strains of a live string quartet playing soft classical music. From the entrance to the cabin, a pathway lit with hanging paper lanterns guided Mei to the lakefront, her heels treading upon a white linen cloth littered with pink rose petals.

At an hour or two before sunset, a golden wash poured over a crystal-blue lake and shone through sky-scraping, ancient trees. An ornate arch of twisted white birch housed the priest, a woman in flowing black robes. Exposed bulb lights strung from poles around the seating area gave a magical glow to the already warm, sandy tones of the evening. Choosing a seat toward the back on the "groom's" side, Mei sat nearest the members of the police force she recognized, including the deputy sheriff, with whom she exchanged polite pleasantries.

The string quartet struck up a quiet, plucked cover of a pop song Mei vaguely recognized but could not name. The processional began when a woman Mei assumed was Reyna's mother walked down the aisle with Ruiz at her side. Dapper in a fitted tux, Ruiz smiled brightly in a way Mei had never seen. She'd seen the sergeant wear a smirk. Maybe a small half smile, if something struck her as truly hilarious. But now her grin could've leapt right off her face. Helping Reyna's mother to her seat, Ruiz took her place in front of the officiant and waited.

Next the wedding party arrived, starting with Morgan. Mei held her breath as Morgan emerged from the mansion with a woman on her arm—one of Reyna's bridesmaids, possibly her sister. Morgan cut a striking figure with her professionally coiffed undercut and black, form-fitting, feminine tuxedo complete with a crisp white shirt, black vest, and pink bow tie matching the dress of her companion. Posing for photos, Morgan's eyes searched the congregants until they found her. Smiling as they met each other's gaze, Mei watched her walk up the aisle and lead the woman to her place. Morgan stood directly behind Ruiz, in front the sergeant's three brothers. She regretted having to turn away from Morgan to watch the bride make her entrance. Of course she looked stunning—Reyna was perpetually model-attractive—but Morgan was the showstopper, at least to Mei. Back at the altar, Ruiz teared up watching her soon-to-be bride approach, and Morgan surreptitiously handed her a handkerchief. They exchanged soft whispers, and Ruiz gave her the soft look Mei learned the grumpy officer reserved solely for Morgan.

The officiant's speech consisted of much of the same spiel on marriage Mei remembered from her own wedding: ruminations on fate and happiness and trust. Allan lived life close to his emotions, so it did not surprise her when he pulled a handkerchief from his pocket to wipe his tears. Of course, in true Allan style, his handkerchief turned into a length of white cloth about fifteen feet long, which he drew and drew and drew, piling at his feet. Mei and their guests burst into laughter except for her mother, sitting stone-faced in the front row, which made Mei laugh harder. It remained her fondest memory of her wedding.

Kissing to loud applause, the new Mrs. and Mrs. Ruiz walked back down the aisle showered with rice, confetti, and rose petals. The guests departed for a cocktail hour, which passed as if it were an entire cocktail day as Mei waited to see Morgan again. She made unbearable small talk with members of the sheriff's office until the DJ thankfully told them to take their seats inside the reception hall.

Once seated for dinner—Mei's placard put her at a table near the front next to Morgan—the wedding party returned. A sexy, bass-heavy Spanish-language song pounded from speakers hid clandestinely in the rafters above. Lesser members of the bridal party entered, dancing toward the center of the room. Morgan and Reyna's maid of honor, a woman Mei learned during the cocktail hour was named Liliana, emerged onto the dance floor, wickedly close. Their hips moved in sync as they crept toward the others in a walk doubling as a tango. Liliana turned on occasion, giving Morgan's bow tie a sultry tug. After a quick twirl and a kiss on the hand, Morgan left Liliana on the bride's side of the line they'd formed, as the newlyweds entered the spotlight for their first dance. The brides swayed to a Spanish love song, and Mei's attention zeroed in on Morgan, who watched with her hands clasped in front of her mouth, overwhelmed with emotion.

Song over, Ruiz and Reyna left the dance floor to another round of applause and the guests took their seats. Finally, Morgan skittered away from the bridal party and dropped herself in the chair next to Mei. Using her cloth napkin, Mei soaked the sweat on Morgan's forehead.

"Quite an entrance," she whispered.

"Anna-Maria made me practice for *weeks*," Morgan lamented. "Fortunately, Liliana is an amazing dancer and a saint for putting up with me during rehearsals."

"It didn't look like she was suffering too much," Mei noted. "How could she when her partner was the most dashing person up there in a tuxedo?"

"Well, thank you, Mei Sharpe. You look…" Morgan trailed off, eyes raking up and down Mei's dress. Taking Mei's hand she squeezed it, bringing it to her lips for a kiss. "You are stunning. That dress looks so incredible on you it almost makes me feel guilty for how badly I want to get you out of it."

Blushing, Mei made a little *O* with her mouth and Morgan winked, giving her knuckles a subtle bite before settling down and turning to the rest of the table.

After a rare, delicious wedding dinner, Morgan left their table to make her speech to the brides. Taking the mic from Ruiz's father, Morgan shoved one hand in her pocket and held the microphone with the other.

"Hi everyone, I'm Morgan, Anna-Maria's best woman. She asked that I not recite any poetry or quote anything from a book, so I'll start by telling you about when Anna-Maria and I met at the academy, and the first thing she said to me was: 'Out of my way, Blondie.' She pushed past me, and absolutely smoked me as we ran our miles. Then, she didn't speak to me for two weeks." Morgan paused for scattered laughter. "Anyone who knows Anna-Maria knows she is an absolute block of ice. She has to be. Three brothers, Army brat, then a brat in the Army, she is a survivor. And survivors do everything they can to keep people out."

Morgan addressed the guests but her eyes stayed glued to Mei, who did her best to stay neutral and encouraging with a smile. "But what she doesn't want you to know is that the reason she keeps people out is because her heart is entirely too large and she is generous to a fault. She likes to claim I made her soft, but the truth of the matter is her strength makes me a better person. And in Reyna she found another incredible human overflowing with kindness, empathy, patience, and a wicked sense of humor. Their lightning-in-a-bottle romance sets the standard for how two people should love and respect one another, and elevates anyone lucky enough to be close to them. And lucky is the word, isn't it? What else can describe when two lives intersect in a way that alters them both forever? How lucky are Reyna and Anna-Maria for finding one another in a world where love is rare and precious? How lucky are the rest of us to be in the presence of their love? I consider myself the luckiest of all to call them my family.

"Now, Anna-Maria asked for no recitals, but I'm going to do it anyway, because she is a fool to think I'd turn down an opportunity to be sappy. Plus, I think she'll make an exception for one of her idols: Bruce Lee."

Clearing her throat, Morgan smiled and gripped the back of Ruiz's chair with her free hand. "'Love is like a friendship caught on fire. In the beginning a flame, very pretty, often hot and fierce but still only light and flickering. As love grows older our hearts mature, and our love becomes as coals, deep burning and unquenchable.' To Anna-Maria and Reyna Ruiz, I love you with my whole heart and I wish you a lifetime of happiness. *Salud, dinero, y amor, y tiempo para disfrutarlos.*"

Teary-eyed, Ruiz stood and enveloped Morgan in a tight hug as the room erupted in clapping and toasts to the new couple. Upon her return, Mei bent forward and pecked her on the cheek. "That was lovely."

"Was it okay? I was so nervous," she whispered. "I had to keep looking at you, otherwise I'd have lost my nerve."

"I'm glad I could assist, but you did wonderfully," Mei replied, reaching up to lightly scratch the back of Morgan's neck. "You got Ruiz to hug you. I'm sure that doesn't happen often."

Chuckling lowly, Morgan shook her head and turned her attention back to the front of the room. "No, it does not. I'm glad there are cameras to catch it because she'll deny it later."

Here, watching Morgan watch her best friend commit the ultimate act of happiness, a new sensation bloomed in her stomach. Like the split-second moment when you step off a curb wrong and your heart leaps in preparation for a fall that does not come. Instead you land sturdily, solidly on the ground, but your heart is racing still. It felt a little bit like falling in love.

A cut cake, rambunctious bouquet toss, and sultry garter removal later, the celebration got truly underway. Spinning an eclectic mix of Reggaeton and dance music, the DJ packed the dance floor in no time. Mei preferred to observe from afar as Morgan and the rest of the party danced to their hearts' content. A staggering amount of liquor flowed, and while Mei nursed a sensible gin and tonic or two, Morgan shot tequila like an old cowboy. She never lost the beat amidst her heavy drinking, dancing with anyone near her. For a time she danced with Ruiz, who then passed her off to Reyna. The new bride was one of the few women in attendance taller than Morgan, and it highly amused Mei to see her look small for once as Reyna twirled and dipped her. Once the brides had their fill and left to dance together, Mei observed over the top of her glass as ladies vied for Morgan's attention in the center of the crowded dance floor. Jacket gone, she'd unbuttoned her vest and then had a few shirt buttons undone for her by Reyna's sister Liliana.

But when the DJ spun a slow song, Mei would not sit idly by as a bridesmaid usurped her place. Leaving her drink on the table, she smoothed out her dress and crossed the dance floor. Mei cut in before Liliana could put her hands on Morgan, claiming her partner with a firm pull on the wrist. Brought into her arms, she held on to Morgan's strong shoulders as her one hand lay flat against the small of Mei's back, and the other hand clasped with Mei's.

"Having fun?" Mei asked over the gentle drone of a 1940s standard.

"Yes ma'am. Food was good, liquor is good, music is good. Gosh, that cake tasted great."

"Yes, I watched you enjoy quite a bit of it," Mei ribbed. "Better than sheet cake, certainly."

"I'm not a cake elitist, unlike some people," Morgan replied. "I witnessed my best friend marry her soul mate. I have the most beautiful woman in attendance as my date—do not repeat that in front of either bride or any of their brothers and sisters or I will be murdered—so yeah, I'm having a great time. What about you?"

After gently twirling around, Morgan brought her in close and Mei smiled up at her. "Yes, it's a great wedding. What a venue. Scenic lake, that ginormous lodge, this incredible barn."

"Reyna knows how to plan a wedding, I'll tell you," Morgan replied with only a little alcohol-induced slur, shaking her head. "I'm so happy for them. It hasn't always been easy, you know? Anna-Maria's family is warm and loving but never fully understood her being a lesbian. Then there was all the transphobia we had to unravel after they met Reyna. A lot of education and patience and love, but boy, it was worth it. They're a dream couple."

"That they are."

The deputy sheriff caught their eyes as he danced with his wife, and he and Morgan exchanged nods. "No regrets?"

"About what?"

"Coming out?"

Mei peered around at the other guests slow dancing, entranced with one another, similarly cozy and contented. None of them noticed Morgan and Mei any more so than other couples. They were two people relishing each other's nearness on a star-filled, romantic night packed to the brim with tender affection. "No. It's nice. It feels normal."

"It is normal," Morgan insisted, dropping a kiss on the crown of Mei's head.

Nuzzling into the fabric of Morgan's shirt, Mei drew a deep breath of her skin. Eyes fluttering closed, she was content to enjoy this soft, slow moment beneath the twinkling lights.

"What will we call each other?" she murmured into Morgan's shirt. "Girlfriend? Partner? We established lover was off the table."

Morgan attempted to pull back but Mei held her tighter. Instead, she rested her chin against Mei's hair and sighed. "Whatever feels good to you, babe."

"Mm, you feel good to me," Mei replied, tilting her head up to kiss Morgan's jaw. "You know, I saw those women tripping over themselves to dance with you. If you weren't otherwise spoken for, you could have your pick, couldn't you?"

"I do have my pick," Morgan insisted. "They're lovely, but come on. None of them hold a candle to you. Believe me, there's no reason to be jealous."

"Oh, I'm not jealous. You want to know what I thought when I saw them dancing with you? 'Go ahead. Dance with her. Get as close as you possibly can because it doesn't matter. You will never get close enough to touch what I touch.' To touch what is—" Mei paused, swallowing as she took hold of Morgan's shirt. "Mine."

Drawing back, Morgan's eyes smoldered—blue-sky irises now a deep, foreboding gray. Their swaying dance came to a slow stop. In a low, clear tone, Morgan gave a command that brooked no argument.

"Come to my room."

Morgan led Mei through the luxurious and cavernous cabin, down a hall to a room on the end. A gorgeous room, Mei noted, in the split second she saw it before Morgan crushed into her and pinned them both against the door. It wasn't so much a kiss as a capture, sloppy and bruising. Backing away for a moment, Morgan bent down and ran her hands up Mei's thighs, hiking her dress up around her hips. In the same fluid movement, she lifted Mei off her feet and turned to pin her up against the wall with enough force to briefly knock the wind out of her.

Pressing into her center, Morgan kissed her again, all tongue and teeth and hard pants of breath. She tasted of tequila and sugar, her scent an intoxicating combination of sweat and cologne. Mei wrapped her arms around Morgan's shoulders and legs around her waist, holding her tightly, body overheated and sizzling. Morgan was not an aggressive lover; passionate, but never rough unless asked. But now, as Morgan's grip dug into her thighs with a bruising authority, it thrilled her to let Morgan have her way, unrestrained.

Carrying Mei with minimal effort—a surprisingly arousing move—Morgan laid her down on the bed with a bit more care and reached behind her head to unclip the barrette in her hair. Sitting up, Mei allowed Morgan to run her fingers through her hair before again crushing them together in a searing kiss. She wished to do the same but it was impossible to get her fingers through Morgan's product-ridden locks. Wanting to find purchase, she moved her hands down Morgan's neck and gripped her bow tie in both hands.

Morgan slid her hand beneath her dress to push it up above her pelvic bone, never breaking their kiss. Somewhere in the back of her mind, Mei's sense of propriety kicked in and she remembered they were fully dressed with their shoes on, but Morgan didn't look like she cared very much. Tearing off her vest, she threw it to the side as if it had offended her. She did the same to Mei's underwear, yanking them down her legs, untangling them from her heels, and tossing them into the unknown. Morgan flattened against the bed and flicked her eyes up for a split second to acquire consent. Frantically Mei nodded, and her desperation put a cocky smirk on Morgan's lips before she buried them between Mei's thighs. Strong hands wrapped over the top of her hips and kept her in place. With her eyes screwed shut, Mei gasped and rolled her hips as much as Morgan's grip allowed, pleasure roiling through her like an angry sea. When she peeked her eyes open, Morgan's gaze burned in her direction. Mei threw her head back as she came, shouting Morgan's name toward the wooden beam ceiling.

Swiping her mouth with her forearm, Morgan got to her knees and moved forward, nudging Mei's knees apart. Ever considerate, Morgan paused for Mei to catch her breath, peppering kisses anywhere she found exposed skin. When her breathing returned to normal she peered down at Morgan, who waited with an arched brow for Mei to assent.

All Mei mustered was a pathetic, "Please."

Plunging inside her deeply and settling into a quick rhythm, Morgan kissed up her shoulders to her neck as Mei keened beneath her. "You're beautiful," Morgan murmured into her skin, biting and laving tender spots beneath her ear. "So beautiful. God, I love you so much."

Under any other circumstance, Mei would've put a regretful stop to this and confronted Morgan about her ill-timed declaration, but the day's emotions welled up inside her and she couldn't deny Morgan this moment. With the blood in her brain rushing south, Mei lacked the sense to respond or give it more thought. She got busy unbuttoning Morgan's slacks and digging out her button-down shirt. Reaching between them, she slid her own hand into Morgan's briefs, but got denied as Morgan used her free hand to grab Mei's and pin it to the pillow behind her.

She kissed the sliver of cleavage exposed above Mei's dress, then bit the flesh and gave it an exploratory suck. Locking eyes, she paused as Mei cupped the back of Morgan's head and pushed her closer. Taking it as an enthusiastic yes, Morgan bit her harder and suckled aggressively, purpling the skin beneath her lips. Mei yelped and gasped, her insides tightening in pleasure. Morgan must've felt her walls pulling in on her fingers because she lifted her head and kissed Mei deeply.

"That's right," she panted against Mei's parted lips. "Come for me, baby."

And dear god if that demand wasn't the most arousing thing Mei ever heard. She crashed into her second climax, her entire body taut and shuddering as Morgan took her time slowing down, still penetrating Mei with long, deliberate movements. Morgan was totally in control of her and Mei didn't mind one bit. This assertive, dominant Morgan matched the fierce, wild feeling inside Mei's chest.

With that in mind she wriggled her wrist from where Morgan pinned her and upon release she promptly returned her hand between Morgan's legs. Inebriated on a cocktail of gin and ardor, Mei touched an unplumbed depth inside herself, full of dominion and passion. She could not process the weight of these feelings and focused the energy on her lover hovered above her in desperate search of release. Eyes shut, Morgan rolled her hips against Mei's hand, and Mei caressed the side of her cheek.

She kept her voice as gentle as her touch. "Look at me."

Compliant, Morgan opened her eyes and Mei stared in wonder, enamored, as if her feelings suddenly materialized between them. Leaning up, Mei placed a feather-soft kiss on Morgan's lips and Morgan came completely undone. She kissed her through the intense orgasm, sharing her breaths and stifling her cries. Morgan rolled over, flopping beside Mei and panting heavily.

"Wow."

"Yeah." Still not yet capable of rational thought, Mei focused on catching her breath. "Wow."

"I should dance with other women more often."

Mei snickered halfheartedly, but she couldn't ignore the heaviness in the room. Coming down from this rush of adrenaline felt different than the other times they'd made love. A shift occurred. A chasm, an ache; a yearning for the woman lying beside her. What existed here was more than belly swoops.

After a few moments of recovery Morgan sat up, unbuttoning her shirt. Though Mei hadn't planned on staying the night, she undressed as well. Shimmying out of her dress, Mei caught Morgan staring at her with a slacked jaw. Self-conscious, she held her arms over her middle and glanced away. No matter how many times Morgan stared at her like she was desirable, the feeling never quite permeated. Shuffling across the bed on her knees, Morgan beckoned her forward and pulled her in for a hug. "Stay with me?"

Peering down, Mei smiled softly at Morgan's face gazing up at her, eyes glassy but earnest. "I couldn't leave you if I tried."

"Mm, good," Morgan replied, placing soft, sleepy kisses across Mei's ribs. "Don't try."

CHAPTER THIRTEEN

When Morgan suggested apple picking as her birthday activity, she did so assuming Mei knew what it was. However, the look on Mei's face as they parked in the dirt lot outside the grove and bought a burlap sack from a smiling farmer, made it hilariously apparent she'd never set foot in an orchard. However, since it was her birthday this week, Morgan got to drag Ruiz, Reyna, and Mei to her favorite fall activity. At the very least, they got a nice day for it. The sky a dazzling, cloudless blue, the temperature stayed brisk enough to only need a light jacket.

As Morgan scaled a tree in pursuit of the perfect apple, Mei questioned her friends from below. "Is this…this is a thing she does?"

"Every year," Ruiz replied. "She's always chasing these childhood experiences she was deprived of, and the apple picking is her favorite."

"And she insists on climbing the trees in spite of all the signage asking very politely that she not," Reyna mused.

"That sign is for children," Morgan called down from between the branches. "I'm not going to break anything. I need this apple that got the sun on all sides. It's so red and shiny."

The tree, not built for the weight of a full-grown person, shook from Morgan's efforts. "Darling, I wish you'd come down. There are perfectly good apples within reaching distance."

With a quick snap, Morgan held her hand up in victory. "Got it!" Leaves quivered and all at once a loud crack echoed through the orchard. "Uh-oh."

God, she hated when they were right. She crashed out of the tree, landing rather unceremoniously on a pile of discarded, rotten apples with a squishy thump. Wincing, she opened her eyes to Mei presumably scanning her for injuries. Morgan thrust the apple at her and grinned. "Saved it."

Plucking the apple from her hand, Mei rolled her eyes and put it in their bag. She helped Morgan off the ground, brushing away the bits of apple flesh stuck to the back of her tartan flannel. "Was that worth it?"

"We'll see," Morgan replied cheerfully, taking the bag from Mei and throwing her arm around her shoulders. Following Ruiz and Reyna down the worn path between the trees, they paused every so often to pull another apple off a tree. Near the end of apple picking season, mid-October, the trees bore less fruit than the ground, but Morgan hadn't taken any time off since the wedding so they seized the opportunity to get out in the fresh air.

However, as pleasing as the day shaped up to be, Morgan retained a tiny nugget of anxiety in her heart. Their relationship had deepened considerably in the weeks since Ruiz's wedding. Mei was less reserved with her affection, and spoke more openly about her feelings, finally catching up to how Morgan felt months ago. So, she had hope her most recent request would at least be considered.

"So, listen. What do you do for Thanksgiving in your family?"

Mei turned, tilting her head. "Where did that come from?"

"It's the next big holiday, besides Halloween. Which I, as a rule, do not celebrate." Most of the police forced shared Morgan's anti-Halloween stance due to the absurd level of civilian hijinks and petty crime that occurred on Halloween. Morgan ritually took the day off to hand out candy to trick-or-treaters, and often volunteered for night shifts to relieve overworked cops. "Just figured I'd ask."

Mei stepped to the side to pluck a ripe apple and plunk it into Morgan's open bag. She put herself back within reach and Morgan slid her arm around her waist as they walked. "Grace took over most holiday duties. Thanksgiving isn't big for us— Allan was a fan, but the rest of us could take it or leave it. We usually do a low-key dinner at her place."

"Okay. Well, um, Thanksgiving is pretty much the only time I see my biological father, so that's what I do."

Stopping in her tracks, Mei pulled Morgan toward her by the shirt. "I didn't know you were in contact with him."

"I am," Morgan admitted, digging her boot into the dirt. "It's…tentative. Over the past fifteen years he's sort of reinvented himself. Sobered up, got a job, got married, had some kids. We text occasionally."

"You have siblings?" Mei asked, eyebrows shooting up.

"Half siblings, yes. Three of them—six, seven, eight. Samuel, Hailey, and Olivia." While Morgan kept her tone light, her anxiety increased. "He contacted me about ten years ago and asked to see me. We went to lunch and I agreed to keep in distant contact. After he starting having kids I said I'd have Thanksgiving with them. I normally spent it alone, so. I guess it's better?"

In reality, it was a mixed bag. Being lonely on holidays didn't start with her mother's death; Charlotte worked most holidays and disappeared for others. Part of her envied the warm, soft family holidays she imagined most people celebrated. The other part of her learned to enjoy the solitude. Or at least, give the convincing impression she enjoyed it.

"What about Christmas?"

"Hmm?" Morgan walked off to pick another apple, placing it in the nearly overflowing burlap sack. "Oh. I take a vacation somewhere new each year. If I don't do that, I work. Lots of overtime on Christmas and it's better for people with real families to be off."

Inwardly, Morgan winced at the pity in Mei's eyes. "You don't have anyone to spend it with?"

"People offer. My biological father asked a few times. Ruiz offers every year—her family is big on Christmas. Mrs. Vern, my upstairs neighbor? She's Jewish, but even she's asked me over. Their intentions are good, but it makes me feel like this pitiful orphan people drag to their celebrations."

"I understand," Mei replied. "I felt that way after Allan died and I got invited to weddings and parties and it felt like...his absence was bigger than my presence."

"Exactly, yeah. I like Christmas parties. Those are fun. You know, wearing ugly sweaters and playing drinking games or whatever. But a real Christmas, a tree-and-presents Christmas... it's awkward. I end up either getting aggressively coddled by Ruiz's *tías* or alone in a corner talking to someone's cat. There is no in-between."

Stepping into her space, Mei ran her fingers through Morgan's hair, sliding her hand down to settle a comforting palm on her chest. "Would you like me to go with you to your biological father's home on Thanksgiving?"

"Would you really? I don't want to take you from your family, but it would be much more bearable with you."

"Sure. I'd be happy to spend Thanksgiving with you." Morgan beamed, bending down to peck a kiss on her lips. "Now, would this be a good time to give you your birthday present?"

She lifted an eyebrow. "Perhaps. I hoped it would be a closed-door affair with you in my bed wearing only a strategically placed bow."

Blushing profusely, Mei eyed the family in the path across from theirs. While their relationship moved along nicely, Mei's level of comfort being publicly out hadn't yet caught up with her devotion. "We can discuss that later. But, no, a regular, publicly appropriate birthday gift."

Shrugging, Morgan adjusted the bag in her arms. "All I wanted was to spend time with you. And get a donut."

"Right, you talked about the donut a lot on the way here," Mei replied. "I do wish you'd have allowed me to get you something more substantial." Digging in her purse, Mei withdrew a palm-sized brown paper bag, folded over once. "I respected your wishes in regard to gift wrap."

"It's wasteful." Morgan put down the apples and dug inside the bag, pulling out a fridge magnet with her name and a picture of the Brachiosaurus from the museum printed on it. Her eyes lit up. "Is this from the gift shop?"

"Yes. They sell a lot of things with names on it, but I felt this was the best one." She tapped on the magnet. "It's Brad."

"It is Brad." Her favorite dinosaur, bought from the gift shop she was never allowed to step foot in. The incredibly considerate gift nearly melted Morgan into the ground. "You're so thoughtful. I love it. Thank you."

Mei smiled, tipping up to press a short, sweet kiss on Morgan's lips. "You're welcome. Happy birthday, darling."

"Ladies," Ruiz called, clearing her throat. "Can we please pay for these godforsaken *manzanas* and get the hell out of here? There are bees everywhere and they're starting to get on my nerves."

Morgan scoffed. "This is their house, Anna-Maria. You're the trespasser stealing their fruit. The bees are our friends."

"Okay, tell your friends I don't even like apples, I only come because you would look very pathetic picking apples on your own," Ruiz replied. "Now, *vamanos*."

"Fine, but I have to stop at the farm stand on the way out because I need fresh cider and donuts."

"Donuts? Plural?" Mei asked as they tailed Ruiz and Reyna out of the orchard and back toward the cashiers. "How many donuts do you 'need?'"

"Well, you *need* at least a dozen to get you through the week. Plus one for the ride home. So, a baker's dozen should do," Morgan reasoned matter-of-factly. "And a gallon of fresh cider."

"You know, you wouldn't have to work out as much or as often if you ate less junk."

"I like working out," Morgan said. "And, if I'm not mistaken, you like that I work out too. You've bought many front-row tickets to the gun show."

Ahead of them, Reyna erupted into laughter and Ruiz glared over her shoulder. "Never say that again or I will arrest you."

"Arrest me for what? I have a license for these guns," Morgan bragged, aiming her biceps and flexing toward Ruiz. "She's jealous I can lift more than her. So competitive."

"I am acutely aware of how much weight you can lift."

With a cheeky smile, Morgan waggled her eyebrows suggestively. "I'm happy to demonstrate that with you whenever you want." Before Mei could respond, Morgan sniffed in the air like a bloodhound. Her hand shot out and stopped Mei in her tracks. "The donuts. They're near."

Just over the orchard ridge stood a nondescript farm stand cobbled together from old planks: the sanctuary of donuts and cider. Morgan pawned off the bag of apples to Ruiz. "What the hell, Kelly?"

"You are buying my apples because it's my birthday," Morgan replied, "and I'm heading straight to Donut Town."

"You're a dork," Ruiz replied, hefting the bag onto the cashier's table. She looked at Mei. "Your girlfriend is a dork."

But Mei merely smiled at her, eyes shimmering with tenderness. "Yeah, she is. Go get your donuts, darling."

Later that night, Morgan insisted they not cook, so they drove to Yumel to pick up dinner. Greeted by the familiar gust of warm air and spices, they stepped inside the cozy restaurant to the tune of bells jangling above their heads.

"Mei-Mei!"

Morgan smirked. After she and Mei frequented their restaurant more often together, Meltem and Yusuf became both aware and loudly supportive of their relationship. Whether she wanted to be or not, Mei was now "part of the family," which included an unsolicited nickname. "Hello, Meltem."

"Happy birthday, Morgana!" Excitedly rushing to her, Meltem grabbed her by the cheeks and squished them together, kissing her soundly on the forehead. "My beautiful little girl growing up."

"I'm thirty-five," Morgan replied quietly.

Meltem ignored her, playfully slapping her cheeks in an affectionate gesture. "I have your order all ready. One moment." As Meltem shuffled away, she caught Mei's impish grin widening. "Don't even, or I'll tell her when your birthday is, too, Mei-Mei."

Within moments Meltem scurried out of the kitchen with two large shopping bags that would easily fit a microwave in each of them. Unsurprisingly, they held enough food to feed around a dozen people. "That is more than I ordered."

Meltem held up the bags with great cheer. "For birthday!"

Taking the bags from her, Morgan smiled as she inspected the wares. "You're always too kind to me, Meltem. Thank you."

"Never too kind," Meltem said with a firm shake of her head. "Nothing is too much for my *kahraman*. My hero."

"I'm no such thing." Morgan pivoted to Mei. "I used to check in every once in a while on my beat, that's all."

Her attempt to circumvent Meltem's storytelling failed miserably and the woman huffed in affront. "Check in? You did not 'check in.' Morgana stopped two men robbing us."

Mei gasped under her breath. "Morgana did what?"

"She did not tell you?" Both women glared at Morgan accusingly, like she'd withheld a large secret. On principle Morgan did not bore people with conversations about her job as an officer; she shared with Mei the emotional aspects of a case, or the logistical details, but never the physical violence or the danger. "Many years ago, we were open late and two men storm in here. Masks over their heads, both of them with guns. They demand all the money in the register. Yusuf told me to go in the back, so I did. I hear them, these men, threatening my Yusuf if he did not get the money faster."

"Oh my god." Mei gasped, her hand on her chest. "That's awful."

"It was scary. Some people, they are not kind to immigrants. They think we are stupid, or that we don't deserve the restaurant, that we steal. These men, they said very nasty things to my Yusuf." The memory visibly upset Meltem and she looked away, taking a moment to settle her emotions. It hurt Morgan's heart, recalling the fright in the eyes of these wonderful people, and her anger upon hearing the robbers disparage them.

"I called the police and Morgana come in less than one minute."

"Alone?"

"Yes, alone."

Morgan sighed, then clarified. "I radioed for backup then responded to the call."

"She pull her gun out and tell the men to lie down on the floor. They tell her they will kill Yusuf if she shoot her gun. Morgana put her gun on the floor, and now I am thinking she is not a very smart person. But she talks to the men, tells them they haven't taken any money yet, so they are not robbers. She says so far it's a *misdemeanor*. If they put down their weapons and surrender, she will tell her boss to give them the lowest charge."

Turning, Mei looked as if she were just seeing Morgan for the first time, her eyes full of admiration and fear. Truth be told, Morgan didn't talk about the robbery because she thought she was going to die. It marked the first time anyone pulled a gun on her, and while it happened several times after, the first time was always the worst.

"They threaten to shoot her. She tell them that is stupid, shooting a police officer will get them life in prison, even if she live." By this time, Meltem's story caught the attention of customers, who stared on in wonder. Morgan fidgeted.

"They put their weapons on the ground and Morgana says thank you. Then they try to rush out the door and she BOOM!" Mei startled, taking a step back as Meltem gesticulated wildly, making punching and kicking gestures. "She took them down! Boom, pow, both of them on the ground. The other police came soon and arrested the men. Morgana told me after she knew those men did robberies around town but she didn't want them to shoot anybody so she lied to them. Very smart, our Morgana."

"Not really. Just good training," Morgan deflected.

"Very brave," Meltem insisted. "She is a hero. The police gave her a medal and Yusuf and I are in her debt. So you see, the food? It is nothing compared to Yusuf and I keeping our lives and our business." Meltem wrapped her arms around Morgan, hugging her hard. She looked helplessly at Mei, whose whites of her eyes shone brightly even in the dim light of Yumel. "Our Morgana is a special girl."

Meltem released her death grip on Morgan and Mei smiled softly. "She truly is."

"Good. You take good care of Morgana, okay?"

"I will."

Upon their return home, Morgan hefted the bags onto the table and reached in to sort through what they'd actually ordered and what Meltem threw in. "Ooh, *za'taar* pitas. Wow, they even made me *mücver*! One time I ate like two dozen of them in one sitting and I don't think Yusuf ever recovered."

Her enthusiastic narration of their food echoed in the apartment. Mei stood a few feet away near the couch, eerily quiet. "Mei? Are you...are you mad at me?"

"Sit down," Mei said, gesturing to the couch. Gulping, Morgan nodded and did as told, heaving a sigh.

"I'm sorry I never told y—" The rest of her sentence perished as Mei straddled her on the couch, grabbing her face and kissing her hard. She squeaked in surprise but kissed back, pulling Mei into her lap. Hot and furious, Mei dropped her hands to grip Morgan's shirt in both fists, tugging them closer with a whimper. When they broke apart, she furrowed her brow at the tears slipping from Mei's eyes.

"Babe, what's wrong?"

"Nothing. I—I hope you know how very, very precious you are to me."

Morgan pulled away, using the pad of her thumb to wipe the tears from Mei's cheeks. "Meltem tells everyone that story. It was not as dramatic as she makes it seem, I promise."

"They had guns," Mei pressed. "They could've killed you."

"I also had a gun. More importantly, I had a lot of training. And look, that doesn't really happen to me anymore. I do paperwork and read through forty-year-old newspapers. I scour abandoned barns and interview regular people about something that happened decades ago. My risk level is low, comparatively. Okay?"

"I know that," Mei countered, exasperated. "But you said that man you brought in a couple weeks ago had like a house full of guns."

"I tell you too much," Morgan teased, prompting Mei to pout. The fear in her eyes, the desperation, exemplified why Morgan never talked about her work. People had left her over the thought of losing her. Consequently, the only real loser was Morgan. "I love what I do, you know that, and there will always be some level of risk. If that's not something you want to handle, better to know now than later."

Brushing some of Morgan's hair away from her forehead, Mei's features drew together quizzically. "What are you taking about? I'm not—I'm not going to leave you because of something I already know. It was a shock, that's all."

"Oh. Well, you wouldn't be the first girlfriend to break up with me because of it. I do sometimes forget how scary my job sounds, and I'm grateful for your concern." What Morgan didn't say—or couldn't—was that she never concerned herself with self-preservation. She put her life on the line without hesitation and not out of bravery, but because of her presupposed expendability. "I promise I do my best to avoid risky situations."

Anxiety temporarily assuaged, Mei took Morgan's hand from her cheek and sandwiched it between her own. "Okay. You are terribly brave."

Morgan deflected the praise with a roll of her eyes, grateful for the release of tension. Running her hands up Mei's sides, Morgan toyed with the top button of her blouse. "Now, would you say my valiant heroics in the face of mortal danger turns you on a little bit?"

"Would that please you? My roleplaying a damsel in distress to your daring superhero?" Mei cocked an eyebrow.

"Absolutely not." Morgan scoffed at this absurdity. "Clearly you'd be my extremely sexy, supposedly 'evil' genius doctor nemesis whose nefarious plans I thwart in sexually charged minor scuffles. Until, one fateful day, we are forced to work together to defeat a common enemy. Our sexual tension reaches a fever pitch and we succumb to the unspoken attraction between us."

Craning her head, Mei narrowed her eyes in suspicion. "You've given this some thought."

"Yes, I have."

She paused. "What is my fantasy PhD in?"

"Bioengineering."

Mei tapped her finger against her chin. "That is acceptable." She cast a glance behind them. "What about all the food?"

"It can wait." Hefting Mei over her shoulders in a fireman's carry, Morgan turned on her heel toward the hallway. Squeaking in surprise, Mei slapped Morgan's back in protest.

"Unhand me!" Mei demanded as Morgan bodily brought her into the bedroom. She lowered her voice. "Like that?"

Morgan grinned, slamming the bedroom door closed behind them.

CHAPTER FOURTEEN

Shanvi reclined in her chair beside Mei, nursing the spiked homemade cider she'd laid out for them. A rare weekend without Morgan, whose murder case had unraveled into a child trafficking ring that subsequently buried her in work, Mei spent a chilly Saturday evening in her backyard with Shanvi. Her patio was peaceful and serene, a respite from the world with a canopy of trees on all sides to shield them from their neighbors. She came here often to think, and Morgan had taken to doing the same thing, thumbing through case files as Mei caught up on a book.

"Anyway, suffice it to say I am not looking forward to another Thanksgiving with Paul's parents. If his mother makes me choke down another one of her green bean casseroles, I might just go for broke and drown myself in it." Shanvi sighed and leaned back in her chair. "Tell me your plans are better."

Fiddling with her cup, Mei divulged, "Morgan asked me to meet her biological father and his family. It appears he's straightened his life out and is trying to have a relationship with her."

"So, things between you are getting serious, huh? Meeting the parents?" Shanvi asked, keeping her tone light but her expression sober. "Good. I think you're good for each other."

Her relationship with Morgan was going so well, she hesitated to voice the nagging thought in her head. "Sometimes...I—I don't know how to say this without sounding awful."

"You saw me through my bleached highlights phase, Mei. You know there is no judgment here."

Letting out a huff of a laugh, Mei continued. "Being with Morgan has made me see my marriage differently. Now, don't get me wrong. I loved Allan. Adored him, really. We had a wonderful relationship. But this is...it's so different. I think about her all the time. It's consuming. And it's so physical. The sex is honestly so good I want to paint it in oils and frame it on my wall."

Shanvi nearly choked. "Please do not misconstrue my shock for anything less than 'tell me more.'"

Mei blushed, rolling her eyes at her friend's exuberance. "Do control yourself. In addition to this, I feel for her something I can't be certain I ever felt for Allan. I don't know how to describe it without sounding melodramatic. She makes me feel like no matter where I am, if I'm with her, I'm supposed to be there."

With Allan, Mei existed on the perimeters of her own life. He fit in anywhere, finding commonalities with people from any walk of life. Mei often felt like the dark moon people tolerated so they could bask in the glow of Allan's sunny personality. But Morgan Kelly shifted her on her axis and pointed her toward the sun, bringing her a joy so contagious Mei spread it to those around her.

Arranging her features seriously, Shanvi put down her drink and leaned in. "Are you worried you may enjoy this new romance more than your marriage?"

"Isn't that terrible? It makes me feel selfish. Like I don't deserve this. Or that—that my marriage was a sham. Maybe I've been queer all along and I faked heterosexuality because that's what my mother wanted."

During her marriage Mei performed sex as a perfunctory part of their union. It was something you did with someone you love, like sharing meals or taking each other to the doctor. She never sought it, but it sufficed and it wasn't unenjoyable. However, nothing about her previous experience prepared her for how ridiculously pleasurable it would be with Morgan, or how she would want it so much.

"Even if you were always attracted to women, that doesn't make your marriage a sham," Shanvi replied. "You loved him and he loved you. That's what marriage is. Now, if you have all that plus mind-blowing orgasms? Well then you're lucky and I resent you rubbing it in my face."

Mei laughed, taking a languid, relaxing sip from her glass. "Fair enough."

"Why don't you talk about it with Morgan?"

"I don't know if I could handle her having insecurities about him," Mei answered honestly. "I mean, she's never even gone inside the house."

"Why not?" Shanvi shrugged. "If you don't give her the opportunity to get over any potential insecurities or issues, you're not being fair to her."

"Maybe you're right. It's probably silly to compare the two, anyway."

Shanvi gave her a sage nod. "Comparison is the thief of the joy of hot lesbian sex."

Laughing loudly, Mei dipped her finger in her drink and flicked droplets at Shanvi. "It's like how I love my children, I suppose. I love them both, but I love them differently."

Shanvi rested her arms on the table between them. "Ooh, you said the 'L' word."

"Lesbian?"

"Love," Shanvi replied. "Do you love her?"

Perhaps for the first time in their many-decades-long friendship, Mei lied to Shanvi. "I don't know. Maybe."

Raising an eyebrow in disbelief, Shanvi gave her a supportive smile. "There is no maybe in love."

"You sound like a greeting card," Mei chided. "It's too soon to say. We've only been dating a couple of months."

"And? Neither of us is getting any younger. We can't afford extensive courting. Trust your gut, Mei. Or, trust your heart."

In contemplation over her glass of cider, Mei gnawed on her bottom lip. The wedding cemented for Mei how deeply in love with Morgan she'd fallen. Her heart was full, bursting with affection, but there was a fear she could not shake. "She told me she loved me once. After Sergeant Ruiz's wedding, quite drunk."

"Did you say it back?"

Jamming her tongue into the side of her cheek, Mei blushed even deeper. "I wasn't…the moment didn't allow for it. We were—it was a moment of passion. She hasn't said it again since. How can I be sure she meant it?"

"That woman adores you and you know it," Shanvi replied. "What does she have to do for you to be sure? Show up outside your house in a trench coat with a boom box blasting Peter Gabriel?"

"You know she was a toddler when that movie came out," Mei informed, jutting out her chin. "She's probably never seen it. I'm going to go through menopause and she'll never have seen *Say Anything*."

"Sounds like you need to show it to her. You know, Paul had never seen *Star Wars*. What white man has never seen *Star Wars*? Not a single Star War, Mei. I almost divorced him." With a weary sigh, Shanvi feigned lament. "Sometimes you have to educate your partner."

Chuckling, Mei tipped back more cider. The smooth alcohol helped calm her frazzled nerves. "I need to tell her I love her, don't I?"

"No offense, but duh." Waving her off, Shanvi repositioned herself on her chair. "Okay, now that the sappy stuff is out of the way, tell me more about this hot sex you want to paint."

After cheering on Morgan at a freezing Thanksgiving charity 5K run, they redressed and began their journey to Morgan's biological father's home miles outside the county. Morgan insisted on driving, as she often did, but was uncharacteristically curt on the road out. The rumble of the engine and quiet folk music provided the soundtrack for autumnal trees shedding their vibrant terracotta leaves outside the window. Every so often Morgan would tug on the sleeve of her sweater—a new one Mei bought her for this occasion—and worry her bottom lip.

With her white-knuckle grip on the steering wheel, her sky-blue eyes remained intently focused on the road ahead. After Morgan took an exit off the highway, Mei attempted a conversation. "You seem nervous."

Morgan spared her a quick look before focusing back on the road. "I am."

"Okay." Mei slid her hand over and cupped Morgan's fingers clutching the gearshift. "Allan was orphaned at five years old, so I never dealt with in-laws during our marriage. He, unfortunately, had to deal with my mother."

"Did they get along? Allan and your mother?"

Mei shook her head. "Not even a little. Which was incredible, because there wasn't a single person Allan couldn't charm eventually. My mother never budged. She wouldn't tell me directly why, but I do know she thought Allan had a 'pedestrian' job. And there's no direct translation for that in Mandarin so it was a feat for her to get across how thoroughly basic she found him."

Perturbed, Morgan glanced her way. "Wasn't he a journalist?"

"Yes, and a good one. But it was a regional paper and it's not like he won any awards," she said, rolling her eyes. "That is important to my mother. Accolades."

Morgan let out a thoughtful "hmm," releasing the steering wheel for a moment to run her fingers through her hair. "Yeah, so, my 'father' hates cops."

"He what now?"

"He hates cops." Morgan slowed down as they approached a cute Colonial-style home on an Arcadian, tree-lined street in an idyllic suburb not all that different from where Mei lived. "I mentioned it when we met. Ah, the second time, at the morgue, while I had verbal diarrhea because the 'uppity doctor' Ruiz brought me to turned out to be the most beautiful woman I'd ever seen in my life."

"Uppity?" Mei sniffed, but she supposed that wasn't the most offensive adjective anyone ever used to describe her. "And yes, I remember now."

"Due to his previous occupation as a drug dealer, he's gotten arrested a lot. Had a lot of bad experiences with the law and he's very vocal about how awful cops are. About how the whole system is bullshit, that sort of thing."

"In front of you?" Mei could already feel her blood pressure rising.

"To me directly," she replied, parking the car near the curb outside the house. Little gel pumpkins and turkeys adorned a wide bay window in the front of the home. "I try to not talk about my job at all."

Ridiculous considering the breadth of Morgan's success, but Mei held her tongue as they walked up the lantern-lined walkway between trim grass lawns. Taking Morgan's hand in her own, Mei knocked solidly on their front door. The thunder of children's feet sounded from the other side, prompting Mei to recall fond memories of her own daughters fighting to answer the door for guests. Grace nearly always won.

Instead of children, a woman opened the door and smiled warmly in their direction. "Hey! So glad you could make it." She stepped forward and hugged Morgan, who returned it with a little less enthusiasm. "Morgan, it's so good to see you. And this must be Mei." The woman extended her hand. She was attractive with wavy, short brown hair and kind green eyes, dressed in an oversized sweater over which she wore an apron with a handmade felt turkey sewn into the center. "I'm Jean, Walker's wife. Morgan has told me so much about you. Well, she's told Walker, and he's told me. Please, come in. Dinner's just about ready."

Despite having three children under the age of ten, the room glistened with a neatly arranged tidiness. Framed photos hung on the mantel above the working fireplace, roaring and warm as they entered the living room. Fine couches and chairs surrounded the fireplace with a large Persian rug in the center. Each part of the home dripped with money like paint on walls.

Olivia skidded into the room first, tall and thin with lots of freckles, lovely short red hair, and sparkling green eyes. She didn't look a bit like Morgan. "Hi, Morgan!"

"Hey, Olivia." Morgan kneeled to hug the young girl. "Gee whiz, how much did you grow? Ten inches since I was here?"

Olivia giggled, shaking her head. "Nope. I grew one inch and one-quarter. Hailey didn't grow at all. Mom says it's 'cause she doesn't eat her veggies. Sammy is two inches taller than last year."

"Two inches? So what is he, six feet tall now?" Another young child, a girl with long brown hair, zoomed in and crashed directly into Morgan's legs. "Oof, there she is. Hailey Hailey Bo Bailey."

"Morgan Morgan Bo Borgan! My new favorite animal is echidnas and not lions," Hailey proclaimed, deadly serious. "Lions are still cute, but echidnas are cuter."

Hailey swung around and jumped on Morgan's back. "Okay, lions are cute but echidnas are cuter. Got it."

The final child, a little boy with a mess of red hair, joined the pile-on until Morgan fell to the ground in defeat, crawled upon by children. Taking a step back, Mei allowed the children more room to wrestle Morgan.

"Ah, the goblins got me! The turkey goblins! They're pecking me apart!" All three Benson children descended upon her with pokes and pretend bites. "Thanksgiving revenge is upon us!"

The youngest, Samuel, paused to blink up at Mei with big green eyes. "You have to save her," he said matter-of-factly amidst the chaos.

"Oh, I do?"

He bobbed his head in confirmation. "Yeah. Mommy said you're Morgan's girlfriend, and girlfriends and boyfriends rescue each other. So, you gotta save her 'fore we eat her, okay?"

"Okay," Mei replied, hiding a smile. She cleared her throat. "Never fear! I'm here to save you from these ravenous turkey goblins!"

Morgan squealed. "No, Mei, save yourself! They'll come for you next!"

"Not if I have my—" Not much around in the way of a weapon, which made sense in a house with three kids. Near the door, Mei spotted a coat stand with an umbrella tucked in the bottom. She hurried to grab it and turned on her heel, wielding it at the children. "Trusty sword!"

"The gravy sword!" Hailey screamed, feigning fright. "She has the gravy sword! The turkey goblin's only weakness! Run!"

"Yes, the gravy sword," Mei announced, jabbing it in their direction. "Stay away from her, you rascally turkey goblins."

In a fit of giggles, the kids scurried away and into the dining room, shrieking with delight. Mei put away the umbrella and helped Morgan up from the hardwood floor. "Thank you for the rescue. Honestly, I love their energy, but it is a little demoralizing they successfully eat me every year."

"I tried to save her with a turkey baster one time," Jean said, placing her hands on her hips. "They refused to acknowledge the weapon. Tragically, she was eaten that year as well."

Behind them, the stairs to the second floor creaked and each woman turned as a tall, striking man came pounding down the treads. Morgan hadn't shown Mei any photos of her father, and by only describing him as a recovered drug addict, she didn't know what to expect. In her mind's eye, she'd pictured an old, grizzled man covered in tattoos and perhaps missing teeth. But her experience performing autopsies on criminals or the drug-addicted did not prepare her for the fact that he looked just like Morgan.

No doubt could be cast upon Morgan's paternity. His eyes reflected her baby blues, his face a map of her dimples and her lovely jaw, identical dark blond hair with its enviable natural highlights, and the same broad build of lean muscle. A resemblance so jarring, Mei completely forgot her manners and stared at him, unblinking as he came around the bottom of the stairs and shook Morgan's hand.

"Good to see you, kiddo. We missed you."

"Good to see you, too, Walker." Morgan withdrew her hand and gestured to Mei. "This is my girlfriend, Dr. Mei Sharpe. Mei, this is my…father, Walker Benson."

Mei extended her hand and shook his. "Nice to meet you, Walker."

"We were so thrilled when Morgan told us you were coming," Jean interjected, sidling up next to her husband. "She speaks so highly of you."

"I'm quite fond of her as well." Hand on her forehead, Mei smiled in embarrassment. "I'm so sorry to stare, but my goodness. You look remarkably like Morgan."

"Don't they?" Jean exclaimed. "I'm always telling them that. You should see...I have some pictures of Walker at Morgan's age and I swear they could be twins. Meanwhile, all our kids look like me, or my mother, god bless them. But Morgan—that's a Benson all right. Her grandfather, Walker's father, looked the same. I'll have to dig up some photos for you."

Walker ducked his gaze awkwardly, much in the same manner Morgan did when embarrassed. Genetically speaking, their similar mannerisms fascinated Mei, as Morgan never learned to mimic them in childhood. "I think maybe it's time for us to eat, eh?"

"Yep. The kids are washing up. Let's go ahead."

The dining room showcased formal touches like gilded scones and a china cabinet, but remained warm and inviting with a charming chandelier hanging over a massive rustic wood dining table. The children filed in as Morgan pulled out Mei's chair and took her own seat beside her. Across the table Olivia beamed ear to ear at the porcelain serving bowl of mashed potatoes, piled high and steaming perilously within her reach.

The maternal warning rose in her throat before Jean spoke up. "Don't even think about it, Liv."

Pouting and deflated, Olivia sat back and waited obediently, if a bit petulantly. Her siblings climbed into their chairs, anxiously anticipating filled plates. "This is such a nice spread."

"Thank you, Mei." Jean smiled as she stood, walking around the table to serve her children. "It's at least a day's work, but it's worth it."

"And this is all Jean," Walker said, digging into the turkey with what looked like a miniature handsaw. "I do what I can— remedial turkey work—but she is a whiz in that kitchen. These kids are real lucky to have her. All I can do is make cereal and a halfway decent grilled cheese."

Talking Morgan through a recipe was one of Mei's favorite things to do on a lazy weekend. Morgan was ruthlessly adorable when she succeeded at a culinary task. "It's never too late to learn. Morgan's got the basics down pat. It's taken a few months of trial and error, but she's getting quite good."

"Is that right?" Walker grinned at his daughter, which Morgan returned halfheartedly. "I'll be damned. I insisted to Jean all these years my inability to cook was genetic, but it looks like maybe I'm an old dog."

"Mei is exceptionally patient," Morgan replied as she scooped modest portions of side dishes onto her plate. She took an offered slice of turkey from Walker, setting her plate down in front of her. "I'm still not great. Mei is like a five-star chef. With her help I've gone from like a zero-star chef to maybe a one-and-one-thirds-star chef."

"You'll have to impart your wisdom to me," Jean said, sitting down in the seat to Mei's right and placing her napkin on her lap. "Then I can try with him."

After passing a piece of turkey to everyone, Walker sat down, tucking his napkin into the front of his shirt. Even for Mei, tangentially related to the situation, it was difficult to reconcile the man Morgan described and this doting father at the head of the table. Morgan never knew him, but on occasion asked her mother, whose descriptions erred more insult than compliment. Manipulative, charming, a con artist through and though. His mood swung with his drug use, making him a wonderful man one moment and an angry tyrant the next. Idly, Mei wondered how much of that man still resided in him. She wondered how Charlotte felt when her little girl started to grow into a miniature version of her delinquent father.

"So, Mei, you're a medical examiner?" Jean asked, popping a forkful of stuffing into her mouth.

"Yes. I work in the basement of the county office, same as Morgan."

"Do you catch bad guys?" Samuel asked from his seat in between Walker and Morgan, who stiffened in her chair. "Morgan catches bad guys."

Walker put the next bite of food in his mouth slowly, chewing deliberately. Carefully, Mei explained, "Ah, no. I work in the morgue. Do you know what that is?"

Olivia piped up first. "That's where the dead bodies go."

Beside her Hailey squirmed in her seat and twisted her face in disgust. "Ew, Livvie, that's gross."

Indifferent, Olivia shrugged and took another bite of her food. It reminded Mei of Grace immediately—the innate sense of authority over her siblings, the careful dismissiveness. "Whatever, it's true. I think it's cool."

"I think it's cool too!" Samuel shouted. Walker snorted, reaching over to ruffle the young boy's hair.

"Maybe it's cool, but not exactly dinnertime conversation," Walker replied, dabbing his clean-shaven face with a napkin. "Hailey, why don't you tell Morgan about your science project?"

Grateful to be the center of attention, Hailey shifted in her seat excitedly. "I made a big poster on dinosaurs. Um, pacifically—"

"Specifically," Olivia corrected.

"Pa—spe—" Hailey grunted, crossing her arms over her chest. Her cheeks grew red and Mei felt a tantrum coming like an animal detects a storm.

"You're good, Hailey, keep going. Sound it out while I see how much mashed potatoes I can fit in my mouth." Forkful by forkful, Morgan filled her mouth with an ungodly amount of mashed potatoes, her cheeks bulging like a squirrel. It severed the tension at the table immediately as all three children broke into fits of laughter.

"Spe—ci—fic—ly I did, um, the Tyrannosaurs Rex and the Stegosaurus. I drew pictures of them and showed my class what they ate and what they looked like. I told my class scientists think lots of dinosaurs had feathers like chickens and not scales like Sammy's lizard."

"No way!" Morgan exclaimed.

Hailey nodded profusely. "Yes way! I 'membered because you told me! And Mommy took me to the library and I checked out two books about dinos. I still have 'em if you want to see 'em."

"Only if you read them to me," Morgan replied. "Gosh, you must've worked so hard on that project. I'd love to see it when we're done eating, if that's okay with your parents."

"Of course, it's up in her room. The teacher was very impressed and only slightly disturbed by how much she already knew about dinosaurs," Jean said.

Mei chuckled softly and Morgan gave her a little jab under the table. "Well, dinos are super-duper cool, so. Makes sense."

After dinner and dessert concluded, the children dragged Morgan upstairs to see the school projects from the past year. Except for Samuel, who didn't have school projects but like every youngest child did have a massive fear of missing out. Unfortunately, this left Mei alone with Walker and Jean cleaning up in the kitchen. Mei took to drying the dishes Jean washed as Walker wrapped up the leftover food, including making a separate collection of leftovers for Morgan.

Walker popped the lid on a plastic container full of stuffing, putting it away in their oversized double-door fridge. Upon the fridge hung selected artwork from the kids, as well as kitschy magnets from tourist locations and family photos. "Normally we send Morgan home with enough food to feed her for a week, but now that she's got you maybe she doesn't need it."

Mei laughed, shaking her head. "She'll eat that and then some, don't worry. No matter where we go for dinner, if it's any place she's been to more than once they send her home with enough food to last months, like she's going away to war. And I always think, 'That's way too much food, she'll never eat that.' Two days later, it's gone."

Beside her, Jean snickered and smiled affectionately, nodding toward her husband. "Bottomless pits, the two of them."

Walker ran his fingers through his hair, the same sandy blond as Morgan with threads of gray entwined at the roots. He had a handsome face, not as rugged as one would expect for someone who did hard time and often under the influence of hard drugs. "So, uh, Mei. Morgan tells us you were married."

Wiping a plate down and placing it next to her, she calmly put the towel on the counter. She hadn't worn her ring, opting to leave it at home to not present a conflicting message to

Morgan's father. "Um, yes. I was married for thirty years, until two years ago when my husband passed."

"How awful," Jean lamented over the run of her faucet. "I'm so sorry, Mei."

"Thank you, that's very kind."

"And Morgan, she—" Walker leaned in the doorway, cutting an imposing figure as his broad shoulders took up much of the frame. Mei indulged Walker's attempt at a Papa Bear routine. A little. "She's the first relationship you've been in since he died?"

"Yes. Why?"

"Just asking," he said. "It must be hard, moving on like that. Especially with someone who has, um, less experience."

Anger rose up her spine, spreading through her veins like fire. Silently, she inhaled a steadying breath and cooled the fire to ice. "Because she's younger than me or because you assume she's been in fewer relationships?"

Scratching the back of his neck, Walker shrugged. "Both, I guess. Look, I don't mean nothing by it. You seem like a nice lady and Morgan is crazy about you. And the Lord only knows where she got it from, but that kid's got a big heart. I'd hate to see it get broken if she's some kinda rebound. I'm just trying to look out for her, is all."

While in this man's own home, Mei couldn't unleash the fury of retorts burbling up inside her, thick and acidic like bile. "I see. Morgan is a grown woman, and an exceptionally smart one at that, so I would trust her to make her own decisions regarding whom she chooses to love. Rest assured, Mr. Benson, Morgan has someone looking out for her: me. I wouldn't let anyone mistreat her. She is not, and never will be, a rebound."

The noise of children and Morgan bounding down the stairs broke the ice between them. An insistent Hailey pried him away from the door and Mei resumed drying dishes. Normally she resented this patriarchal delegation of duties, but the monotony calmed the unexpected storm raging inside her. Without it, that man might've gotten one of these decorative turkey serving plates to the side of the head.

"He isn't a mean man," Jean muttered. "He's…haunted. He lives with a lot of regret about not being there as a father for Morgan."

Doing her best to cool her temper, Mei sighed. "I think perhaps I assumed he interrogated me because of my age. Not that it's any of his business, but I would understand if he thought I'm too old for her. I'm sure I would feel the same if it was one of my daughters."

Jean turned off the faucet and peered around Mei to watch Walker happily chasing the kids around their couch, pretending to be a dinosaur. "It has nothing to do with age. Walker was in prison so long, secluded and deprived, he would find that sort of thing petty. He sees a lot of himself in Morgan and worries for her. He does his best for the kids, but he's troubled. And I think Morgan's troubled too. You can see it in their eyes, can't you? Just out of your reach, this sadness that never goes away. Walker knows how easy it is to give in to the sadness."

That was precisely what Mei saw in Morgan. An unreachable pain beneath her unflappable friendliness. A pain she wanted to soothe. A pain that drew her in like a siren in a sea storm.

"They were kids when Charlotte got pregnant. Both of them only sixteen, both with a lot of problems aside from the drugs. Morgan is pretty tight-lipped about her childhood, at least to me, and that leads me to believe it wasn't a good one. I don't imagine it would've been much better with Walker around, in and out of jail as he was."

"Right, Morgan mentioned he did hard time and isn't thrilled about her occupation."

At this, Jean sighed and crossed her arms. "Walker believes many of his charges were trumped up by the cops. I have no idea if that's true, but a lifetime of battling the law gave him a distrust of the police. I can't say I blame him for that, but I do blame him for letting it affect the tentative relationship he has with his daughter. They got into a fight last year about it."

"A fight?" Mei couldn't imagine Morgan raising her voice, never mind getting into a full-blown argument.

"The kids asked Morgan about her job and Olivia became so enthralled by her she would've joined the police academy if she hadn't been seven at the time," Jean said with a chuckle. "They adore her, all three of them, but I think Olivia's taken a special shine to Morgan. It took me five months of telling her she's not allowed to have an undercut until she's sixteen for her to stop asking."

Snorting, Mei gestured for her to elaborate. "And Walker took an exception to this adoration?"

"Yes, he was livid. When the kids went to bed, he accused Morgan of trying to brainwash them with pro-police propaganda. Obviously, she had done no such thing. I tried to talk them down, but the two of them went at it."

"I've never seen Morgan angry," Mei replied with an astonished look in her eyes.

"More disappointment than anger. She didn't care that he hates cops, she was upset he thought she would try to manipulate our children." Jean peeked into the room with Mei, watching Walker crawl in his hands and knees with Hailey and Sammy, while Morgan quietly explained something to Olivia in a corner, using a makeup brush as a pretend fossil-dusting tool. "Morgan loved the kids instantly, but you can tell it pains her to see them living the life she never had. It breaks my heart, and it breaks Walker's too. After they fought, I wasn't sure we'd ever see her again and it tore him apart. He texted and called her and apologized, but she never responded. But then she met you and she spoke to him again. She told him she met someone wonderful and how happy she was, it…it meant so much that she wanted to share her happiness with him."

Shaking her head in amazement, she caught eyes with Morgan in a moment of reprieve from Olivia's attentions, and the younger woman smiled brightly at her. "I'm glad to hear that. She makes me happy too."

"What else do you need, you know?" Sammy came running at Jean, who scooped him up into her arms and gave him a hug, blowing a raspberry on his cheek. "Sure, maybe the age difference is complicated, and I can't even begin to imagine what you went through losing your husband. But when you find joy, hold on to it as tightly as you can. The rest will fall into place."

As the night wore on and Morgan assisted putting each of the children to bed, Walker brought out a vintage whiskey he kept in his basement. Mei declined the offer, as did Jean, but he and Morgan enjoyed a few glasses as they relaxed in the living room.

"Tell us how you met," Jean chirped, sitting back in her recliner and smiling at the two of them cozied on the couch. "We never got the full story from Morgan."

Morgan sipped the whiskey, the strength of which Mei could smell quite clearly. "Um, well, the first time was on the highway. Mei's car had a flat and I saw her on the side of the road, so I offered to fix it."

"We were in a blizzard and I thought she was going to murder me," Mei added, to Walker and Jean's laughter.

"The second time was at work," Morgan replied uneasily. "I assisted Ruiz on a case and we asked Mei for an update on the victim. I didn't know we had already met."

Jean clapped her hands enthusiastically. "That's so romantic! Two chance meetings. And? Then what happened?"

"Three months later," Morgan said, casting a sidelong glance at Mei, "we started dating."

Walker gestured between the two of them with his drink. "So, y'all work together, is that right?"

The arm Morgan slung over her shoulder tensed, and Mei placed one hand on her thigh. "We work in proximity to one another, yes. The morgue is in the basement of the county sheriff's office, and Morgan's office is down the hall."

Jean's features scrunched together. "In the basement?"

Rubbing her palm against her jeans, Morgan deliberately stalled by drinking more whiskey. "Yeah. I was promoted earlier this year and transferred to the county office. I run the cold case unit."

"You got promoted? Oh, that's exciting," Jean gushed, visibly restraining herself from getting up to hug Morgan. "Congratulations."

"Thanks."

"She's also gotten a commendation from the state for her work within this past year," Mei tacked on. Walker scoffed under his breath and Mei zeroed in on him like a fighter jet.

"It's not a big deal," Morgan said, wriggling in her seat. "I'm just doing my job."

"No, go on ahead," Walker replied, sitting down on the arm of his wife's chair. "I'd love to hear what they're handing out awards for now."

"Because," Mei enunciated, narrowing her eyes, "Morgan's exemplary work solving a child murder also solved a string of sexual assaults on minors, and branched out to expose a child pornography ring running since the eighties."

This information left Jean appalled, Walker unjustly suspicious, and Mei so angry she wanted to slap the look right off his face.

"That's great, Morgan," Jean said, breaking the tension with a smile.

"It is great," Mei insisted. "It was an incredible amount of work she completed in a matter of months."

"What a horrible business," Jean lamented. "Do you two work together at all?"

At this, Mei felt Morgan let up some of the tension in her body. "We don't work directly together, no. But I badger her all the time for advice. She's a genius."

Despite Walker's obvious discomfort, Jean valiantly continued to show support. Mei admired it and resented Walker even more for foisting this emotional labor onto his wife. "I think that's wonderful. What a team you must make."

"Yeah, what a team of crime stoppers," Walker said, raising his glass in a salute Morgan did not return. "How'd you end up on cold cases, anyway? Isn't that for washed-up old detectives? Last I heard you was running up the ranks at your old place."

"I got transferred," Morgan murmured.

Walker laughed and shook his head. "Did you now? What did you do to piss off the pigs? Forget to cross your t's and dot your i's? Forget to shine your shoes?"

"I turned in my partner for evidence tampering and witness intimidation," Morgan revealed. Mei watched the shame sweep across Walker's face, and she kept her own reaction neutral. She hadn't actually known why Morgan was transferred, having assumed it was because she sought a promotion. "Brass opened an investigation and found more offending officers, up to and including our captain. My partner was fired and a couple officers were suspended without pay. The chief of police officially reprimanded the entire precinct. Needless to say, it made me extremely unpopular and other officers harassed me constantly and tried to sabotage my cases. When the sheriff put out feelers to see if anyone would want to lead the cold case unit, my captain pushed my promotion and sent me away."

Morgan trembled in anger, but as Mei lowered her hand to comfort her, she stood up and put her glass on the table beside them. "So now you can choose what you hate more about me: that I'm a cop, or that I'm a rat. Excuse me." Mei considered going after her, but chose to stare down Walker as he peered into his glass.

Jean stood, forcing her husband's attention to her. "You're going to lose her, Walker."

Even for a man who spent a lot of time in the penal system, Mei couldn't imagine a more painful punishment than losing Morgan.

Once Morgan returned, she and Mei retrieved their coats and said their goodbyes. Mei lingered near the door as Morgan sleepily trundled down the walk. Once she moved safely out of earshot, Mei spun to face Walker and Jean in the doorway.

"You know," she began, "it's not like she doesn't understand why you're angry, she doesn't understand why you're angry at her."

"I'm not angry at her," Walker said stiffly.

"How is she supposed to know the difference?"

"I don't know, I—"

"Look, before I go, let me give you two pieces of advice, from someone with *experience*." Willing herself calm, Mei unclenched her jaw. "One, as a parent: if you keep this up, she won't come back. Our children do not belong to us; they are not obligated to be in our lives once they're out on their own. She is choosing to be here. She is choosing to have a relationship with you. Morgan is one of the most extraordinary people I've ever met, and every day I wonder what I could've possibly done to deserve her, and most days I come up empty. And yet that amazing person chooses to bring *you* into her life. Do you have any idea how lucky you are?"

Walker looked past her to his daughter, who stood on the sidewalk fumbling with her keys. The keys hit the ground and Morgan let out a whispered, "Aw, shoot."

"I do," he said, returning his downcast gaze to Mei.

"Good. Two, not as a parent but as the woman who loves your daughter: don't you ever demean her like that in my presence again. I was polite once and I will not be polite twice." Mei pivoted sharply to Jean. "Thank you for inviting me to your home. It was a lovely dinner, and your children are wonderful. I do hope to see you again."

Mei tugged her coat and headed toward her girlfriend, who stared down at her keys with intense, adorable confusion.

"Let me drive, Morgan." Mei reached for the keys. Petulantly, Morgan held them away from her. "You've had a lot to drink and you look like you're about to fall asleep."

Dramatically, Morgan groaned and dropped the keys into Mei's open palm. "Fine, but go easy. She's got a couple miles on her."

"The sexist way you talk about your car is baffling."

"Who said I was talking about the car?"

With a cheeky giggle, Morgan slid into her passenger seat. Leftovers securely fastened in the back, Mei smoothly rolled out down the street and back toward the highway.

"It's unexpectedly sexy to see you driving my car. I mean, it's not unexpected that you're sexy, because you always are, but it's strangely erotic."

"Is that so?"

"That is so." The lilt of a female singer-songwriter buzzed from the speakers controlled by Morgan's phone, which she distractedly tapped as Mei drove. "Thanks for coming with. I'm sorry it got bad."

"I can empathize with strained parental relationships," Mei replied. "You had every right to be angry with him. I—I had no idea you were transferred for whistleblowing."

"S'not really a panty-dropper," Morgan explained with a humorless scoff, tone dripping with self-loathing. "I would never tell him, but...I wish we could be like, a daughter and her dad, you know? It could be cool, I think, to have a real dad. I wish he...I wish he liked me."

While Mei debated turning the car around and driving it through Walker's front window she replied, "He did attempt to give me the 'if you hurt my daughter' talk. Maybe I should've let him."

"If you'd let him get away with that, you wouldn't be you," she said with an affectionate, sleepy smile, gazing down at her phone where she swiped through photos taken of and by her half siblings.

"Morgan, may I ask you a question?"

"Yes you *may*, Mei." Morgan snickered to herself.

"You get one pass on making that joke." Wrapping her fingers around the steering wheel, she inhaled sharply. "Do you want children?"

Having almost dozed off, Morgan blinked her eyes wide open. "What? Where did that come from?"

"Nowhere. You..." Mei trailed off, gesturing at her phone. "You're so comfortable with kids and they respond to you. Seeing how effortlessly you charm them, it made me curious, is all."

Morgan snuggled into the supple leather of her seat. "Nah, I don't think so. I feel like my vibe is more 'cool lesbian aunt' than 'mom.'" Warily, she eyed Mei. "Why, do you want more kids?"

"No, no. I wouldn't—I wouldn't begrudge you that desire, that's all. It's not as if I dislike children; I enjoyed raising my own," Mei replied, flustered.

Out of the corner of her eye, Morgan smirked. "Oh, man. You wanna make little gaybies with me, don't you?"

"That is not what I meant," Mei said, chuckling and shaking her head. "You're ridiculous. '*Gaybies.*' Who even? Forget I said anything."

"Can't say I blame you," Morgan replied, yawning. "I would make adorable gaybies."

Reaching over, Mei fondly ran her fingers through Morgan's hair. "I don't doubt it."

Dark and familiar roads guided them from one set of suburbs to another. Mei turned away from the claustrophobic lights of the city, the ones that led to Morgan's neighborhood, and toward her own spacious neighborhood. She pulled Morgan's sleek car into her driveway, turning it off and letting the engine shudder to rest.

"Darling, wake up."

"Hmm? Did I fall asleep?" Adjusting to the darkness with a series of blinks, she stared out the windshield, confused. "Where are we? Did you kidnap me?"

"This is my home," Mei said, exiting the car with Morgan's food in her arms. Darkened homes stretched in either direction on the idyllic street, save for a few windows emitting flickering blue lights. More cars parked by the curb than usual because of the holiday, but not a single soul in sight except for Mei, shivering in the cold as Morgan oriented herself.

Unsteadily, she gazed at the unassuming home Mei and Allan fell in love with as newlyweds, then swiveled her head to take in the surrounding neighborhood. "You live here?"

"Yes."

"Here? On the set of *Desperate Housewives*?"

"Hilarious. Come, it's cold out here." Inside was as dark as outside; only a handful of inset nightlights lit the hardwood floors and the treads up the staircase. Kicking her shoes off, Morgan tiptoed inside, as if afraid of spooking a ghost. "I'll put the food away. My bedroom is upstairs, second door on your left. The master bathroom adjoins it. There are extra toothbrushes under the sink."

"Your bathroom is in your bedroom? Gosh." While Mei stacked the containers, Morgan yelled down the stairs. "Your tub is huge! And the shower is separate! Wow, it's like one of those HGTV Dream Homes in here."

Chuckling, Mei followed Morgan's incredulous voice up to her bedroom. A warm lamp lit the room, highlighting Morgan as she gazed around in wonder. The inebriated woman plunked down on the end of the bed and Mei rummaged through her drawers for clothes Morgan could borrow. Producing a few items she considered oversized for herself, she handed them over. "Let me know if these are okay."

Morgan shrugged, pulling off her shirt and folding it neatly on a dressing chair near the closet. Accustomed to Morgan's physique, Mei hadn't given much thought to the scars pockmarking her skin. Her occupation or experience as an athlete could be the origin of any one of them. Now, though, Mei considered the possibility each mark represented a dot in the timeline of Morgan's harsh childhood. It pained her to think someone could have ever intentionally hurt Morgan, especially the mother she adored.

"I'll make do. I always do."

Leaving Morgan to undress, Mei stared at herself in her bathroom mirror and started her nighttime facial routine. Though anxiety riddled her nerves, she knew it was time. Buck up, be a grown woman, and have some courage. Morgan deserved to know. She needed to know.

When she returned to the bedroom, Morgan lay under the covers with the television on. It struck Mei all at once that this marked the first time anyone else would sleep in her bed. She'd bought an entirely new mattress, frame, and headboard after Allan passed. New sheets and pillows, nothing to smell like him or remind her of the voided space beside her. It was a relief not to stare into an empty bed, but one with someone who cared for her in it.

Shaking the thoughts from her head, Mei slipped under the blankets. Morgan seemed more awake now, eyes less glassy than before. "Thank you for bringing me here. You have a nice house. Well, what I could see in the dark looked nice."

"I'm sorry I didn't invite you over sooner. You've always welcomed me into your home and I should've extended the same courtesy to you."

Morgan snorted. "It's really okay, my apartment is nothing. I understand the significance of this, and I appreciate it."

Propping herself up, Mei peered into the wide, adoring eyes looking into her own. The bluish hue of the television and the glow of moonlight coming in from the window did nothing to diminish the simple beauty that was Morgan. Heart swelling, Mei cupped Morgan's cheek and smiled. "I hope you know how much I admire you."

"You do?"

"Yes. I'm so proud of the person you are. Brave and resilient, caring and kind. You work so hard and selflessly for others, always doing the right thing even if it's extraordinarily difficult. I'm proud of you, and I'm proud to be your partner."

The scrunched look on Morgan's face smoothed out and her eyes became watery, shimmering in the light. Unable to resist, Mei kissed her with conviction. Morgan responded sluggishly but assuredly, and when Mei broke away she could see a tear coming down her cheek. Self-conscious, Morgan swiped the tear away. "Sorry. Nobody's ever—nothing. Just, sorry. A-and thank you."

With her hand still on the side of Morgan's face, Mei swallowed the lump in her throat and her fear along with it. "I love you, Morgan. I'm very much in love with you."

Morgan's bottom lip quivered and she craned up to kiss Mei with soft urgency. Normally, Morgan would take the lead and push Mei onto her back, but she instead held her close, neither deepening the kiss nor pulling away. An innocent kiss suffused with profound affection. "I love you too."

Of course she did. Her wedding confession aside, this came as no great revelation. Everything Morgan did was an act of love; her actions spoke of a devotion transcending the simple act of exchanging I love yous. Loving in a way Mei found insurmountable, but it came easily to Morgan. She dropped a kiss on her forehead, and this prompted Morgan to settle her head in the crook of Mei's shoulder and slink her arms around her middle. While Mei often took the position of little spoon, Morgan needed the comfort of Mei's protection. "Tired?"

"A little," Morgan replied in a small voice. "What about you?"

"I'm all right."

Scrolling through the apps on her television and subscriptions she barely used, Mei bounced between available options before finally settling on a film. She combed her fingers through Morgan's hair as the film opened. "Have you seen *Say Anything*?" Morgan shook her head. "Good. I think you'll like it. It has Bebe Neuwirth and John Mahoney in it. It's about—"

"Say no more. You had me at Bebe."

An hour into the movie, Mei giggled out of nowhere. Sleepy blue eyes blinked up at her. "Nothing. I just realized the irony of Walker naming his child Olivia Benson."

Morgan snorted, snuggling deeper into Mei's arms. "Jean chose the name."

"I knew I liked her."

CHAPTER FIFTEEN

Big homes made Morgan feel small. Tall and broad since seventh grade, everywhere she went she felt like she took up too much space. But in big houses, the ones with high ceilings and spacious rooms, perfect paint jobs and matching photo frames, she felt minuscule. Like Alice in Wonderland, too oversized or too undersized. Like a puzzle piece someone carelessly tossed into the wrong box.

Mei's house felt like that. Before sunrise with Mei still asleep, Morgan gave herself a tour of the home. Three other bedrooms completed the second floor, a bedroom each for Mei's daughters, and the third a nondescript guest bedroom. Grace's room reflected what Morgan knew of her: neat and tidy, with few mementos of her youth other than two shelves boasting trophies. Technically next door but otherwise a world away, Lara's bedroom typified an angsty teenager: posters of musicians and actors on the wall, all women, as well as colored bulb Christmas lights strung around her bed.

Morgan envied them. Once in all the moving during her childhood did she have her own bedroom. Only a converted laundry room, but the sole taste of privacy Morgan had until college. Other nights she spent on floors, sharing a bed with her mother, or tucked into a bunk bed in a crowded foster home. She'd have wished for a bedroom of her own, but asking to keep the roof over their heads used up all her wishes. Demanding more from her mother was unfair.

After passing an enormous bathroom, Morgan walked downstairs and inspected the archipelago of framed family photos on the wall. Their wedding, the births of the girls, various vacations, and lots of school photos. Not many with Mei in them. She must be behind the camera more often than not, which was a shame. Expensive-looking furniture and tasteful rugs sat around the family room, but one of those weird family rooms without a television in it. An enormous kitchen led into a formal dining room too fancy for Morgan to dare tread upon it. Too cold to wander outside, Morgan pressed her nose against the patio's glass doors and peered out into the yard. Not a blade of grass out of place, from fence to fence expansive and well kept.

Only two doors remained. One led to the basement, where Morgan did not venture with Mei still asleep. Finding your girlfriend rummaging around in your basement on her first time sleeping over seemed creepy. Or worse, quirky. The other door intrigued her more, closed with an Arizona Diamondbacks plaque affixed on the front. Since Mei could barely stand to watch a single at bat of a baseball game, Morgan assumed it must be Allan's office.

Though this room remained locked away, Allan's touch spread through the rest of the house. His shoes waited by the door, his huge physique and contagious smile appeared in every photograph, and his clothes hung on the right side of the bedroom closet. His presence loomed like the shadow of a solar eclipse. By nature Morgan was not a jealous person; those who grow up destitute know how easy it is to lose everything, so she never learned covetous inclinations, least of all toward another person. Besides, how could she resent the man who loved the woman she adored? No, Morgan wanted to know his likes and dislikes, what Mei loved about him and what she didn't. If Allan lived on as her roommate in Mei's heart, Morgan wanted to know all about him.

"Morgan?" Rubbing sleep from her eyes, hair tousled and clad in silk pajamas, Mei had no business looking as beautiful as she did standing at the top of the stairs. She radiated poise and elegance, strength and beauty, even unkempt from sleep. Morgan often fought the overwhelming feeling she did not deserve to behold Mei at all. "Hey, you're awake early."

"Never been good at sleepovers. First nights are always the hardest."

With a soft chuckle, Mei descended the stairs. "Unless it's me at your apartment and I sleep so well I don't leave for days."

"Not entirely your fault. The Morgan Kelly Experience has exhausted many women."

Stopping on the last step, Mei put her hands on her hips as Morgan approached her. At this height, Mei could stare directly down into Morgan's eyes. Placing her arms on either of Morgan's shoulders, Mei tilted her head. "And how many tickets have you sold to the Morgan Kelly Experience? Is it more exclusive than 'the gun show'?"

"Why?" Eyebrow raised, Morgan leaned in with a little smirk. "Do you have a jealous streak, Dr. Sharpe?"

Idly dragging her nails along the shorn hair on the back of Morgan's neck, Mei shrugged. "I like to think it's a balanced amount of jealousy. Enough where I keep you to myself because you bring me joy, but I do not keep you from what brings you joy."

Morgan pushed up on her tippy toes to press a kiss against Mei's lips. "Ah, so your possessive bit at the wedding?"

"My possessive bit?" Mei inquired archly, blushing up a storm. "You gave me a hickey. I couldn't wear a low-cut shirt for weeks."

"Don't deflect," Morgan chided. "We both know what you were after on that dance floor."

"Fine. I may have been a tad jealous of your admirers at the wedding, yes. But ultimately, I was fully confident I would have the last dance. And I did." Mei played with the hem of

Morgan's borrowed tank top strap. "Would you like me to make you breakfast?"

"Baby, I'd like you to be breakfast," Morgan replied easily, sliding her hands around Mei's waist to cup her butt through her silk shorts. "But I would settle for pancakes."

Dipping her hand between them, Mei took Morgan's chin and lifted it. "There is ample time for both."

Eyes ablaze, Morgan bit her bottom lip and gazed up in unadulterated desire. "God, I love you."

With two successful charges awaiting conviction and a total of three solves on cold cases under their belt, Morgan and her team worked like train engine operators going full steam. Their dungeon was now outfitted with real desks and state-of-the-art computers. Even her own standing within the department rose—they included her in supervisory meetings and office-wide celebrations. It left little time to do much else, but thankfully Mei had sort of taken up living with her on those long weeks. Mei watered her plants and ironed their clothes. Morgan made sure to take care of their laundry, as Mei stayed over so much she practically had a full wardrobe in Morgan's closet. This casual domesticity was wonderfully grounding. Spending her days sifting through brutal old murders, having something normal and reliable to come home to at night kept her from spiraling too deeply into her caseload.

Cleaning up after dinner at Mei's, Morgan stared out the window at the falling snow. Hands dunked into soapy water, she daydreamed about the first night they met up outside of grief group and how beautiful Mei had looked in the glittering snow. The trajectory that landed them here in Mei's house was not what Morgan expected, but infinitely better than the several months of pining and agony during those first three months.

"Morgan?"

"Hmm?" Turning her head, the annoyed but affectionate look on Mei's face led her to believe she'd accidentally ignored her girlfriend. "Sorry, zoned out a little. What's up?"

"I asked if you'd made any arrangements for Christmas."

"What do you mean?"

"You said you normally go on vacation. I assumed you were doing the same this year."

"Oh, no," Morgan said, waving her off. "I got so busy I didn't ask for the time."

"Ah, okay." A pregnant pause built between them as Mei rested her hip against the counter. "Would you like to spend Christmas with me and my family? Now, I know you are hesitant to do a big 'present thing' with other people, and I respect that. I won't be upset if you say no. I will also say, as a warning, my mother will be there. Take that as you will."

Shifting her weight, Morgan gazed into the stainless steel sink as she contemplated the offer. On the one hand, it meant great progress in their relationship. Mei's family didn't know about them yet, and Morgan possessed no plans to press her on it. On the other hand, the thought of sitting through someone else's family holiday filled her with dread.

Beside her, Mei grew fidgety at the lack of response. "Like I said, you're free to say no. We could see each other the day before, or that night, if you want."

"So, um, you want to tell them about us?" An attempt to be casual, but she couldn't deny the tiny wellspring of hope burbling inside her.

"Yes. I—I will speak to my daughters and my mother before Christmas to be sure you're not a surprise. Besides, it's long past time for them to know I'm in a relationship. My absence at Thanksgiving was evidently an event and they've become rather suspicious."

"Suspicious of what?"

"Of what or whom is making me so happy." Mei pecked Morgan on the cheek.

"Oh?" Morgan closed the dishwasher and set it to run, nabbing Mei by the hips to pull her in close. "They think you're getting laid, don't they?"

"If they do, they would never say it outright."

"They're like, 'Damn, Mom's been so happy recently. I bet her partner knows how to lay that pipe.'"

Mei balked away from her, but Morgan gripped her tightly. "I would certainly hope if my daughters discussed my sex life they'd avoid a term like 'laying pipe.' I would hope they'd avoid talking about it altogether." Half-scandalized, she cast sidelong glances at Morgan. "'Lay pipe.' Who even says that? Honestly."

"I love that little blush you get when you're embarrassed." Shimmying out of Morgan's reach, Mei skittered away and giggled as Morgan chased her through the house and bounded up the stairs. "Wait up, we need to do some plumbing."

"You're a monster!"

Rolling up to the curb, Morgan threw Dorothy into park and scrambled out of her seat. Twenty minutes late to Christmas with Mei and her family, she vaulted up the steps of Grace's porch in a panic. Taking a moment to settle herself, she swiftly knocked and waited, taking deep breaths. She didn't even have time to look at the house in full—she could tell it was big, white with black trim, sparse holiday decorations other than warm yellow string lights along the porch and a single wreath on the door.

From the other side, Morgan heard an unfamiliar voice. "Always been a lightweight, just like—" The door swung open and Morgan prepared her biggest smile. "Daddy."

Her smile fell and she furrowed her brow in confusion. The woman must be Lara, Morgan figured, based on the telltale tattoos and extremely queer vibe. She bore a striking resemblance to Mei, with her angular features softened by the genetics of her father. "Excuse me?"

"Jesus, sorry, I wasn't calling you 'Daddy,'" Lara replied, flustered. Her eyes, the same twinkling brown as Mei's, trailed her from head to toe. "Not unless you want me to."

Barging in behind Lara appeared another woman, taller and equally as beautiful. The genetics in the Lin-Sharpe family were truly something else. "What she means is, 'Hi, Morgan. I'm Lara, resident gay disaster. Would you like to come in?'"

"You're Morgan? Our mom's girlfriend, Morgan?" Lara asked, turning to face the other woman, presumably Grace, who nodded once. "Well, shit. She told us to expect you for dinner but she didn't tell us to expect..." Lara gestured at her. "All this."

Peering down at herself, Morgan looked up and shrugged. "Ah, well. I can't be anybody else, unfortunately. I left my other skin suit in the car and I'm already twenty minutes late."

Lara barked out a laugh, stepping back and out of the way. Bookended by Mei's daughters, Morgan awkwardly kneeled to remove her boots, making quick work of her laces and placing them near the collection of shoes by the door. The interior of Grace's home was unsurprisingly fastidious, tastefully decorated with objet d'art from around the world. Near the fireplace, tucked into a brown leather recliner that looked like it cost more than Morgan's car, sat Jui-Yu, Mei's mother. Next to her stood a handsome man with short, curly black hair and deep green eyes. He strode forward with a big, toothy grin and relieved Morgan of her coat and hat.

"Hey, Merry Christmas, Morgan. I'm Mateo, Grace's husband. It's great to meet you. Mei's told us all about you."

"Oh, boy." Morgan smiled back at him. "Nothing too incriminating, I hope."

"Nah, but she did mention you have a seventy-one Cyclone?" he ventured, folding her coat over his arm to shake her hand.

"Yeah, I do. Would you like to see it?"

Grace scoffed, striding across the room to perch herself on the arm of Jui-Yu's chair. "He would love nothing more. Maybe you can trade toys or whatever it is gearheads do."

"I have a sixty-eight Camaro SS in the garage," Mateo replied, unperturbed by his wife's teasing.

Morgan whistled. "That's a beauty. Does she run?"

"Oh, yeah, like a dream. Anyway, we can talk shop later. Let me put your things in the guest room," he said, scurrying out of the living room.

"Also detach our children from their presents and tell them dinner is ready," Grace called after his retreating form. "Thank you."

Standing in the living room with Lara, Grace, and Jui-Yu, Morgan felt like she'd been thrown into a cage ring. Thankfully,

Mei emerged from a hallway and smiled brightly at Morgan as she crossed to her.

"Hello, darling," Mei greeted, taking Morgan by both her hands and subtly appraising her. She'd worn one of the nicest outfits she owned that wasn't a suit: a cranberry button-down shirt with the sleeves rolled up her forearms, tucked into a pressed pair of form-fitting, smoke-gray slacks. She'd even taken the time to apply makeup, something she hadn't done since Ruiz's wedding. In her distress, she'd snapped a photo of herself and sent it to Reyna, who'd given her stamp of approval. However, the growing look of concern on Mei's face caused her heart palpitations.

"You have grease on your face."

Eyes widened, embarrassment and resignation made her stomach tighten. "Oh, geez, I'm sorry. Big holidays tend to be a magnet for car trouble. People get stressed out and ignore the warning signs of malfunction. I saw some folks broken down and I can't let them sit there, not on Christmas. One was a flat, but then I came across a family having engine trouble. Anyway, that's why I'm late. I'm so sorry everyone, to keep you waiting."

"Come here," Jui-Yu called from her seat.

Stepping around Mei with a wary look, Morgan strode to Jui-Yu and knelt next to her chair. Despite her diminutive stature and seated position, Jui-Yu had a command over the room, and Morgan knew she made the right call by getting eye-level with her. "It's an honor to meet you, Mrs. Lin."

"Let me see you." Without any other direction, Morgan remained still as Jui-Yu narrowed her eyes at her in silent inspection. "Okay. Go clean up. Everyone is hungry. My great-grandchildren are starving."

"Yes, ma'am." Morgan stood, holding her hand out to Grace. "It's nice to meet you, Grace. Your mother speaks very fondly of you and your sister."

"She spoke fondly of you as well, the one time she mentioned you," Grace remarked with an arched eyebrow. "You may use the bathroom next to the kitchen."

Mei intervened, taking Morgan's arm. "I'll show you." Escorting Morgan through the warm and fragrant kitchen, she corralled them into the powder room and breathed a heavy sigh against the closed door. "Sorry about that."

"About what? Everyone was polite considering how late I am. I really am sorry. I had to help those folks. You know I have to try."

"It's okay, I know, my lovely caped crusader," Mei soothed, wetting a washcloth to rub the grease from Morgan's face and arms. "It's only dinner. It's still warm and it'll be as good now as it would've been twenty minutes ago. I'm just glad you're here."

"Me too." Once the last of the grease disappeared from Morgan's face, Mei tilted her head up and kissed her. Morgan slid her arm around Mei's waist and held her close, nuzzling their noses. "Merry Christmas, babe."

"Merry Christmas. Now, I will apologize in advance for what my daughters and my mother will say to you or at you over the next few hours. Mateo is wonderful and will be a normal person, but all of those in my bloodline are suspect."

Chuckling, Morgan swept some of Mei's hair behind her ear. "Duly noted. It can't be any worse than what I put you through on Thanksgiving."

"Oh, my darling, it can be much worse. My one daughter is an uptight stickler who will grill you without mercy, and by the looks of it, my other daughter might want to eat you alive." Mei sighed. "It's astonishing to think perhaps my mother will be the least problematic."

"I think you're underestimating my ability to woo the Lin women. It happened once, it can happen again." Clearing her throat, Morgan puffed out her chest and offered her arm. "Now, let's get out there before your family thinks I'm debauching their mother in the bathroom."

Dinner began smoothly; she exchanged small talk between herself and Mei's family. Grace's children, precocious and smart, fell into an easy rapport with her about Harry Potter. (Julia a proud Ravenclaw, Nathan a Slytherin, and Morgan considered herself very much a Gryffindor.) Meanwhile, she could feel the inter-generational stare of the Lin women on her at all times, ranging from cold scrutiny to warm interest.

"Morgan," Lara began, narrowing her eyes. "Have you ever been on a stakeout?"

Tearing her attention away from Mateo and a promise to let him drive her car, she nodded to Lara. "Yep. A few times when I was a detective, why?"

"Were you ever on a stakeout near the city college? A couple years ago?"

Though uncommon, any stakeout assigned to her blended together into a monotonous string of late nights and bad coffee. Mentally flipping through her inner file cards of cases, she finally landed on the right one. "Oh, yeah. It was a suspected drug ring, if memory serves. Turned out to be bogus, but my partner and I sat out there every night for a week." After another long pause, Morgan laughed. "You were that drunk girl, weren't you?"

Lara returned her laughter with a nod and raised her drink. "Guilty as charged, officer. I cannot believe my mom is dating Detective Dimples."

"I'm sorry, what?" Mei glanced between them, bewildered. "I'm dating who?"

"It was one of Lara's many crushes," Grace supplied with an eye roll. "That year she was prolifically horny and exceptionally gay."

The children—and Mateo—giggled, and Mei shot Grace a withering look. "Grace."

"I can't believe that was you," Morgan said, grinning. "You had much shorter hair then, which proved helpful when you threw up on me."

"Oh, Lara," Mei admonished.

Despite Mei's embarrassment, Morgan recalled the incident with delight. "I'm astounded you remember it at all. You were pretty wasted."

"I remember," Lara elaborated, "because you were so nice to me. Even after I aggressively came on to you and then threw up on your boots. You still made sure I got back to my dorm safely."

"Of course." Morgan shrugged it off. "That's my job."

Lara shook her head. "No, most cops would've given me a citation or sat me in the drunk tank. Trust me, because that happened, too. Only once did someone treat me with any care.

You got me to my dorm, laid me on my side so I wouldn't choke on my vomit, and left me a bag to puke in. I couldn't thank you for it, but I never forgot it."

"Don't sweat it," she said, giving Lara a smile. "All that matters is you were okay."

One down, Morgan thought, as Lara's eyes glimmered with affection. Mei's other daughter, made of glacial ice, would be harder to melt. Grace, with Mei's poise and her father's looks, rolled her eyes. "We do love your drunk and disorderly tales, Lara."

"Everyone does regretful things in college," Morgan said.

"Oh, really?" Grace raised an eyebrow. "And where did you go to school?"

"Michigan State," Morgan replied. "And then to Oxford for my Master's as a Rhodes Scholar."

"Where's Oxford?" Nathan inquired.

"England," Morgan said. "Like Hogwarts, but not nearly as cool. Instead of magic there's just a lot of rowing."

Julia scrunched her face. "What's a Rhodes Scholar?"

Lara leaned in conspiratorially toward her niece. "It's a scholarship program for smart kids. They get to study at Oxford University, which is a really prestigious school."

"I wanna be a Rhodes Scholar," Julia announced.

"I bet you could," Morgan said, gesturing around the table. "You're super smart, like the rest of your family, you work hard in school, and your grandma told me you do volunteer work, too."

Julia nodded vigorously. "I tutor and Nate helps out the coaches at the community center."

"That's great! I hope you're both extremely proud of yourselves. Being a Rhodes Scholar is amazing, but honestly, doing the work to get there was as rewarding as getting the opportunity. I got to do a lot of great community service for the city."

Grace peered at Morgan over the top of her glass, suspicious and calculating. "So, that's your thing, hmm? Being an upstanding citizen? Community service, public servant, rescuing my delinquent sister and then my mother? Next you'll tell me you scoop kittens out of trees and read books to shelter puppies."

Switching gears, Morgan hardened her gaze as she focused on Mei's other daughter. "My occupation often puts me in a position to help others. I would be remiss not to. Plus, I like it."

"Is that so? Am I next?" Grace tipped back more wine and lifted her eyebrow again. "Any plans to carry me bridal style out of a burning plane?"

With a good-natured chuckle, Morgan shook her head. "That implies you somehow mishandled the piloting, doesn't it? I have to imagine the chances of that are pretty low. Mei told me they recently held a dinner in your honor as part of a celebration for your five years of exemplary service. You must be an incredible pilot to have such an astonishing record so young."

Caught off guard, Grace went silent for a few long beats as she considered all of what Morgan had said and how best to pivot away from the compliment. Mateo piped up first. "Grace is incredible. You should see how she handles the pressure, cool as a cucumber. I sat in the jump seat for one of her flights once and it was amazing."

This prompted a boisterous story from Nathan and Julia about flying in the plane with their mother piloting, and Morgan felt Mei squeeze her thigh under the table in a tiny show of support. Gesturing toward Morgan, Jui-Yu spoke up for the first time in over half an hour, speaking to Mei in Mandarin. Once finished, she nodded at Morgan and returned her attention to her grandchildren with a relaxed smile.

Worried, Morgan lowered her voice. "Was that about me? Does she hate me? You can be honest; I'm ready to hear it. I mean, I'm not, it'll devastate me, but I'll cry in the shower at home and not in front of everyone."

"She's impressed. You didn't cave under my daughter's rudeness and you didn't overuse the soy sauce." Fork in hand, Morgan froze. With a smile, Mei leaned in and nudged her shoulder. "It's a compliment. She thinks Americans use too much soy sauce."

"Oh. I didn't even know that was a test I had to pass." Morgan shook her head. "Are there others?"

Glancing around the table at all the personalities in her family, Mei shrugged and nodded. "Probably."

After receiving a slice of cake, Morgan retreated to the living room to hand it to Jui-Yu, who took it with a smile. "Sit."

Morgan wanted cake for herself, but she dutifully sat on the coffee table across from Jui-Yu. They regarded each other in silence for a few beats. Jui-Yu resembled Mei quite a bit, especially the same lovely eyes Mei and Lara inherited. She had a similarly commanding presence, capturing respect and attention without speaking at all.

"You love Mei-Ling."

Well, at least her interrogation started easy enough. "Yes, ma'am."

"It was not a question, I know this," Jui-Yu remarked. "Your job, it's a good job? Steady job?"

"Yes, ma'am."

"And this job not going to kill you? My Mei-Ling already a widow once. Not again, that is too much."

Morgan tilted her head. "Oh, no, it's—it's pretty safe."

"Good. Money is not a problem, my Mei-Ling have a lot of money."

"Um, okay. I don't want her mo—"

"When is your birthday?"

Morgan looked around as if the answer existed in Grace's living room. "October fourteenth."

"What year?"

"1985."

Jui-Yu stroked her chin. "Hmm. Ox."

"A Wood Ox," Morgan added. "Mei's talked to me about it a bit."

"Do you want children, Morgan?" Jui-Yu asked abruptly.

At this moment Grace walked in, eyes huge and stifling a chuckle. When Morgan looked to her for relief, she found none. "Ah, no, not really."

"Why not?"

"I didn't have a good childhood, so I don't know how to give a kid a good life," Morgan replied, holding a smile on her face like a fragile vase.

Jui-Yu contemplated this with nearly closed eyes. Worried she fell asleep, Morgan reached for her but the woman spoke up loudly and Morgan retracted her hand in fear. "Where is your mother?"

"My mother passed away when I was fifteen."

"Not natural," Jui-Yu stated, not asking. Morgan shook her head. She patted Morgan on the knee and gave her one nod. "Okay."

Both Morgan and Grace waited for something else to happen, but Jui-Yu seemed satisfied with that answer for now. "That's it? Just okay?" Grace rounded the chair, sipping on eggnog. "*Wàipó*, that's it? You grilled Mateo for an hour the first time you met him. He cried the whole way home. You asked Mom if she was sure about Dad, like, every Christmas."

"I ask more questions when people lie. I ask Mate-oh until he stop telling me what I want to hear and tell me the truth. I ask Allan about Mei-Ling, and Mei-Ling about Allan."

"Sure, but you asked, like, every year."

"I never like the answer," Jui-Yu replied. "Always lies."

With a white-knuckle grip on her drink, Grace's entire person shook. "What are you talking about? Dad loved Mom."

"Allan was a good man and my Mei-Ling had love, yes, but that is not everything. A good match is more than love. A good match is completion. You cannot be complete if you live with lies. Only truth bring true love."

"And what, this is true love? They've been together what, four months?"

"Six," Morgan corrected softly.

"I ask Morgan and I know what she want from Mei-Ling, what make her complete." Jui-Yu opened her eyes fully, crinkling them in a smile. "To belong. My Mei-Ling want that, too."

Swallowing the lump in her throat, Morgan blinked away tears as she sat back. Scowling, Grace aggressively put her glass down as Lara cautiously walked into the room, eyes shifting between the women like she'd stumbled into a standoff. "Is everything okay?"

"Everything is fine. *Wàipó* decided Mom's new girlfriend—whom she only told her actual family about, like, last week—is somehow a better match for her than our father, whom she was married to for thirty years."

Lara rolled her eyes. "And? So what if she did? *Wàipó* can think what she wants. Maybe she's right, you don't know."

"How can you say that?"

The plate full of cake in Jui-Yu's hand slipped as she dozed off and Morgan scooped it up, leaving it on the coffee table. Standing, she offered Grace an apologetic smile, desperate to diffuse what was rapidly becoming a situation. "She was just being nice."

"No, you don't know *Wàipó*," Grace replied. "And how could you? You only met her two hours ago. I guess it doesn't matter since you're suddenly Mom's soul mate. But trust me, she meant what she said. She isn't nice. Especially not for no reason."

"I'm sure she didn't mean to offend you or your father."

Lara stepped closer in an attempt to intervene. "Dude, chill out."

"Oh, please. You were as skeptical as I was until she got here and now you want to fuck her." Agape, Lara flushed and crossed her arms defiantly over her chest. "Don't look at me like that, we all know it's true. And that's, that's fine. That's classic Lara, so whatever. What's not fine is *Wàipó* shitting on Dad and telling Morgan she 'belongs' when the only reason she's here is because Dad is dead."

"And what, you've decided to become the family bigot?"

"Don't turn this into a gay thing, you know I'm not homophobic."

"Do I?"

"Oh, sure, now I'm a homophobe because I resent the implication Mom's rebound with Lady Oedipus here is more meaningful than her marriage to our father."

"Grace."

All three women swiveled to look at Mei, standing in the doorway to the living room, incensed. Lara shrank back, taking a step or two away from them. Her sister, however, remained unbowed. Behind Mei, Mateo shooed the children down a hallway and away from the escalating tension. Any hurt Morgan experienced from Grace disparaging her dissipated the moment pain appeared in Mei's eyes. A rare, intensely hot anger burned inside Morgan's chest.

"I think you owe your mother an apology."

Grace balked, whipping back to glare at Morgan. "Are you fucking kidding? Who are you to say that to me? Maybe Lara wants you to be her daddy, but I do not."

"What the hell, stop dragging me into your dramatic-ass confrontations," Lara whined.

"You hurt her feelings and you should apologize," Morgan said flatly. "You're welcome to be skeptical of me; you're right, we barely know each other. But what you say and what you think matters to your mother. She asked me to come today because she loves you, she trusts you, and she wants you to be a part of this facet of her life."

"You don't know the first thing about me, or my relationship with my mother."

"Maybe," Morgan replied, the restrained rage causing a band of pain to wrap around her skull. "But I know what it's like to lose a parent. I know the hurt and the pain and the regret, the loss of stability. I carry it with me every day. Sometimes, it makes me so, so angry. It makes me angry with her for leaving, for changing my life without my consent. For putting me into situations I never should've been in. Like the one you're in now, having to reconcile the fact that someone besides your father is in love with your mother. I know that dissonance. But. Being with me is your mother's decision, and you at least owe her the dignity of respecting that decision, even if you disagree."

Moving across the room silently, Mei arrived at Morgan's side and placed a steadying hand on the small of her back. Defiantly, she waited for Grace to say anything in response. The hard, angry look in Grace's eyes waned. Now shame crept in, and perhaps even a speck of understanding. Still, it would not be that easy.

"I chose my words poorly," Grace said slowly. "I'm sorry, Mom. I should not have disrespected you or your relationship. I am happy you've found someone who loves you and makes you happy. But I…I don't think I'm ready to accept this as a reality yet. And that's not your fault or Morgan's. I encouraged you to date, but I didn't consider if I was ready to accept it or not. I need more time."

"Apology accepted," Mei replied in a soft voice. "*Wàipó* can be unintentionally insensitive, and you should know better than to let her get under your skin."

"Yeah, and you say I'm the sensitive one," Lara cut in, wiping tears from her cheeks. Grace tilted her head. "I'm not crying because of *Wàipó*, I'm crying because I'm so happy someone upbraided you right in front of me. It's a Christmas miracle."

"You're impossible. Where are my children?"

"Mateo took them to the basement to play with their toys when he caught the vibes coming from in here," Lara explained.

Grace sighed, rubbing the crease on her forehead. "I'm going to talk to them."

Once Grace exited down the stairs, Morgan turned to Mei. "I think I should go."

Regret and discouragement fleetingly crossed Mei's face, but she nodded in understanding. "Okay. I'll get your coat."

Head pounding, Morgan knelt down next to Jui-Yu and tapped her on the knee. Big, dark brown eyes blinked at her and crinkled at the edges. "It was great to meet you, Mrs. Lin. Thank you for letting me come to your family's Christmas. It meant a lot to me." Jui-Yu smiled but didn't say a word. Morgan strode to the door, jamming her feet into her boots. She spared a glance toward Lara. "So, that went okay, right?"

Lara laughed, tipping back her beer. "Grace is a mean drunk."

"I'm sorry she embarrassed you. I met enough of my mom's 'boyfriends' to understand where she's coming from, but there was no reason to call you out."

"Oh, trust me, that had nothing to do with you." Lara gave a dismissive wave. "That's been Grace our whole lives."

Morgan grimaced in sympathy. "Yikes. I always envied people with sisters and brothers, but having siblings sounds like a lot of work."

"It has its ups and downs. Grace isn't so bad, but she misses Daddy. And for a second there, everyone liked you more than they like her, and that is against the rules," she ribbed.

"Thanks," Morgan said, scratching the back of her neck. "I appreciate you trying to come to my rescue. I'm sure this isn't easy for you both."

"Are you kidding? This is the easiest thing ever. My mom is happy. Do you know how long it's been since she was genuinely happy? Years, even before Daddy died. What's not easy is seeing she snagged a unicorn in the lesbian dating community. But of course she would, because she doesn't settle for anything less than the brass ring."

Morgan scoffed. "Trust me, that's not true. I'm batting way out of my league with Mei."

"Ugh, stop it. You can either be humble or attractive, but not both. I only have so much resistance to your whole *thing* here and I'm already several beers deep," Lara said. "Look, she talks to us more. She sees us more. She calls me just to ask how I'm doing. I thought she was getting laid on the reg, but now I see it's not only that. I mean, it's clearly a little bit that because, sweet Sappho, look at you!"

Snorting in amusement, Morgan blushed. "She doesn't have the easiest time connecting with or sharing her emotions, but it's always been clear to me she loves you both so much."

"And she loves you. The way she looks at you…god, Morgan, I've never seen her look that way before. So, for what it's worth, you have my support. And *Wàipó* is apparently ready to make you her special dumplings, and that's the equivalent of putting you in the will."

Mei approached them from behind, handing Morgan her long wool coat and hand-sewn beanie, snatching her own coat from the hanger next to the door. "Thanks, Lara. I'm glad we got to truly meet this time."

"Me too, Detective Dimples."

Chuckling, Morgan buttoned her coat. "It's lieutenant now."

Lara paused. "All the nicknames coming to me will scandalize my mother. As much as I do love that, I will refrain in the spirit of Christmas. Good night, Morgan."

"I'll walk you out." Looping her arm through Morgan's, Mei led them out into the chilly winter's night. An unimpeded darkness stretched from the heavy gray clouds to the shiny black asphalt, shrouding Grace's tranquil side street. Next to Morgan's car, Mei pulled her in. "I'm so sorry about that."

"There's no need to apologize."

"Yes, there is," Mei replied sternly. "I brought you here because I—well, you know why. I knew this wasn't going to be easy, but I didn't expect my mother's acceptance of you to trigger my daughter. That is literally the last thing I thought would happen."

"It's all right. If there's anything I understand, it's a kid being protective of their parent. But hey, they met me, right? They got to know me a little and hopefully saw how much I care for you, and that's the best takeaway. It's only fair we let them deal with the rest themselves." Mei smoothed the collar of Morgan's jacket before pulling her down and into a kiss. By now, Morgan figured out the nuances to Mei's kisses, growing confident translating their intent. This one ached with affection. As they broke apart, Morgan's gaze drew upward, flinching into the snowfall. "Wow, that really is our thing now, isn't it? Oh! Speaking of."

From her passenger seat, Morgan retrieved a green-and-red plaid box tied with a red satin bow and handed it to Mei with a big grin. Mei took it, admiring the handiwork of the neat ribbon. "I thought we said we'd exchange gifts this weekend."

"We will," Morgan said. "I didn't want to wait for this one. Full disclosure: Reyna tied the ribbon and picked out the box. They both came with me to get the gift because neither trusted me to wrap it myself."

Snickering, Mei untied the ribbon and opened the box, lifting up the bed of cotton keeping it safe. Inside sat a gold bracelet with a flat, rectangular tag on the top, connected on both sides by minuscule chain links. Engraved on the tag was a series of numbers, many digits long, one set on top of the other. "Oh, Morgan. It's stunning."

"The numbers are the longitude and latitude of the spot on the side of the road where your car got the flat tire." Anxious, Morgan shoved her hands in her pockets. "I know we 'met' in the office, but I thought it would be nice to have a reminder of where we were when...when I met the woman who changed my life."

Closing the bracelet back into the box, Mei plopped it in the bag before throwing her arms over Morgan's shoulders and kissing her until she could hardly breathe. She hoped Mei would wear the bracelet, at least occasionally, to carry a bit of Morgan with her. Not a ring, but it would do. "I love you," Mei said, lowering back onto her heels. "I love you. Will you be home tonight?"

"If you want me to be."

"I do." Mei cupped her cheek. "Wait up for me?"

"Always."

CHAPTER SIXTEEN

Last year on Valentine's Day, Morgan found herself on the ground in the snow, changing a flat tire. Drawn to the woman whose tire it was, she'd nursed disappointment upon their parting, knowing she had to return to her awful date and the never-ending purgatory of being a single lesbian.

This year on Valentine's Day, Morgan found herself on the ground in the snow, having fallen flat on her ass trying to ski down a bunny slope. Since it was not normally in Mei's nature to make romantic gestures, Morgan couldn't say no when Mei told her she'd booked them a long weekend getaway for the holiday. She figured a weekend in a private, cozy cabin with the most beautiful woman in the world was worth revealing to the aforementioned beautiful woman that she was a woefully dreadful skier.

They arrived at a picturesque resort with a few dozen cabins tucked away in the mountains, each a private respite from the rest of the resort. To the right stood tall mountains blanketed in fresh powder for skiing, as well as smaller ones for tubing and amateur skiers. At the top of a ski lift sat a glass-enclosed restaurant with breathtaking 360-degree views of the mountain range and the resort itself. Everything about the location radiated beauty and magnificence, and Morgan was determined to enjoy herself despite the very glaring problem of not being able to ski to save her damn life.

On her back in the snow, skis perpendicular to the ground, Morgan crossed her arms over her chest. "Babe? I don't believe this is going to turn out to be one of my talents."

Skiing over to where Morgan lay, Mei reached out her gloved hand. "It's all right. It can take years to get good at it, and—" A child whizzed by, finessing through the snow and spraying Morgan's body with powder. Face full of snow, she leveled an unimpressed look at her girlfriend. "That child has probably skied since before they could walk."

"I guess. I didn't have a 'ski' childhood. I had more of a 'use an upside-down trash can lid to slide down a snowy embankment and try not to accidentally coast into a busy street' childhood," Morgan replied, getting up with great effort. Mei bit her lip, barely suppressing a grin as she brushed snow from her face. "You're enjoying this, aren't you?"

"Let me have this one thing," Mei said, laughing as she held Morgan's shoulders to steady her. "You're such a gifted athlete, and I finally found the one physical activity I'm better at than you. Indulge me."

With exaggerated steps and wobbly legs, Morgan trundled toward their cabin. "Fine, but I'm getting the biggest hot chocolate they have when we get back. And so help me if there are not extra-large marshmallows in it."

"What?" Mei asked, looping her arm through Morgan's to help her cross the terrain. "You'll throw a little fit?"

"Yes." Morgan sniffed. "I might throw a little fit."

Once out of their skiing gear and into regular clothes, they walked back to the lobby, inside which a cute bakery served baked goods and coffees. They approached the counter and Morgan beamed at the cashier. "Becca, how's it going?"

The cashier glanced up, smiling back. "Good, Morgan, how are you?"

Mei looked between them. "How do you...You know what, never mind. Based upon your pastry case I will assume Morgan has been here at least twice since we arrived one day ago."

"Three times," the cashier corrected, adjusting her Coke-bottle glasses. "What can I get you?"

"The biggest hot chocolate you have," Morgan replied. "Topped with the most absurdly large marshmallows you can find."

The woman beside her chuckled and started on Morgan's order, drizzling chocolate syrup into a cup. Becca tapped the touchscreen register. "And for you?"

Mei shook her head. "I'm fine, thank you."

Morgan stepped closer to the register as Mei left to peruse the pastry case and head toward the barista counter to wait for Morgan's beverage. Handing over the money, she asked, "Your day going okay?"

Becca nodded and produced her change, which Morgan dropped into the tip jar along with another couple bills. "Yeah, actually. My girlfriend dropped off flowers for me before my shift. It had a cute little card and everything. It's our first Valentine's Day together."

"Oh, nice! Are you doing anything tonight to celebrate?" Morgan clapped giddily. "Dinner? Date? Dinner date? Movie? Rock climbing?"

"No, we're both broke as hell, so we'll just be staying in," she said, remorseful. "We work a lot so it's nice just to even have the night off."

Being a hungry, broke college student was a memory that lived in the forefront of Morgan's mind. She could distinctly empathize. "I hear you, that must be tough. But flowers at work is pretty cute. What's your girlfriend's name?"

"Lynn," Becca revealed with a shy smile. "I really wanted to take her out tonight. I never get to treat her like that. We're so busy with school and textbooks cost a billion dollars, but hopefully soon I can do something nice for her. Get her a necklace or something."

"Sure, but you know what J-Lo says: love don't cost a thing."

Becca frowned. "But she's a millionaire. Nothing to her costs a thing."

"Hmm, fair." Morgan opened her wallet and withdrew a couple large bills. "Tell you what. Take this and treat Lynn to dinner tonight."

Wide-eyed at the money, Becca shook her head. "I couldn't. We don't—you don't even know me."

"I don't? You're Becca, I'm Morgan, and we're both queer and in love. That's enough for me. Please, take it. Buy her something, whatever you want. Just use it on love, that's all I ask."

After more hesitation, Becca slowly took the money and tucked it into her apron. She cast a glance to Mei, whose eyes bulged at Morgan's massive hot chocolate sliding across the counter toward her. "Is that your wife?"

"No," Morgan replied with a wistful sigh. "I wish. My girlfriend."

Becca tipped forward onto her toes to see Mei more clearly. "Maybe soon? Lots of people get engaged here."

Gazing at Mei, Morgan allowed herself a moment to fantasize about being married. The ring on her finger one Morgan bought for her, going home to a place they owned together, and the simple joy of looking Mei in the eyes and calling her, *my wife*. She shook the thought away. "If it were up to me, maybe."

"You could always ask her?"

"Ah, can't do that."

"Why not?"

Morgan smiled sadly. "It might kill me if she said no."

Eyes comically wide at the sheer magnitude of Morgan's hot chocolate, Mei walked Morgan's beverage to her, using both hands to transport it. Pressing a kiss against Mei's temple, she took the cup from her and slid her arm over Mei's shoulders, sticking a grin on her face at her giant hot cocoa. Affectionately, Mei rolled her eyes. "Happy?"

"Always." Casting a parting glance at Becca, Morgan gestured toward the lobby. "Shall we?"

The lobby's vibe was more relaxed than Morgan would assume for an upscale resort centered around what she considered a rich-people sport: skiing. On the drive up, she'd imagined it more yuppie, more "powerful business couples on a mandatory vacation." However, regardless of what she assumed must be an extravagant expense, the resort radiated comfort. A warm fire crackled in a giant hearth, and people in big, cozy sweaters sat around and drank in front of it, chatting quietly amongst themselves. Morgan liked it, despite feeling outclassed.

She slurped her steaming hot cocoa, using her teeth to grab a marshmallow, and happily chewed the large confection as Mei waited for the receptionist's attention.

"Good afternoon," she greeted with mechanical friendliness. "How can I help you?"

"We'd like to make a seven o'clock reservation for dinner tonight at Black Mountain," Mei said politely. "For two, please. We're in the Foxtail Cabin."

She tapped away at her computer, nodding as Mei spoke. "Wonderful. And I should put it under the name on the booking? 'Sharpe'?"

"That's fine, yes."

Bobbing for marshmallows, Morgan observed silently as the woman booked their reservation. "Okay, you're all set. How has your stay been so far, Mrs. Sharpe?"

Morgan rolled her eyes, and Mei coolly replied, "Dr. Sharpe, and our stay has been lovely, thank you."

"Is there anything else I can do for you?" The receptionist briefly glanced at Morgan. "Will you be needing a cot for your cabin?"

Morgan stilled. She thought perhaps she'd misread the glances from the receptionist, but her instincts were right. They often were, disappointingly so. Mei, however, appeared perplexed. "Why would I need a cot? There's a king-size bed already."

"I'm double-checking you have all the accommodations necessary for you and your…guest."

"My guest?" Mei followed her gaze to Morgan, whose jaw flexed as she clenched it. "Oh. No? We're fine. Just the dinner reservation."

Wiping her nose on her forearm, Morgan encroached upon the counter and narrowed her eyes. "Actually, Kelsey, is it? Kelsey, if you wouldn't mind sending a bottle of champagne to the cabin around ten tonight, that would be great." Sliding her arm over Mei's shoulder, Morgan continued with a sickly sweet smile she'd forced onto her face. "It isn't Valentine's Day without a bottle of bubbly, right?"

Kelsey cleared her throat, losing eye contact with Morgan to stare at her computer and clack against the keys. Cheerful expression gone, she fixed her eyes on Mei. "I'll have that arranged. Anything else?"

"Anything else?" Morgan repeated, swiveling her head to look at Mei. "No, I'm good. You good? This 'guest' has everything she needs."

Angrily grabbing her hot chocolate, Morgan stormed out of the lobby, scowling under her breath. A tight band of pain wrapped around her forehead, her temples pulsing. Once Mei caught up with her, she stepped in front of Morgan to slow her down.

"Are you going to tell me what that was?"

"She knows we're together," Morgan gritted out, shaking her head.

"Who does? That young woman?"

Jaw tight, Morgan stopped in her tracks and stepped out of the way of other guests walking the trails between resort areas. "We have a romantic cabin booked for the weekend of Valentine's Day. It has one bed. It has a Jacuzzi that only fits two. You just made a dinner reservation for two people. She knows we're together, and she tried to send us a bed."

Trying to maintain her calm, Morgan's knuckles turned bright white around her hot chocolate. "Yes, I suppose it confused her when she realized we are both women. She probably expected a man. She didn't seem very bright," Mei said.

Morgan opened her mouth to speak, then clamped abruptly. Closing her eyes, she willed herself more patience. "You don't get it, do you?"

Her attempt to not give in to her anger meant her tone came out clipped and condescending. Mei's soft features drew into hard angles. "Clearly I don't, so why don't you explain it to me?"

Impatient, Morgan rubbed her forehead with her free hand. "I sometimes forget you've never experienced homophobia."

"No, just sexism, racism, and xenophobia. But not homophobia, no." Mei bristled, posturing herself defensively.

"Sorry, that's not what I meant," Morgan said, softening. "I meant that...you aren't equipped to recognize that specific micro-aggression. Well, more than a micro-aggression, since she forcibly tried to make us sleep in separate beds. But that little erasure of our relationship right in front of our faces? That's purposeful. I bet if we'd been the same race she'd have asked if we were related. They *love* to ask if you're related."

"Who's 'they'?" Mei asked. "I don't think I understand. You're saying that woman intentionally tried to send us a free cot because she's a homophobe who wants us, as lovers, to sleep in separate beds?"

"Yes. It's her way of showing disapproval. A low-key way to demean us without outright calling us dykes." Mei flinched. Morgan never, ever used that word. It was like the c-word or the b-word: off-limits. But of all the indignities Morgan was willing to suffer, homophobia was not among them. She did not tolerate cowards. "It's the twenty-first century, you know? Gay marriage has been legal for years now; gay culture is a major part of the zeitgeist. Yet these jerks want to act as if we're unwanted 'guests' in our own society. It infuriates me, the gutless way they try to make us feel less than."

Mei slid her hand around the back of Morgan's neck, rubbing the little vertebrae soothingly. "I'm sorry, darling. I did not realize she was homophobic. I genuinely thought she was just an idiot."

"Well, I guess we're both right."

"This is an LGBTQ-friendly resort, you know. I checked. Also, we're not even the only gay couple here." The pain in her head waned slightly, but she could still feel her heartbeat in her ears. "Will it make you feel better if I storm in there and go full 'let me see the manager' on her?"

"Better? No. Turned on? Without a doubt," Morgan replied, a smile finally breaking on her features. She took Mei's hand and pivoted them in the direction of their cabin. "I want to finish my hot chocolate, take an aspirin, and pout about it for a while in our hot tub."

"All right." Mei gripped Morgan's hand in hers. "How about this? If we see her in the restaurant, we can do that spaghetti dog thing you're always asking about."

Mouth agape, Morgan halted. "You'll do *Lady and the Tramp* with me?"

"Am I the lady, or the tramp?"

"It would be very obvious to you which one you are if you'd watch it with me."

Tipping up in her boots, Mei pecked a kiss on Morgan's jaw. "One milestone at a time, darling. You do still owe me a viewing of *Say Anything* since you fell asleep last time."

"I did not 'fall asleep,'" Morgan replied. "I merely rested my eyes."

"Uh-huh. Remind me, which one of us is the senior here?"

Refreshed from their weekend away, Mei and Morgan dug back into their demanding work schedules. Unless Morgan went out of town for work, they stayed at her apartment during the week, as it was closer to the office. Weekends they retreated to Mei's house. The arrangement worked for them, as they resisted giving up their individual domains but wanted to spend as much time together as their schedules allowed. Truth be told, Morgan wanted to move in with Mei, but neither of their homes suited them as a couple. Mei's house was big and overwhelming, and the constant presence of Allan made Morgan feel like the other woman. Her apartment, on the other hand, erred on the small side, and Morgan didn't want to assume Mei would be willing to part with her memories, both tangible and not, to share a smaller home with her. So, like every adult with a traumatizing childhood, she buried those feelings and moved on. The snows melted, the morning frosts turned to dew, and spring once again bloomed between Morgan's home near the city and Mei's house in the suburbs.

This particular morning differed from the others, as Morgan had a rare weekday off and spent the night at Mei's. Instead of exercising she slept in, cozied in the blankets as Mei woke up and quietly started her day.

Forcing herself fully awake, she drowsily padded into the bathroom, rubbing the sleep from her eyes. "G'morning."

Mei smiled at her in the mirror. "Good morning."

Wrapping her arms around Mei's middle, she kissed the back of her neck. "How'd you sleep?"

"Very well, darling, thank you. Do you want me to start breakfast before I go?"

"Nope. I have to practice my pancakes." Morgan pressed dry kisses on the exposed part of Mei's neck near her hairline. As Mei bent down to spit out her toothpaste, Morgan stepped back and leaned against the doorframe. "By the way, have you seen my Oxford sweatshirt? I couldn't find it last night."

Dabbing her mouth on the face towel, Mei nodded. "It's in the wash." Backing into the bedroom, Morgan sat on the edge of the bed and flicked on the television while Mei dressed. As Mei buttoned her blouse, she inquired, "Any plans for the day?"

"Ah, only to sit in on a lunch meeting Ruiz set up with a guy who works with cadaver dogs," Morgan replied, shrugging. "She's picking me up later to bring me home, and then we'll go from there."

Tightening the belt on her slacks, Mei tilted her head. "Why would you need to go home first?"

"I can't go looking like this." Sleeping sweats might be appropriate for Ruiz, who'd seen Morgan in nearly every state of undress, but not to meet a fellow professional. She might've grown up poor, but she had enough decorum to know that.

"Right, but why don't you change here so Ruiz doesn't have to drive all over the county?"

"I don't have any clothes here," Morgan explained. "Not anything I can wear to a professional lunch, for sure."

In Morgan's home, Mei's presence commanded every room. The rug at the base of the bed, a fraction of her wardrobe in Morgan's closet, her own toothbrush, towel, and robe in the bathroom, a candid photo of them at Ruiz's wedding framed and sitting on the bedside table. They stocked Morgan's fridge with food Mei liked to eat and prepare instead of a freezer stuffed with frozen dinners and a cabinet full of protein powder. A few of Mei's DVDs tucked into Morgan's collection as if they were her own. Here, all of Morgan's worldly possessions amounted to nothing more than a toothbrush and an overnight bag.

Evidently, Mei only now realized this. "Oh."

"It's all right, Ruiz doesn't mind. Besides, then I can water my plants." Morgan followed her downstairs to the kitchen, where Mei dumped out a fresh mug of coffee and retrieved her bento box from the refrigerator. "Why do you do that?"

Mei looked down at the box. "Eat lunch?"

"No, the coffee. If you're not going to drink it, why not stop brewing it?" It always struck Morgan as odd that Mei set the coffeemaker at night and then threw it away in the morning. Mei preferred tea, as far as Morgan understood, so the entire appliance didn't serve much purpose.

However innocuous Morgan considered her question, Mei's entire body became taut with tension. Any levity in her expression dissipated, and she leveled an almost suspicious look at Morgan. "Why? Does it bother you?"

Blinking in surprise, Morgan stopped. "No, no. Just thought I'd ask. It looks like an expensive coffee to be tossing away every day."

"How I spend my money isn't any of your business, Morgan," Mei stated with a chill that could've frosted the windows.

Tentatively, Morgan inched toward Mei like one might approach an angry dog. "Hey, I'm sorry, I didn't mean anything by it."

The silence made Morgan's stomach churn. She didn't know what else to say; she'd never drawn this much ire from Mei before. While she desperately searched for a resolution, Mei tilted her wrist to look at her watch. "I have to go. I'll see you tonight."

Morgan watched her depart from the kitchen window, eyebrows furrowed in confusion. She picked up the mug into which Mei brewed the coffee. While blank on one side, when Morgan turned it she spotted the text scribbled on the other in child's handwriting: "we love you daddy."

Replacing the mug beneath the coffeemaker, Morgan exhaled a long breath. Allan's mug, of course. Allan who drank the coffee each morning and Mei continued the tradition in his absence. That…was fine.

Determined to clear her mind, Morgan used the rest of her morning to attempt to make a pancake. Mei made it look effortless, creating picture-perfect pancakes on demand. Morgan's success rate hovered around thirty percent, but she considered creating any edible pancake an improvement. She ate all of them, including the rejects, out on the patio, listening to the quiet rustle of wind through the trees and the nonstop call of birdsong.

Ruiz considered on time as late, so she knocked on the front door and let herself in about half an hour before Morgan anticipated her. "Kelly?"

Coming in through the sliding glass doors, Morgan waved from the kitchen. "Just a second." It only took her a minute to clean her plate, loading it into the dishwasher and snagging her bag from where she'd left it on the kitchen island. Without looking up, she could feel Ruiz's judgment about her attire. "This is why I asked you to take me to mine."

"Yeah, you look like a gym rat." Turning on her heel, Ruiz led them out as Morgan locked and alarmed the door behind her. "You don't have anything here decent to wear?"

Tossing her bag in the back seat, Morgan got into the passenger side of Ruiz's truck, buckling herself in. "No. I usually bring a bag. We don't normally do weekdays here because my place is closer to work, but I didn't feel like having her drive me home last night."

"That still doesn't answer my question as to why you don't have clothes there," Ruiz replied. "You two practically live together. You loaded the damn dishwasher."

Gazing out the window at the passing homes, Morgan shrugged. "I mean, not really. She's got loads of stuff at my place, but we don't spend a lot of time at hers."

"You should probably make it easier on both of you and shack up already."

She snorted. "Then who would throw out Allan's coffee every morning?"

Shifting gears, Ruiz's dark eyes grew wide. Cutting remarks were not exactly Morgan's MO—usually Ruiz provided the snark between them. "What? Is everything okay?"

"Yeah, it's fine. Mei also didn't know I don't have clothes there. And, like, how could she not know? There's no room for my clothes anywhere. Her closet is mostly full and the other side of her closet is Allan's stuff."

"His clothes are still in there? What is she gonna do, gain a hundred and fifty pounds so she can wear them?" Ruiz rolled her eyes.

"I don't know. I've never asked her. It seemed private." Off Ruiz's look, Morgan sighed. "I know. The coffee thing is what got me thinking. Like, she buys this coffee she never drinks, goes through the effort of making it, and then throws it away. Keeping his stuff I can understand, but brewing his coffee? It's so…"

"Domestic," Ruiz supplied. "It's like she's still going through the motions of being married." Ruiz deliberately slowed down as they neared the exit to Morgan's house. "You two definitely need to talk."

"It's hard," Morgan replied. "She's gotten better about sharing her feelings, but not about him. He's off-limits." Ruiz took the turn onto Morgan's street, tires crunching over the gravel of the trendy side street. "I'm not jealous, but I can't help but feel like when I'm in her house I'm an invader in their marriage. You know, today, for the first time, I realized she doesn't have a picture of me anywhere. I'm not even the lock-screen on her phone."

"In that *palacio* she doesn't have any photos of you? How many bedrooms she got? Four? Five?" Pulling up outside

Morgan's, Ruiz put the car into park and looked over at her. "C'mon, Morgan. You have to know you deserve more than that."

"Do I?" All the hurdles she and Mei had to leap for their relationship to work, Morgan feared this would be the one Mei wouldn't jump. "I've worked so hard to make our relationship solid. The last thing I want to do is give her a reason to leave me."

"Leave you for what? Wanting to be a part of her life?" Scoffing, Ruiz stared ahead at the road, tense. Morgan could count on one hand the number of times she witnessed Ruiz become angry; all of them because someone else had been wronged. Her temper could flare like a reflex, but genuine anger was hard to come by. "You're right, you've put in a lot of effort to make this work and she can't even spare you a dresser drawer. She's got walls full of old memories and not a single picture of you anywhere. How much effort is she putting in?"

Screwing her eyes shut, Morgan vehemently disagreed. "She puts in effort. She loves me. She supports me. She's…she's kinder to me than anyone I've ever been with. And I—I don't know what I'd do without her. So if she doesn't want me to put stuff in her closet, fine. I can deal with that. And who cares about photos, anyway? I have, like, four in my entire apartment."

Her dizzying spiral tempered Ruiz's anger, and her friend placed a conciliatory hand on her thigh. "Hey, calm down, okay? I'm not trying to ring any alarms. I'm only saying it's okay to have needs."

"I need her, that's all I need."

"*Escúchame, manita.*" The affectionate term of address stalled Morgan's descent into anxiety—it was a badge of honor she'd earned after winning Ruiz's friendship and becoming a de facto member of the her family's large brood. "Let me tell you something, okay? Everything I know about love I learned from you. You love without conditions, you give everyone the benefit of the doubt, and you put so much of yourself out there I'm surprised you have anything left in the tank." Reaching over, Ruiz braced her hand on the center of Morgan's back. "You remember Soledad? The woman I dated before Reyna?"

Morgan groaned. Of course she remembered; she took an aspirin every day they were together. "Ugh, yeah. I didn't like her at all."

"Yeah, and annoyingly you were right," Ruiz replied, smirking. "A few days after we broke up she begged me to take her back. I was fucked up and lonely and I probably would've done it, but I remembered something you said to me and it clicked."

"Don't date anyone whose favorite movie is *Saw*?"

"No, but that was weirdly good advice," Ruiz relented. "You said: 'I can't tell you how to love, and I can't tell you who to love, but I can tell you one thing for sure. All love is give and take, not give and be taken from.' I never forgot it, and neither should you, okay?"

Dejected, Morgan nodded, reaching behind her to grab her bag. "You're much sappier since you got married."

"Yeah, I know. And trust me, I'm not happy about it."

CHAPTER SEVENTEEN

The arrival of their one-year anniversary took Mei by surprise. It hadn't felt like a year since she showed up on Morgan's doorstep, desperately seeking her affections. A year since she took a chance on this crazy notion that she might be in love with a gorgeous lieutenant with sapphire eyes. And now this silly woman ruled her heart.

She never cared much for anniversaries during her marriage, and she told Morgan they could just as well eat at Yumel or have a quiet night in. But Morgan insisted they do something fancy for a change and booked them a table at an upscale restaurant out on the lake. The restaurant bustled around her; Mei watched from her perch on a stool at the swanky bar as quick, efficient waiters hustled to and from the kitchen. A text from Morgan indicated she was running a little late, so Mei bided her time nursing a gin and tonic, smoothing out the wrinkles in her nicest red cocktail dress.

"Can I buy you another drink?" Looking up from her phone, Mei took stock of the man sidling up next to her. Handsome enough, around her age, maybe older. Dressed well in a neat tuxedo with a Rolex wrapped around his wrist.

"Oh, no thank you," Mei replied, turning her attention back to her phone.

The man continued to linger around the bar, his eyes fixed on Mei. Exasperated, Mei gave him her attention again with an impatient stare. Undeterred, he smiled. "Are you waiting for someone?"

Mei, like every other woman, was trained in the art of shooing away persistent men. No foolproof method, of course, but a few statistically more successful ones. "Yes, I'm waiting for my husband." She lied easily, using her left hand to take a sip of her gin.

His eyes darted down to her hand, her ring, and raised his drink at her. "Ah. Well, lucky guy. Have a good evening."

Mei turned to watch him go and spotted Morgan only a foot or so behind her, standing ramrod straight.

"Sorry I'm late."

Sliding off her stool, Mei adjusted her dress and took a moment to appreciate Morgan's outfit. Deep emerald-green ankle-length slacks and blazer hugged her body, with a neatly pressed white button-down shirt and matching green tie, and gleaming black loafers on her feet. This was partly why Mei didn't protest too much at Morgan's insistence on a fancy dinner—she loved to see her dressed up.

"Our table is ready," she said before Mei could greet her. Although it wasn't offered, Mei took Morgan's hand as the waiter escorted them to their table. Fresh white linens lay draped over the table, topped with a vase stuffed with dainty flowers and a jar encasing a gently flickering candle. Next to their table a line of open windows gave an unobstructed view of the lake, shimmering with the light of reflected stars, like a cache of loose diamonds on a black velvet cushion.

Settled in their seats and drinks ordered, something strange lurked in Morgan's expression. "Lots of traffic. Hope you weren't waiting long."

"No, no." Mei smiled to relieve a tension she hoped she imagined. Morgan attempted half a smile but it didn't quite reach her eyes. Even with her attention turned to the menu, uneasiness emanated from her. "Are you okay?"

"I'm good," Morgan stated, and every syllable rang with untruth. One of Morgan's many wonderful qualities was her inability to tell a convincing lie. She could put on an act at work if necessary, but otherwise she was an open book. "I'm just a little tired."

A public restaurant was not the place to hash out whatever bothered Morgan, so she took it at face value and returned her attention to the menu. "If you want to go home, I'm more than willing to skip the dinner and have a night in."

"No, this is fine." It didn't look or sound fine, but Mei respected her privacy enough not to pry. At least for now.

The rest of their evening went smoothly, if a little stilted. Morgan's usual warmth was tempered and Mei felt its absence acutely, like a cozy home with an unexplained draft. When Morgan shockingly declined a massive dessert menu and settled their tab, her supposed lethargy became less likely. Irritation colored her posture as she tailed Mei to the car, eyes staring directly down at the ground and her hands jammed in her pockets, fidgeting.

Next to Mei's driver-side door, Morgan exhaled sharply. "Listen, I'm going to go home and turn in. I have an early meeting tomorrow."

"Oh. That's all right. There are other nights." She reached out, touching Morgan's wrist above her pocket. "You can talk to me, you know. If something is troubling you, I'm here."

Morgan backed away from her touch and Mei's chest hurt. "Thanks, but I'm fine. I'll see you tomorrow." Taking a half step forward, Morgan kissed her on the cheek and turned away quickly, stalking toward her car. Paralyzed by the atypical behavior, Mei stood rooted in place as Morgan's car roared to life and she abruptly sped out of the parking lot.

Windows down and radio on, Mei sat in her car and let the breeze off the lake chill her skin. She could go home, draw a bath, have a glass of wine, and let Morgan work through whatever upset her. But her instincts knew better. If something else upset Morgan, she'd have told Mei. Whatever the root of Morgan's unhappiness, it had to do with Mei. She wasn't totally oblivious—an unknown discontent had gnawed at Morgan for months now. The only thing Mei noticed was Morgan's subtle preference for staying at her own apartment as opposed to Mei's house. Otherwise, their relationship remained the same: loving and fun.

For the better part of an hour, Mei loitered in the parking lot, gaining and losing the courage to drive to Morgan's. If she went home, she wouldn't sleep. She'd been like this with Allan too, unable to go to bed angry or upset. On the rare occasion they had a disagreement or the even rarer occasion Allan was in a bad mood, Mei would force him to stay up with her and talk through it. Maybe it had something to do with early childhood memories of sitting on a cot in a one-bedroom apartment hearing her parents quietly, but fiercely, spit venom at each other in another room. Maybe the scientist in her needed to work a problem through to a solution. Whatever the motivation, the answer would not come if Mei didn't do anything. So, she drove.

Morgan's apartment was dark, save for the standing lamp in her living room; the amber glow of it illuminated the drawn curtains on her front windows. Knocks on her door went unanswered, so Mei rang the doorbell and patiently lingered at her front door. When Morgan finally answered, Mei nearly gasped aloud. Bloodshot, puffy eyes, rimmed red from crying, regarded her with suspicion. In her free hand she gripped an open bottle of what smelled like strong whiskey. "What are you doing here?"

Not the welcome she expected, and Mei stuttered before replying. "There's obviously something wrong, and it must have to do with me since you're unwilling to talk about it. That's not acceptable. I want to talk about it, whatever it is."

Morgan snorted in a sneering amusement and Mei's jaw opened. It was…it was *mean*. Morgan was never mean. "Sure." Leaving the door ajar, Morgan deserted her and skulked back into her house.

Following her in, Mei closed the door behind her and kicked off her heels. Morgan sat on her living room chair, slouched, nursing the whiskey bottle. She'd removed her suit jacket and shoes, tie loosened around her neck.

Cautiously, Mei walked to her side and sat down on the couch. "Please, darling, tell me what's wrong."

Putting the bottle down, Morgan wiped her lips and locked eyes with Mei. Her heart squeezed in her chest to see the pain written across her face. Pain, and anger. "You told the man at the bar you were waiting for your husband."

Taken aback, Mei folded her hands in her lap. "I did, yes. It—it's what I tell men so they'll stop bothering me. Telling them I'm married usually works without me having to repeat myself."

Morgan laughed, but it wasn't a real laugh. It came out ugly and rude, and Mei shrank back. "Yeah, oh, I know. Despite how exceptionally homosexual I look to anyone with a brain, men make that mistake with me too." She grabbed the bottle and took a more aggressive swig of it. "But the thing is, I'll say I'm married, or that I'm waiting for my girlfriend, or my partner, or sometimes my wife, if they're persistent. But I don't"—she hiccuped—"I don't pretend to be straight."

Aggression rolled off Morgan in waves as she shot up from her seat, pacing the floor. For the first time, Morgan elicited fear in her heart. "Is that what you think I did? That's why you're upset?"

"Is that what I *think* you did? Or is that what you did?" Morgan asked, tilting her head. "You didn't have to say husband, but you did. Words matter."

"I could have said husband and still been bisexual," Mei replied, raising an eyebrow.

"But you don't have a husband, Mei! You have a girlfriend. You have a partner. You have me, but you didn't think of me, did you? You thought of him." Terror took root in Mei as Morgan waved the bottle around. "And that's emblematic of the real issue. The real issue is you've been one foot out of this since we started dating. And I—I ignore it because I'm crazy about you, but I can't anymore. It's been a year and I *can't* anymore."

Mei's heart battered against her rib cage. "I don't understand. I've been—I love you. I'm…I'm in this with you. I'm out, I told my kids, I don't see—"

"No, of course you don't." Morgan slammed the bottle down on the coffee table and startled Mei in her seat. "You know why you think you're 'in this with me'? Because I let you in. Into my home, into my heart, into my life. But in your life, Mei, where am I? You've never invited me to keep my things at your house. You don't have a single photo of me anywhere, not even on your phone. You didn't defend me to Grace. And look, all of that? I can get over it. But to hear you erase me to a complete stranger? I'll put it this way: my mother shot herself in the fucking head to get away from me, and this hurts more."

Inwardly, Mei winced, but she maintained her composure. It was one of her few remaining possessions. "I'm so sorry, darling. I never meant to hurt your feelings. I see how thoughtless my actions have been, and I promise you I can do better."

"Can you? Because I can't." Mei blinked in surprise. "I love you with all that I am, and it's never enough because in your head, and in your heart, you're still married to him."

Her accusation hit Mei like an open-palm slap. "That's not true."

"Isn't it? You still wear your ring," Morgan accused, pointing in her direction. "You brew his coffee like you're expecting him to wake up next to you and what am I supposed to do with that? All I asked for, all I want, is to be in the next part of your journey. But you refuse to move forward and I don't know why. Is it guilt? Is it the gay thing? Is it the age thing? Honestly, I have tried to figure out what the fuck is wrong with me and why you won't love me."

Roughly wiping her eyes with her forearm, Morgan continued to pace. All of this animosity at once was like getting gagged with a chloroform rag of her stupidity. That's what had built for months—her refusal to replace Allan's presence in her life with Morgan. However, Mei resented the implication she did it intentionally. "I do love you. I didn't know you were upset I wear my ring. You never mentioned it."

"For god's sake, it's not the fucking ring, Mei," Morgan shouted, voice cracking. "You won't make space for me. I try and I try to make myself as small as possible, but I don't fit. Not in your home, or in your heart. The former I can accept; homes have never been reliable for me, anyway. But the latter? That kills me."

"I don't want to keep hurting you, but it's not as if I can throw away thirty years of marriage."

"You know that isn't what I want." Morgan exasperatedly tossed her hands in the air. "I want you to love me wholly, not just the fragmented pieces of you that aren't buried with him."

"Maybe I can't do that," Mei choked out. Morgan clamped her mouth shut, eyes watering. "Maybe I don't know how, okay? Maybe I'm...maybe I'm scared."

"Scared of what?"

"Of what we will become."

"What the hell is that supposed to mean?"

"You have no idea," Mei replied, inhaling a deep, shaky breath. "You have no idea what it's like to lose someone you were supposed to spend your life with and have to start over. But you will. You will learn that because I'm twenty years older than you. Twenty years! I'm ten years away from retirement and your career is rising. You'll be solving crimes and earning promotions and I will be home, doddering over my puzzles. Not to mention I'm overdue to hit menopause. And what then? What then, when I can no longer keep up with you, physically or sexually? I'm going to get old and sick, and you'll be stuck taking care of an invalid while still in your prime. You'll hate me and resent me for it."

"That won't happen," Morgan dismissed, crossing her arms.

Scoffing, Mei wiped the tears streaming down her face. "No? You think the alternative is better? Because the alternative is that we are happy, we are content, and one day I die and leave you here alone. You'll be sad and angry and hurt and so, so lost. And I won't be here to help you make sense of the world without me." Breathing in a shuddering breath, Mei implored her. "Don't you see how I can't do that to you?"

Morgan stopped pacing. Turning slowly, her jaw slipped open. Devastated didn't begin to cover it; her eyes conveyed an open, raw sadness that could only be described as ruination. "You don't want to put me through what Allan put you through, so instead you break my fucking heart. Make me miserable now, so I'm not miserable later. Nobody can say you're not efficient."

Lip quivering, Mei quietly added, "To watch the person you love most in this world die, it is an indescribable pain."

"Oh, I am very familiar with pain," Morgan said, her voice hot and wet. "Everyone who has ever loved me has left me. Over and over, they get close and they leave. Why? What's so wrong with me, huh? Why doesn't anyone stay?" Choking out a sob, Morgan stared down at the ground in defeat and asked in a small, anguished voice, "Why doesn't anyone want to keep me?"

Returning to her chair, Morgan buried her face in her hands, stifling sobs into her palms. Numbness seeped into Mei's blood, spreading up from her toes to her heart. A feeling reminiscent of years ago, staring down at Allan as the machine keeping him alive droned out a long tone. An emotion so great, so enormous it became incomprehensible, like trying to fathom the size of the universe.

"Morgan, please. I only want what's best for you."

"No, no, no, fuck you," Morgan snapped, ripping her face away from her hands. Mei gasped, holding back tears in the face of Morgan's anger. Using both hands, Morgan aggressively massaged her temples, wincing. "You don't get to say what's best for me. You don't get to say what I want. Because what I want is to spend my whole life with you. And I'm such a fucking idiot for thinking that's what you want, when all you want from me is an out."

From within her pants pocket, Morgan withdrew a small box and tossed it on the table. Mei didn't have to open it to know what waited inside. Pocket-sized, round, velvet. A ring box. "So go ahead. Have some courage for once in your life and take your out."

Picking up the bottle from the table, Morgan stormed into her bedroom. The subsequent slam startled Mei and shook a photo frame off the shelf with a clatter. In shock, Mei stood in the center of the living room, unable to move, staring down at the ring box. At a proposal that never was, that never would be. Without much control over it, her body managed to get to the front door, put on her shoes, and walk out into the night. The drive came to her automatically; she didn't remember making a turn or pulling into her driveway.

Once home in her bedroom, staring at a sweatshirt Morgan left, she allowed devastation to overcome her. Holding the sweatshirt against her chest, she collapsed sideways on the bed and let the tears fall freely. *It was the right thing to do*, a voice in her brain screamed. *It was right. It was right. It was right.*

If you have to tell yourself you're doing the right thing that many times, chances are you're not.

CHAPTER EIGHTEEN

It came as three revelations.

The first arrived, as many do, while under duress. Brokenhearted and numb, Mei parked herself in front of her fireplace and peered into its sooty depths for several nights in a row. The longer she observed, the more she developed a strange affinity for the chimney. She, too, existed as a cold, hard shell requiring others' passion to keep warm.

That's false, a voice whispered to her, sounding suspiciously like Morgan. *You just don't let anyone close enough to feel your warmth.*

She resented the Morgan voice in her head. Optimistic and encouraging, willfully ignorant of Mei's desire to be self-deprecatingly pathetic. It did, however, illuminate a rather obvious conclusion, the first revelation: Mei needed Morgan, and she committed herself to making that happen.

The first revelation begot the second: she had to go to therapy.

On the scale of eschewing cultural traditions, marrying a white man and coming out as queer did not rank as highly as admitting she needed help. The stigma around mental illness and the unfair insinuation of brokenness prevented her from seeking therapy when she endured post-partum depression after Grace's birth and again when reeling from the loss of her husband. It would be disrespectful to her parents, she reasoned by way of deeply entrenched ideals, and it would bring shame to her family. What type of weak-willed person can't handle two of the most ubiquitous of human experiences—birth and death?

However, directly through Morgan, Mei understood weakness and vulnerability as a strength all their own. Her attentive ear and singular ability to open Mei up sparked the realization her trauma grew lighter when shared. Morgan was not a therapist, of course, and so while she received and validated Mei's feelings, she was not the place for Mei to unload the emotions and memories she'd used as weights to drown herself.

Armed with preconceived notions of bonded leather chaises and disinterested Freudian kooks, Mei entered into therapy brimming with skepticism. However, instead of lounging and interpreting dreams, Mei stared down the barrel of the hardest work of her life. For two hours twice a week, she emptied her soul. Easy hours sailed by, chatting about her past and parsing through her relationship with her mother and the relationship she didn't have with her father. Other days stalled, cutting through the tangled vines of grief, guilt, and fear that bound and squeezed her. The inability to recognize she deserved another chance at love, the chance denied to Allan.

Her therapist encouraged her to return to the group grief meetings. Working through grief, she'd told Mei, was much like climbing a mountain: much easier in a group.

She didn't want to. Everything about the meetings reminded her of falling in love with Morgan. Witnessing the chipper detective shed her layers and present to Mei the tender, damaged woman beneath. The stunning moment of realizing this woman, of all the billions of people inhabiting the planet, saw directly into her soul.

Tonight, that woman was somewhere else and Mei stared across the semicircle at an empty folding chair. Its unironic symbolism of the gaping hole in her life did not amuse her in the slightest. Morgan's continued absence also did not amuse the seniors, whose icy glares she fended off as Sister Laura navigated the meeting. Mei had not come to share—only Morgan made her comfortable enough to display her feelings in public—but rather to listen to the others. Their candor and naked truths pulled Mei out of her own head after weeks of individual therapy.

After most of the members shuffled out, Mei timidly approached Sister Laura. "Dr. Sharpe," she greeted warmly. "Glad to see you back. Can I do something for you?"

"I think so, I..." Mei turned her cheek, embarrassed. "I was hoping to speak to you for a little bit, privately, if you didn't mind."

She smiled. "Of course. Help me get these tables tucked away and then we can talk."

Chatting idly, Mei assisted Sister Laura in breaking down folding tables and packing up the extra goodies. The appearance of dessert made her miss Morgan; she recalled with painful accuracy how her lovely eyes lit up at the sight of any treat and the unfiltered joy she derived from something as simple as sugar.

Once they safely tucked away the tables and chairs into the school's musty closets, Sister Laura escorted Mei outside toward a spectator's bench near the soccer field. They sat together in companionable quiet as Mei attempted to organize her thoughts. Sister Laura inquired softly, "I can do you a favor and assume you want to talk about Morgan. Is that right?"

"Ah, sort of," Mei replied, wringing her hands together. "I've been seeing a therapist since, um, since Morgan and I broke up. One of the reasons for that is because part of our breakup included my fear of doing to her what happened to me when Allan died."

"And what happened to you when Allan died?"

"Well, I—I was heartbroken. I was lost." Impatient with herself, Mei sighed. "My life has been a series of planned events. Despite my attraction to two rather eccentric souls, I prefer order and predictability. But Allan's death took me completely by surprise. I never admitted it to him, or anyone else for that matter, but I didn't believe the cancer would kill him. He was so strong and so vital, I thought surely he'd recover. Nobody loved life like Allan...if anyone deserved the chance to survive the odds, he did. But, obviously, he didn't make it, and the entropy overwhelmed me to the point that I think I ignored it entirely. How can I put someone else through that? Especially someone who has already dealt with such enormous loss?"

Bright spotlights on the wrong schedule shone down on the damp grass, giving it a backlit sheen like a white-hot field of fire. Beside her, Sister Laura shifted to face Mei. "I don't mean to be presumptuous, but is it possible this is not about saving Morgan from some terrible fate, but about your disbelief you're worth taking that risk for?"

Mei blinked hard, caught somewhere between indignity and embarrassment. "I suppose."

"Based upon what you've shared with us in our meetings, I believe part of your struggle with grief is survivor's guilt. You believe Allan relished life and he deserved to live, but you don't deserve the same. I can see why that would cause problems in your relationship, especially with someone who believes in you more than you do."

"She did believe in me, and I broke her heart so she could move on," Mei admitted. "She was already angry at me for a host of other reasons, and it seemed easier to just...leave."

Running her fingers through her hair, Sister Laura let out a short noise that was both a snicker and a snort. "This seemed easier? How challenging the rest of your life must be for this to seem easier."

"Easier than spending many happy years together, only for her to watch me die," she replied. "This is—she'll get over me. She'll move on to someone younger, someone who can provide more healthy years, someone who isn't a coward. She'll be fine." Inside her mind she watched a flashback of herself on Morgan's lap, confessing how much she wanted her. How earnestly Morgan told her she never stood a chance of getting over Mei. She wondered if that was still true. "She'll be fine."

"And you? You'll get over her?"

No use in evading the truth. "No, I don't think so."

Sister Laura ingested the information with a sage nod and thoughtful pause. "You know, a lot of our talks here revolve around grief, obviously. Many who come have recently lost someone close to them and the grief is still new. It affects everything they do, like a drop of black ink in a bucket of white paint. But when Morgan started coming to these meetings, her grief was old. Her mother died two decades ago, and while Morgan continued processing her grief to some extent, it was not central to her struggle. And I think for you it's similar. It isn't about the grief, it is about the after. The void that exists between the death of the person you love and the moment you move on with your life." Placing her palms on her thighs, Sister Laura leaned in. "The real kicker is people are not afraid of the void. They like the void. They're comfortable in the void. It's leaving the void that scares them, it's the moving on that scares them. The realization you've left the comfort of the void and your heart is open again. Love, my dear, is scarier than death."

"Love is..." Drawing her brows together, Mei stared at Sister Laura. Unassuming, with her thin smile and a twinkle in her eye, but good lord. Like a miner with a sharp pickaxe, she got right to the heart of the matter. "Do you know how much my therapy costs and you said that for free? God, you're good."

"Me? I got that from you." Off Mei's perplexed look, Sister Laura elaborated. "'The normalcy is frightening' is what you said your first night here. That stuck with me for a while as I ruminated on Morgan's thoughts about living with the void. She perceived the void as the absence of her mother, but I believe the void to be the absence of grief. When you find something to pull you from the void—love, or whatever else it may be—the normalcy can indeed be frightening."

This all sounded very logical, but the same question remained. "So, what do I do?"

"It isn't my place to tell you how to proceed; only you and God know the path forward from here." Sister Laura flicked her eyes upward to the stars she believed held the secrets of the heavens. Mei envied her the comfort she took believing in this benign watchful eye. "But out of all the fears to face in the world, I can't think of a more joyous or rewarding one than love."

In direct opposition to facing her fear, her therapist advised avoiding Morgan for a while longer. The easiest of all tasks as Mei literally never saw her. Dorothy arrived in the lot before Mei and remained long after she left. She even waited in her car one night to catch a glimpse of her, but by nine o'clock the waiting verged on stalking and she gave up before it got excessively pathetic. Only once, during a drive by her house around midnight sometime in July, did Mei spot a lone blue light coming from Morgan's home, flickering against the walls. Mei told her therapist how helpless it made her feel. How she longed to be in that room cuddled close to her. She wanted her heart close to Morgan's heart. She wanted to feel her breath against her skin. She wanted to be the port in a storm. It broke her heart all over again to think of Morgan by herself in her apartment, feeling abandoned and unloved.

She would not consider the idea that Morgan wasn't alone.

In August, when the dog days of summer peaked and the sun stubbornly refused to set, Morgan's car was absent in the lot for nearly a week. By Thursday Mei grew worried and decided it was perfectly acceptable to check on her. With Morgan's car pulled deep into her driveway, the truck parked near the curb intrigued her. Disregarding the excellent advice of her therapist, Mei slowly walked to the door. All five of her senses yearned for Morgan with a longing she had never felt, a longing she thought no one should ever feel. The kind of ache that cracks fissures in your heart and leaves it perpetually on the verge of implosion.

Using the lights on inside as an invitation, Mei knocked on the door, her chest filling with hope and anticipation. The belly swoops.

Ruiz opened the door wearing a loose, slouchy black T-shirt, low-slung dark blue jeans, and the coldest expression Mei had ever been on the receiving end of. "Dr. Sharpe."

"Hello, Ruiz," Mei greeted sheepishly. Surely by now Morgan disseminated the tale of how Mei broke her heart, and any good will she'd earned with Morgan's best friend had evaporated. "I—"

"Kelly's not home," Ruiz interrupted in short tones.

"I know," Mei replied, and Ruiz raised her eyebrow. "I wanted to make sure she's okay. I noticed she wasn't at work this week, and I got worried."

Ruiz scoffed at her and shifted her gaze to the door, fingers gripped around the edge in anticipation of slamming it. But Mei's desperation and pitiful resignation seemed to prompt Ruiz to step back instead, gesturing with her head. "Come in."

Entering the apartment proper flooded her with memories, triggered by the scent of Morgan hanging in the air. Her apartment was usually filled with the sound of music or the din of her television, as well as Morgan's jovial presence, which made it feel like home. Now, a surreal sense of nonexistence unsettled Mei. A sudden onset of déjà vu stopped her, and she struggled to pinpoint the memory. She gazed around at Morgan's belongings, for the most part neatly organized, and it hit Mei like a bullet: coming home after Allan's funeral. Realizing he no longer lived in the house even though his cologne hung in the air and his smile beamed at her from every photo on the wall. A similar sense of loss carved into her, despite Morgan's continued corporeal existence.

Ruiz led her to the kitchen where Reyna was in the midst of misting Morgan's plants. In lieu of a dog, which is what Morgan truly wanted, Mei bought her a harem of plants she tried to keep alive. The little thicket of starter succulents basked in the sunlight on the windowsill above her sink. Reyna turned, giving Mei a sympathetic smile. "Hi, Mei."

"Hello." Reyna watched her wife walk into the room with peculiarly careful observation. Mei followed her line of sight to the round protrusion of Ruiz's belly over the top of her cinched belt. On the edge of her emotions for weeks, Mei nearly burst into tears at this revelation. "Are you two expecting?"

Finally, a smile broke on Ruiz's face as she nodded, wrapping her arm around Reyna's waist. "Yeah. I'm three months."

"That's wonderful. Congratulations."

"Thank you. How have you been?" Reyna asked, sitting down at the kitchen table and motioning for Mei to sit as well.

"Not great," Mei replied with a wet laugh. "I'm sure it's no surprise to you two, but I feel like I made a huge mistake."

"You think?" Ruiz didn't sit, instead crossing her arms and casually slinging one leg in front of the other as if interrogating a perp. "No offense, but why are you here?"

"I honestly don't know. My therapist tells me I should keep my distance, but I miss her so much. She hasn't answered any of my calls or texts, which, you know, makes sense and she shouldn't. But I do want to know how she's doing."

Emotion creeping up on her face, Ruiz glanced away. Bearing or witnessing Morgan's pain deeply afflicted Ruiz, Mei knew, though Ruiz was loath to express it openly. They possessed a truly profound bond. "How do you think she's doing? She's busted."

"Right. Of course."

The tension in Ruiz's body gave away the anger she hid in favor of stilted civility. "So, I'll ask you again: why are you here?"

No way Mei could slip out of this interrogation. "I'm normally not this selfish, but I wanted to see her. I want to talk to her, to apologize. Basically, I'd like to beg her to take me back."

"Oh, that's all? Why didn't you say so? Let me call her up and—" Ruiz cut herself off and leveled a withering look in Mei's direction. "She'd be the kinda idiot to say yes, too, and you know that."

"You have to understand," Reyna began, reaching across the table, "Morgan has a lot of abandonment issues."

"I know."

"Do you?" Ruiz cocked an eyebrow and stomped off into the other room. Upon her return, she dropped Morgan's mother's case file on the table in front of Mei. "Have you ever looked at this?"

Mei grimaced at the file like an unappetizing meal. "No. It didn't seem like Morgan wanted me to."

"No, probably not," Ruiz replied. "I'm sure she's told you the same tale about her mother's death being a murder."

She stared at Ruiz quizzically, unsure of where this was going. "Yes. At first she told me it was a murder, but when... another time she inadvertently revealed to me it was not."

"Yeah." Ruiz's anger dropped, shoulders sagging. "She's never opened up to me about it, and trust me, I've tried."

"We've always felt that if Morgan could open up about what her mother did, about her childhood in general, she might be capable of healthier relationships," Reyna said.

"So, a couple years ago, when Morgan went away on one of her Christmas vacations, I took the case file and asked Cap if I could look into the case. Unofficially. I did, and...Look, I was thorough. I looked at every angle. I investigated it like Kelly would've done. Like I'm sure she did, even though she's never admitted it. Nobody murdered her, that's for sure. And whatever Kelly told you about her childhood, the reality is much, much worse."

Digging into the box, Ruiz pulled out the coroner's report and laid it in front of Mei. It felt like a violation of Morgan's privacy, but Mei's professional curiosity got the best of her. Only a few pages to skim; clear suicides never have thick folders. No bruising, no defensive wounds, nothing but an exit wound through the top of the skull. The toxicology revealed a cocktail of hard drugs in her system—remarkable, in fact, that it hadn't killed Charlotte before the gun did.

However, Ruiz's perception of the case matched the coroner's findings. Self-inflicted gunshot wound to the head. Blood and gunshot residue on the right hand. Rigor mortis set in, curling the hand permanently around a trigger. A suicide as clear as day.

"The tales Kelly tells about her mother and the cold facts about her childhood rarely line up. All over these files is evidence of her mother abandoning and abusing her. Charlotte was heavy into drugs and alcohol. A working drug addict, but a user. Kelly's *vago* father is one of Charlotte's many dealers-turned-boyfriends. She only stopped the drugs during her pregnancy. After that? Right back on the horse."

All of this information stood incongruent with Morgan's stories of a doting mother. Those long Sundays Morgan walked alone in the museum were colored differently now, less an impromptu education and more blatant abandonment. Mei spared a glance at the dinosaur magnet on Morgan's fridge, which used to hold up a photo of them. Now only the magnet hung askew. "Oh my god."

"They were in and out of trailer parks, halfway houses. For a while they lived at the battered women's shelter here in the city. Every so often her mom would date some *puto* and he'd put them up until Charlotte either broke up with him or swindled him and they'd have to leave. Many of the volunteers at the battered women's shelter suspected her mother physically abused her. God only knows what other kinds of abuse she suffered."

All the scars, Mei remembered. The dark round spots that looked like burns, faint brown lines of old cuts and scrapes. No wonder Morgan could never move on from her mother's death. Charlotte was painted all over her.

"And then just like that—boom—her mother domes herself. Leaves her brains blown out everywhere for her fifteen-year-old daughter to find." Eyes glossy, Ruiz sniffed and shook her head. "She took and took and gave Kelly nothing."

Reyna wiped the tears falling from her eyes. "Morgan's built a big house of lies to keep herself from accepting the fact that her mother willingly left her."

The walls of that house came tumbling down behind her, and Mei glanced into the room at the former scene of their ugly confrontation. As clear as day she could see Morgan's anguished eyes, the rage and desolation battling inside her. *I'll put it this way: my mother shot herself in the fucking head to get away from me, and this hurts more.* Mei shuddered.

"Haven't you ever thought it's weird how she keeps her stuff in boxes?" Ruiz gestured around the room. Certainly it looked lived in, but despite having lived there many years several items remained packed, as well as moving boxes leaning next to a closet door. "She's never had a real home."

"Our point being, you need to be careful. Morgan has a lot of issues to work through before she can get into something romantic again," Reyna explained softly.

"But I'm worried about her," Ruiz murmured. "She drinks a lot, and considering both her parents were addicts I worry she's going down the same path. She has all this anger bottled up she's never fully expressed. Instead of taking it out on someone else like her mother did to her, she keeps it inside and takes it out on herself."

"Well, where is she now?" Mei asked, feeling impatient.

"DC. She's at a conference and going to interview for a position with the FBI."

Agape, Mei politely closed her mouth to not look as dumbstruck as she felt. "She's…she never told me about that. I—I'm going there tomorrow for the conference as well."

"Yeah, it's one big law enforcement lovefest." Ruiz rolled her eyes. "She got headhunted again a couple weeks ago. It would be a big step up for her—"

"We don't want her to go," Reyna lamented, peering up at Ruiz. The sergeant attempted to stay neutral, but ultimately nodded in agreement. "Not to stand in the way of her career, but without any of the support she's built here—us, you, even her father and his family—we worry about the kinds of self-destructive behavior she'll get up to. We want her to be safe."

"So, if you happen to see her," Ruiz began with an air of nonchalance, "at the Washington Hilton on Connecticut, Room 402, you could talk to her. I know she wants to see you because I told her to text me or call me when she has the urge to contact you, and she texts and calls me *constantly*. But talk only, okay? No asking to get back together, no makeup sex, none of that. Kelly is one of the strongest people I know, but she's weak right now, and she is especially weak for you. So you need to be strong for her, okay? *¿Comprende?*"

Standing from her chair, Mei nodded. Though not exactly the conversation she hoped to have, it did give her a bit of confidence to know Ruiz didn't want her to fall off the face of the earth. They walked to the door together and Mei couldn't help but steal another look at Ruiz's tiny baby bump. "I'm thrilled for you both. I bet Morgan is beside herself."

"I haven't told her yet. I didn't want it to affect her decision to take the job or not. Don't tell her when you see her, please."

"I won't." Mei rubbed her forehead. "How do you know what room she's staying in?"

"I found the booking," Ruiz admitted, slightly embarrassed. "I thought about flying out myself to make sure she didn't do anything reckless. She's in a dark place, Mei. I only saw her like this once before, when she discovered her partner was a dirty cop. She is…hard to reach."

A chill trickled down Mei's spine, recalling the mean, sneering Morgan whose heart she broke in their last fight. "Do you think it's a good idea for me to see her?"

"Do I think it's a 'good idea'? No, I don't. But I also know it doesn't matter. You are gonna end up seeing each other again eventually, so the when and where of it is pointless."

"And you—you don't think it's too late? Or that I don't deserve her because I broke her heart?"

"I'm not gonna give you shit so you can feel better." Ruiz reclined against the door. "If you were anyone else, I'd have slammed the door in your face and made damn sure you never saw her again. But you and Kel—you and Morgan, you've got an inevitable kind of love. The kind of love you can't hide from. The kind of love that isn't easy, but worth the work. So, no, it's not too late, because that kind of love waits."

CHAPTER NINETEEN

Cop conferences were like frat parties—Morgan hated them and they smelled bad. Lots of mostly white men carousing around, talking shit about their wives and boasting collars over the din of salesmen selling ridiculous SWAT gear nobody outside of a warzone could use. However, the date of this conference coincided with her job interview, so Morgan took Corporal Gilland with her and they flew to Washington DC to suffer together.

Interviews didn't faze Morgan at all; she excelled in the personal, the one-on-one, and enjoyed her work enough to want to talk about it. Plus, she'd been specifically headhunted by the director to join the program. Her interviewer, the director herself, was a woman in her late forties, with smoke-gray hair with a single stripe of black near her crown, and eyes so brown they were almost black. Stern and intelligent, she grilled Morgan on her credentials and her interest in the program. It reminded her so much of Mei she almost threw up on the desk. Lots of older, attractive women attended the conference—her type, according to Ruiz—but Morgan couldn't scrounge up interest if she tried. Since breaking up with Mei, her romantic desires vanished overnight. In fact, most of her desires vanished. She didn't go on runs in the morning, or get a treat at the café. Most days she forgot to eat at all. But, she showed up to work at the crack of dawn, drowned in cases until nearly midnight, then drank herself to sleep. It left no time for romance or friendship, or anything requiring her heart.

People noticed. So, she saw people less. Only Gilland knew about Mei, so Morgan kept up the pretense of detached professionalism with Polzar and Daniels. Her lack of enthusiasm surely didn't go unnoticed, but as their boss, it did go unquestioned. At least, to her face. Ruiz and Reyna proved more difficult to avoid. She kept in contact via text, using Ruiz as her sounding board when she got the urge to talk to Mei. This kept them off her back generally, until a particularly bad night in late July. Within minutes of making a desperate call to Ruiz, she nearly broke down Morgan's door and didn't leave until Morgan agreed to see a therapist.

A long road lay ahead, but at least she was on it.

With her interview over, Morgan spent the rest of the conference in and out of different panels. Her captain urged her to take meetings with anyone who asked—hobnobbing, as it were. Morgan hated hobnobbing. Schmoozing wasn't in her nature. But, this was a dream job. Not only would it be away from the sheriff's office and local law enforcement in general, but also she could make a difference on a large scale. With field offices all over the country, she'd have her pick from well over a dozen locations to live and work out of. The locations spread out far and wide, but one of them was close to home. *Home.* Morgan snorted. As if she ever had one.

With their next panel not until late afternoon, she and Gilland met at a local pub for lunch, and to exchange panel information. While Gilland nibbled on a club sandwich, Morgan drank her tall beer and signaled the waitress for another.

"So, what's next?" Morgan asked, tapping the schedule on the table between them.

Gilland eyed her drink. "Did you even eat breakfast? And you're chugging down a liquid lunch?"

"Sorry, Mom," Morgan replied, rolling her eyes. "I'm not hungry."

Disbelieving and wary, Gilland eyed her for a long moment, but Morgan offered nothing. Sighing, she returned her attention to the schedule. "Back-to-back panels on racial bias."

"Surprise, surprise. They'd need several weeks' worth of panels to undo all of this white machismo," Morgan said, nodding to a table not far from theirs populated with six bald dudes. "Okay. Well, we should at least go to one. Anything else look good?"

As Morgan looked back to her own table, Gilland quickly turned her phone screen off and pretended to be engrossed in her sandwich. "Not really. After those panels we're pretty clear."

Morgan narrowed her eyes. "Who were you texting?"

Gilland placed her sandwich back on the plate. "I don't think as my boss you're allowed to interrogate me on my texting habits, Lieutenant."

"We're on the clock, Corporal."

"We're technically on lunch?" When Morgan didn't let up, Gilland sighed. "Sergeant Ruiz asked me to keep in touch and make sure you were okay. And I know, I know, you're a grown woman and you can make your own choices, but you're making really shitty ones and all your friends are worried about you."

"Yes, all of my one friend is extremely concerned," Morgan shot back. "Two, I guess."

"Three," Gilland replied softly. Mid-sip, Morgan put her drink down and released some of the tension in her body. "We're coworkers, I understand. And I know you're here for a job interview and there's almost zero chance you don't get it. But, I care about you too. I think a lot more people give a shit about you than you think. And look, these past few months have been really hard on you and I get that. Love sucks. It's why I don't bother with it."

This made Morgan chuckle, dropping her gaze to her lap. "Sounds like the right idea."

"For me? Definitely. But for you? Absolutely not." Peering up, Morgan found Gilland's normally pinched features gazing at her openly. "This isn't you. You love love, Lieutenant. You're a complete sap, there's no two ways about it."

"Geez, c'mon, kicking me when I'm down?"

"These are not insults, these are facts. You're a loving person who enjoys loving others. It's part of what makes you an excellent detective. You just…get people. And people are so drawn to you, you don't even see it." Gilland sat up straight. "Everywhere you go, you leave a place better than you found it. I'm sure that's fucking exhausting and I do think you deserve a break once in a while. But not like this. You're too good for this."

Firmly put into her place, Morgan sat back and folded her hands in her lap. "Was 'reading me the riot act' on the schedule?"

Gilland smiled. "No, but I can pencil it in."

"That's all right, you've made your point." Breathing out hard, Morgan screwed her eyes shut and attempted to ingest what Gilland told her. She was right about all of it, annoyingly enough. Keeping these walls up exhausted her. The waitress arrived with her beer, setting it down gently on the table. "Sorry, miss, would you mind taking this back? I'll pay for it. In fact, I'd love to buy a round for the staff, if that's possible. And instead, may I have one of those amazing fig and goat cheese flatbread pizzas?"

Perplexed but compliant, the waitress shrugged. "Yeah, sure. Can I get you something else to drink?"

"A water would be amazing, thank you." Morgan paused. "Is the blue-raspberry lemonade only for children?"

The waitress laughed, shaking her head. "I'm sure I can sneak one out for you."

"You're a legend," Morgan replied, grinning back. As the waitress left with the beer, Gilland gave her a nudge under the table. "I'll try not to be so sad all the time. I just miss her."

"Well," Gilland started, turning the schedule around and pushing it toward Morgan. "She is doing a panel at four."

And there it was, in plain black ink on soft white paper: DR. MEI SHARPE—THE EVOLVING SCIENCE REGARDING TIME OF DEATH ANALYSIS

"Anyway, I'm not saying storm into that panel in some gross romantic gesture. However, if you wanted to see her? Maybe… test the waters of how it makes you feel? Could be worth it."

"Plus, this panel is sure to be the best one of them all," Morgan replied, shrugging. "Worth it just for the knowledge, to be fair."

"Yes, dork, it's also worth it for the knowledge."

Skulking in a crowded hallway, Morgan waited until a large group of people entered the conference room before she followed suit. Taking a seat in the back, she waited with restless energy for the talk to start. The conversation around her mostly centered on other panels, but a few people spoke on their excitement for hearing Mei speak. It warmed her heart and made her proud, despite having no claim to Mei's intelligence or success. Mei deserved these accolades, even if she didn't think so.

A fellow medical examiner from Quantico introduced Mei, listing her impressive credentials and other papers Mei wrote on several key elements of forensic examination. When she walked in stage, Morgan held her breath. She looked tired. Stunning, of course, gorgeous and poised, dressed in a casual, black suit with a baby blue button-down shirt. A vibrant color for Mei, she thought affectionately, remembering her closet of neutrals. But, despite that, she looked tired. Her posture held weight to it, her voice not its usual bell-perfect tone. Who cared for her, now that Morgan could not? Who looked her in the eyes and told her to get some sleep, and really meant it?

See how it makes you feel, Gilland had said. How did she feel? Like she had an ache in her bones; like the night before you come down with the flu and just existing costs energy. Did Mei feel that way too? Did she miss Morgan in the same full-body way Morgan missed her?

Morgan had a lot of questions and none of them appropriate for the half-hour Q and A following the talk. No cool way to ask, "Hey, are you still in love with me?" in the middle of a professional conference, though the sap in her considered it.

Instead, she watched Mei hastily make for the exit with her papers tucked into a slim briefcase.

She toyed with the idea of trying to find Mei in the hallways but decided against it. Seeing Mei fatigued her, and now all she wanted to do was sink into her hotel bed and shut the world off for a while. She didn't expect all her feelings to rush back at her at once in overwhelming waves of longing and affection. But there they were, these feelings she'd buried, bursting out of their graves like malcontent zombies.

Back in her room, Morgan sunk into her pillow and conjured Mei in her mind. She imagined meeting eyes with her in the conference; would she get that look in her eyes that she used to get when spotting Morgan across the room? Like she'd finally found what she'd been searching for? Or would she be angry? Or worse, disinterested? Sniffling, Morgan let hot tears roll off her cheeks and onto the pillow, soaking into the starchy white cotton.

Morgan didn't like to cry. As a child, her mother detested her crying and would often dole out a punishment to get her to stop. When she was good, smiling and happy and nice, her mother lavished her with attention. So she internalized early on that crying got you nothing, but kindness could get you attention. And, sometimes if you were really lucky, kindness got you love.

But she deserved this cry. Suddenly, the tears became less about Mei and more about everything else. Her mother, her father, Gemma, the thought of leaving Ruiz and Reyna and moving away…misery compounding misery until she ran out of tears.

She didn't look up when the door opened and closed, just peered out of the corner of her eye. Gilland strolled in, staring down at her paper. "So that's all the panels for today. Do you want to get dinner? There's a place nearby that—" She looked up, stopping short. "Oh, shit."

"Sorry," Morgan said, rubbing her face. "I sort of started letting it all out."

"Don't let me stop you." Gilland tossed the paper on a desk in the corner. "I'll order us dinner into the room tonight. Shitty Italian or shitty Mexican? Or, halfway decent diner breakfast-for-dinner? Capital of the damn country, you'd think the dining might be better than what I used to eat in Nowheresville, Ohio."

"You're from Ohio?"

"Yeah, don't spread that around. People either hate Ohio or start talking to me about football, and in both instances I'd rather cut off my own foot," Gilland replied, perusing the takeout menus the hotel provided. "I'll try to find the least offensive cuisine."

"Thanks." Sniffling, Morgan grabbed a towel and a robe. "I'm gonna finish this cry in the shower."

"Good call."

Morgan heard a knock on the door over the sound of her shower. Dinner, she thought hopefully, and she quickly rinsed out the hotel conditioner. Wrapped in a robe, she emerged into their room, ready to pig out. But instead of finding delicious food, she found only Gilland on the floor doing push-ups in sweatpants and a loose-fitting T-shirt.

"Dang, that wasn't the food?"

"No, that was Mei."

Morgan paused. "I'm sorry, that was what?"

"Dr. Mei Sharpe."

"And you…" Swiveling her head back and forth between the door and Gilland, she nearly yelled, "And you didn't let her in?"

"She didn't want to come in!" Pushing off the floor, Gilland stood up and shrugged. "She asked where you were, I said you were in the shower. She thanked me and she left."

If not firmly attached by her optic nerve, Morgan's eyes might've shot straight across the room. "What? You answered the door looking like that, and told her I was in the shower? Oh my god."

"What?" Gilland looked at herself, trying to see what Morgan saw. "I was doing my bodyweight circuits, is that a crime?"

Shoving on her hotel-issued slippers, Morgan wrapped her robe tighter around her waist. "No, Gilland, it looks like we had sex. You're sweaty and basically in loungewear and I was in the shower."

"Ew, gross. I'm not even your type. I was born way after Desert Storm." Gilland snickered to herself until finally Morgan's unrelenting look of ire made her clamp up. "Shit, sorry. Uh, you can probably catch her? She literally just left."

"Jesus, lead with that next time!"

Sprinting out of the room, she headed straight for the elevator and smashed the button. A glance up revealed it was in the lobby, and Morgan did not have the patience to wait for this ancient elevator to rise again. Bursting through the stairwell door, Morgan padded down four flights of stairs as quickly as she could without wiping out in her slippers, which severely lacked tread.

Outside, Morgan flinched at the humid swamp heat. Near the curb stood a slender woman in a black suit with her back turned, her cocoa hair pinned up into a bun, rolling a suitcase behind her with a briefcase strapped to the top. Morgan's belly swooped.

"Hey, Mei! Wait up!" Sweating and breathing heavily, Morgan nabbed her elbow and turned her around. "Mei, hey! Uh-oh."

"Can I help you?" the woman, not Mei, asked in a clipped voice.

"Oh, geez, I'm so sorry. You looked…" Morgan withdrew her death grip on the woman's elbow. "I thought you were someone else."

"Someone else you were going to accost in your bathrobe?"

Ducking her head sheepishly, Morgan had no response as the woman huffed and turned, getting into her taxi with more haste. As the door closed and the taxi pulled away, Morgan's heart dropped. She'd missed her. Mei came to see her and they missed each other.

Then, Morgan heard her name. Looking up like a dog who'd heard a whistle, she glanced around and spotted Mei halfway in a taxi, three cars down from where she stood. "Morgan?"

"Mei!" Jogging over to her, Morgan breathlessly stopped in front of Mei and her taxi. "Hey, wait, don't go. It's not…it's not what you think."

"Morgan, you're in a robe."

"The shower is not a sex thing," she blurted out, panting.

Mei froze. "What?"

"It's not a sex thing. It's not like a 'we had sex so I'm taking a shower' thing. I was in the shower because I was crying," Morgan explained in a rush.

"Oh. That's fine. You have a life to live. I didn't leave because I thought you—I'm not here to police what you do with your body. It's—"

"I'm not sleeping with Gilland, nor with anyone else," Morgan interrupted in a soft voice. "You didn't have to leave."

"Well, I did. I have a flight to catch."

The taxi driver shouted at them to hurry up and Morgan scowled in his direction, taking Mei's suitcase out of the trunk and slamming it closed. Holding the handle of the rolling suitcase, Morgan impatiently asked, "Why are you here?"

"I was invited to speak at a panel," Mei replied stiffly.

"I know. I was there."

"You were?"

"Yeah," Morgan admitted, rubbing the back of her neck. "I snuck in and sat in the back. It was a great talk."

"Thank you," Mei replied, lifting a small smile.

"Anyway, I meant more…why did you come to see me?"

Mei stubbed the ground with the toe of her shoe. "I wanted to see how you were."

"As you can tell by my crying in the shower, I'm great." Morgan scoffed.

"I know, I'm sorry. I'm sure you don't want to see me and I don't blame you for that. You don't owe me anything."

"No, I don't." Morgan's voice was stern. "I hope you aren't here to ask to be friends."

Mei chuckled feebly. "Oh, god no. I think it's well established we make good friends, but we are inevitably much, much more than that."

"Yeah." Crossing her arms over her chest protectively, Morgan shrugged. "So, what do you want?"

"I—" Whatever words were coming to Mei, they ultimately failed her. Morgan's hope began to deflate. "I don't know."

Morgan sucked in a sharp breath through her nose. "Right. So, you came to tell me nothing changed."

"No, I—"

"You what? Nothing's changed, Mei. You don't know what you want, or you do and you're too scared to admit it." Wearily, Morgan held back tears, managing to hold on to her composure by the tips of her fingers. "I started seeing a therapist a few weeks ago, before I got the call about the interview. I've been…I've been drinking a lot and I caught myself contemplating suicide and realized I need to change before I end up like my mother and blow my brains out."

"Oh, Morgan." What Morgan wouldn't have given to give in to Mei's comfort, to let her wrap her arms around her and tell her it was okay.

"That's obviously not your fault, so don't think this is me blaming you for that. I just never got that close before, and it was scary."

"I'm sure."

"Part of my therapy is coming to terms with…who I am, and who my mother was, and why she—why she killed herself. Why she left me. Well, not that, not really, but I'm starting to understand it's not my fault." Morgan didn't quite believe that yet, but she was getting there. Clearing her throat, she moved on. "But, uh, the rest of it is you know, me talking about my other fun trauma or how I'm pretty bad at loving myself. Some of it is about you."

"I talk about you with my therapist too," Mei said softly.

Morgan's eyes widened in surprise. "Good for you. I mean, for seeking help, not for talking about me."

"Yes, well, she told me not to do this. Not to see you, to jeopardize the progress I'm making, but I—I couldn't stop myself. I have to apologize to you. I'm so sorry for what happened. I'm sorry I ever made you feel like you weren't loved.

Because you were. You are." Tears slipped down Morgan's face, and she glanced away from Mei. "I need you in my life, and I guess I came here hoping you want me in your life too."

Agonizing silence followed, punctuated only by insistent taxi honking. Wiping her tears on her sleeve, Morgan let out a sad laugh. "That's the only thing I ever wanted."

Hope passed through Mei's eyes like sand through outstretched fingers. "But?"

"But you're not ready yet. I can see you're still scared." As usual, Mei appeared to take this as an affront, as she often did when Morgan presumed to know how she felt. "What we have is…it's extraordinary. Looking at you now, Mei, it's like no time has passed at all. It's taking everything within me not to kiss you right here and start all over again. That's crazy, isn't it? That's… love is wild."

"It is 'wild,'" Mei agreed, attempting to smile. "Ruiz called it an inevitable love. For a supposedly hard-ass detective, she is quite soft."

At this Morgan genuinely laughed. "That's because you missed all her Spanglish rants about what she was going to do to you after I told her what happened. It was like listening to a very aggressive, homicidal Ricky Ricardo."

Taking a small step forward, Mei touched the hand Morgan had on her suitcase. "I'm not giving up on us, not as long as you don't want me to."

"I'll be ready when you are." Morgan shivered despite the intense heat outside and nudged the suitcase toward Mei. "I should go in before I get arrested for flashing our nation's capital. Have a safe flight home."

"You too, darling." Flustered, Mei blushed. "Oh, dear. That's a reflex. I'm so—"

"Don't apologize," Morgan pleaded. "I missed hearing it."

Smiling softly, Mei nodded. "Okay. I'll see you soon."

"See you soon."

CHAPTER TWENTY

Like a lot of widowed spouses, Mei went through the motions after Allan died. Most do, as many pamphlets explained, and it was a natural part of the grieving process. As Mei described it to her therapist, it was like floating underwater. And when you're suspended in the water, not drowning and not swimming, it's easy to see the others floating alongside you. Some struggle to reach the surface, the fighters who refuse to drown. Others, like Mei, content to swim down. The water carried them along and the movement mimicked living. And while existential and metaphorical, Mei also understood the science. We do not measure life in movement; even the most desolate, barren planets spin on their axes and orbit a star. They move, but they do not live, nor contain life. Life is measured in energy, in combustion, in change. Life is moving, not being moved.

Now, at this juncture in time, Mei was being moved again. She took off her shoes at the security check, placed her items in a plastic bin. She stood while a machine puffed air into her clothes as a woman waved a wand over her outfit. She gathered her things from the bin and returned them to her person. She waited. She boarded her flight. She sat in her assigned seat. She ate a complimentary bag of pretzels and drank a ginger ale. She thanked the flight attendant. She stared out the window of a taxi. She unpacked, started her laundry, made something resembling dinner, and ate it in her bedroom in front of the television.

Then, on Monday morning, she called out sick for the first time in years. After requesting the week off, Mei put down her phone and didn't look at it again. Approved or not, she intended on staying away from her office. She had work to do, but not the kind for which she'd need a lab coat and a scalpel.

This time, Mei fought the current. She breached the surface and breathed deeply.

With fresh eyes, Mei wandered through all the rooms of her house. Her home had become a museum to a life she no longer lived. Allan's office left untouched, even the glasses he refused to wear sat on his desk waiting for him to pick them back up. His side of the closet remained packed with clothes. The old, ratty sneakers he used for lawn care sat parked by the front door, tremendous in size. Mei and Allan were frozen in this home. Except Allan didn't know and couldn't change it. But Mei could.

So, she did. It began easily enough, tossing out the newspapers Allan accumulated into a blue recycling bin and canceling the subscription. Putting his old sneakers in the garbage. Methodically, carefully, lovingly, she divided his items into what could be donated to charity, what was garbage, and what she would keep. It took longer than she anticipated—many times she had to pause and collect herself, the grief springing up fresh.

Wrangling her daughters away from their busy lives, Mei invited them over to sort through their childhood bedrooms, as well as taking whatever belongings of Allan's they wanted to keep. As emotionally exhausting as the cleanup was to do alone, it became three times as exhausting with her daughters, who each had strong connections to their father. Despite the emotional gravity of the day, Grace and Lara acted suspiciously amicable. No petty squabbling, no intentional barbs, no passive-aggressive remarks. Mei felt like she was sitting in the eye of a hurricane—the quiet, yellow-tinted moments before the storm raged in again.

Once they'd gotten through the bulk of their work, Mei ordered takeout from Morgan's favorite local Thai restaurant and they ate in the kitchen, perched on stools around the kitchen island.

Chewing in silence, Mei watched her daughters exchange wary glances until finally she got fed up with their clandestine nonverbal conversation. "What? You two have been playing nice all day and it's extremely suspicious."

"It's fucked up me and Grace can't be nice to each other without drawing suspicion, you know," Lara replied.

Mei didn't relent. "What is it?"

Grace put her container on the countertop. "Are you moving?"

With a tilt of her head, Mei replied, "No. I told you, it was time to get your father's things together. And your rooms are weird little shrines to you as teenagers."

"No, I understand," Grace said. "I know it was Dad's thing to want to keep our rooms. I just…why now?" Her eyes dipped to her food guiltily. "Is it because of Morgan?"

"I haven't spoken to her in weeks," Mei replied in a controlled voice. "I'm sure Lara told you."

"She did. And I—" Inhaling a deep breath, Grace pursed her lips and aimed an even gaze at her mother. "I'm sorry if my behavior contributed to your breakup. Lara told me about what she said about not having space and I—I didn't make space for her either. It was unfair of me, and I'm sorry."

Glancing at Lara, who didn't look nearly as shocked as she should be, Mei narrowed her eyes. "Did Lara put you up to this?"

Lara huffed. "Mom—"

"No," Grace interrupted. "That's fair. Yes, I've been talking to Lara a lot. And Morgan had a valid point. I was out of line for objecting as strongly as I did. Morgan was…Morgan seems great. I regret not getting to know her better."

"She would've liked you, I bet," Lara said.

Grace raised an eyebrow. "Why?"

"Because she likes Mom, so she must be into bitches."

Laughing as Grace nearly shoved her off her stool, Lara sighed. "I joke to cover my deeply-seated jealousy."

Turning her attention to her mother, Grace waved her fork around. "You know, *Wàipó* barely speaks to me because of what happened at Christmas. Has she talked to you about all this?"

"Unfortunately. When I told her Morgan and I broke up she was not surprised," Mei replied. "Because she was certain I would ruin that relationship."

Her empathetic daughter winced. "She is so harsh."

"Yes, she is. However, she did tell me not to worry because she knows there is *yuánfen* between Morgan and myself, and it will work out in spite of what she sees as huge gaps in my ability to love another human being." With a sigh, Mei had to admit, "She's not totally wrong there either."

"Where did you and Morgan leave things?"

Poking in her bowl, Mei shrugged. "She told me I wasn't ready for a relationship with her yet, but she would be waiting for me. So, I guess I finish this and see?"

Grace stabbed a chunk of pineapple with her fork, and then pointed the fruit at her mother. "You want her back, right?" Mei nodded. "So, you can't do nothing. You have to do something."

"Grace, she can't force Morgan to suddenly want to be together again. If she's not ready emotionally, they'll end up right back here," Lara explained.

"That's not what I'm saying. I'm saying all this preparation has to be for something, right? Like, you don't win a girl back by sitting on your ass."

Lara gasped. "Oh my god. Grace. Are you suggesting Mom do a big, gay, romantic gesture? Because I am on board."

"I don't know anything about that," Mei replied, blushing. "It was your father who knew how to woo someone."

"You had thirty years with the man!" Lara groaned, exasperated. "Besides, you are romantic, in your odd little Virgo way. I will start brainstorming ideas. How do we feel about costumes? Yea or nay?"

"Hard nay." Grace curled her lip in distaste.

"Yes, I second Grace's 'hard nay.'"

"Ugh, you're both no fun. I don't know why Morgan would prefer either of you fuddy-duds over me."

Grace snorted. "And yet, we all know she would."

"Shut up," Lara replied, chuckling and tossing a cashew at her sister. "You're not even queer."

"Yeah, luckily for you." Pretending to sigh, Grace put on an air of wistfulness. "What a shame. I bet I'd do well as a lesbian."

Lara moaned. "I hate you, and I hate how true that is."

The following afternoon Mei took to sorting through Allan's clothes. This was more intimate than his office, or the photos. There was a detachment there. Those were Allan's things. These...his clothes, these touched his body. These protected him from the sun, warmed him in the cold. All these stupid plaid shirts and silly cargo shorts, the one pair of cowboy boots he owned for absolutely no reason at all. Mei lovingly boxed and bagged them, marking them for donation and placing them on the curb for a local charity pickup. She couldn't bear to throw them out. But to know somewhere, someone would wear what once was his, brought Mei solace.

Dusting off her hands, she looked up as her neighbor Evelyn crossed into her yard. Mei tensed. "Hello, Evelyn."

"Mei! Long time no see. Doing a little spring cleaning?" As they both glanced back toward the curb, Mei watched it dawn on Evelyn's face, the contents of those boxes. "Oh, I see. I'm sorry, that was insensitive."

"No, it's all right. It was about time," Mei replied, smiling. "It's not like his clothes were ever going to fit me."

Relieved, Evelyn laughed. "Certainly not. He was a big man, huh?"

"In size and personality." Planting her hands on her hips, Mei canted her head toward her home. "I should get back to it."

"Right, right, sure." As Mei took two steps toward her house, Evelyn cleared her throat. "I hope it's not an intrusion, but I wanted to ask you about your girlfriend, Morgan? I haven't seen her around in a while."

Mei's entire body seized up, but she turned around and presented a neutral face. "When did you meet her?"

"Oh! One morning I tried to clean the gutters. You know how Henry hates to get on the ladder. His hips." This was not information Mei kept readily in her brain, but bobbed her head in agreement. "Morgan was out here changing your oil and offered to help me. I declined but she insisted. We got to talking, and by the time I realized it, she'd cleaned the gutters all the way around the house. It was awful nice of her."

"That's Morgan," Mei said affectionately. "But um, we…we aren't seeing each other at the moment."

"Aw, what a shame." Evelyn sounded like she meant it. "She's lovely. And gosh, she was so keen on you. Well, anyway, I know that's none of my business, but I do hope things work out. If you don't mind the opinion of an old lady, you seemed a lot happier with her around. For all the tragedy you've had, you deserve to be happy. At least, I think you do." Evelyn beamed at her, eyes crinkling. "Take care, Mei."

"Same to you, Evelyn. And, hey, um, is there any chance you'd like a coffeemaker? I don't drink coffee, and it's such a nice machine. I'd hate to see it go to waste. I know you and Henry like to have a cup on your lanai in the morning."

Eyes shimmering, Evelyn clasped her hands in front of her in restrained emotion. Unused to eliciting such a reaction from anyone, never mind her neighbor, Mei smiled unsteadily. "Oh, I'd love that. Ours is such an old model. Henry is too cheap to buy a new one. But I will only take it under the condition that you join us one morning."

"Sure," Mei answered. "As long as I can have a tea."

Beaming from ear to ear, her neighbor nodded. "Of course."

After exchanging the machine and agreeing on a coffee date, Mei returned to her home, now emptier than before. Most of the pictures still hung on the walls, others she took down and gave to Lara and Grace. Any boxes they couldn't fit in their car waited near the doorway, their names scribbled on the side, ready to go to their homes and become part of their memories.

Slowly, she ascended her stairs to her bedroom, her first floor deconstructed and cleaned. A pristine office divested of its ghost, one side of the closet empty and vacuumed, a reorganized basement—even the cabinets in the kitchen reflected Mei's taste, having removed the food only Allan ate.

With great effort, she slid off her ring with a gentle tug. She tucked it between powder-blue velvet rolls inside her jewelry box, closing the lid and pressing the tips of her fingers against the wood. A thin band of indented, lightened skin went around her finger, contrasting the tawny shade above and below. Soon it would darken and the flesh would return to its shape. The world would continue to turn. Her marriage would still exist and her love for Allan would not diminish, it would merely hold a different shape.

The most important revelation of the three came last.

Memories were not made of mass. Memories were gaseous, amorphous, and they expand, change shape, and fill the space in which they are held. If you allow it, they will fill you up entirely and leave no room for anything else. Condensing her memories did not dilute them; it merely made room for those who needed the space. Around her wrist, she secured the bracelet Morgan gave her for Christmas, grazing her thumb over the coordinates. The first place their lives intersected, the moment in which the trajectory of Mei's life changed forever.

Having received all the revelations, the trumpets sounded and Mei was ready for the next, and final step.

She called Shanvi.

At an outdoor café on an abnormally brisk afternoon, Mei sipped her tea and stared at Shanvi, waiting for her to respond. Her normally quick-witted friend silently brooded in deep contemplation, weighing the ramifications of Mei's proposal.

"It's desperate."

"I know."

"It's dramatic."

"Yes, it is."

"And this was your idea?" Shanvi raised an eyebrow in reasonable suspicion.

Mei rolled her eyes. "It was the brainchild of myself and my daughters."

Shanvi sat back and exhaled a long breath. Then, slowly, she smiled. "I love it. Do it."

Bolstered by this vote of confidence, Mei tapped away at her phone. The message had to let Morgan know in no uncertain terms that Mei wanted to get back together, that she wanted to be with her, and only her, for as long as she could.

I'm ready.

The answer was almost instant.

Me too.

CHAPTER TWENTY-ONE

As a child of abuse, the child of a narcissistic drug addict, the child of a desperately lonely person, life forced Morgan to be resilient. Nobody wants to be resilient. Resilience is a badge you earn trying to survive. A badge someone else gives you when they realize you should be broken but you miraculously remain whole. This resilience carried with it a specific bravery, one born from repeated trauma and genetic recklessness. With this auspicious background, Morgan was rarely bereft of courage.

Today, she was scared out of her mind.

Since Mei sent her text, Morgan spent every available moment agonizing over it. Morgan allowed only the tiniest amount of cautious optimism based on a text she'd received from Lara a few days earlier: a photo of Mei's kitchen with no coffeemaker on the counter.

But fear and bravery are not mutually exclusive, so Morgan drummed up her fortitude and wrapped her fear in it. Resolute, she washed her face and stared at herself in the mirror. The changes she'd made since coming back from Washington

DC reflected back at her: sober, her cheeks no longer flushed and bloated from alcohol; her skin cleared up and her energy returned after resuming her exercise regimen; she'd gotten her hair cut and styled in the way she'd always kept it. She smiled, and it didn't hurt.

Back in her kitchen, Morgan thrust her hands into a sink full of soapy dishwater and washed the bowls and pans she'd used to make lunch. As she squeezed the spray nozzle to rinse them, Mrs. Vern yelled from upstairs. "Morgan, what's that noise? Is that you?"

"I'm not doing anything, Mrs. Vern," Morgan called out the open window.

"You're not playing music?" In fairness to Mrs. Vern, it was not unlike Morgan to loudly play somber music and curl into a ball for a few hours over the past few months.

Shutting off the faucet, Morgan wiped her hands and listened for what Mrs. Vern heard. A light melody blew in from the street. "It's probably a parked car playing music."

The pound of Mrs. Vern's feet as she scuttled across her living room sounded overhead, and Morgan chuckled as she dried her dishes. Much faster, the scuttling returned to the window. "There's a suspicious woman outside, Morgan. Go be a dear and see what she wants."

With a sigh, Morgan walked to the front door, swinging it open to reveal what she presumed would be a delivery driver trying to mail a package. Mrs. Vern's threshold for what she considered suspicious was very low.

But it wasn't a delivery driver.

It was Mei.

It was Mei, wearing a knee-length beige trench coat over a graphic T-shirt and blue jeans, which scrunched at her feet above a pair of basketball sneakers. Hoisted above her head a monstrous boom box rattled, blasting Peter Gabriel to not only Morgan, but most of her neighbors. A few of them poked their heads out of their doors and windows.

Morgan wrung the dishtowel in her hands, then hung it over the railing and started down the steps to her short walk.

Heat rose behind her eyes and she swallowed the lump in her throat. Valiantly, Mei held the boom box over her head and stared directly into Morgan's eyes. Once within arm's reach, ears bleeding from the volume of "In Your Eyes" playing in her face, Morgan reached up to press stop on the stereo.

Lowering the boom box, Mei attempted not to look feeble as she placed it carefully on the ground. They stood in silence, a cold, early-autumnal wind picking up around them. It rustled the leaves and trees, providing a gentle backdrop to their staring contest.

"How did you even find a boom box that big?"

"I'm old, Morgan, I own a boom box." Mei smirked. "It was in my attic. Surprisingly in working condition. But, they made things to last back then."

"Tell that to my Walkman," Morgan replied. Sniffing, she looked around before settling on Mei again. "Before you... before you say what you want to say, I need to tell you something first."

"Of course."

"I got the job."

"Okay."

Morgan tilted her head, face twisted in confusion. "Okay?"

"Yeah. Okay. That only slightly changes what I'd like to say to you."

Everything, every single thing, hung by a thread. Their past, their present, their future, the ghosts haunting their souls, the heartache living inside them, the doubts, the assurances, the love, the disappointment. All of it hung in the balance.

"Take the job," she said, and Morgan's heart plummeted. She wanted to totally unravel but hardened her expression, hardened her heart just enough to give Mei one firm nod. In an instant the abandoned, scared teenager inside Morgan emerged. "Take the job, but take me with you."

Looking up from the ground upon which she'd firmly planted her gaze, Morgan cautiously peered up. "What?"

Mei arranged her features into absolute confidence as she spoke. "I want to be with you. I want to be with only you. I want to go where you go. I want you to unpack all your boxes and live with me. I want us to find a place that's ours, together. I want to argue with you on what color to paint the walls. I want to fill a closet with your clothes, the ones that smell like you, and hold them close to me when you're away. I want to get you a dog, some pitiful rescue you'll fall in love with immediately and I will reluctantly adore. I want us to make a home together. I want you to be happy. I want to be part of the happiness in you. I want to be a place you feel safe to be sad but also share in your joys. I want to put in the work to be with you, because you are worth the effort. I want you to let me choose you. I want you to let me keep you for as long as you'll have me." Mei exhaled. "If you're ready, of course."

Nothing could prevent the tears falling from her eyes. The old fear—the ancient one, born in youth and reborn every time someone loved her and let her go—rose inside her. "I'm ready, but there needs to be space for me."

"There is," Mei insisted, voice firm despite the glossiness in her eyes. "I always had space for you, and it scared me to see it. But I'm not scared anymore. Well, not of that. I still do not like mummies."

"That's still so weird because you see dead people all the time."

"As I've explained before, that's exactly why. They're not supposed to *do* that, and the putrefaction alone—" Mei sighed. "That is not the point."

"I didn't think it was, it's just adorable," Morgan said. Slowly, her smile dropped and she implored Mei. "Are you sure? You have to—you have to be sure."

"I'm sure," Mei replied without a hint of hesitation.

"Okay, you have to be sure because I am going to kiss you. And if I touch you again I may not be able to stop."

After huffing out a laugh, Mei nodded. "Then I am definitely sure."

Closing the gap between them, Morgan cradled Mei's face in her hands and yanked her in for an ardent kiss. She dropped her hands to Mei's waist, and Mei slid her arms up and around

Morgan's shoulders. Lifting her into the air without much trouble, Mei giggled into their kiss and held on tightly, wrapping her legs around Morgan's butt. Breaking apart, they rested their foreheads against one another and shared oxygen. Crimson and orange leaves fell around them, dozens upon dozens, swirling and gently landing on their heads and at their feet.

"Not snow," Morgan whispered. "Not quite our thing."

"Maybe it can be our new thing." Mei pulled back, running her fingers through Morgan's hair as she was held aloft. "Are you sure? Is this...am I what you want?"

Placing Mei gently on the ground, Morgan stared down into her eyes and smiled. "I have become uncertain about a lot of things in my life recently, like my mother and my career and my friendship with Ruiz after she waited months to tell me she's pregnant."

"Aw, but aren't you excited?"

"Of course I'm excited. I'm completely floored by the prospect of my two favorite people combining their genetic material to make the world's smartest and most beautiful super-baby, but that doesn't make me less angry she waited so long to tell me," Morgan said with a petulant pout. "However, out of all the places in my life upon which shadows of doubt have been cast, you are not one of them. I have always, always been certain of you."

Mei kissed her again, keening against her body and holding Morgan as tightly as possible, as if she feared Morgan would untether and float off into the sky. Drawing back, Mei breathed out a few panting breaths. "I know we still have work to do, both as a couple and separately. I...I feel like I'm ready to do the work with you."

"Me too," Morgan said. Stepping back, she admired the incongruent outfit Mei put together. "I'm so impressed by the commitment to an accurate cosplay, by the way. After you left your *Say Anything* DVD here, I watched it a lot because it reminded me of you. I got very familiar with Lloyd's outfit."

"Lara sourced the outfit." Mei shook her head. "This is Grace's trench coat."

"A team effort." Touched, Morgan grinned ear to ear. "I knew eventually I'd woo the Lin women."

"They didn't trust me to pull off a romantic gesture on my own," Mei admitted. "I think I did pretty well."

"Sure, I mean, you got the girl, right?" Morgan bent down to press play on the stereo. Standing to her full height, she offered her hand. "In keeping with the romantic aesthetic, may I have this dance?"

Taking Mei's hand with her left, Mei waited as she ran her thumb over the skin where her ring used to be. Morgan spun her and reeled her in, pressing them heart-to-heart. Mei laid her head on Morgan's chest as they swayed to the tune of the soft rock melody, showered in cascading leaves of change.

TWO YEARS LATER

"Kelly, if she throws up on you, I'm not dry-cleaning that shirt."

Lying back on the grass, Morgan chuckled as she tossed the baby a few inches into the air and caught her, much to her delight. "You would never throw up on *Tía* Morgan, would you, Alicia?" Alicia giggled and wriggled in her hands, and Morgan tossed her up one more time. "No, no, you would never, you'd—" Before Morgan could finish her sentence, Alicia burped and a droplet of a milky substance plopped onto Morgan's shirt. "Oh, you would. Well, that's okay, because *Tía* Morgan loves you and your gross baby puke."

After placing a kiss on Alicia's nose, she passed her over to Reyna as Mei handed her a napkin. "We did tell you not to throw the small child," Mei chastised.

"But she likes it so much," Morgan whined, wiping the vomit from her shirt. "Didn't you hear her little giggles?"

"Yes, I heard her little giggles. I also heard her surprisingly thunderous burp."

"Kid's got a killer burp," Morgan agreed. "Small price to pay to be Alicia's favorite *tía*."

"You know Reyna has four sisters," Ruiz said, handing her wife a wipe to clean their daughter's face. "Plus all those *primas*. It's tough competition to be Alicia's favorite *tía*."

Jaw open in shock, Morgan feigned insult. "How dare you. Tell her, Alicia. Tell her *Tía* Morgan is your favorite *tía*."

Mei watched the baby scrunch her nose and giggle at Morgan's face, reaching out her fat baby hands to try to grab her. "If not, you could be the second Ruiz's favorite *tía*," Mei suggested, jerking her thumb toward Ruiz's protruding stomach.

"Oh, I plan on it. You'll tell her, won't you, Alicia? Or him. Or them. You'll tell your younger sibling of unknown gender identity that *Tía* Morgan is the best of your *tías* and definitely the coolest *tía* and certainly the most good-looking." Morgan allowed Alicia to grab her finger and squeeze it, eliciting another round of squeals from the toddler. Her phone rang from within her pocket and she frowned at the baby. "Excuse me, young lady." Fishing out her phone, Morgan pushed herself off the grass and walked a few feet away. "SAC Kelly."

Mei plucked a grape from their picnic basket, which they'd laid out in the middle of a beautiful park near Morgan's field office. Warm from spring, Mei breathed in as the breeze ruffled her hair. Reyna caught her hand, admiring the ring on her finger. Three gems, one diamond and two sapphires, on a plain platinum band. Mei blushed under the attention, but Reyna was all smiles. "Have you picked a date?"

Shaking her head, Mei followed Morgan with her eyes. They'd tossed around a few ideas for dates, but never committed to one. Morgan agreed as long as they stayed engaged, she'd allow Mei time to get comfortable with getting remarried. "No, not yet. We'll be waiting a bit. Neither of us is in a rush to return to the altar, but there was no way I could tell her no."

"I understand," Reyna replied, bouncing her daughter on her lap. "How's the new condo? Getting settled okay?"

"Oh, it's wonderful. It's right on the water and next to a lovely park where Morgan goes on her runs with Eddie. Plus, it's not too far from Grace and the grandkids." Crossing her legs, Mei popped another grape into her mouth. "You'll have to come by for dinner soon. Morgan's gotten pretty decent at dim sum. My mother's teaching her some ancient technique. Though I'm afraid if they spend any more time together, my mother might get the idea to move in."

Ruiz narrowed her eyes. "Wait, did you say *neither* of you are in a rush? When the hell was Kelly at the altar the first time?"

Mei pursed her lips, eyes wide. "Did I say neither? I misspoke."

"Like hell you did. You know how much shit she gave me for not telling her about my pregnancy? And now she was married before and I don't know about it?" Rolling side to side, Ruiz valiantly tried to get up from the grass but ultimately was unable to right herself, like an overturned turtle. "If I could get off the ground without help, I would go over there and kick her skinny white ass."

Jogging back to them, Morgan's shoulders sagged in defeat. "Regretfully, I have to get back to the office. But thank you for the picnic. Always great to see my three-point-five favorite Ruizes." Morgan knelt next to Alicia, shaking her little baby hand. "*Adiós, mi princesa.*"

"*Adiós, Tía Mentirosa,*" Ruiz remarked, pitching her normally toneless voice into that of a small child. Though her wife smacked her good-naturedly, Ruiz maintained her pout.

"What?" Helping Mei from the ground, Morgan aimed a confused look in her direction. "Why am I a liar?"

"I might have accidentally let it slip about your previous elopement." Mei reached up to straighten the collar on Morgan's shirt and rested her hands on Morgan's sternum.

"Oh." Morgan cast a glance at Ruiz. "Uh-oh."

"Yeah, so you're telling me that story later and I never want to hear you moan again about how I 'hid my pregnancy' from you," Ruiz said. "Go back to work, *Federale.*"

Ignoring Ruiz's attitude, Morgan smiled as she gazed adoringly into Mei's eyes, cupping her cheeks and pecking a kiss on her lips. "Do you want me to drop you off at work or at home? We do need to take Eddie out for his walk."

"Well, what I truly want is for neither of us to work and instead go home together." Mei tugged on Morgan's shirt to pull her in for a longer, deeper kiss before breaking apart. "I miss you when you leave."

Ruiz groaned. "*Dios mío*, go already before I throw up on your shirt too."

"Do you mind taking the picnic stuff?" Mei asked, looking back toward the others.

Reyna waved her hand. "Go ahead, I think we'll enjoy the weather a bit longer. Plus, it will take at least five minutes for my wife to get up off the ground and the fewer witnesses to that, the better."

"All right. Later." Morgan wrapped her arm over Mei's shoulder, escorting her across the courtyard and toward the parking lot.

Arm around Morgan's waist, Mei walked blissfully unaware of any passing glances their way as they approached Morgan's car. Her focus remained on all the places their bodies met, the warmth passing through Morgan and into her, the warmth she continued to siphon but drew from a never-ending supply, which Morgan was always willing to share.

"You know, why didn't you ever tell Ruiz you were married?" Mei wondered aloud as they arrived at the passenger side of Morgan's car. She turned and rested against it as Morgan stepped into her space, linking their fingers together.

Bashful, Morgan peered down between them to stare at the asphalt. "Oh, it's silly. It's no big deal."

Tilting her head slightly, Mei used her free hand to hold Morgan's jaw between her fingers and connect their gazes. With a sly smirk, she inquired further. "That's uncharacteristically opaque."

"Well, I…" Huffing, Morgan peered up into the blue sky, a faint wrinkle between her brows. "I decided the only person I would tell is the person I could see myself marrying. After Gemma, I was sure that person did not exist. But then I met you and I thought it was worth the risk. If it was going to be anyone, it was going to be you."

Of all the possible answers to that question, Mei didn't expect that one. Taken aback, she allowed this avowal to marinate, coating her heart and soaking into her soul. "How? How could you have known? That was before—how?"

"I told you," Morgan said, tucking Mei's hair behind her ear and smiling widely. "I feel the connection instantly. Maybe it was fate, or maybe it's inevitable like Ruiz said. All I know is I was certain of you. I wasn't certain of how or when, but I was certain of you."

"You were certain of me when even I wasn't certain of me." Mei looped her arms over Morgan's shoulders. "How did I get so lucky?"

"You didn't," Morgan replied, pressing her forehead against Mei's. "Lucky is when you're given something you didn't earn."

"True, and as a wise stranger once told me on a snow-covered side of the road: love is not given, love is earned."

Morgan placed a single, soft kiss against Mei's lips. "Hmm, she does sound pretty wise. You ought to marry her."

"I plan on it."

"But first date her for three months without realizing it."

"Wow, I'm never going to live that down, am I?"

"Absolutely not."

Bella Books, Inc.

Women. Books. Even Better Together.

P.O. Box 10543
Tallahassee, FL 32302

Phone: 800-729-4992
www.bellabooks.com

Patchwork Farm

CPSIA information can be obtained
at www.ICGtesting.com
Printed in the USA
JSHW021437230122
22188JS00001B/3